SENTENCED TO TROLL 2

S.L. ROWLAND

AETHERVALE
PUBLISHING

ALSO BY S.L. ROWLAND

Tales of Aedrea

Cursed Cocktails

Sword & Thistle

The Halfling's Harvest

There Be Dragons Here

Pangea Online

Pangea Online: Death and Axes

Pangea Online 2: Magic and Mayhem

Pangea Online 3: Vials and Tribulations

Sentenced to Troll 1-6

Path to Villainy: An NPC Kobold's Tale

Collected Editions

Pangea Online: The Complete Trilogy

Sentenced to Troll Compendium: Books 1-3

Sentenced to Troll Compendium 2: Books 4-6

Sign up for S.L. Rowland's Newsletter

For signed copies and advanced chapters visit Patreon at patreon.com/slrowland

 Formatted with Vellum

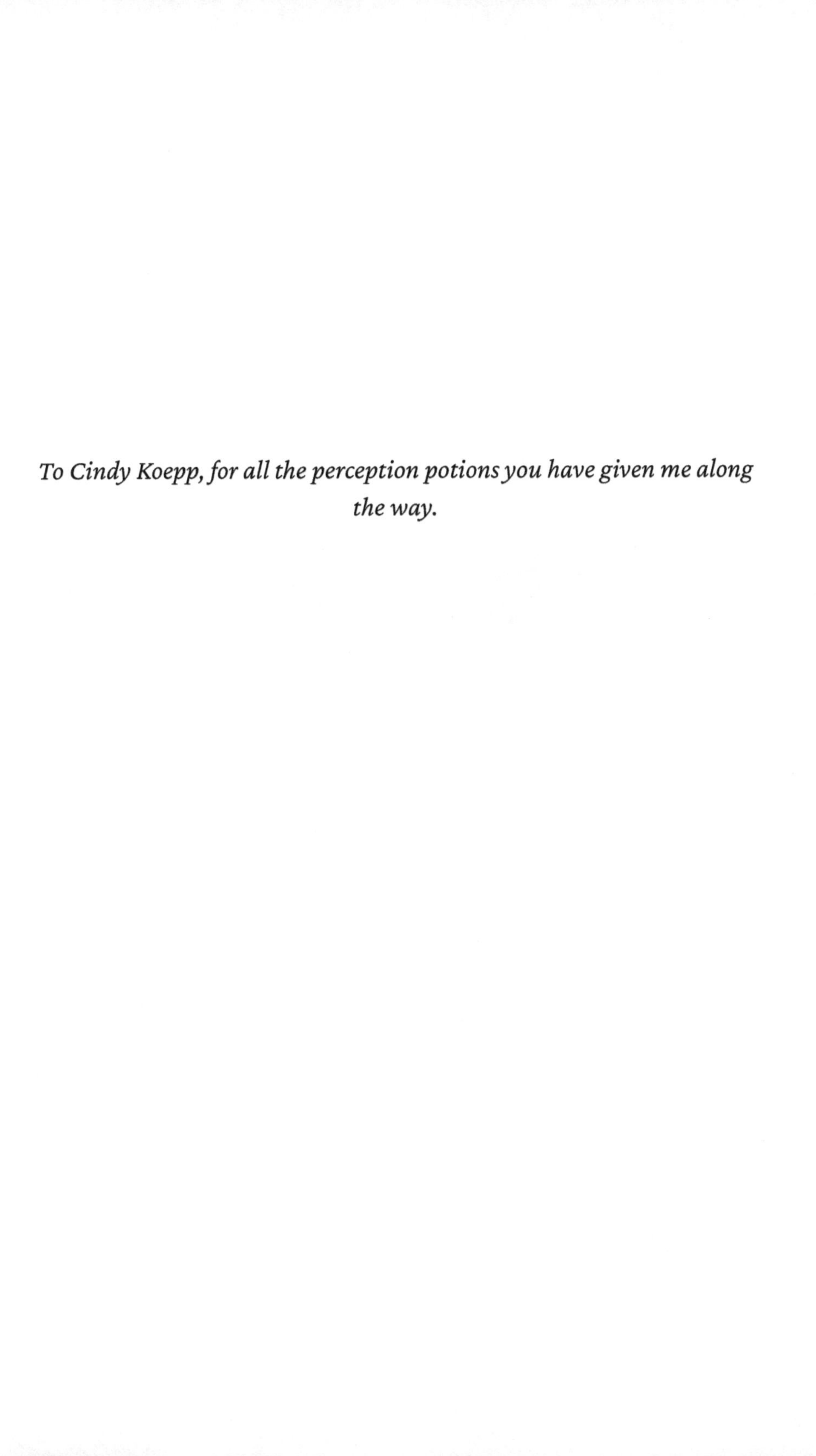
To Cindy Koepp, for all the perception potions you have given me along the way.

PROLOGUE

"I'm going to kill him." Jude sat in the corner of the Green Giant Inn. He wore boiled brown leather armor and cleaned his fingernails with a dagger. Funny how he was in a game, yet dirt and blood still crept underneath his nails just like in real life. This was some next-level shit, and it certainly beat prison.

"You're starting to sound like Glenn." Michael had no need to clean his nails. As a paladin, the holy light seemed to follow him everywhere he went. Just one of the benefits of his chosen class. "And you know what happened to him. I'd leave this troll alone if I were you."

"I don't get how you're just cool with it. He attacked us without provocation." Jude stabbed the dagger into the wooden table. "And yes, I know the meaning of word. It's what happened. We cleared the dungeon and were walking back home when him and his little troll buddies ambushed us. They took our items, our levels, and killed two NPCS. And no punishment." He leaned back against his chair, crossing his arms. "And now they want peace? I'll give him a piece of something."

"You've got to know when to pick your fights," Michael tried to reason. "We let our guard down, and we paid for it. This game is not that different from prison. Someone new comes in and they either fall in line or do what needs to be done to take a spot at the top. He made you his bitch."

"And what about you?" Jude picked up the dagger and twirled it around his hand.

"I'm not the one sulking."

Jude stared at his reflection in the blade. *Jude Duggan is nobody's bitch.*

CHAPTER 1
VANARIA

Two SHARP CLAWS grip my tough blue skin as Limery perches on my shoulder. The small red imp looks at me with his bulbous yellow eyes. "Is we there yet, Chods?"

Is this what having a kid is like?

"For the thirtieth time, no, we are not there yet. I know you have a map like the rest of us. Pull it up and look for yourself."

Gord erupts in violent laughter, his gleaming nosering swaying back and forth. Limery takes flight from my shoulder, his leathery wings flapping like sails as he flutters toward the massive green troll.

"Did you put him up to this?" I ask. For someone who hated me when I first showed up at the village, Gord has gotten pretty good at pressing my buttons for his own amusement.

Ismora places a hand on my arm. "Let them have their fun. It has been a long time since we have had reason to joke."

I flash her a smile, knowing all too well what she says is true. It wasn't that long ago that she lay on the floor of Jira's hut, the wound from a cursed blade nearly taking her life. A life she wouldn't respawn from like me. She still bears the scarred handprint on her throat from where Limery cauterized the wound with his fiery hands. The handprint is just one of many scars displayed against her hunter green skin, so new that it has not yet lost its luster.

Between Ismora's fighting skills, Gord's brute strength, and Limery's fire magic, we've got a pretty good party. Not to mention the horrors I can summon. The only thing we're lacking is a healer, which is surprisingly hard to come by in this world. At least we have a fair supply of health potions that I helped brew before we left the village. Potion-making is one skill I have been able to build up nicely in the short time I've been here.

We make our way across the sprawling golden plains to the south of *Isle of Mythos*, and I can't help but think about the circumstances that led me here.

Before I logged out from my thirty-day sentence, I sent the human king a letter on behalf of the forest trolls. At the time, I didn't know if or when I'd be coming back to *Isle of Mythos*. With my sentence served, I was a free man. Yet here I am, because the system started crashing the moment I logged out. Something about me led the AI to think I was part of the system and it couldn't function without me.

If I log out, the system resets. Everyone I've met since coming here dies. How could I possibly sentence them to death when I have nothing waiting for me on the other side? Each and every one of them has a history, a personality, quirks that make them unique. They are more than just lines of code.

This doesn't feel like a game anymore. So, I chose to come back and save the lives of these characters instead of living my own life. They don't know that, though, and I'll be damned if I ever tell them.

They call us heroes because we don't truly die. Really, we're just fully-immersed in this game world. We get respawns. They don't. As far as they know, I'm on an adventure from another world, sent to protect and guide my fellow trolls.

That's fine by me. The friends and adventures I've had here over the course of the month beat anything I ever experienced in real life. The only person I missed was Taryn. My best friend.

Valery said she would find a way to get Taryn into the game. That was my only condition for staying immersed and saving the system they have poured years of time and effort into. She was willing to make the deal, because if I log out before they track down the source of this problem, the system will reboot. That means everything is wiped to square one.

A week has passed, and I still haven't heard anything. Considering it's a top-secret rehabilitation project designed to reform violent felons, and created by the biggest name in esport gaming, I'm sure there's tons of red tape for them to wade through. Without a way for me to contact them or log out on my own, I'm just waiting. Well, waiting and adventuring.

What the hell did I write in that note?

I still can't recall. I remember putting on the Kingly Crown that I won defeating the specter king at Paltras Ruins. The +10 Charisma gave me that familiar high that always accompanies increased Charisma, telling me that anything was possible while simultaneously encouraging me to make bold and reckless decisions. And then I started writing. Before I knew it, the letter was finished, and when I took the crown off, I had a hard time recalling what I had written.

Whatever it was, it worked, because the king responded, asking for a meeting with me, Chod, now known to most humans on the island as 'Hero of the Forest Trolls.'

Chief Rizza sent me—along with Gord, Ismora, and Limery—south to the castle at Vanaria. It'll be their first time visiting anything more than a small town. Their first time in an actual human city. With Gord's abrasive personality and hulking physique, I can only imagine the looks we'll get. Not that I look much different aside from my blue skin, but at least I can act civilized. Plus, I don't have a nose ring. Old people hate nose rings. I hope he's on his best behavior for once.

Our destination is Vanaria, the mighty castle where the human king rules over the southern half of the island. Geographically, it's about as far away from Seascape, the dwarven kingdom in the north, as possible. Midway between the two is a giant mountain pass, the Greystone Mountains, and just below that, the forest where the trolls call home.

Where I call home.

I have no idea what to expect when we meet the king. Peace, hopefully. A truce to let us live our lives in peace. The trolls have earned it. Centuries of hatred have left their mark on the forest trolls. For too long, we have been viewed as monsters. It's high time we be reinstated in the world as equals.

The king would be a fool to provoke the trolls. If he wants us at the castle, he most certainly wants peace.

There's no doubt he'll want to talk about Lynchton. Not that I did anything worthy of reprimand. I simply did what needed to be done, storming the town and spawn-camping Glenn, another player, another Hero, all the way to level one without hurting a single NPC. Just because Glenn holds the title of hero, it doesn't mean he acts the part. He had it coming after everything he did to the trolls since he logged in. The man is a psychopath, and I'm glad I put him in his place before he could hurt anyone else.

By the time we were finished, the entire town had seen him for what he truly was. A monster. I wonder what the townspeople did with him after witnessing his vitriolic madness. Locked him away, if they were smart.

We still need to be vigilant as we come upon the castle. Even though we were invited, we still have a negative reputation amongst humans. Anyone who doesn't know our business with the king could attack us on sight, and the last thing I want to do is kill someone because of a misunderstanding. I may be a barbarian, but I'm not a savage. I take no joy in killing innocents.

Moving the needle from hated to untrusted with one town has done little to change our reputation on the large scale. Maybe the king can change that. His word is law after all, among humans, at least.

A herd of bison stampedes across the prairie, leaving a trail of dust in their wake. Stopping to fight them would be some nice experience, but I'm anxious to meet the king and would rather make as few detours as possible.

The crackle of fire draws my attention, and I turn just in time to see a fireball soaring across the sky towards the bison. It sizzles as it hits one of the slower creatures, leaving a scorch mark on its backside.

Limery leans back and cackles.

"Just make sure you catch up to us when you're done," I shout at Limery as he takes off in search of his prey.

"I'll follow him." Ismora turns in his direction, the fading sun gleaming off her black hair that's pulled into two ox-horn buns. "If he manages to defeat the beast, I'll bring back the meat for dinner. My Boots of Swiftness will allow me to catch back up with ease."

Gord and I continue our march in silence as the sun draws closer to the horizon.

"Do you think this king can be trusted?" His thunderous voice finally breaks the quiet.

"I don't know, but I feel it is our best option. If we spurn him, it only proves us to be the unreasonable savages they already despise us as."

I grip my staff a little tighter. Every time I think about the meeting with the king, my chest tightens. There is a lot riding on this meeting.

Gord adjusts the massive black shield that hangs over his shoulder. The shield is engraved with a ram's head, complete with massive curling horns. "And the chief, she has authorized you to negotiate with the king?" His eyes question me. Even though we have grown closer since our first meeting, he still has his doubts.

"Within reason. I have a seat on the council and have been granted special privileges for our mission." I can negotiate for peace as long as it benefits the village.

"I still don't understand why the chief didn't come herself," he booms.

That's the real issue. The chief is the leader of the village, someone Gord greatly admires. He believes she should be squaring off with the king.

"Because if something goes wrong, if this proves to be a trap, then I'm the only one who will not truly die." The words say what I don't. If this is indeed a trap, then Gord, Ismora, and Limery aren't going home.

I can't allow that to happen. I didn't come back here just to let them die. This has to be a peaceful mission.

As we carry on, the plains transform into rolling hills scattered with billowy trees covered in pink and white flowers. The wind wages war against the trees, speckling the landscape in a fantastical array of petals while simultaneously covering us in fragrant confetti.

My jaw drops when we reach the crest of the hill and Vanaria comes into view. Beside me, Gord can't hide his wonder. Even from so far away, the city is magnificent. The keep in the center shimmers with a pearlescent sheen, with towers that rise high into the sky and disappear among the clouds. Whatever material it is constructed from gleams even in the fading daylight. Even after growing up in New York City, where skyscrapers are a way of life, the magnitude of the castle astounds me. Hundreds, if not thousands, of homes and buildings are packed between the curtain wall and inner walls. I wouldn't be surprised if half the island's population resides here.

Obsidian walls protect the city, gleaming with a dark fervor that dares anyone to challenge their protective power. Fires from the guard towers posted every few hundred feet reflect off its surface, and soldiers clad in white and blue patrol the parapets in between.

So this is how the other half lives.

The flap of Limery's wings bring me back from my astonishment just in time to hear Ismora's own gasp of admiration.

"It's beautiful," she gawks, but I can also see the uncertainty in her eyes.

I can only imagine what it must be like for them. A month ago, they had never left the forest, and now they are looking at a castle that's more like a work of art than a fortress. Just like all the small-town actors who came to New York to make it big, only to be swallowed by the city and eaten alive.

"Let's camp for the night and we will enter the city first thing in the morning."

We find a wooded area to make camp, having a dinner of roasted bison. Even though our passive ability Savage allows us to eat raw meat, it tastes so much better cooked over an open flame.

Limery tucks himself beneath my arms and Camouflage kicks in, concealing us from prying eyes while we sleep.

As I slowly drift to sleep, I can't help but think of what kind of king could live in a castle so opulent. How could someone like that ever understand the plight of the trolls?

Did I make a mistake by coming here? There are five tribes of trolls. I should have at least tried to band them together first. The seaside trolls turned me down, but that didn't mean the others would. If I'd known that this was Vanaria, I would have tried.

I led the forest trolls against an attacking town, against a psychopath, not this. We aren't prepared for this.

CHAPTER 2
ALL THE KING'S MEN

THE EYES of the guards bore into us as we approach the gate. High above the obsidian wall, arrows and crossbows point in our direction. None of them have fired, which tells me that they are expecting us at the very least. I take a deep breath and soldier on.

"Just keep calm." I try to sound confident, but the truth is that I'm just as nervous as they are. My guts rumble in that familiar way that would always come before class presentations. I never showed how nervous I was, but on the inside, it was turmoil.

Regardless of the invite, this is hostile territory. Men and trolls have been at war for thousands of years.

Gord adjusts his massive shield, and Ismora straightens her back. Nervous movements. Limery silently holds tight to my shoulder. I wait for him to say something, anything to relieve the tension, but it doesn't come. He's more worldly than any of us, and his silence only makes my heart race faster.

The portcullis is open and a handful of armed guards wearing blue capes stand beneath the entrance to the city, checking passers as they enter. Carts loaded with wood, produce, and other necessary items for a big city grind against the cobblestone road. None of the humans have spoken to us as we walk, but I hear whispers, and they've all given us a wide berth.

"Trolls, in the city—"

"Stand back, son. We don't know what they are capable of."

"Why are the guards not attacking?"

"I never thought they'd be so big, and that blue one—"

For this being a meeting for peace, I am strangely on edge. I feel for the mana that runs through my body and it comforts me a little knowing I can summon my horrors at a moment's notice if something goes down. These people have no idea what we are truly capable of.

A farmer checking in a wagon loaded with produce tries to speed up his inspection when we get too close for his liking. The guards watch us with suspicion, always one hand on their weapons.

One guard steps forward. He has a blue plume sticking out of his silver helmet that the others do not. His armor glitters in the morning light, and his cloak is spotless. Whoever he is, he lives well.

Captain of the City Watch. *Level 25.*

Twenty-five levels on an NPC is no joke. Gord had ten when I first met him, and he could have ripped me apart. This man could probably kill any one of us if he felt threatened. Perhaps all of us. Most of the soldiers surrounding him range from level ten to fifteen. These must be the best fighters in the land.

"Who are you and what is your business in Vanaria?" The man's voice cuts like ice, and Limery's claws dig a little deeper into my tough skin. The captain stands tall, but there are bags under his eyes. How long has he been waiting for us?

"I am Chod, councilmember and hero of the forest trolls. King Favian has requested a meeting." Certainly, he must know all of this already. Why else would he allow us to stroll right up to the gate unimpeded?

"Very well. Hand over your weapons, and I will escort you to the king."

I translate to Gord and Ismora, and they reluctantly relinquish their weapons. The cloak Ismora wears conceals more weaponry than any of us thought possible. Some of the guards murmur between themselves when she finally finishes emptying it.

I hand over my staff. I don't need it to summon my horrors, but these guys don't need to know that.

The captain whistles, and several dozen men march around the corner and appear in two columns adjacent both sides of the gate.

"All this for us?"

"It's for safety." He points toward the line for us to get moving.

Ours or his, I wonder.

From inside the city, the castle seems even taller than before. Several of the keep's ivory towers are visible, but most of it disappears above the clouds. No matter where someone is in the city, the keep towers above it all, a constant reminder of who is in charge.

Ismora sticks next to me, while Gord grunts at guards who step too close to him. I swear one of them flinches at the sound of his deep voice.

"I do not like this at all," he rumbles.

Nor do I, but it's the cost to play ball. If the trolls are going to finally be able to travel the island trading, adventuring, and exploring without risking certain death, this is the only way. Well, maybe not the only way, but we could never win an all-out war against an enemy like this.

It makes my decision to invade Lynchton feel all the more foolish. The king could want retributio—

Brown liquid splatters on the street before us, and I look up to see a woman emptying a bucket from the second-floor window of a dilapidated building. The smell of human waste assaults my nose as we enter the first line of streets. Disgusting.

A guard mumbles "absolute filth" as we step through it.

"This is the outer bailey. Most people call it Rat Row." The captain finally decides to show some hospitality. "Home of the peasants and other filth who dwell within the city. I'm sure trolls at least have the decency not to shit where they eat." He steps over a pile of what might be mud or excrement.

These are nothing more than well-guarded slums.

We pass through several rows of the same rundown buildings before we come to another obsidian wall. The soldiers guarding the entrance move aside as we approach.

On the other side of the wall, the buildings and streets are much cleaner and less ragged.

"This is the inner bailey. Those with a trade or some valuable skill live inside this wall, as well as soldiers and members of the guard."

"Why doesn't it stink on this side?" I ask.

"There is plumbing to carry waste away to the river."

"Why doesn't the outer bailey have it?"

He scoffs at me before answering. "What's the point? They live, die, and breed in filth. That's about all they are good for." A couple soldiers laugh at his words. "But even if that wasn't the case, the plumbing was installed before the outer bailey was populated. The castle was crafted by magic thousands of years ago, back when crafting was handled by the nimble of mind instead of body. Those ways are lost to us now."

The inner bailey bustles with activity, alive with excitement like every fantasy RPG I've ever played. There are stalls filled with fruits and vegetables where people hunt and haggle for the best produce. A blacksmith bangs against his anvil, and smoke plumes into the air from his forge. I spot shops selling fabrics, spices, medicine, and many more that stretch around the corner.

This is the reason people will play *Isle of Mythos*! This is the experience I have been missing. I can't wait to—

A figure clad in black exits the apothecary and looks in our direction. I recognize him as one of the men we killed after they left the underground dungeon.

Jude Duggan
  Level 14
  Fighter
  Human

He has gained back the level we took from him.

"You!" he snarls before running at us.

Gord lets out a roar that startles some of the soldiers and townspeople alike.

The guardsmen take a defensive stance, spears pointed toward Jude.

Wait, what? Why are they protecting us?

The captain steps forward, his hand on the hilt of his sword and a scowl on his face. "You will turn back now, or else I will send you to your next life before you form another breath."

Jude stops, but his eyes still cut at us. "They killed me. Me, Michael, and two soldiers. What the hell are they doing here?"

"Their appearance is none of your concern. I will not warn you to be on your way again."

"This isn't over," spits Jude.

Just as he turns to leave, Michael the paladin exits the blacksmith, a massive warhammer tossed over his shoulder. He looks at us, but Jude pulls him around the corner.

I feel this isn't the last we'll see of those two.

"Thanks for that," I tell the captain.

"I didn't do it for you." He releases his grip on his sword, and the other guardsmen fall into line.

Well, screw you too, buddy. We could have handled him on our own.

We're making our way through the business district when I notice a wheelbarrow loaded with kegs being pulled by a short, but rather stout man. A braided red beard hangs down his chest, and he wears an apron with the sigil of a beer mug over two crossed warhammers.

"Is that a dwarf?" I ask. Since I've been in *Isle of Mythos*, I've only seen humans and trolls. I know dwarves exist because they have a kingdom in the far north, but I've yet to see one.

"Indeed." The captain looks fondly at the dwarf, the first break I've seen in his icy exterior. "He is here on a trade exchange with the dwarven kingdom. They brew us beer and we send several of our vintners north to help them produce wine. The coastal climate in the north is surprisingly well-suited for a variety of grapes."

The dwarf slows his pace as he comes closer. Several jeweled metal clasps adorn his beard and clink together as he walks. "I'll be looking for ye after yer shift, Captain. The new lager be ready for tasting."

The captain only nods, and we continue our march towards the keep. Gord looks like an owl as he twists his head to watch the dwarf pass by.

"Are there more? Dwarves, I mean." I look down the streets and alleys, but there doesn't appear to be any other races.

I still remember the many races to choose from when I created my character. They were all blocked out to me, but that means they have to exist somewhere. If not on the island, maybe another continent.

"There are some. Most prefer their homeland. They are not great adventurers, the dwarves. They much prefer to toil for the good of their kingdom. Something those in the outer bailey could use a good dose of."

"Chods, look!" Limery seems more like himself as he points to a band of street performers juggling and walking on stilts. A crowd has gathered around them. They toss coins to a small monkey wearing a vest and hat. "Can we watch, Chods? Please," he pleads, hands clutched together.

"Do you mind?" I ask the captain.

He looks around—for what, I'm not sure. "Five minutes."

His men fall into position around us, leaving room in front for us to watch the performance even though we are several feet taller than the guards and have no problem seeing. When some of the townspeople notice us, they step aside, eyes wide and clearing a path. The performers continue their show as if nothing is happening. A man in purple and yellow clothing with a painted face tosses bowling pins into the air. Limery's bulbous eyes are alight with wonder.

He flies from my shoulder and hovers in the air next to the juggler. His palms crackle and a fireball appears in each hand. The crowd gasps and takes a step back. With a flick of his wrist, the fireballs jolt into the air, the hot flames distorting the air around them but remaining intact. Quickly, he conjures another fireball and adds it to the mix, mimicking the juggler's routine. The crowd looks on in a mixture of fear and wonder.

They must not see a lot of imps around here. Or is it magic they're afraid of?

When the juggler finishes, the man on stilts walks through the crowd to 'oohs' and 'ahs' as he fakes losing his balance. He makes eye contact with me and winks, his eyeball disappearing beneath the painted eyelid.

"Time to go," orders the captain.

As we turn to leave, the juggler calls out to us. "Hey, troll!"

The guardsmen block his way as he approaches. Something gleams in his hand, and with a flick of his thumb, it flies through the air, over the guards, and I catch it.

It's a golden coin with the head of a lion engraved on one side.

"Thanks for the show." The juggler winks and places a finger over his mouth, signaling me to keep quiet, before returning to his group.

I analyze the coin and can't believe what I see.

Item. Underground Circus Coin. *An enchanted coin used by the secret society. It will allow you access into areas otherwise unattainable.*

"What is that?" asks the captain, eyeing the coin.

I don't know why, but I get the feeling I shouldn't tell him.

"A coin. I guess he was happy with Limery's performance." I stuff the coin in one of the pouches on my belt before he can inspect it. I'll look into it further when there aren't so many prying eyes.

He looks at me suspiciously but doesn't press the issue.

We make our way through the inner bailey, past much nicer houses and buildings. The closer we come to the keep, the more opulent the homes become. Many are made of stone and are draped in banners emblazoned with their house sigils. Above them all, the shimmering keep towers over everything. Those that walk the streets wear clothing made of the finest threads and materials. Most of them do not carry weapons.

Finally, we come to the stairway that leads into the mighty keep. Beautiful white marble gleams in the sunlight, giving the keep a heavenly radiance. Eleven guards in silver and blue plate armor wait at the base of the stairs, blocking all entry. They stand stoically, unmoving sentinels. Their armor is intricately designed, with small engravings carved throughout. On each of their chests is a silver griffin with a blue jewel for the eye. This isn't the plain armor of a warrior. No, this armor is a symbol. I focus on one of the guards and his stats appear.

Kingsguard. *Level 22.*

Not quite as experienced as the captain of the city watch, but eleven of them could fight off almost any threat to the king. The captain walks to the kingsguard in the center and says something. That's when I notice that particular kingsguard wears a blue cape draped over his armor.

Captain of the Kingsguard. *Level 30.*

Wow! He's eleven levels higher than me. The amount of work it must have taken for an NPC to gain that many levels, I can't even begin to imagine.

The captain of the kingsguard instructs his men to make way, and my three companions and I ascend the stairs. The captain of the city watch takes his men and disappears back into the city.

It's like we're a baton being passed from one captain to the next.

"Follow me," he instructs. His voice is smooth and strangely youthful. I would expect a warrior of his stature to be gruffer, to be older.

Two other kingsguards flank us on both sides. There's no small talk as we ascend the stairs. Why would there be? This man has one job, and that's to protect the king with his life.

At the top of the stairs, two magnificent silver doors engraved with twin griffins facing one another bar our way. Sapphires the size of my fist dot their eyes and an array of diamonds add glitter to their wings.

"Pretty," mumbles Limery, his eyes greedy, reminding me of

the first time we met when he tried to steal my pendant from around my neck.

Please don't steal anything while we are here.

With a groan, the doors open and a gray-bearded man in blue robes waits on the other side.

CHAPTER 3

BLOOD PUDDING

"WELCOME TO VANARIA." The wizened man sweeps his arms to the sides, inviting us into the castle. Silver tassels hang from his robe, cinched tightly around a belly rivaling that of an expectant mother. The tassels match the color of his long, flowing beard. "The king is indisposed at the moment, but I will be entertaining you until he returns." The edges of his mustache rise slightly, hiding a smile underneath.

He looks like a lovable grandpa, but I keep my mana on edge just in case.

"Returns?" The captain of the kingsguard lets out an exasperated sigh.

"Not now, Warwick. You've made your feelings known, but he is the king. You know as well as I that we can't tell him anything unless he wants to hear it. Now, you lot, come." He motions to our party. "I'm sure you are famished from your travels." He starts walking before abruptly stopping and pressing a ring-covered hand to his face. "I'm sorry. Where are my manners? I am Lord Kassidy, advisor to the king. You must be Chod. Word has spread fast about a giant blue forest troll who can speak the common tongue and summon monstrous creatures. You should be proud of your notoriety. I'm looking forward to learning more about you. And that would make you Limery." He extends a finger for Limery to shake. "I had the pleasure of meeting your mother. A wonderful imp and extraordinary conversationalist."

"Pleased to meets you." Limery flashes his sharp teeth. His small hands linger on the old man's rings a little too long as they shake.

"As for you two, I'm not sure I am acquainted."

I turn to translate, but Gord is already answering. Lord Kassidy must have a communication stone.

"I am Gord, son of Guilda, guardian of the forest trolls."

"And I am Ismora, master of weapons for the forest trolls."

"Pleased to meet you. Now, if you don't mind, let us carry this conversation forward in the dining hall."

What a strange man. He appears more concerned with eating than the three trolls and imp standing before him. Not the least bit worried or hesitant that we are here. He is actually...friendly. His jovial nature is a bit infectious, causing me to let my guard down slightly, but I'm not entirely sure it's warranted. Who the hell is this guy? When I try to focus on his level, all I see are question marks.

Servants scurry through the castle as Lord Kassidy leads us to the dining hall. The table in the center overflows with food displayed on silver platters. Cornucopias spill fruits across the blue silk tablecloth next to roasted fowl, bread, vegetables, and an assortment of pies and puddings. A giant roasted pig dominates the centerpiece. There's enough food to feed a small army.

"Have a seat." Lord Kassidy pulls out a chair for Ismora before seating himself.

All of us, except for the kingsguard, take a seat around the table. The extravagance of the dining hall reminds me of some of the parties my mother and father would bring me to when I was young. Fancy tablecloths, silver spoons, and foods so rich that my stomach would hurt for hours. It wouldn't be complete without giant paintings of old men on the walls. They were always such boring affairs, too. Men in black ties holding martinis and talking about business. I was left alone with the other kids to entertain ourselves for hours.

The guards stand watch outside the entrances to the dining hall. We all sit there, waiting for instruction, when Lord Kassidy bursts out, "Oh, don't be shy. Dig in," before scooping himself a massive helping of pudding.

I reach for a grape and toss it in my mouth, expecting the deliciously tart and sweet flavor I love. Instead, I'm greeted by juices so bitter that I almost spit it out.

"Something wrong, Chod?" asks Kassidy.

"Uh, no, nothing at all." I pull off a leg of roasted goose and bite into it. Delicious and savory. Next, I take a small portion of green beans, but they have the same bitter taste as the grape. Is it possible my taste buds have changed since entering the game? It's not entirely out of the realm of possibility. It did take me some time to adjust to the size of my new body, why wouldn't I develop the palate of a forest troll?

I check on the others. Gord, Ismora, and even Limery have piled nothing but meat on their plates.

"This is a beautiful city." I try to make polite small-talk since we are their guests.

"Truly a work of art." Globs of mashed potatoes coat Lord Kassidy's beard. "You know, Vanaria was formed on the remains of a dormant volcano. Long ago, earth mages pulled obsidian from the earth to form the walls of our great city. The ivory towers were taken from the heart of the volcano itself. Blessed with divine power by a powerful cleric, the towers prevent necromantic activities within our city walls even to this day."

That's surprising. One of my options when I chose my summoner class was necromancy. If this is true, then I definitely made the right choice. "Is that a problem? Necromantic activities?"

"Not here, no. But I'm sure you are familiar with the great wizard that closed the fast-travel portals between continents. Well, let's just say he would have a hard time laying siege to our castle."

Interesting. "So, he was a necromancer?" I don't remember Limery's mom mentioning that.

"He was many things. Powerful in several branches of magic, but that was long ago. Losing access to fast-travel was a small price to pay to be rid of a threat so dire."

"He's still out there, though, isn't he? A powerful wizard like that doesn't just disappear to go die."

Kassidy looks up from his food, and there's a wildness in his eyes. Storms rage behind their gray surface. "I pray to the gods that we never find out." Just as quickly as it went, his jovial nature returns. "Let us enjoy dessert and then we can go up to wait for the king in the viewing chamber."

Remembering the grape, I try to object. "Us trolls aren't really one for sweets." And I'd hate to vomit on this nice tablecloth.

"Nonsense, I had our chef look through some of our ancient books for recipes of old. I quite think you will enjoy this one." He snaps his fingers, and the food on the table vanishes.

Gord scoots back in his chair, a roar of alarm sounding in his chest. Ismora rises to her feet, and Limery flutters into the air with a screech. The kingsguard rush into the room, swords drawn. I'm the only one who seems unphased by the action.

"Oh, sorry. I didn't mean to frighten you." Another snap and a black pudding appears in a bowl in front of each of us. It's going to take more than a nice meal to get these three off-edge. "No need to worry. I only use my powers for good."

"You're a wizard?" I ask.

Gord slowly readjusts himself at the table. Aside from Jira, I haven't seen any other magic users that weren't players.

"Indeed. Teleportation is my specialty. It has so many uses, but that's neither here nor there. What's important is the dish in front of you. I've been told it is a troll delicacy."

Blood pudding. *+3 Strength and Constitution for one hour.*

I pick up the spoon and dip it into the black glob. Gord and Ismora are unsure of how to use the cutlery, holding the spoon facing downward like they're about to plant a stake in the earth. I dip my spoon and take a bite, then they follow my lead. The thick pudding coats my mouth, and I anticipate the bitterness of sweets, but it's actually delicious. Like a cool meaty treat. A small jolt of power flows through my body and my muscles pump gently, the bonus Strength and Constitution taking effect.

"Wow, this is good," I say between bites.

Ismora echoes my enthusiasm.

"Oh yes, Limmy likes. Limmy likes." The imp runs his tongue against his blood-covered teeth.

"The blood was freshly drained this morning," Kassidy laughs. "I'm glad you like it. Now, what do you say we find the king?"

Lord Kassidy leads us to a wide spiral staircase that ascends into what I believe is one of the giant towers. Warwick, captain of the kingsguard, and his two men follow closely behind us.

The wizard sucks in air with each step as we ascend, and I wonder if he needs help. He could be attempting to look weak so that we underestimate him. With his level being hidden from us, there is no way to know how powerful he truly is.

Still, he's a teleportation mage. Couldn't he just teleport

himself to the room we are going to? Maybe that's why he is so out of shape.

A lazy wizard. I can't help but smile at the thought.

As we climb the stairs, we pass different levels with doors leading to various rooms and hallways. Occasionally, there is a window that looks down onto the kingdom below.

Our party halts as the wizard comes to a stop, keeling over to gasp for air.

"This man advises the king?" Gord leans in so that he isn't overheard, but his booming voice carries nonetheless. Gord's remark goes unnoticed by the wizard sucking at air, but one of the kingsguard snickers.

"It certainly seems so."

"How can a man who cannot care for and strengthen his body expect to care for a kingdom?"

For a dumb brute, Gord has a good point. The wizard does seem a bit simple-minded.

"Is we there yet?" Limery asks, fluttering down next to the wizard.

Kassidy resigns to his defeat at climbing the stairs. "Hardly. Warwick, lead them the rest of the way." With a snap, the wizard disappears.

"Typical," scoffs Warwick. "I take it you are all in good shape, so let's pick up the pace. I'd have this over with sooner than later."

We move up the tower at a near jog, the metal plates of the three kingsguards clanking with each step. By the time we reach the top, my muscles burn and sweat beads down my shoulder blades. Limery is the only one who's not sucking for air. The endurance of imps still amazes me.

The top of the tower empties into an open-air room above the clouds. Kassidy sits on a large sofa eating strawberries with his feet propped on a pillow.

"I'm glad you are comfortable," quips Warwick. The other two guards take position outside the entrance, not that I think anyone else is making the journey up those stairs ready to fight.

I'm certain we climbed over a hundred flights of stairs to be this high.

Warwick removes his helm, revealing a youthful face and black hair drenched in sweat. His eyes are as dark as coals. He can't be older than his early twenties. And already level thirty. He sits the helm on a stone bench and walks over to the ledge, gazing at the clouds. We're so high that they conceal the ground below.

"Oh, have a seat, will you?" Kassidy bites another strawberry and the juices run through his beard. "The king will be back when he is back. Staring off into the abyss won't bring him any sooner."

"This is foolish." Warwick doesn't turn around.

Something is definitely up between these two. And why are we up so high waiting for the king? What could he possibly be doing?

"The king can handle his own, you know this."

"Then why have a kingsguard at all?" Warwick turns, his face set in stone. "These heroes can't be trusted! All they need is one stroke of luck and the king is gone forever. If I am not around and something happens to him..." He lets the words drift off.

"You worry too much. These heroes are no danger to the king."

Knowing what I know, I wouldn't be so certain about that. I keep my opinion to myself, though.

"You lot." Kassidy points a strawberry in our direction. "Join me and relax your legs. I'm sure the climb up was terrible."

We take a seat on a sofa across from Kassidy. Sitting there, it's the first time I've been aware of the comforts of the real world that the trolls are missing. Not that we need them. Our tough hides and Constitution allow us to sit or sleep almost anywhere in comfort.

"There are a lot of ways to get the king's attention." Kassidy ponders eating another strawberry and then places it back in the bowl. "But taking over a town and then sending an imp-delivered letter straight to the top of the tower, that's a bold move. Probably the only reason you are here now and not six-feet under."

I had no idea Limery's mother delivered the letter all the way up here. I'll have to give her something extra for that.

"I only did it be—"

A monstrous screech cuts me off as a giant winged creature with the head of an eagle and the body of a lion flies into the room. It lands with a grating slide as its claws dig into the stone. Warwick dives out of the way, his armor scraping against the stone floor. The creature squawks at us, revealing its sharp beak and razor-like talons. Its dark gray wings flap in agitation.

Griffin. *Unique monster. Level: ??? Known as the 'King of Beasts,' the griffin is one of the oldest and wisest monsters. Both proud and intelligent, they will only fight with their masters, not for them.*

Upon its back sits a man wearing simple boiled leather.

Kassidy sits up, casually eating another berry. "Welcome home, Your Highness."

CHAPTER 4
PEACE OFFERINGS

THE LEATHERS that the king wears is simple and rustic. Aside from the griffin branded on his chest, nothing hints at the nobility of the man beneath it. A pair of goggles obscure his face, and short, brown, windswept hair gives him an air of adventure.

Warwick crawls to his feet. "Do you have to do that every time?" The exasperation in his voice tells me this isn't the first time he's been knocked on his ass.

The king laughs off the comment as he dismounts from the massive griffin. With a huff, the griffin stalks to the corner of the room and lays down. I try to analyze the king, but I get nothing.

King Favian. *Level: ???*

"So you're the troll who has the entire kingdom in an uproar?" He approaches with a confidence that tells me his level isn't visible most likely because it is too high for me to comprehend. There's a gentleness about him, but underneath it all, I can sense a raw power. He could kill me before I ever lifted a finger.

Gord and Ismora rise as he approaches. They have no weapons, but I know that if anything happened right now, they would die for me. For their tribe. It's my job to make sure that doesn't happen.

"That was never my intention." I stand beside them, and Limery's body feels strangely hot against my shoulder. After Lynchton, I felt invincible. Defeating Glenn and storming the town without losing a single troll, I was a big fish in a small pond. How little I knew of the world and the other powerful beings that dwelled within it.

"Don't let it trouble you too much. They hate that which they do not understand, and it has been far too long since trolls and humans have understood one another."

I let out a sigh of relief, and Gord unclenches his fist. For now, at least, it seems we will talk.

"Why did you ask me here?" There's no point in beating around the bush.

He smiles at me for a long moment, as if sizing me up. "Partly to see the troll that said he would tear this entire kingdom to the ground if his people weren't left in peace." Gord and Ismora both let out an audible groan of disapproval. "But mostly to meet the hero that would do that for his people. You see, I've met the so-called heroes of my people. Some are noble, some are...not so. Warwick thinks I do not recognize them for what they are, but the truth is that I see all too well. They will do my bidding for gold coin or valuable items, but I do not think any of them would risk themselves out of sheer selflessness for my people, for those who do not come back from death."

The king certainly is no fool. Still, what is his motivation for bringing me here?

"You want peace?" He lifts his goggles and piercing blue eyes stare at me.

"That is all we want. The ability to live our lives like any other race. Freedom to travel outside of the forest to trade or adventure without risking certain death."

"Then let us cut right to the chase. Kassidy, Warwick, will you accompany Chod's party out of the room? I'd like to speak to the hero troll alone." His lip curls up around the edge in a mischievous way, and my chest tightens. What is he up to?

Kassidy and Warwick make for the door, but Gord and Ismora remain.

"Come," orders Warwick.

A fierce growl rumbles in Gord's chest. "I will not leave my brother alone."

"It's okay, Gord. I'll be fine." At least, I hope so.

His eyes flitter between the king and I, untrusting.

"Are you sure?" asks Ismora.

"Yes, I will find you when we are done." It's not like I have a choice in the matter. It's either talk to the king or fight our way out.

"Be safe, Chods." Limery hugs me before jumping from my shoulder to Gord's.

A few moments later, it's just the king, his griffin, and me alone in the room. King Favian takes a seat on the sofa and folds his hands together. I still can't get a read on the man.

He lets out a long sigh before leaning back.

"It's not easy being king, you know. There's so much responsibility. As a child, I thought it was all hunting trips and lavish parties, but more often than not, its council rooms and closed meetings. I take to the air every chance I get. It's the one thing that allows me to clear my mind." He sighs. "My father was lucky he didn't have to deal with heroes. Hundreds of years pass after the great war and then suddenly, immortals show up out of nowhere." He leans forward and looks me square in the eye. "Part of me thinks I should kill them all. Round them up before they are too powerful and kill them. Much like you did in Lynchton. I know they get weaker when they die. That's their one vulnerability. I could kill them and lock them all away and they'd never be a problem."

My body tenses at those words. Maybe he brought me here for just that reason, to lock me up before I become a real problem. Could I make it to the ledge before he stopped me? One long drop and I'd respawn in the forest. But I can't leave my party. They trusted me, and I'm not that big of a dick.

He still seems rather calm, so I abandon the thought of suicide for the moment. "Why don't you?"

He runs his fingers through his hair. "I'm no fool. They will all have their part to play before all is said and done. If heroes are here, it is for a reason. Something is brewing. If not on the island, then somewhere in the world. What, I'm not sure of yet. Mythos has a way of balancing itself out, at least historically. So I find myself in a chess match, where I am forced to guide the heroes to power while at the same time protecting my people. Only I don't know the end goal. Do you?"

"Do I what?"

"Know the end goal?" He rubs his eyes. "Of course you don't."

"Why did you bring me here?" I ask again.

He sits in silence for a moment, as if questioning if he should really tell me. "Because I want to wage war on the dwarves."

That is about the last thing I expected him to say. They're trading partners, so what could he possibly have against them? "The dwarves? Why?"

"Their kingdom sits on one of the largest ley lines on the island. It's so powerful that it influences the metal they mine with magical properties. We have the fewest number of enchanters in the kingdom since I was born, making it difficult to forge many rare and powerful items. The dwarves make them every day. I want what they have, and you are going to help me acquire it. Once the dwarven kingdom is mine, you and your trolls shall have your freedom."

He can't seriously be asking this. It's suicide. The forest trolls are a small tribe as it is, and war would push us to extinction. Perhaps that is his goal—to take over the dwarven empire and rid the forest trolls in the process. There is no way the chief would agree to this.

Anger boils inside, and my mana rages at my fingertips. Would summoning a Horror of Vitality slow him enough that I could tackle him off the ledge? Would the fall be enough to kill him?

I hold my hand for the moment, hoping I can talk my way out of this. "Why do you need the trolls for this? Can't you fight your own battles, reward the heroes to fight for you?"

He smirks before answering. "As far as I know, the dwarves have yet to receive a hero. I find that very strange. Two dozen human heroes and one troll, but no dwarves. It's almost as if fate is tipping the scales in my favor. With enough rewards, every human hero will fight for my cause. Add in your army of trolls, and don't think I forgot about the wyrms you've been training, and I'd lose less than a tenth of the men I would in open combat. I have no misconceptions about how the strength of a troll compares to a human. One troll is worth at least four men, and that's not counting your precious little monsters." He seems to be relishing the victory before the battle has even started. "With the dwarven kingdom under my rule, the entire island would be mine. You and your trolls would be greatly rewarded for your role. Refuse my offer, and the trolls will forever regret the day they attacked my village."

He's not leaving any gray area. Greatly rewarded! Ha! If any of the trolls survived.

We sit in a long silence. The king watches my face intently, and I wonder if he can see the internal struggle raging underneath.

There has to be another way! I can't agree to making my people slaves for a would-be conqueror. Gord, Ismora, and Limery will likely die if I run, but I have to make it out of this castle. The one thing I can't do is allow myself to be captured. I have to alert the chief. If I can manage to warn some of the other troll tribes, hell, maybe I can even warn the dwarves, then we might have a chance at stopping this tyrant.

"I'm sorry, but no." I say it clearly and calmly, though my stomach is in knots. I know nothing about this man other than that he is more powerful than me. Even so, I have to try to escape.

"No?" he asks, and the mischievous grin returns.

As worried as I am for what happens next, I stand my ground. "I came here for peace, not to become pawns in a war we have no part in. If you force us to fight, then we shall, but it will not be on your terms."

He opens his mouth to respond, but before he does, I cast Horror of Vitality and the small monster summons in a puff of smoke. The rotund, furry monster with orange and blue stripes charges the king at the same time as I bolt for the ledge. The sofa I'm sitting on flips backward with the force of my lunge. The black ram's horns of my horror lower as it charges, and I pray that its sharp tusks inflict at least some damage to the king as I leap into the abyss.

Gravity quickly takes hold and the rush of air beats against my skin. Clouded sky is all I see as I plummet towards death. The thought of breaking every bone in my body scares me more than I would like to admit. Even with my tough skin and Constitution, it may be the worst pain I've ever felt in my life. The only consolation is that at least I will respawn in the forest.

My thoughts are with Limery and the others as I fall. Will they be killed for my transgressions or will the king hold them hostage? They are the very reason I came back into this game. I wanted to save them, but I failed.

I fall through a voluminous cloud, everything white as I'm engulfed in its misty embrace. Then suddenly, there's a strange presence around me, like I've been wrapped in a shield. The clouds disappear, and I collide with a hard surface, knocking the air from my lungs.

Stars dance across my vision as I gasp for air. My surroundings come in and out of focus, and I can barely make out two brown boots standing before me. My mouth tastes of blood. I try to push the stars from my vision so I can stand, but as I try to rise, I lose my balance and stumble to the ground once more.

I roll onto my back and look up to see the king. He holds my horror by one of its horns as its arms and feet claw at the air.

CHAPTER 5
DIRTY DANCING

So, the fuck-up fairy decides to make another appearance.

What have I gotten myself into?

My head clears and I realize I'm on the floor of the room I just jumped from. The stone is cool against my back, matching the icy dread in my chest. How did I manage to fuck up killing myself? One job. I had one job, and I screwed it up. Who is going to warn the chief about the king's plans now?

Some hero I turned out to be.

The king still holds my Horror of Vitality by the horn as it thrashes against his grip. I could explode the creature, but I doubt it would do more than scratch the king. He's staring at me with a look of what...amusement?

I want to smash that look off his face.

"What happened?" Kassidy's voice comes from behind me. Had he been in here the entire time without me realizing it? He must have teleported me back as I was falling.

"He tried to jump. Turned down my offer and then jumped off

the ledge." He looks down at the horror as if he's not sure what to do with it. The creature continues to snarl.

"What offer?" Kassidy frowns. The way he says the words makes it sound like he doesn't know the king's plans.

"Oh, you know. To invade the dwarven kingdom." A half-smile creeps across his face.

"You didn't?" gasps Kassidy. "These aren't nobles in your kingdom that you can just toy with for amusement." He sounds serious, the first time he's acted like an actual advisor. "For all you know, this could be considered an act of war."

"I doubt that. This troll has more honor than most of the men on my council, yourself included." Kassidy lets out a harrumph at that. The king finally looks at me, still holding the horror. "Can you call this thing off now?"

I have no idea what the hell is happening. "What's going on? Are you not attacking the dwarves?"

He waves the horror at me, and I call off its attack. It quits thrashing, and King Favian drops it to the floor.

"I have no plans to attack the dwarves. I simply wanted to understand what kind of troll you were, what your intentions were, and what you would do for power if it was offered to you."

"And what kind of troll do you think I am?" There's a bite to my voice that I don't try to restrain. He toyed with me, and it's not something I'll soon forget.

"The kind who would not put his people at risk for something he did not believe in." The king extends his arm to help me to my feet. "Bring the others in."

Kassidy makes a motion with his hand, and a few moments later, I hear the clank of Warwick's armor before everyone enters the room.

The horror puffs out of existence, his life force depleted, and I catch looks of befuddlement from my party as they join me.

Once we have all gathered in the center of the room, the king clears his throat. "I was surprised today. Surprised that a troll, a race most of my population would consider a monster, showed me what it truly means to make a tough decision. He displayed the true meaning of the word hero. It is my hope that you become not only a hero of the trolls, but a hero for Vanaria and all of Mythos. I pray that you do not hold my methods against me. You want peace, Chod? Then you shall have it."

Regional Alert! *King Favian has struck terms for peace with the forest trolls. Any unwarranted attack upon a forest troll by a Vanarian will be treated as an attack against a fellow citizen.*

Peace. It actually worked. I set out to do something and I actually did it. This will affect the lives of every troll in the forest. I catch sideways glances from the rest of my party. A demonic smile graces Limery's face. We actually did it.

"This won't solve all your problems." He takes the time to look and acknowledge each member of my party and for the first time since meeting him, I see him as a king. As youthful as he may look, he has that undeniable presence that says he is no mere man. "The hate and distrust will not vanish overnight, and there is very little I can do to change the hearts of my people, but I hope that in time, they will see you as equals. My advice is to travel north and make peace with the dwarves, then together, we can work toward a brighter future and prepare for what is coming."

The turn of events has my head spinning. I accomplished what I set out to. We have peace. I should be happy for that. But I just went through a mental obstacle course. I mean, I thought I was sacrificing my friends, for fuck's sake!

"You're an asshole!" I blurt it out without thinking, and the room goes silent.

The king stares at me for a long moment, and I'm suddenly conscious of every sound in the room. Gord's heavy, barbarian breathing. The gentle shuffle of the griffin's feathers as it settles itself in the corner. My own racing heart.

I'm an idiot. The king offers me peace, and I insult him in the next breath.

"I'm—" I start to apologize, but the king's laughter cuts me off.

"Asshole," he chuckles. After a moment, Kassidy joins in. Soon the whole room is laughing, Limery's shrill laugh carrying above it all. Even Warwick has a smirk on his face. "Asshole. I like that. I'll have to use it the next time I'm forced to entertain Lord Reynolds." He comes closer and stands directly in front of me. "I'm sorry if my methods were a bit unconventional, but I feel we will have a great relationship between our people. If I recall correctly, there are more than one tribe of trolls?"

"You are correct." I take a deep breath, trying to release some of my anger as I list them off in my mind. Mountain, seaside, desert, arctic. I've met the seaside trolls, but I have no idea what to expect from the others.

"Do you think they would be interested in peace? I am willing to come to terms with the other tribes so that our races may trade together. I am certain they have products we need, and I am willing to bet that a little bartering would go a long way with easing the hearts of my people."

I would hope so. Even the seaside trolls, who want nothing but to be left alone, might reconsider if it meant peace. "I can't speak for them, but when I return, I will let the chief know. We will do what we can to reach out to the other tribes."

"Very good. Then I think that is enough politics for one day." He tosses his goggles on a marble table. "We can negotiate the final terms of peace tomorrow. Tonight, I would like to host an evening of revelry in honor of the forest trolls. But first, Kassidy, did you save me any dinner?"

Warwick escorts my party and I to our quarters for the evening. We each have a separate room in one of the smaller towers of the keep. The giant center tower that touches the clouds is only for the royal family. A lot of tower for one family, if you ask me.

We have a few hours to kill before the party, so Gord, Ismora, and Limery all gather in my room while I recount the events with the king.

"You were going to leave us to die?" Gord's nose ring reflects the candlelight of the stone room as he scowls at me. "I take back every nice thing I ever said about you."

"When have you ever said anything nice about me?" I point a taloned blue finger at him. "You would have done the same thing. It was the only option. I had to warn the village."

"We know, Chods." Limery hugs me. "I's glad yous didn't die."

"You did the right thing," echoes Ismora. "I will be glad to be back in the forest. Trolls were not meant to be caged away in stone fortresses. There is no life when the ground is made of stone."

"If all goes well, we will be back on the road tomorrow." The quicker we can be back in the forest, the better. We may have peace, but the work has only just begun.

Limery flies up to the candlelit chandelier and latches on with his feet, hanging upside-down. "Limmy likes the city. Lots of peoples for him to watch."

"If by watch, you mean pickpocket, then sure." Sometimes, he's like a child in the candy aisle, in constant need of supervision. All those years stealing magical items to power their home has made thieving second nature to him. "You know, with the magic returned to the forest, you don't have to steal magical items anymore, right?"

He bats the lids of his bulbous eyes at me sheepishly. "Limmy knows."

"Then how about you keep your hands to yourself."

They each return to their rooms to 'clean up' and look 'presentable,' as Kassidy calls it. I don't know how the man can judge us when he always has something in his beard. Nevertheless, I scrub away the dirt and debris of our journey, and the new leather clothing they provide fits surprisingly well. In lieu of my normal loincloth, I wear a leather vest and kilt. It offers no bonuses, but the deep brown leather looks remarkable against my blue skin.

I sit on the bed, waiting for the others to finish. A large tapestry depicting a man riding a griffin and battling a dragon catches my eye. There are so many details in the threading that I could lose myself in it for hours. While the man rides his griffin through the sky, his army battles against a force of armed skeletons on the ground.

A knock on the door interrupts my focus. It's time to party.

A trumpet blares, announcing our arrival to the great hall, and the dull chatter of guests comes to an abrupt halt as we enter. The room is packed with hundreds of people, all wearing fine garments. The bright colors look like a rainbow vomited all over them.

"How do they move in such things?" Ismora stares at a woman in a ruffled gown that billows out twice as wide as she is.

In her slim-fitting gray tunic and pants, Ismora is nothing like the frilly women that surround us.

There are several gasps and whispers as Kassidy leads us to the head table where the king stands surrounded by several members of his guard. To his left sits a beautiful brunette and two young children. I can feel the eyes of the nobles on us as we walk, eyes filled with fear, wonder, and a million other emotions these people must be feeling.

This might not have been such a great idea.

The king has changed out of his riding clothes and now wears a royal blue tunic embroidered with silver thread. It has the same griffin on the chest I have become accustomed to seeing. An ornate design of silver vines runs down both arms. Upon his head, a jeweled crown glitters in the candlelight.

We step up to the head table and the king raises a hand, bringing silence to the hall.

"By now, all of you have received the notification detailing our kingdom's peace with the forest trolls." There are grumbles at this, but the king continues. "It is a peace that I believe will benefit both of our races for many years to come. As the nobility of this fine kingdom, you hold sway over the opinions of the common people. I implore you to see that the trolls are not that different from us. I present to you: Chod, Gord, Ismora, and Limery the Imp, our honored guests. Eat, drink, be merry. Celebrate peace, and when the time comes, make our guests feel welcome."

The king extends a hand to me. "Georgia, Maximus, Delania, meet Chod of the forest trolls." All three stand and bow.

"Nice to meet you." My deep voice causes the young girl to jump.

"Give it time." The king places a hand on my shoulder. "Now, let us celebrate."

We take our seats as food is brought out by the servants. Mountains of meat are set before us. Roasted deer, boar, and many types of fowl, the king spares no expense. I notice that the vegetables and fruits stay clear from our area of the table this time.

While we eat, minstrels play music, and entertainment is brought into the center of the hall. I recognize the juggler from the town center as he tosses balls into the air to the delight of many. I had almost forgotten about the coin he gave me. It's still tucked in one of the pouches I left in my quarters. Limery has an inkling to go down and join the entertainment, but I convince him to stay put this time.

After the food is cleared, people take to the dance floor. Gord and Ismora firmly refuse when I invite them to go down.

"That is not dancing." Gord looks at the crowd in disgust. "That is a mating call."

Remembering the tribal dance I saw on my first day in the forest, I can see why they have the misconception. This is fluid and elegant, with one movement blending into the next. The tribal dance was full of stomping, beating chests, and roaring. It was primal in a way this could never be.

"Fine, suit yourselves." I make my way down to the dance floor, and the flap of Limery's wings lets me know he's following.

I'm not sure what the dance is called, but it seems pretty easy to do. A few steps as they spin clockwise around the floor. I'm not that great of a dancer, but as a member of the council, I feel it's my duty to act stately as best I can.

I glance back at the table and find Gord and Ismora engaged in conversation with Kassidy. At least they aren't sitting alone giving mean looks to the other guests.

The song ends and another begins. I wait for an opening to join in, but one never appears. The dancers seem glued to their partners all of a sudden, unable or unwilling to switch off. I ask several ladies for a dance but receive excuses of sore feet and full stomachs.

King Favian said it would take time, but I didn't think I'd be shunned at a party thrown in our honor.

"It's okay, Chods. Limmy will dance with you." The small imp flutters in front of me, arms outstretched. I'm sure he's experienced his own share of dislike for being an imp.

"Mind if I cut in?" Queen Georgia appears beside us, extending a hand to me. "And I have a partner for you too, Mr. Imp." She smiles. Princess Delania mimics her mother's motion to Limery.

"I'd be honored." I take her dainty hand in my own, swallowing it in my grasp.

We take to the dance floor, and I try to ignore the daggers being stared in our direction, instead focusing on every step so I don't crush the queen's feet with my own. The queen is dancing with a troll. I can't imagine the thoughts running through their ignorant minds.

The queen is miniature compared to me. My massive hand wraps around her side as we waltz, and she has to stare straight up to make eye contact.

"My husband told me about what happened. I hope you won't hold it against him. He has always had an odd sense of humor."

Our eyes meet, and when she looks at me, it's not with hatred or disgust but wonder, almost childlike. Her blue eyes match the hue of her dress.

"I will do my best."

We spin around the dance floor and little by little, I forget that the other people are in the hall. I never went to any of my school dances. They seemed stupid. Or maybe I just didn't have the confidence to ask any of the girls out. But here I am now, my first dance ever, and it's with a queen.

"When I was a child," she begins, and I have to lean down closer to hear her. "My mother would always read me stories about princesses, but every now and then, when father wasn't busy with travel or business, he would read to me. He read me ancient stories about the heroes of old. About Timofy Stillblade, whose sword was so fast it appeared not to be moving at all. About Davos the Wrathful, the dwarven berserker who mined an entire mountain by himself. Even Brod the Vanquisher, the famous troll who cleared the great forest of werespiders."

The song comes to an end and we stop dancing. She looks up at me. "I am not afraid of trolls nor heroes, Chod. I believe we all have our parts to play in this world, you and yours included. I am just sorry it has taken so long for us to correct mistakes of old."

After meeting the royal family, it's a relief to know that these two rule Vanaria. Perhaps things will turn out okay after al—

A sharp pain shoots through my shoulder, and screams ring out all around me. I grasp at the source of the pain and find a dagger lodged in my back. Just as I pull it out, another dagger connects with my ribs. The site of the wounds goes hot and begins spreading through my veins. Poison.

Who would attack me here? Did the king betray me?

I'll kill him!

My head spins, and I can hear Gord's battle-cry and the crackle of Limery's flames in the distance. Who would attack me? Here of all places? I grasp my Tiger's-Eye Pendant and the burning liquid vanishes from my blood, allowing me to think clearly again.

I look up just in time to see Jude the Fighter move between guests in a blur, leaving a shadowy trail behind him. Something glitters in his hands, and I step in front of the queen, determined not to let anything happen to her.

Calling my mana, I cast one of each horror back to back, sending the crowd into even more of a panic. The horrors charge at the cloaked man.

Jude raises his arms in a flash, throwing the three glowing daggers in my direction. As they soar through the air, a trail of darkness follows each blade. I raise my arm and brace for impact.

The daggers vanish from sight. Jude screams in pain and falls forward, shaking violently as he collapses to the ground. Three daggers stick out of his back. My horrors rush to him, but before they make it, he vanishes, respawning only God knows where. All that remains are the daggers and his black clothing.

"Chods! Is yous okay?" Limery hovers before me, eyes full of concern. Gord and Ismora race to the spot where Jude died, only to find he is gone.

Warwick calls out above the frantic crowd, "Everyone out! Clear the great hall!"

Several kingsguards surround the king as he rushes toward his queen, while others usher the guests out of the hall.

Kassidy leans over Jude's remains, holding one of the daggers that killed Jude. "Dammit! I shouldn't have killed him. He could be reborn anywhere." He looks at me. "Chod, do you know this man?"

"Yes, he's another hero, Jude Duggan. We ran into him on our way into the city. He and I have a bit of a history."

"Warwick," Kassidy orders. "Put out a call to the city watch. Jude Duggan is to be apprehended on sight."

"Are you okay?" King Favian holds his wife and daughter tight, combing their hair with his fingers. "That man will pay for this! To attack an honored guest, in my great hall of all places. It cannot be allowed!" He releases his family and joins Kassidy. "How could he have made it past the guards without an invitation?"

"Heroes have their ways. Chod, let us get your wounds tended." Kassidy takes me by the arm.

"He will pay for this," the king reaffirms. "After Chod's wounds are treated, I want him and his party taken to their rooms. Post a guard outside of every door. We will talk tomorrow after we know more."

Of all the ways I imagined this night ending, attempted assassination was at the bottom of my list.

CHAPTER 6
SNEAKY SNEAKS

THE GUARDS ESCORT me and my party to our separate rooms for the evening. Gord, Ismora, and Limery are all on edge, and I don't blame them. I'm just glad Jude attacked me and not one of them. With the bonus critical damage from Kassidy's teleportation sneak attack, the hit was deadly enough to kill Jude with his own weapons. I'd rather not think about how it all could have went down. We can rest easy knowing that it wasn't some elaborate assassination attempt, just an asshole hero with a score to settle.

There's also comfort in knowing he has a bounty on his head. No human city will welcome him until he's been captured, and then he'll be dealt whatever punishment the king sees fit.

I still can't believe he attacked me in the king's castle. With so many people and guards around, he had to know he wasn't making it out of there alive. Maybe the thought of killing me was worth the risk. That's probably the thought process that landed him in prison in the first place. Was it worth enough to risk a hard-earned level?

The more I think about it the less sense it makes. The only

logical explanation, aside from him hating me so much that he would do anything to see me dead, is that he was hoping to start a war. If I died at the king's party and had no idea who was responsible, were they hoping I might think it was the king?

This is a fantasy game, but somehow, it's all politics. There's always someone in a dark alley pulling strings. Whatever happened to dungeon diving and monster slaying? Once I get back to the forest, I'm going to take some much-needed time for rest and relaxation.

I sit on the edge of the bed and find myself staring at the tapestry again. The griffin, the dragon, the army of the dead. Is it from history or a fairy tale?

There's a noise from the other side of the stone wall that startles me. It comes from behind the large chest-of-drawers that sits just below the tapestry. A grating, scratching noise that's muffled through the thick stone.

Not wanting to take any chances, I summon one of each horror and wait for the cooldown to cast more. If someone is trying to sneak into my room to murder me, one, they are doing a terrible job of sneaking, and two, they have another thing coming. I will not be attacked unaware twice in one day.

My horrors scurry towards the wall, sensing something on the other side. The Horror of Power takes the lead. It walks on all fours, wide-stanced like a pit bull with a massive head, sharp teeth, angry red eyes, and tusks that shoot out of its jaw like a warthog. Its fur is golden with a black mane that surrounds its head. A barbed tail with four spikes swishes through the air like a mace. It is my primary damage dealer, with each Horror of Power having twenty percent of my Strength. My hands glow faintly after the summon, the bonus from casting it granting my next attack double damage.

Behind the Horror of Power, the Horror of Vitality creeps

forward. The twenty percent of my health it receives makes it perfect for tanking. There's also the bonus Area of Effect it has that slows anything in its vicinity. Whatever is on the other side of that wall isn't going anywhere fast if we meet it. The black ram's horns and protruding tusks give a menacing quality to its otherwise cuddly orange and blue fluff.

The Horror of Finesse brings up the rear. The smallest of the three, its strength is in its speed. The blue, gangly creature is not much bigger than Limery. It has long pointy fingers, huge bat-like ears, and a dog snout. Basically, a blue imp without wings. With twenty percent of my attack speed, its sharp claws are deadly. The bonus heal it gives on my next attack isn't too shabby, either.

With three horrors active, I gain a three-percent bonus to Strength and Constitution. The bonus stats feel like a shot of adrenaline. I'd like to see Jude challenge me with a full army of horrors at my disposal.

My minions move closer to the wall, where the scratching continues, growing louder. Something has to be trying to get in.

A crack forms in the stone wall so thin it is almost imperceptible. It goes straight up and then cuts horizontally, like a door. Then, the stone pushes outward and bangs against the chest-of-drawers. Someone mumbles something from the other side.

It's been so long since I have been in battle that I don't have enough rage to use any of my barbarian abilities. When my horrors attack, it'll give me the rage I need to cast Bite or Claw or whatever else I need to seriously fuck up whoever is on the other side.

I pull back the chest-of-drawers and it screeches against the stone floor. The hidden entrance springs forward, pulling down the tapestry, and two bodies tumble to the ground covered in the fabric artwork.

My horrors descend on the bodies, biting and clawing and goring them with their tusks.

"Stop! Oh god, please stop!" a voice squeals, and I temporarily call off the horrors.

"Who the hell are you and why are you sneaking into my room?" I add a little extra roar to my voice for effect.

"Please don't kill us, Mr. Troll. We didn't mean any harm, honest." The bodies squirm underneath the tapestry like a dog caught in a sheet. "Hawkin sent us. He said you had a Circus Coin and that we was to lead you to the circus."

"Is everything okay in there?" a guard yells from outside my room. The door jostles as he attempts to enter, but the wooden beam that runs across the door frame keeps him out.

"Yeah, everything is fine. I fell off the bed." The mention of the Circus Coin has me intrigued, at least for the time being. One wrong move, and I'll explode my horrors on these two dingbats.

After a moment of silence, the guard's footsteps announce his return to his post.

"Who is Hawkin?" I return my attention to the intruders.

There's movement underneath the tapestry, and a freckled-face boy with red hair pops out from underneath. Several scratches run along his cheek. Dressed in tattered clothing, the boy can't be more than ten or twelve years old. Why the hell are they sneaking through the castle walls?

"He's the one who gave you the coin." The boy pulls the tapestry off his companion, an almost identical boy, only with jet black hair and a smudge of dirt on his cheek.

"The juggler?"

"Oh, Hawkin is much more than a juggler, isn't he, Brock?" The two exchange a knowing look.

The black-haired boy, Brock, responds with enthusiasm,

"Truly. Now, come with us and we'll show you the way. Make sure you bring the coin, Mr. Troll. You'll need it to get in."

This seems like a terrible idea, but I want to know more about the so-called Underground Circus and why these children are crawling through hidden passages in the castle.

Throwing caution to the wind, I follow them into the secret entrance. "If this is a trap, I'll kill you both."

The boys' eyes go wide before they turn and exit into the tunnel.

Inside the passageway, it's a tight fit. My shoulders are so broad they scrape the walls and I have to hunch to avoid hitting my head. Whoever's idea it was to install these in the castle, they were most assuredly not a troll.

Brock carries a torch to light the way, but with my night vision, I don't need it. The tunnel twists and turns, winding through the underbelly of the castle, occasionally criss-crossing with other hidden passages. We go up and down stairs, and at several points, candlelight flickers through the thin cracks in the stone.

With so many secret entrances, how is it possible the king is unaware?

Eventually, we enter the drainage pipes far beneath the castle. Water drips from the ceiling and trickles down the stone walls. Rats and other creatures scurry away from our presence, their eyes glowing ominously from the torchlight.

At the end of the tunnel, moonlight glows from beyond, casting a silver ring around the entrance. The tunnel empties onto a rocky cliff overlooking a wide stream. It's at least a twenty-foot fall from the tunnel to the stream.

The two boys grip the edge of the tunnel and exit, attempting to scale the cliff.

"Don't fall in the water, Mr. Troll. It's full of jabberfish," the red-haired boy warns before disappearing out of view.

"What's a jabberfish?" I dig my claws into the rock and slowly follow their lead.

"Oh, you know. The big, ugly fish with two mouths full of sharp teeth. My cousin got bit by one once; he lost three toes." He curls up his lip in disgust.

Sounds lovely.

When I'm out of the tunnel, the entrance disappears, blending into the rocky terrain.

"Is it some kind of enchantment?" I ask.

"Very old magic," says Brock. He climbs the hillside like a monkey, jumping and swinging along the steep cliff.

I release my grip on the tunnel and fully commit to my first-ever attempt at mountain climbing. Dirt and debris fall into the stream with each step, and I wish for the first time since coming here that I didn't weigh hundreds of pounds. I keep my eyes on the boys and try not to think about the demonic piranhas waiting in the depths below.

Before I know it, we've scaled the cliffside and find ourselves in the outer bailey, far away from the castle. I'd know it was the outer bailey even if my eyes were closed because of the stench. The center tower looms over us, its pearlescent exterior catching the glow of the moonlight.

No wonder no one knows about the hidden passages. Considering you can only get to it via the outer bailey and it has an enchantment over the entrance, there's not much chance of discovery. It can't be that often that people go scaling cliffs around here. But how does the king not know? Was the entrance lost to history?

The streets of the outer bailey are mostly empty at night. They have a sinister vibe to them, the way everything is covered in shadow. Cats prowl along the rooftops and every so often, a hooded figure disappears into a dark alley. We stay to the shadows to avoid the searching eyes of the city watch as they patrol the walls above.

The two boys take off and motion for me to keep up. They walk stealthily, like little ninja versions of Oliver Twist.

"Where are we going?" I follow close on their heels, but they both shush me.

They come to a halt at the end of the street where it connects with the main road.

Brock turns to me. "When we tell you, run to the other side, but not until we say."

He peeks around the edge of the house, up towards the gated entrance to the inner bailey. Of course, a blue troll walking through the outer bailey would surely alert the guards, and more likely, the king.

Brock reaches into his satchel and pulls out a large rock. He tosses it with a heave towards the guards. "Run!"

We take off across the road and I look up to see the guards all facing the other way. Classic misdirection, no magic necessary.

They take me down several small streets filled with houses that look like a strong wind might tear them apart, and we stop at one with a red lion painted on the door. The paint is faded and scratched, barely visible in the dim light of night.

The red-haired boy opens the creaky door and waits for me to enter. Inside, the house is empty. A small lopsided bed sits in one corner and a frayed rug covers the dirty floor. Aside from that, nothing. Brock moves the rug out of the way, revealing a cellar door.

He knocks three times and the door opens from beneath. Loud music and bright lights flood the small room we're in.

Did I just wander into a fantasy speakeasy?

"Mr. Troll, time to use your coin." Brock flashes me a wicked smile.

CHAPTER 7

THE UNDERGROUND CIRCUS

A LARGE MAN wearing a black tunic emblazoned with a red lion's head blocks entry into the next room. His eyes are mismatched colors, with one eye brown and the other sky blue. It's almost mesmerizing to look at him. He extends a gloved hand. "Coin, please." A thick black beard twitches when he talks.

Brock and the red-haired boy place a golden coin in the man's hand, and I follow suit. The doorman moves aside, and we enter a world full of swaying candlelight and whimsy.

Dozens of people shuffle through the room, holding large mugs filled with frothy liquids. Some of them bubble, others smoke, but the people drink them down with smiles on their faces.

There's something strange about the lot. Something...off. A woman with a long, hooked nose covered in boils shuffles past me. She passes by a man with splotched skin—the ivory tone is dark brown around his eyes, giving the appearance of a mask. A black man with bright red dreads dances about, his hair swaying like the flames of the candles. Next to him, a woman drinks a bright blue liquid and then bubbles spout from her mouth and waft through the air.

"Mr. Troll!" A voice enthusiastically shouts for me and I turn to see the juggler, Hawkin, flashing me a wide grin. "I was hoping you would make it. Such a crazy turn of events at dinner tonight. I'm glad to see you are okay."

He leads me across the room to the bar, and my two traveling partners vanish into the hustle around me. Hawkin holds up two fingers, and in a flash, a mighty mug filled with amber liquid appears before each of us.

Item. Underground Tonic. *-3 Intelligence for one hour. Useless, but it feels good.*

The stats remind me of the imp mead that Limery's mother served me at her cave.

"What is this place?" I ask. How is it possible that something so lively is going on just below the surface, yet none of it can be heard from above?

"First, we drink." We lift our mugs and they clink as Hawkin taps his against mine. I still don't know why he wanted me to come here, but so far, I'm not feeling any danger. "To the Underground Circus, may she never fade."

Hawkin takes the first sip, and when I'm sure it's not poison, I take a swig of my own. The warm amber liquid is surprisingly creamy and malty. It goes down easy, even with my new troll palette. Bubbles fill my chest and a warm happy feeling winds its way through my veins.

"That's the spirit." Hawkin takes another long gulp. "Welcome to the Underground Circus. The most secret guild in all of Vanaria."

"Guild?" This doesn't look like any guild I've ever seen.

"Yes, guild. Otherwise known as a collective of individuals

indebted to one another for the advancement of a common goal." He winks at me and takes another drink.

"I know what a guild is," I laugh. "I was more wondering, how is this one? It looks like a party room to me."

"Who says the two have to be exclusive?" He raises an eyebrow.

I'll give him that. "What common goal are you trying to advance?"

A woman steps up between us and orders a drink, stopping our conversation. "Lion's Roar Elixir, please."

The barkeep pours her a small mug filled with fiery red liquid. She takes a sip and then turns toward the room and lets out a roar that would rival my own. The crowd cheers at her performance, and she downs the rest before returning.

"Acceptance," says Hawkin. He points at the crowd of people dancing and drinking. "We all have our struggles, something about us that the outside world would call freakish. They praise us when we perform, because then it's okay. Then, it's entertainment. But let them catch us on the street in their part of town at a late hour and who knows what may come. Many of our brothers and sisters have scars, both inward and outward, from our run-ins with society." He takes out a gold coin and flips it in the air. "I thought a troll might know a thing or two about that. Perhaps I was mistaken."

"You weren't." I take another drink. He's right. More than he knows. It's the entire reason why I made this journey, why I'm fighting for my people. Acceptance.

"Thanks for the coin, by the way. Does everyone here have one?"

"Members of the guild have one, senior officers may also give out coins to non-members for one-time visits. Each coin is enchanted. The red lion on the door, no one can move past it unless they have a circus coin."

"Are you all performers?" I recognize some of them from the party tonight, and others from the street performance yesterday.

"Not all, no. Some are lucky in that their abnormalities are easy to conceal, but I'll not out them. If you are truly interested, you may discover yourself." He drains the rest of his drink and sets the mug on the counter. "I must disappear for a few moments, Mr. Troll, but please, enjoy yourself."

"Before you go, I need to ask you something." It's been on my mind every time I've thought about the coin.

"Yes?" Hawkins raises an eyebrow.

"Why me? You gave me the coin without knowing anything about me. I could have given it away to the guards. If the secrecy of your guild is so important, then why risk it on someone you don't know? Trolls are supposed to be evil monsters, you know?"

He smiles so wide it makes his eyes squint. "Why, indeed?" he laughs. "Enjoy yourself, Mr. Troll."

As he leaves, I analyze him for the first time. Seeing him juggling in the street, I never gave him a second thought, but now, I feel he may be more than a simple performer.

Hawkin. *Level: ???*

What? That can't be right. There's no way a juggler can be in the same league as Kassidy and the King, is there?

I scan the room, analyzing the crowd, and sure enough, one in every four has the same question marks as Hawkin. Are they all that powerful, or is there something I am missing?

"You look confused." It's the roaring woman from before. I examine her more closely this time. Pale features, dirty blonde hair that drapes down her shoulders like a lion's mane. Her level unreadable.

"I am a bit. How is it that many of these people are able to hide their level?"

She looks me over, as if taking me in. "Some of us value our privacy more than others. It's more of a risk to pick a fight with someone if you don't know their level, don't you think?"

I grunt in approval, remembering the first time I met Kassidy and the King. But how do they do it?

"Some say it's not worth it. Guards can see through the Conceal of anyone who is inside the kingdom, but we don't do it for the guards." She taps a finger to the barkeep, and he fills her glass again.

An ability that hides your level from those around you. That could be invaluable. "How do I learn it?"

"It requires fifteen points in Wisdom." She leans in closer. "Most people would rather spend their points on something more practical, but when you make your living on the streets, what is more practical than Wisdom?"

Charisma maybe, but I'm not going down that road ever again if I can help it.

"I see your point. By the way, what's your name?"

"Leona." She smiles. The lion, how fitting. She takes a swig of her new drink and lets out a vibrant roar. "You're turn—?"

"Chod."

"Your turn, Chod." She nods toward the crowd.

I hesitate for a moment, afraid that unleashing my roar might cause a panic, but then I remember where I am. We're all outsiders here.

I roar. It silences the crowd and the music, my ferocity echoing off the walls, deafening. I haven't roared like that since the forest, since Glenn. Tension flows out of my body. The silence that follows makes it all the more powerful. Somewhere in the back, a glass drops and shatters.

Then, applause. Hoots and hollers and laughter. The music resumes and people dance. For the life of me, I can't force away the smile.

"Well done." She pats me on the shoulder. "What I would do for the ability to do that." She looks at me with admiration, like I'm some prized jewel. I can't help but think that maybe peace with the humans might work after all. "It was nice meeting you, Chod."

"Likewise."

With a flourish of her dress, she disappears back into the crowd.

Fifteen Wisdom to learn Conceal. It's been a while since I allocated my stats points, maybe I have enough. I pull up my stats page to take a look.

Chod, Level 19 Barbarian/Summoner Forest Troll
  HP: 4255/4255
  Mana: 5000/5000
  Rage: 0/100
  XP: 308,249/355,000

Strength: 36
  Dexterity: 24
  Constitution: 37
  Intelligence: 10 (-3)
  Wisdom: 10
  Charisma: 6

6 stat points.

1 ability points.

The Petrified Staff offers a bonus of +3 Intelligence and +3 Wisdom, but I don't have any of my weapons since entering the city. My Intelligence has really taken a hit from the Underground Tonic, too. Luckily, Leona said I only needed Wisdom to learn Conceal. I have six stat points, but since I don't have the staff equipped, I'll have to use five of them to learn the ability.

Whatever. It's not like I have any better plans, and hiding my level might make Jude and the rest think twice about attacking me next time. I put all five ability points into Wisdom, bringing it up to fifteen.

Two new abilities appear amid the slew of old abilities I haven't unlocked.

Conceal (Passive). *Hides level from anyone who is not a guard on city grounds.*

Perception. *For 10 minutes, gain increased awareness of your surroundings. Spot hidden objects, as well as unusual sounds, odors, and tastes. Cooldown: 6 hours.*

Oh. No wonder most people don't conceal their levels. If given the choice between hiding a level and increased perception for ten minutes, who wouldn't want to understand the world around them better? Especially for a hero, using Perception after a boss fight might show hidden doors or missed treasure, or lead to escape when lost in a dungeon. For me, though, the ability to conceal my level could have a major impact going forward. I can always invest in Perception later.

I select Conceal. Nothing happens. No glowing light, weird sensations, or anything telling me it worked.

"Ah, thinking smarter already." Hawkin returns, carrying a

fiddle in one hand and a bow in the other. "I knew you were a smart one."

"Did it work? Is my level concealed?" How am I supposed to tell if it is active?

"It's as gone as the daylight. Now, come, it's my turn to play." He puts the fiddle to his neck and pulls the bow across the strings.

Dull light emanates from the fiddle, pulsating with each pull of the bow. The notes ring out across the room, overpowering the rest of the music. They carry over conversations until everyone stops what they are doing. The light of each note flows out from the fiddle in visible soundwaves, and when they touch the guests, each note infuses their bodies.

A note hits me in the chest. There's very little resistance as the purple soundwave disperses into my being. When it does, I feel healthier, more alive. I pull up my stats and sure enough, I have a bonus point in Constitution as well as a notification.

You have been targeted with Aura of Vigor. +1 Constitution for 2 hours. All debuffs have been cleared.

The negative bonus from the Underground Tonic has disappeared as well.

The red-haired boy's words come back to me. "Hawkin is more than a juggler."

He's a bard!

The melody bathes the room in a watercolor fog. Hawkin plays as he walks, the folksy notes of the fiddle winding through the crowd, carefully selecting their targets. It's relaxing, calming. For several minutes, he walks and plays. Some people sit on the ground, others embrace one another and sway with the rhythm. I half-expect someone to start clapping and singing Kumbaya. When the song ends, he spreads his arms and takes a bow to the applause of the crowd.

When his spotlight is over, I catch up with him. "You're a bard.

Why do you perform in the streets when you could be out adventuring?" With a talent like that, I'm sure plenty of heroes would want him in their parties.

He leads me over to the bar, where he orders another drink. "I imagine the same reason why you are in Vanaria instead of out exploring some dungeon." He sighs. "The world's not always safe for people like us. And even more so for people like them. These are my people. I do what I can for them."

"You should leave then. Take your circus on the road. There are enough small towns that I'm sure would want a break from their boring lives. You could even stop by the forest. It would be a great gesture for peace." If what he says is true, if it's really that hard for people here, then they should go somewhere else. Let the city see what life is like without entertainment.

Hawkin puts his fingers to his chin, as if pondering the idea for the first time. "Perhaps, but I don't know if the small towns and villages have the coin to pay."

"They will pay. Trust me. And if they can't pay, they will at least feed you." My mind races with history lessons about traveling caravans from the middle ages, of the circuses of the 1900s, of fairs and carnivals. People want entertainment.

"Thank you, Mr. Troll. You have given me a great deal to think about." The crowd begins to gather their belongings. Hawkin's Aura of Vigor must have been the finale to clear the alcohol and other elixirs from everyone's systems. "I hope you have enjoyed yourself. Brock and Neville will escort you back to the castle. I'm certain our paths will cross again someday." He extends his hand and we shake.

The boys lead me out of the house, bypassing the guards with another act of subterfuge before we arrive at the cliffside of the outer bailey.

I'm about to scale the cliff when a message flashes along the side of my vision.

Incoming Message (Admin): Chad, I'm sorry it has taken so long for me to respond. There was a great deal of red tape for entering a player into the game without a court order. Fortunately, that is all behind us now, and your friend Taryn will be entering Isle of Mythos *soon. We have also drafted a payment arrangement for you as well. You can find it in your inventory. Read it over and if the terms are agreeable, we will begin drafting money into your account. I will update you when we have more information regarding Taryn's arrival. We have also added in a protocol for you to message the admins. Focus on the icon of parchment next to your stats and it will transcribe your message. Remember, the world is in your hands. -Valery*

Holy cow! Taryn's logging in! I can't believe it. My best friend is going to join me in the coolest game on the planet. It's going to be awesome!

The excitement doesn't wear off for some time. Not until I've made it back to the castle and lie in bed. I can't wait to share what I know with Taryn. We'll adventure and explore, and I can help him level up. Now that I've negotiated peace for the trolls, maybe I can finally have some fun.

CHAPTER 8
THE GOD OF CHAOS

I'm still asleep when Gord's giant fist booms against my door. After my adventure with the Underground Circus, I was pretty late getting in.

Wiping the sleep from my eyes, I stumble to the door and remove the board that locks it. I usher him, along with Ismora and Limery, into my room and close the door behind them. I quickly abandon all thoughts of sleep. "You'll never guess what happened to me last night."

The only part I leave out is the message from Valery and the expected arrival of Taryn. By the time I'm finished with my story, they are all three scowling at me.

"You left the castle with someone you didn't know?" Ismora clenches her fist and I get the impression she wants to punch me. "After the attack at dinner? They could have taken you hostage, tortured you, killed you. How foolish are you?"

"Yeah, Chods. You is not smart. What if they takes you away?" Limery pleads with me, his bulbous eyes full of concern.

Gord snorts. "Why they put you in charge, I have no idea."

This is definitely not the reception I was expecting. "Don't you see the bigger picture here? We have allies. There are those who don't hate the trolls."

"The king doesn't hate the trolls. We have peace. Who cares if a few puny humans want us dead?" Gord stands up and walks over to the tapestry, searching the wall for the hidden entrance. He runs his fingers along the stone, but it doesn't open, only accessible from the inside. "We are the only allies we need. Even if they hate us, they have to follow the law or suffer the consequences."

"It's not that simple." I find myself getting annoyed by his brutish behavior. Why make the world our enemy if we don't have to? "Is it not time for breakfast?" I just had an amazing evening and they want to shit all over it. Nothing bad happened, so I don't know why they are so worried. It's not like I can't take care of myself anyway.

There's another knock on the door, and I open it to find Kassidy. His mouth is full of some berry pastry as he attempts to speak. "Breakfast," he mumbles between chews, "is ready in the dining hall." He takes a final bite of the pastry, and before he has fully swallowed, another one teleports into his hand.

All that power and he chooses to be a glorified fast food worker.

Warwick and several other guards stand outside the dining hall. Inside, King Favian and his family wait for us at the table. The king and his son both wear silver tunics embroidered with a blue griffin. The ladies wear silver gowns with blue ornamentation down the sleeves. They all stand as we enter. There are several empty seats along the king's left-hand side, and his family sits to his right.

"Good morning. Please, have a seat." He motions for us to sit. "Chod, if you would," he says sternly. His hand stops at the seat next to him.

I take my seat in front of the glorious plates of food. Eggs, bacon, and sausage cover our half of the table. The king stares at me as I fix my plate, his blue eyes gazing deep into my soul. Is it possible he knows I left the castle last night? Certainly not. If he knew, then why wouldn't he try to stop me? Still, I get the feeling that something isn't right.

My companions stuff their faces like they have been starved. Limery grunts with each bite.

"Once again, I can't begin to apologize for last night." The king's face softens a bit. "An honored guest, attacked in my own home. You have no idea the shame I feel."

"Don't worry about it. It was another hero. I hardly blame you for the anger of someone else." Though I appreciate his worry, my real concern is Jude. "Is there any word on his whereabouts?"

"My men combed the streets, but there is little to go on. He was staying at the Green Giant Inn, but apparently moved his belongings elsewhere yesterday before the attack." The king stares off into the distance. "There is a warrant out for his arrest, and he will not be welcome in Vanaria or any town under my rule until he has answered for his crimes."

Sucks for him. "What will you do if you capture him?"

"When, not if," he corrects me. "When he is captured, he will be shown the error of his ways. Fortunately for him, you did not die, but I will make sure he knows what is and is not permissible under my rule. Hero or not, I am the king. It is my hope that I may be able to correct his behavior and put him on the path to right-eousness. As I told you before, I believe the heroes will have a part to play before all is said and done."

Sounds like a slap on the wrist to me. Let me catch Jude out on the road and he will rue the day he ever tried to stab me in the back. I have no intention of losing any more levels, and once Taryn is in-game, I'll finally have another hero to watch my back. It doesn't matter if it's Jude or Glenn or someone else, if they mess with me or my people, then they will pay.

Over breakfast, we discuss plans for our two sides now that we have negotiated peace. We are free to trade with any of the towns or villages that have need of our supplies or services.

"I don't know how willing they will be at the start, but if you play your cards right, then you may very well find some nice propositions. It'll take time for prices to settle as you each gather the value of the other side." He takes a bite of a strawberry and seems lost in thought. "The forest belongs to the trolls. If I were you, I would set up a station along its boundary and sell permits to local hunters for starters."

That's not a bad idea. We could make money to buy goods simply by opening our borders. We could probably even sell back the weapons we've looted from all the soldiers who have attacked over the years. If we could transport the mana, we could even offer mana-infusion services. "I'm sure we'll think of something."

"If any of your people wish to train in Vanaria, let me know and I will have our masters work out an exchange program. I would very much value an ambassador of my kingdom to go and learn more of troll customs as well." He leans forward and looks down the table at my partners. "That goes for all of you. The trolls are entering this world and for my part, I will do what I can to make sure you do not fall behind."

Gord, Ismora, and Limery all issue their thanks.

"What about our children?" asks Ismora. "I think it would do well for some of them to learn the ways of the world."

"Send them and it shall be done."

"We are grateful for everything you are offering." This trip truly couldn't have gone any better. "Aside from your so-called test..." At that, he laughs. "This has been the start of something good between our nations."

"What are your plans from here, Chod?" the queen finally speaks. "We would love to show you more of the city if you have time. There is so much more than this castle to Vanaria."

"It will have to wait for another time, I'm afraid. This trip is strictly business. Though she has already received word of the truce, I need to inform the chief of the details. The beginning stages will be the most important for ensuring that this peace lasts." I finish off the last bit of sausage from my plate. "But once that is taken care of, I would greatly enjoy a chance to adventure once again."

"I bet you would." She laughs. "Take care of yourself out there. And, Limery, you keep an eye on him."

"Yes, ma'ams. Limmy is on it!" He gives her his trademark demonic smile.

The rest of the meal is spent in polite small talk as we tell the royal family about life in the village. For once, Gord and Ismora do the majority of the talking, and I'm able to sit back and listen. Gord is a proud troll and boasts of the accomplishments of the village and the other guardian trolls. Ismora talks of her training with the young trolls and her position as weapons master.

As they talk, my mind wanders for a bit and I find myself watching Kassidy as he shoves even more food into his mouth. He eats enough for two full-grown trolls. Honestly, I don't know how he doesn't weigh five hundred pounds. I focus on him and his level appears, still unreadable. I wonder if he or the king have noticed my newest ability or if they are able to see through Conceal just like the guards.

Is it possible that the king and Kassidy are not as powerful as I originally thought? Of course they are powerful, but just how powerful? Warwick is level thirty and is responsible for protecting the king. It wouldn't be too farfetched to think that the king's level isn't too far off. If that's the case, he has more to fear from the heroes than I originally thought.

"Are you sure you don't want the guards to escort you out of the city?" The queen has her arm entwined with the king's. The two children stand beside them at the top of the staircase. They look resplendent in their matching silver attire as they look down over their kingdom.

"If it's okay with you, we'd like to enjoy the view out of the city without armed security. To see what it's really like when people aren't being watched."

"Very well." The king nods. "Take care of yourself and your people, Chod. I look forward to our paths crossing again."

The morning sun warms my skin from above, and the pearlescent tower reflects onto the city streets below. It's kind of freeing, walking through the city alone. Especially after my adventures last night. I do wish we could stay longer, but it's important to get back and talk things over with the council.

The streets are alive with the early morning bustle. Workers race to their jobs while the wealthy stroll along the cobblestone, making idle chatter. We're given a wide berth everywhere we go and catch glances from far away. Some people are even bold enough to point. A grunt from Gord is enough to put a stop to it more often than not.

The occasional child we pass is what puts it all into perspective. Not yet old enough to hate, they stare at us with wonder until they are popped on the wrist and told to look away.

"I am ready to be home," rumbles Gord. "Two days in the city is more than enough. The stench of these people..." He fakes a cough.

"Oh, come on. You've got to admit that there is a certain elegance to this place. Maybe not the outer bailey, but up here, the castle. Just think of all the work that went into constructing that."

He scoffs. "If this is elegance, then I do not care for it."

We pass a street vendor selling meat on a stick. Whatever the mystery meat is, it smells divine.

"Can we haves some, Chods?" Limery salivates.

The old man stares at us with wide eyes, but he holds up a meat skewer. "That'll be three bronze."

Shit. I don't have any coins. We've been so used to providing for ourselves that we've never had the need for money. "I'm sorry. I just realized we don't have any money."

The man's wide eyes turn into slits. "Well, this ain't a soup kitchen. We're not giving away food for free. Go on, now. Get!"

Even though Gord can't understand what the man is saying, he can sense his reaction and steps forward with a growl. The old man jumps back, dropping the skewer to the ground.

"It's okay, Gord. We're supposed to pay for things in the city. We'll have to wait until we get back to the village to trade for coin." I can't believe we didn't bring any coins with us since we knew we were going into the city. With all the humans that have died in the forest over the years, I'm sure there are coins tucked away in a chest somewhere.

We turn to leave, and I can hear the man mumbling something about 'stupid trolls' and 'if this is the way things are going to be.' I try my best to tune him out.

"I'm sorry, Limery. We'll hunt for food once we are outside the city gates." He gives me his puppy dog eyes. "I'm sorry, but there is nothing I can do until we trade for coin."

"But Limmy has moneys." He reaches in his small pouch and pulls out a handful of gold coins.

"Where in the hell did you get those?" I know for a fact he didn't have any gold when we came into the city.

He bats his eyes at me sheepishly. "Limmy finds them. Can we eats now?"

I bury my head in my hand for a moment, contemplating who he managed to steal a sack of gold coins from. Certainly, someone from the party had their pouch a little lighter by the time the evening was over.

"You're going to be the death of me. Go get your food."

He flutters off toward the food cart. The man is about to tell him to get lost when he spots the gold coin in Limery's hand. Then his eyes bulge with greed and he licks his lips as he listens patiently to Limery's order. After a few minutes of talking, Limery returns, struggling to carry a large platter of meat. The man waves him off with a smile. Is there anything that a little money can't fix?

Limery bobs and weaves through the air, the food throwing off his sense of balance.

"You bought the entire cart?" We just ate breakfast not even an hour ago. How hungry could he be?

Gord takes the platter from him, and Limery shoves a skewer in his mouth. "Limmy hungry."

The imp has been hanging around Kassidy too much. I'm sure the gold coin he paid for all this food was more than the man typically makes in an entire day, maybe longer.

Not one to look a gift horse in the mouth, I partake in the grilled meats as we stroll through the inner bailey. With food in hand, it almost feels like I'm watching a show as the people around us carry on with their lives. The anvil of the blacksmith and the clop of horse hooves echoes through the streets.

I come to a halt when I see a large brown building with green shutters. For it to be in a nice part of town, it has a downtrodden look about it. Dark, heavy curtains cover the windows. The logo on the door has a tall green man holding a sign that reads, "Green Giant Inn."

The inn where Jude stayed before attempting to assassinate me.

"I want to go check it out." They look at me like I'm crazy.

"I thought you wanted to hurry back to the village?" Ismora plants her hands on her hips. "The king will deal with Jude."

She's probably right, but I can't let this opportunity pass me by. "Just give me a few minutes. I'll be in and out before you know it."

Inside, the curtains block out the sun and the room looks no different than it would at night. Candle chandeliers offer the only source of light, illuminating the room, but not enough to reveal anyone who might be sitting in the shadows. It's the perfect place for lowlifes and criminals to congregate. My night vision has no problem spotting the faces of the men with their cloaks pulled over their heads.

A balding man with a belly stands behind the bar on the far side. A few people sit at tables, eating plates filled with sausages and bread. A heavy-set woman with curly blonde hair carries two mugs of ale to a group of men huddled together in the corner.

Seems a little early for drinks, but it's none of my business.

"Can I help you?" the man behind the bar barks at me.

As I make my way over, the silence in the room tells me that the others are all watching me. Not a single fork scratches a plate. News has probably spread that a group of trolls are in the city, but I doubt any of them expected me to show up here.

"I'm looking for a man—"

"He ain't here." The bartender cuts me off.

"I know that, but—"

"He ain't here." He cuts me off again, and places both hands on the bar. He looks remarkably like a bulldog as he stares me down, one of the few humans not intimidated by my size and presence.

"Sir, if you would just give me a—"

"He. Ain't. Here. I ain't gonna say it again. The king's men come here, scaring my patrons. And now you. He ain't here. Now order a room or be off with you."

My blood boils at the man's response, and I have a mind to smash my fist through his bar. But instead, I turn and stomp across the room. Ismora was right, I shouldn't have come here. I reach for the door handle when I hear a "psst" from a cloaked man in the corner.

I focus on him and his stats appear before me.

Richard Hummel
  Level 17
  Cleric
  Human

Another criminal. And also a cleric. This seems like an awfully sketchy place for a man of faith to hang out. He motions for me to come over, and I take a seat on the bench next to him. The bartender is engaged in conversation with the barmaid and doesn't notice me when I slip to the side.

The cleric wears dark red robes, and a black chain hangs from his neck. He keeps his cloak pulled over his face, concealing all but his mouth. "You the one Jude tried to kill?" he whispers.

I nod. "Do you know where he is?"

"What's it worth to you?"

"Are you seriously trying to hustle me for information? You're a cleric, for gods' sake."

His lips curl into a devious smile. "I serve the God of Chaos. Now, what's it gonna be?"

CHAPTER 9

THE ROAD LESS TRAVELED

THE CLERIC'S LIPS CURL UP AS he waits for my answer. What is it worth for me to know where Jude is? I don't know. Will he stop coming for me unless I shut him down? I don't know if I should try to handle him myself or wait for the king's justice.

"I don't have any gold." Limery has the pouch he stole, but I'm not using it to pay for this. There has to be another way.

"Items then?" He stares across the room towards the bar.

I take out my items and let him examine them. "My weapons are with the guards. This is all I have on me."

Item. Phoenix Feather. 10% resistance to fire-based attacks. A very rare item, phoenix feathers can only be gathered if they are willingly given by the host. Feathers plucked from unwilling birds turn to ash.

Item. Tiger's Eye Pendant. Removes one debuff. Cooldown: 10 minutes. A rare stone believed to ward off evil and bring balance to life.

Item. Aquatic Boots. Allows user to walk on water.

There are also a few health potions and perception potions I crafted on the journey from the forest to Vanaria. Luckily, my Kingly Crown is stored safely in the forest. I wouldn't want that falling into the wrong hands. I don't have much, but maybe it's enough to get me a little information.

He eyes the items unappreciatively before settling on one. "I'll take the Tiger's Eye Pendant. In addition, you will owe me one favor, usable at the time of my choosing. You are an honorable troll, yes?"

"I am." And yet here I am making a deal so I can track down a man and punish him. "But I will not do anything that harms the troll population or brings shame upon my people."

He licks his lips. "We can work with that." He extends his hand, waiting for the pendant.

It dangles from my hand, but I can't seem to let it go. Chief Rizza gave me that pendant. Back when she barely knew me, when the entire hopes of the forest trolls rested on the adventure I was about to begin. Would she approve of this?

I wrestle with the thoughts as the pendant dangles precariously from my muscled blue fingers. With Glenn, I had no choice. I either had to make a stand or continue eating shit for the rest of our lives. I did what had to be done and it paid off. But this...this feels wrong. What do I have to gain from this? "I'm sorry. I can't."

"Very well. One thing I know about chaos is that it's always around. And it seems to favor you." He leans back into the darkened corner and I take my leave.

"Did you find answers?" Ismora narrows her eyes at me.

"No. You were right. Let's get back to the forest." I need to do a better job of listening to my companions. I've got a hot head and it has gotten me in trouble more times than I would like to admit. If the cleric hadn't asked for an item the chief had given me, I might have gone through with the deal.

The market square bustles as usual. In the center, I spot a

giant archway on a raised platform. It has runes engraved around its edge, and the center of the arch is blocked with stone. No one goes near it, and I can't seem to make out what it is for, so I ask one of the merchants.

"That's the fast-travel portal. Hasn't been active in ages." The merchant pushes a few of his items closer to me, hoping I'll take a look.

As we walk away, I can't help but think how nice it would be to have fast-travel. I could be at the forest in a minute instead of days. People could come from all over to buy items from the capital. I imagine there would be a lot more diversity if the different kingdoms were all connected, not to mention what's out there in the rest of the world.

By the time we pass from the inner to outer bailey, we've polished off the last of the meat skewers. Just in time for the stench of Rat Row to turn our stomachs. I wonder if every exit in the outer bailey is so run-down, or if we just happened to pick the shittiest one. A few hundred yards from the city exit, a group of vagrants loiters next to a dilapidated shanty. They wear tattered clothes and toss dice in the street. They're scruffy, scraggly, and I can smell them from a mile away.

"Aye, lookit this, boys. We got us a couple-a monsters in our city streets." One of the dirty men taunts us. "We best go get our swords and axes."

The others laugh, displaying rotting teeth and wicked smiles.

I can feel trouble brewing, but since Gord and Ismora can't understand them, I elect not to translate. Only a few hundred yards stands between us and the open plains. There's no need to lure Gord into a fight. Not after all we have accomplished.

"Just ignore them," I tell Limery. He clings tighter to my shoulder, and I can feel his feet radiating heat, calling to the power that dwells within him.

"What is it?" asks Gord.

"Nothing. We're almost out of the city. No need to start trouble now."

The vagrants are low level, every one of them a one or two. Even if they attacked, they wouldn't cause much damage. The disrespect for me and my companions is what gets me. No matter how much I want to cave their skulls in, we are on peaceful terms with all of Vanaria.

"Oh no!" one of them screams as we approach. "Call the city watch!" The others burst out laughing.

As we pass them, something small and lightweight hits me in the back of the head.

I turn around and see a stale piece of bread lying on the ground. Every cell in my body wants to summon a horror on top of their ignorant heads.

"What? It wasn't me," one of them says, lifting his hands to his shoulders.

"Me neither."

"Wasn't me."

Gord cracks his knuckles menacingly. He doesn't have to understand their words to know their intentions.

"Let's go." I usher them towards the gate.

Laughter echoes behind us as we walk.

The guards hand us our weapons without incident, and just like that, our adventure in Vanaria is over.

We cross the bridge that leads to the city and come to a crossroads. Ahead lies the hills and plains that we traveled through to get here. To the left and right is, the Mythroad, the road that connects all of *Isle of Mythos*. Travelers pass us by as we stand there.

"Are you ready?" I ask.

"For what?" Gord searches our surroundings for impending

attack, holding his axe at the ready.

"For what comes next." I take the road to the right and my party follows. "That's one small step for troll, one giant leap for trollkind."

They all just look at me like I'm stupid.

For the first time since entering the game, we're able to walk along the main roads without risking certain death. The days of hiding as we travel through the countryside, hoping against hope that we don't run into any other travelers, are over. We are a part of this world now.

But this is where the real test begins. Now, we face people who aren't under the vigilant eyes of the city watch. People who only face punishment if we make it back alive. We'll have to be alert.

The first few miles of the Mythroad are fairly busy, not by New York City standards, but it's busy compared to empty stretches of grassland, or the roads outside of Lynchton.

Those on horseback increase their pace to a gallop to pass us. In one instance, a man with a wagon full of lumber takes it off-road to avoid us, nearly spilling his load. I hope these sorts of actions change in time, but for right now, I need to get used to them.

"You think they believe we'll eat them?" A smile curls on the edge of Gord's lips. He is the only one who seems amused by everyone's fear.

"I don't know what they believe." I sigh. "They think we're all savages and monsters."

"We are monsters." Ismora shrugs. She says it so matter-of-factly that it catches me off guard. "We're not human. Why should we act like it? We are one with nature and the monsters that dwell within it. We live and die just like they do. Our village is one with the earth. Humans are the only ones that wish to tame the world. We only want to live in it."

It's the first time since being here that I really see it that way. They are monsters. Their customs and their behaviors have been so tribal that I've always compared it to my knowledge of tribes in the real world. But the truth is that they aren't human at all, only I am. I need to be more aware that every decision I make for the village is tainted because I am human underneath this giant mound of blue muscle. I want to help them, but I don't need to change them.

Maybe it's time for me to step down from the council. They have peace, so why not allow the chief to decide how to enforce it?

I'll settle that another time. For now, I'll enjoy the journey back.

Up ahead, Limery flutters through the air, flipping one of his stolen coins. I still can't believe he pickpocketed at a royal event. For the guards or Kassidy not to notice, he must be pretty good.

The road runs beside a stream that bubbles with small rapids. It's beautiful. Water so clear that the rocks and fish below the surface are completely visible.

The way the stream gently bubbles, it reminds me of a water fountain, bringing back distant memories.

"You know, Limery, where I come from, it's good luck to toss coins into water sources."

They all stop in their tracks as I say this. Maybe it's because I never talk about the real world.

"Really?" His eyes dart between his precious coin and the flowing stream.

"Yeah, you make a wish and then if you toss in the coin, it's supposed to come true. You can't tell anyone what the wish is, though."

His eyes light up and he flies over to the edge of the stream.

I remember going to the mall as a young boy. We were shopping for new clothes for school, so I had to be there. That was one of the few times Mom had taken me with her. To make sure I looked presentable. There was a giant fountain in the middle of the mall, and I saw other children tossing in pennies. I asked what they were doing, and Mom told me that they were making wishes. She said that if you paid off the gods, that it was supposed to make it come true. She gave me a penny and I tossed it in, wishing for more trips with her to the mall.

I guess the gods must have been busy that day.

Limery closes his eyes and I can see the force with which he is making his wish. He flicks the gold coin and it enters the stream with a splash. As soon as it enters, something rushes up and grabs it before disappearing in a silver blur.

CHAPTER 10

KEEP YOUR SECRETS

WE SEARCH for the gold coin, but it seems to have disappeared. The clear water offers no trace of its whereabouts. Whatever took the coin vanished in a flash, not even disturbing the silty bottom of the stream as it zipped away. The irony of the pickpocketed coin being stolen isn't lost on me.

Limery frowns at the tranquil water. Hopefully, his wish wasn't stolen along with his coin.

As we are leaving, a splash of water soaks the back of my head. A moment later, Limery, Gord, and Ismora are doused as well.

We turn to see an amorphous blob rising from the stream like a water ghost. Its watery exterior ripples in the breeze, sending a spray of mist in our direction. The gold coin shimmers in the center of the blob like a heart of gold.

Water Elemental. *Level 12. One of the four major elements, the water elemental is difficult to destroy, especially in an open water source. Being bodiless, the only way to defeat a water elemental is to completely destroy the element itself.*

Great. A water elemental in a flowing stream. The smart thing would be to just let it be. Even at level twelve, there's little we can do to fight it.

The water blob morphs its body, mimicking the shape of a troll. It rises taller and flexes its watery muscles.

"Is this thing taunting us?" Of all the things I thought would mock me, a stream was at the bottom of the list.

In answer to my question, another ball of water hits me in the face, and the elemental morphs into a tiny imp.

Limery cackles at the creature. "Look, Chods. It's Limmy!" A watery fastball hits Limery in the head, silencing his laughter. "Hey! You no hit Limmy. That's not nice." Fire crackles in his palms, and he offers his own brand of justice, slinging a fireball at the elemental.

The fireball heads straight for the watery imp, but at the last moment, the elemental disperses, forming a hole in the center where the fireball passes straight through.

Gord roars with laughter at Limery's frustration.

"Not funny!" Limery tosses another fireball and the elemental dodges it again, this time countering with a barrage of water projectiles that soak Limery and Gord both.

Unable to do anything, they both stand there fuming.

I summon a Horror of Power and send the demonic lion toward the elemental. The elemental morphs around the horror, letting it pass through, but right as it is surrounded by the elemental, I cast Kamikaze and the horror explodes, sending a spray of water as the elemental bursts into mist.

"Surprise!" I shout, content to have actually damaged the thing.

The elemental rises from the stream as a ghostly blob again, the gold coin floating on the end of one of its appendages. It flips the coin in the air with one appendage and flicks me an obscene gesture with the other before vanishing into the depths of the water.

We all exchange surprised looks before bursting into laughter. This world never ceases to amaze me.

Incoming Message (Admin): *We are in the final stages of bringing Taryn into* Isle of Mythos. *You should be hearing from him within a couple of days. -Valery*

I focus the message away. Two days have passed since I received it, and I still haven't heard anything from Taryn. Could there have been some kind of holdup, an issue keeping him from logging in? I hope not, because I can't wait to hang out with him again. We used to have so much fun staying up late and pigging out on pizza and energy drinks until our eyes were bloodshot and our hands shook from the caffeine. On nights like that, we never left a quest unsettled until it was completed or we died. With our teamwork, very rarely did we die.

Looking at my map, we're still about three days from the forest's center. I don't know why I didn't ask the king for a wagon or something to make the trip easier. Traveling by foot isn't that bad when you're adventuring and making stops to gather herbs or fight monsters, but when you're on official business, it's a real drag.

I could never be a businessman like my father. All he does is travel and go to board meetings. Where's the fun in that? Maybe I'll stay in *Isle of Mythos* forever, shirking all my responsibilities in the real world. It's not like Mom or Dad would miss me. It might be a few years before they even realize I didn't come home.

We do our best to pass the time as we travel. I taught Limery how to play "I Spy," and we've been playing for a few hours now. When it's Gord's turn, he always picks the closest bush or tree. I'm not sure if he truly grasps the point of the game or if he just picks the thing closest to him. Or maybe he's trolling me. Either way, he's pretty terrible.

"It's a good thing you're strong," I tease, and he makes a very trollish gesture.

As the sun begins to set, we stake out a place to camp for the night. The area we are traveling through is pretty wooded on both sides, offering plenty of cover from passersby. Not that we need it with our Camouflage. A few miles ahead, there's a small town called Dundee, but I'm hesitant to stop there. It looks to be about the size of Lynchton. I'm sure it has an inn, but we don't have any money, aside from what's left of Limery's criminal enterprise, and I don't want to encourage his behavior by spending his gold.

The smart choice is to make camp away from the road again tonight and avoid the other settlements for now. Let them see us from a distance and get used to the idea of trolls in public. The way I see it, our best bet will be to start trading with Lynchton first since we have something of a relationship. Start small and then branch out from there. We don't have to engage the entire island all at once.

When I wake the next morning, I find that I have a new message.

Incoming Message (Taryn): *Dude! This is so cool! I can't believe you had to go to prison to get in here. I know a few guys who would commit a crime just to be able to experience a game like this. Thanks so much* *for hooking me up with the job, too. The money they are paying me to be here is going to help out the family so much. It still seems surreal. Getting paid to play a game. Wow!*

Sorry it took me so long to reach out after getting in-game, I started my tutorial as soon as character creation was over, and it wouldn't let me message until I completed it. I'm free to travel now, though. Picked up a couple of quests in the city until I hear back from you. Hit me up and let me know where to find you.

Hell yeah! He's finally here. I don't waste any time responding. I focus on the message interface and it appears translucent over my vision. As I think the words, they appear in the message.

Message (Chod): *Taryn, that's awesome! What character did you pick? And what city are you in? I'm on my way from Vanaria back to the forest; we should be there in two to three days. I can't wait to meet up and tell you everything I know about* Isle of Mythos. *It's unlike anything I've ever experienced. Also, how did you get a tutorial? I was dropped in the middle of the forest.*

We gather our belongings and set out toward the village. I read over his message several times, trying to garner any information I can about his whereabouts. What city could he be in? There are only two major cities on the island, Vanaria and Seascape. Is it possible that he was in Vanaria at the same time as us? And how the hell did he get a tutorial? My tutorial was being smacked in the head by an ogre.

It sounds like he is off to a good start, though. He already has a few quests. That's one thing that I'm looking forward to about adventuring. There are surprisingly few quests in the troll village.

"What has you so happy?" roars Gord.

I guess I must have been smiling without realizing it. "Oh, nothing. Just looking forward to being back in the village."

He slaps me on the back. "Me too, brother."

A faint ding lets me know I have a new message and I focus on the glowing icon of parchment.

Incoming Message (Taryn): *You probably didn't get a tutorial because you are a deviant. Valery filled me in on your character and what's happened in-game so far. Sounds like you have the potential to be pretty OP. And you know I'm totally calling you Chode, right? It'll take me a little while to reach the forest, but I'll message you when I do. I can't believe there's no fast-travel in this game. Somebody should really try to reopen those portals.*

Anyways, I've got a quest to finish and then I'll be on my way. I'm going to try and level some along the way so you aren't carrying my noob ass. Don't try to ask for details about my character, I'm not saying a word.

Message (Chod): *Alright, scrub, keep your secrets. I'll make sure to rest up for a bit since I know my back will be hurting from carrying your weak self. Seriously, though, hurry up. I've missed you, bud.*

Even though I know we'll make it to the forest before him, the excitement of seeing my best friend has me walking a little faster. There's a lot to take care of once I return. I don't want to rush through it, because it's setting up the future for the troll race, but the quicker it's taken care of, the quicker I can meet up with Taryn.

The others are ready to be back home, too, so they keep to my pace, only stopping for food and bathroom breaks.

After we enter the boundary of the forest, I send Limery ahead to find his mother and ask her to come to the village. I have an idea that just might be able to help both the imps and trolls.

Tension seems to melt off my body when we finally return to the border of the troll village. The massive mana-infused flowers drape the village in a fragrant aroma. I didn't realize how tense I had been out on the open road. Luckily, we didn't have any issues once we made it out of the city. Integration might go more smoothly than I had originally thought.

Most of the village is waiting for us when we return. Chief Rizza stands in front of the others, with Jira and Tormara by her side.

There's a loud crash against a nearby tree, and two mana-infused wyrms tumble through a bush, coiled together. The legless dragons break apart and both rise, taunting one another like cobras before slithering back into the forests depths.

They've grown bigger in the time I've been gone. The three wyrms the village has are the only survivors of the regional event I unlocked after defeating the mana-infused wyrm that was blocking the ley lines. The other heroes managed to kill the rest, but the event was still a failure. The penalty for failure was that the remaining wyrms would lay eggs, starting an infestation that would destroy crops and towns across the island. But since these wyrms are all bonded, there's no threat of them laying eggs. Bonding with a troll means they lose their ability to mate.

The chief's golden eyes radiate pride as she pulls me in for an embrace. "You did it, Chod. Once again, you accomplish the impossible." Her green skin is warm against my own. She releases me and I make my way through the crowd, exchanging pleasantries with each troll in turn.

Jira grasps me on the shoulder, his white-tipped dreadlocks swaying with the movement. "This is a new day for trollkind. One day, we will look back and remember this as the beginning of something truly great. Well done."

Tormara holds a young troll against one hip, its hair the same bright red as her own. I expect one of the snarky comments I've grown accustomed to, but instead, she simply nods. "Good job."

Gord boasts of our adventure to his mother, the gray-haired Guilda. Though she is old and wizened, only her hair betrays her age.

Ismora embraces Yashi, the smallest of the trolls, for a long moment, and I wonder if there might be something going on there I wasn't aware of.

Several of the guardian trolls—Jojin, Watu, and Malak—offer me congratulations and speak of their excitement to adventure beyond the forest.

For everyone here, peace will change so much of their lives.

I gather the chief and the other council members. "Can we convene a council meeting? There is much to discuss."

The other council members agree, and we schedule a meeting after dinner. Before returning to the village, I instruct the guardians to watch for Limery's return and to send him and his mother to me when they arrive, even if we are in a meeting.

For dinner, I have some of Kea's famous stew. It boils twenty-four-seven, and Kea constantly adds new ingredients as the old are depleted. I also grab a leg of roasted boar and take a seat against a tree to devour my food.

Gord sits next to me. He turns his bowl up and slurps the stew like a savage. When he finishes it, broth runs down his chin beneath both massive tusks. One tusk is broken off at the end, and I realize I never asked him how it happened.

"How did you break your tusk?"

He rips off a chunk of roasted boar and responds with a full mouth. "I was very young," he mutters. "There was an attack on the village. Father rushed into battle, and being young, I did not yet understand the dangers of combat. A human must have thought I was an easy target, for it isn't often that humans meet trolls other than our guardians on the fields of battle." He cracks the bone in half and sucks at the marrow. "His sword caught me in the tusk and lodged there. If not for my tusk, he probably would have taken my head off. After the battle, when the sword was removed, the rest of the tusk cracked and broke."

"Well, I think it gives you character." I tap my roasted boar in his direction, mimicking a cheers. "Whatever happened to your father?"

"He died several years later. He was a mighty troll. He fell in battle against a horde of ogres, killing five of them by himself. If not for him, they would have caused great damage to the village." He talks of his father with great reverence. As the son of a great warrior, now I know why Gord carries such a chip on his shoulder. He has a lot to live up to.

"Sounds like one hell of a troll. I'm sure he'd be proud of the troll you've become."

There's a glisten in Gord's eyes for a moment and just as quickly, it fades away. He stands up and tosses his bones into the forest. "It has been an honor to travel by your side, brother, but it is now time for me to guard our boundaries once more."

With a final glance in my direction, Gord disappears amongst the trees.

CHAPTER II
THE FINAL COUNCIL

Twilight grasps the forests in its dark embrace. The fire that crackles in the center of the council area gives off an unholy vibe as light darts across our faces, momentarily keeping the shadow at bay. We look more primed for war than peace.

In the distance, the light of the mana-infused flowers twinkles on and off as someone walks through the forest.

Chief Rizza stares at the fire, her dark braid winding down her neck and chest like a serpent. Her long, lithe arms rest against her thighs. She is the epitome of a strong leader. Her mana-infused wyrm curls around the base of her living throne, now big enough to fully encircle it. The mana-infused ooze that coats its scales glows a dull blue in the dim light, and its electric blue eyes search the forest.

Across from me, Tormara strokes the hardened snout of her own wyrm. It licks at the air and leans into Tormara's hand. The only wyrm not present is Yashi's, who is not on the council. The three wyrms have grown a great deal in the weeks I've been gone.

In a few months' time, I imagine they will rival the size of the adult wyrm that was obstructing the ley line before I defeated it.

Before long, the legless, wingless dragons will be the greatest defense the village has. With three of them bonded to female trolls, I'm less worried about leaving, knowing that such strong protectors will remain.

Guilda is the last one to arrive, taking her seat to Chief Rizza's right. Next to me sits Kina, the only female troll that doesn't wear her hair in a braid or bun. Women back home would kill for her voluminous blueish-black locks. In the chair beside Tormara, Sonji twiddles her thumbs. Jira stands opposite Chief Rizza. Though he is not a council member, he attends every meeting and offers his advice when needed. As the only magic-wielder in the village beside myself, his shamanistic abilities are viewed with reverence.

"Let us begin," says the chief, bringing one hand to her heart. "We know that peace has been granted, but do not yet know the details. Chod, if you would, please fill us in on your journey."

For the next little while, I tell them of our trip to Vanaria. About my meeting with the king, jumping out of the tower, and even the attack on my life at the feast. They all sit in silence, hanging on every word as I describe the Underground Circus and the suggestion I made to Hawkin about taking his act on the road. I try to impart the way the humans looked at us, leaving no misconception that true equality will take time.

Once I've caught them up, I sit back and wait for their comments.

"Do you trust him?" asks Chief Rizza. "The king?" Her gaze is penetrating. Everything she has helped to build in this community is at stake, and it's my word she's trusting.

"I do. He seems like a genuine man, with a longing for adventure and an easy disposition. He doesn't strike me as one who desires war."

She sits in silence for a moment, her mind elsewhere.

"Then I believe the best thing for the trolls is not to take peace and hide away in the forest, but to make ourselves a part of the world once again."

The council erupts at her words.

"They can't be trusted." Tormara's words cut like daggers.

"It is not wise." Guilda's words are lost amongst the madness.

"I think it is for the best," says Kina.

Sonji sits quietly, tapping her fingers against her chair.

"Enough!" roars Chief Rizza. The council falls silent. "We have all lost loved ones to the humans. Over what? Ancient history. A war between humans and trolls that cost too many lives and left us isolated while our kingdom slowly crumbled. I will not doom our children to the same fate because I was afraid to work for progress." Her eyes fall on each one of us in turn. "If you do not agree, that is your choice, but trollkind will move forward with or without you."

Jira steps forward, requesting permission to speak.

"Go on." The chief nods.

Jira takes in a deep breath. The feathers that hang from his neck swish in the evening breeze. "I agree with the chief. It may not be easy, but the time has come for the trolls to embrace the future, or we will surely perish. Tough times may be ahead, but it will lead to a brighter future."

Tormara clears her throat. "I do not agree. Our place is in the forest, where we may grow stronger, not spread so thin so that we may fall apart. I have said my piece, but you are the chief. If this is your decision, then I will support it. I pray it does not come back to bite us." She slinks back into her chair. Tormara is spirited, but she has great respect for the chief.

"Very well. It is settled."

Night comes, and we spend the next several hours outlaying a plan for the future. Several of the young trolls will be sent to Vanaria to learn the ways of humans in order to better understand one another's culture. Tormara agrees to join as chaperon. I'm glad to not be a part of that debacle. I can't imagine her listening to anyone who is not a troll. We decide to open the edge of the forest to human hunters. They will be granted a permit to allow them to hunt, but the troll village is to remain off-limits.

Our remaining stockpile of human weapons and armor will be traded to Lynchton and then we will begin bartering with them for supplies we may need.

"I do not know how I feel about offering mana-infusion—" Chief Rizza is cut off by approaching footsteps.

Gord appears from the darkness. Limery sits on Gord's shoulder, with Lillith, his mother, fluttering behind them.

"What is the meaning of this, Gord?" asks Chief Rizza.

"It's my fault." I stand, acknowledging our new guests. "I requested they bring Limery and Lillith here the moment they arrived. I have a proposition that may help both imp and troll in this new endeavor. I would like the council to hear me out."

She gives me a questioning look. "Alright then, out with it."

I really hope this idea is as good as I have imagined. "I believe that the biggest struggle for our two sides will be the ability to communicate. Not very many humans outside of large cities have communication stones, nor do the trolls. I am proposing that we reinstate the IMS, Imp Messaging Service. They can serve as translators at the market, in exchange for a small fee. They can also deliver messages between you and the king, keeping a line of communication open. It will serve to make the transition easier, at least until some of the trolls learn the common tongue." I look to both Chief Rizza and Lillith. "What do you think?"

Lillith is the first to speak. "There aren't many imps left on the island. Many were trapped on other continents or went into hiding when the portals closed. I can reach out to those that I know of and see if they are interested, but know that many of them have suffered a similar wrath as the trolls over the years. They may not be willing. As for me and my family, we will help in any way we can."

Chief Rizza smiles. "I am grateful. For this and everything you and your brood have done for us so far. Limery has played no small part in where we find ourselves. Please, reach out to your people. We will be grateful for any who take up the cause."

Lillith bows to the chief. "Then I will take my leave and return when I have answers. Limery, let's go."

"Actually," I interrupt before they leave. "I would like it if Limery could come with me." He flashes me those demonic teeth in response.

"You have a communication stone," says Lillith. "I'm sure he could be of greater use elsewhere."

"I'm sure you're right, but there's something else I want to talk to the chief about." I turn to her and she seems to have a knowing look on her face. She had to know this moment would come eventually. "I don't really know the best way to say this, so I'm just going to come right out and say it. Trollkind is at the beginning of something beautiful. A new day is approaching, and I look forward to watching it all unfold. You are an amazing leader, one that the forest can be proud of." I take a deep breath before continuing. "It is your time to lead. I brought magic to the village. I met with the king for peace. I am a hero, and it is now my time to do what heroes do. I need to leave the forest in search of adventure. The council is more than capable of handling the politics without me. I will always be a hero for the trolls, but it is time for you to lead them into a new age. Therefore, I will be vacating my seat on the council so that someone who has lived and breathed this village for far longer than I can help you going forward."

They sit in stunned silence. Tormara raises a hand, but then it falls to her lap.

Chief Rizza nods several times. "I knew this day would come. I just didn't think it would be so soon." She intertwines her fingers, as if searching for the right words. "Chod, you will always be welcome in the forest. You are a member of this village now and that is not something that I nor anyone else can take away. I pray that your adventures lie elsewhere, and that though you are more than capable, this is the last we need of your services." She pauses. "When do you plan to leave?"

"Tomorrow. If I may, I would like to offer a recommendation to replace my seat on the council."

"Very well. Share your thoughts." She wears a half-grin, and I can't quite tell if she is amused.

"In my short time here, I have witnessed the importance of this council. They weigh in on every decision you make, offering varied points of view, giving you insight you might not normally have. Only sometimes losing their temper." I nod to Tormara, and I swear she blushes. "When my predecessor fell in the battle with Glenn, I was given the opportunity to offer my own advice. In the coming years, it will be important to have someone with experience, but also who isn't afraid to speak their mind. Someone who loves this village more than anything in the world. Someone like Gord."

Everyone except the chief bursts into chatter. Gord's eyes are as wide as I have ever seen them and his jaw hangs slack. I hope I didn't break him. I raise my hand for them to let me finish.

"I know I was the first male to ever sit on the council. It would not have happened if I hadn't completed the quest to clear the ley line. But be that as it may, you are entering a new age. Why not have a council that speaks for all trolls, and for all points of view?" I stand up from my council seat. "Think about it. He's not as dumb as he looks."

CHAPTER 12
FAREWELL

WHEN I WAKE UP, I'm not nearly as well-rested as I would like. Thoughts of whether or not I made the right decision kept creeping through my dreams all night. In the dreams, the village was bombarded with secret attacks and the sky rained fiery arrows. I stood there, watching it all unfold but unable to help. In the end, the bodies of everyone I cared for in this game lay scattered over the forest floor, and I sat all alone in the burnt aftermath.

I sit up and rub my eyes. It's not like I've been at the village every second since I've been here anyway.

They're just dreams, nothing more. A manifestation of my worries. I know the village will be fine without me. Chief Rizza and the others are more than capable, and for the first time in ages, they have peace. Besides, I didn't come back into this game to sit around and babysit them. I need to continue leveling up, because if there ever comes a time when they do need me, I want to be the baddest motherfucker on this island.

A light knock interrupts my thoughts. Limery hovers at eye level when I open the door.

"Morning, Chods." He beams at me, holding a roasted leg of some small animal in one hand.

"Good morning. Want to come in?"

"I thought we was leaving?" He tilts his head like a confused dog.

"Soon. There are a few things I need to wrap up before we go. After that, it's all adventure. You excited?"

"Limmy can't wait to see the world with Chods." He rips the last of the meat from the bone and contemplates throwing it on the floor.

"Don't you dare." I scold him.

He gives me a sheepish grin before stuffing the bone in a small pouch.

I pack what few items I have into my satchel and prepare to say my good-byes. "I need to go see the chief before we leave. If you want, you can go say good-bye to the others and I'll come find you when I'm done." I know for a fact that he and Gord grew pretty close over our adventures together. He's really grown on the rest of the village, too.

Once I'm finished with the chief, I plan to say my farewells to Gord, Ismora, Yashi, and Tormara.

One of the troll children runs through the village center, a small wooden club tossed over his shoulder. I stop him, and he points me in the direction of the chief.

The spicy smell of incense greets me long before I enter Jira's hut. Smoke wafts out of the chimney. He must be meditating extra hard today.

The chief's wyrm guards the entrance to Jira's hut but moves aside to let me pass. Inside, I find Jira and the chief leaning over a golden chest. The same chest where they plucked items for me and my party before our journey to Paltras Ruins.

I clear my throat and they both turn around.

"Chod." Chief Rizza nods at me. For a moment, we just look into one another's eyes. I hope she doesn't view this as me abandoning the village. I want to spout off all the reasons why I can't stay, anything and everything to justify why I must go. Why must I feel so guilty for doing what needs to be done? Our gaze breaks and she looks past me. "Morning has come too soon. It seems like just yesterday you came to us, and now it is time for you to leave."

"I will always be around if you need anything. All you have to do is offer me a quest, and I will know to return right away. But before I go, I just wanted to say thank you. For taking a chance on me when I was just finding my way in this world. This village has made me into who I am."

She smiles. It's a smile of both happiness and sadness. "Before you go, we have a final gift for you."

Jira pulls out a small pouch and it jingles as he hands it to me.

Currency: *10 gold.*

"You've got better things to do than trade leather. Plus, your leatherworking skill doesn't seem to have improved much." Jira grins. "I don't know if it is a lot or a little, but I hope it serves you well."

Once again, their generosity astounds me. I find it funny, that for the majority of my time here, currency was never an issue. The trolls have a village that is built on community. For my first thirty days, gold never crossed my mind. Not until I entered a human city.

I have a feeling ten gold will go quite a long way in these smaller towns. "Thank you. Both of you."

They both embrace me before I leave, and I'm certain it will not be the last time we meet.

When I step out into the courtyard, everyone is gone. Even Kea has left her stew unattended. The children that normally train to the other side of Jira's hut are nowhere to be found.

"Where is everyone?" I ask the chief, but she doesn't answer. Instead, she says, "Follow me."

I follow her out of the village center and into the forest. We walk in silence, dead leaves crunching under our feet. We come to the spot where we battled Glenn's army, the broken trees the only reminder of the chaos. It's then that I see the translucent figures of the entire village as they sit stone silent in two rows facing one another.

A loud crack echoes as each of them claps their hands and rises to their feet. They all take a step back, making a path for me to walk.

At the end of the line, closest to me, Malak and Jojin face one another. They stomp their feet, then beat their chests. As they finish, the two trolls closest to them repeat the action. Then all four of them stomp their feet and beat their chests. The next two repeat the action. The thunder of their movements grows with each new addition. Then all six continue the cycle, with two more joining in. The cycle continues until the entire line of trolls has joined and their movements rumble the very ground.

Chief Rizza nudges me forward, and they all fall silent. As I step in front of Malak and Jojin, they all let out a roar so loud that the birds in the trees take flight. They begin another beautiful tribal dance, filled with stomps and thunderous chest-beats, thigh-slaps, and roars that clear the forest of animals for miles. I let the sounds and vibrations wash over me.

At the very end of the line, Gord and Tormara face one another. Gord's nose ring flicks with each movement, and Tormara's braid whips like a viper. I step past them, and they all fall silent once more.

Far behind me, a song erupts. It's a song without words, but a guttural cry as Chief Rizza wails into the sky. It's a song of power and melancholy. A song of farewell.

Suddenly, my body erupts in electricity. For a moment, shockwaves course through my veins, threatening to explode out like lightning. Then just as quickly, it fades away.

You have been blessed by the forest trolls.

CHAPTER 13

MYTHOS' MOST WANTED

THE FAREWELL DANCE will be burned into my mind for as long as I live. Much like the dance I witnessed my first night in the village, the power and might in those movements resonates in my bones. Maybe the dance called to something primal in me, to my very troll nature.

Aside from the notification telling me I had been blessed by the forest trolls, none of my stats have changed. Not like when Hawkin hit me with his Aura of Vigor. Still, there was something powerful about the blessing. Something happened, I'm sure of it. How else do I explain the electricity that seemed to course through my veins?

"Did you feel it?" I ask Limery. He sits perched on my shoulder watching colorful birds as they jump from limb to limb.

"Feels what?" His eyes are locked on the birds. He conjures a fireball, and I know exactly what is about to happen. A moment later, a bird is engulfed in flame and falls to the ground. Limery hops from my shoulder to claim his prize.

I guess it was just me who was affected by the chant. I wish I could have stayed to ask, but after such a mighty performance, I didn't feel like I should hang around and ask questions. When a moment like that comes around, I think it's best not to ruin it.

Even if there was no buff, the gesture itself was momentous. The entire tribe sending me off like that, it really shows the impact I made in my short time there. Not to mention the impact they had on me. I may not ever understand what it's truly like to be a troll or have the history they have, but I know that I will always be a forest troll, even if I go back to the real world.

Now that I have no obligations, I feel both free and lost at the same time. It's a strange feeling, not having anything to do. Since I first came into *Isle of Mythos,* I've had one quest right after another. And not just "help me clear these wolves that keep killing my livestock" quests, but big, world-spanning quests. Now, I finally get to experience the game without an entire race depending on me. It's nice. I'm a free troll with nothing but time to kill until Taryn shows up.

Speaking of Taryn, he has to be getting close by now.

My first order of business: travel to Lynchton. I'd like to get the lay of the land and remind everyone there what I am capable of, so that they are on their best behavior when the first envoy of trolls arrives. There will definitely be a transition period, but if Lillith comes back with enough translators, things will go a lot smoother. The least I can do is give the village some warning of what to expect when the trolls arrive.

I pull Petrified Staff from my satchel and cast a Horror of Finesse. The blue, imp-like creature falls in line behind me. Since I've got some time to kill, I might as well do a little leveling.

Most of the creatures in this forest are far below my level now, but every little bit helps. Once Taryn levels up more I'd like to find some higher level areas, wherever they may be.

The first unlucky creature to cross my path is a deer. The

young buck squares off with me, antlers lowered, and begins his charge. When it's several yards out, I cast Horror of Vitality, and the bonus effect of the summoning slows the charge. The Horror of Finesse bites and claws at the creature, while the furry Horror of Vitality lowers its own horns and collides with the deer's antlers. The collision disorients the deer and breaks off one of his antlers. With a few swings of my scepter, my XP bar moves a small amount. I loot the corpse of its hide and antlers.

Limery returns from bird killing just as I finish removing the hide.

I'm contemplating whether I should save the meat or cook it now when I hear a loud crash from beyond a thicket of trees. Branches crunch and something grunts in disapproval.

We follow the source of the noise and find an ogre pulling trees from the ground and breaking them in half. The small-headed, lumbering fool grunts to itself as it carries on its meaningless work. I focus on the monster and view its stats.

Ogre. *Level 6. Big, strong, and ugly. Ogres are quick-tempered, powerful brawlers.*

It turns at our approach, revealing a set of crooked brown teeth. The top row is dull, but the bottom row is jagged and sharp. It's draped in an assortment of furs, and a bone necklace dangles across its pasty yellow chest.

I've seen that necklace before. That's when I realize that this isn't just any ogre; this is the asshole that killed me!

His bloodshot eyes cut at me. "You!" he roars. Thanks to my communication stone, I can actually understand him this time.

"Hey there. Long time, no see, big fella. I love what you've done with your hair. How do I get it to come out of my nostrils like that?" I taunt him. If we're going to fight, I might as well get him angry beforehand.

He lifts a tree trunk and charges, his ogreboobs flopping with each step.

"Limery, stay back. He's mine." Limery lands on a tree limb to watch the carnage unfold.

I cast three more horrors in rapid succession, bringing my total to five.

"Bad troll!" the ogre shouts, spittle flying from his mouth. Each fat roll jiggles as the monster rushes towards me. He's taller than I am, and definitely weighs more, but he's about to get payback from our first encounter.

I use Sacrifice, and all five horrors vanish, a portion of their energy flowing into me. I gain +1 Dexterity for each Horror of Finesse, +1 Strength for the Horror of Power, and +1 Constitution for each Horror of Vitality. My muscles bulge and heart pounds with the sudden increase of stats.

"Bad troll," he says again, displaying his extensive vocabulary.

He swings the club, and I dodge it with ease. The force of the attack knocks the ogre off balance. I rake my claws along his side as he stumbles, and he cries out in pain as thick black blood flows down his side.

He regains his balance and swings again, but my high Dexterity is too much for the level-six cretin. I duck under the blow and land a right hook to the side of his pea-brained head. He staggers back and forth from the punch.

"You might want to get a colonoscopy after all this butthurt." I taunt him again, but the effort is lost on him.

"Get him, Chods!" Limery cheers me on.

The two attacks have dropped the ogre's HP to fifty percent. Even though he's a significantly lower level than me, he still has a high Constitution. I really was an idiot to try and fight him when I was only level one.

The follies of youth.

When the ogre's head quits spinning, he tilts it head back and roars. His HP slowly begins to regenerate.

"That's a nice trick."

I put away my Petrified Staff and pick up a wooden club off the ground. We're going to finish this the old-fashioned way. With blunt force.

He pulls back his club to swing, and I do the same thing. Our clubs collide with a violent crash, exploding into debris and sawdust. The ogre mumbles something unintelligible as he scrambles for another weapon. He leans down to pick up a tree trunk, and I plant my foot against his ass, sending him sprawling to the forest floor.

I find a nearby boulder and lift it above my head. "Sorry, dude. It's not business, it's personal." I drop the boulder and score a critical hit.

In the aftermath of the fight, I realize the ogre shit himself. The realism of this game never ceases to amaze me. Even though the ogre could speak, I don't feel bad about killing him. Not after the story Gord told me about his father. The fewer murdering nitwits we have roaming the forest, the better.

"Good job, Chods. Yous kicked his butt!" Good to know I'll always have one cheerleader everywhere I go.

The bonus stats from Sacrifice wear off and I feel like my normal self again. I try to imagine what it would feel like if I had a full army of horrors when I used the ability. +20 Strength, Dexterity, and Constitution. Could Warwick or Kassidy stop me if I were that powerful? Too bad the buff only lasts as long as the remaining time on each horror. Would it make more sense to keep my strength spread out among my horrors since they don't decay in battle rather than have it all on me?

Questions for another time. For now, I'm going to enjoy the sweet taste of revenge.

There's not much to loot from the ogre's corpse. The furs he wears are mangy, and I couldn't be paid enough to eat that meat.

Limery and I follow a deer trail through the forest, making idle chat about what happens next.

"In a few days, there's someone I want you to meet." I duck below a low branch. "He's an old friend of mine."

"Really?" His bulbous eyes go even wider. "Chods's old friend?"

"Yeah, he comes from where I do. Once we meet up, we can all go adventuring together."

"Oh yes, Limmy loves adventures." He grins.

"Now that we don't have any quests, is there anything that you want to do?" Since I met the little guy, he's followed me practically everywhere. I'd like to do something he wants for a change.

"Limmy just wants to adventure with Chods."

We camp for the night near the edge of the forest. Even with the newfound peace, I don't want to show up to Lynchton's gate at night in case I frighten them. Limery tucks himself under my arm, and the sounds of howling wolves lull us to sleep.

The next morning, sun beams through the boundary of the forest, bringing the day to life. All around us, the forest erupts with sound. Birds chirp, bees buzz along the forest's edge, and critters scurry along the underbrush.

Something tickles my arm, and I look down to see a bright red lizard licking at my skin. Smoke plumes out of its nostrils. A flick of my wrist sends the creature soaring into a bush.

Limery wakes with groggy eyes and stretches his small arms overhead. I have the strong urge to rub his tummy, but I refrain.

"Ready to explore?" I ask.

"Oh yes! But first, Limmy needs to eats." He rubs his stomach and takes flight. Fire crackles as he sets out in search of breakfast.

After devouring some roasted fowl, we step out of the shadows and into the open stretch between the woods and Lynchton. Several wagons are already entering the city, loaded with the day's produce.

I walk confidently towards the town, as if entering the city is the most normal thing in the world. We catch several glances, but my reputation precedes me, and no one says a thing.

A familiar face greets me at the gate to Lynchton. Jameson, the soldier who awoke to a hundred trolls demanding entry the night we spawn-camped Glenn, stands guard at the gate along with another young soldier. Their armor isn't as polished and pristine as the soldiers in Vanaria. This is armor that is used both for training and battle, armor that is mended when dented and passed down from father to son.

"Morning." I nod, gauging their response.

"Come to humiliate me again, have you?" He cocks an eyebrow but offers no resistance as we enter.

Several pieces of parchment nailed to the gate catch my eyes. They're wanted posters, and I recognize the men pictured.

Jude Duggan: *wanted for attempted murder and breaking out a prisoner.*

Glenn Orickson: *wanted for escaping the town dungeon.*

Their faces stare at me from the yellowed parchment. This is not good. This is so not good.

"What happened? What does it mean that Glenn escaped?"

Jameson lets out a long sigh. He waves a wide-eyed man driving a wagon through the gate after his partner inspects its contents.

"A couple of days ago, this fellow in black shows up at the dungeon, demanding that he be let in. The guard on duty immediately recognized the wanted mark on his head, but before he could sound the alarm, the man stabbed him and took the cell keys. He and Glenn disappeared into the night."

"And what about the guard? Did he survive?"

"Barely. He's lucky that their shifts changed only minutes after the attack or else he would have bled to death all alone." Jameson shakes his head at the thought. "Truth be told, I don't care that they're gone as long as they stay the hell away from here."

Fat chance of that. Seems like Jude is recruiting for his troll-hating army. "Was there a paladin with them? Big guy, golden hair, silver and blue armor?"

"Not that I've heard. As far as I know, he was alone. Why? Should we be expecting more?" Jameson jabs the butt of his spear into the ground.

"No. He got what he came for." For now, at least.

I struggle with what to do with the news. At level one, it'll be some time before Glenn is strong enough to form any sort of attack on the village, but I still need to let the chief know. A warning could be the difference between life and death.

If Jude is running the show, then I'll be the one they're after. But that doesn't mean they won't go through the village to get to me. They know how much I care about the other trolls. There's not a bone in my body that believes they wouldn't hurt them.

At least they won't be able to buy anything from towns or villages. That'll slow them down some. Without access to a blacksmith or tailor, they'll probably resort to killing travelers for items. Anyone who meets them will know they are wanted by the crown. I'm sure they'll either head for the wilderness, or somewhere the king's justice doesn't reach.

North, perhaps. The wanted mark might not even work outside of the king's borders.

I turn away from the wanted posters, back to Jameson. "There will be more trolls coming in a few days to trade with the village. Make sure that you let them know about these two so that they can prepare."

Jameson flashes me a fake smile. "More trolls. Great."

I don't blame his reticence towards the trolls. He had to have gotten a pretty strong talkin- to after letting us all into the town that night. Not that he had a choice.

"Good seeing you, Jameson." I leave him to brood by the gate as we enter the town.

The last time I was here, the moon shone overhead. The town is even more quaint by daylight, igniting my desire for adventure. The blacksmith, tailor, and apothecary are to my left. To my right are the stables, The Dancing Donkey Inn, and a market. The market is filled with people at this hour, and the smell of roasted meat wafts through the air, causing me to salivate. Farther down, there are several buildings that sell everything from pottery to spices. The steeple from the town church rises high into the sky from the center of town, and farther back are the houses with their thatched roofs.

"Excuse me." I try to get the attention of a woman walking by with a basket of fruit. She jumps at the sound of my voice before running off.

Several people stare at me, covering their mouths as they whisper between themselves.

I walk over to one of the stable boys and try again. The young man with curly brown hair struggles with a horse as he attempts to saddle it.

"Excuse me, but do you know where I might find the mayor? I'd like to have a word with him."

The man looks up from his work and does a doubletake. He lets the saddle drop to the ground, abandoning the attempt for a moment. "Uhm. Probably at the Spice Emporium. Everybody knows he fancies Ms. McGee." He shuffles back and forth. "Say, you're that troll, aren't you? The one who did that to Glenn?"

"Yeah, about that—"

"I, for one, am glad you did it. He deserved it for what he did to my brother." A fire burns behind his brown eyes. "Tucker never was a fighter. He fancied himself a poet, and yet, somehow, that bastard convinced him to go off and fight your lot. My brother wasn't the only one either. Lots of folks who normally wouldn't do such a thing followed him to their deaths." He takes off his gloves and extends a hand. "If you ever need anything in Lynchton, come to me and I'll do my best to get you sorted. Name's Luka."

"Nice to meet you, Luka. I'm Chod. This is Limery." He shakes Limery's small hand. "We need to see the mayor, but thank you for your kindness."

The staring townspeople don't bother me as we walk to the spice shop. I can't stop thinking about what Luka said about his brother. How is it that Glenn was able to convince so many people to join his cause? People that normally wouldn't. And not just once, but multiple times.

"Chods, we's here." Limery snaps me from my thoughts.

I open the door and a little bell rings, announcing our arrival. There's a sharp intake of breath that I suppose I should be getting used to, and a woman wearing a pink frilled dress clasps a hand over her mouth. The wrinkled old sot I remember yelling at me just before I executed Glenn leans against the counter.

"Can I help you?" the woman squeaks.

"Actually, I'm here to see him." The tension visibly leaves her body.

"Ah, yes." The mayor stands away from the counter. "I assumed I would be seeing some of your ilk around here eventually. Congrats on your peace. I hope your days of mischief are over."

"It would seem you have enough mischief without me. I see Glenn managed to escape."

"I've alerted the king. As long as he stays away from Lynchton, he's no longer our concern." He hands the woman behind the counter a few coins and takes a jar of orange spice. "If you'd follow me, we can speak in private. I was actually looking forward to our first contact with trolls. I'm the only one in the village with a communication stone." He lifts his head a little higher, like a strutting peacock. "Perks of being the mayor. No one here speaks troll either. It's a very harsh language, wouldn't you say?"

I ignore his rude comment and carry on with business as we walk down the street. "I actually may have a solution for that."

"Is that so?" He leads us into a stone cottage next to the church. Inside, it's well kept. Several pieces of parchment litter a table. There's a leather couch and a fireplace. A bottle of amber liquid sits on a smaller table in front of the couch, and a fire fizzles in the fireplace. "Please, have a seat. Can I offer you a refreshment?"

I decline, but Limery eagerly accepts.

The mayor fills a pot with water and stokes the flame of the fireplace. After a moment, it roars to life and he hangs the pot from an attachment over the fire. Once it comes to a boil, he adds a sprinkle of the orange spice and pours himself and Limery a cup. "What is it you have in mind?"

I tell him my plans for the Imp Messaging Service and the propositions that the forest trolls have for the forests. "I wanted to give you a warning so that perhaps the other trolls are not greeted in such a manner as I was."

"Not much I can do about that, I'm afraid. Living so close to the forest, our people have had more than their fair share of run-ins with trolls over the years. I don't think I have to tell you that they haven't been the most pleasant. And the whole debacle with Glenn. Right or wrong, a lot of our men lost their lives. It will take time."

I can't really argue with the logic of that.

"But I have a plan," he continues. "As a gesture of good faith, I have a quest for some of the trolls who will take it. Monsters have been harassing some of our farmers. They've destroyed acres of crops, killed livestock. If something isn't done about them, soon it'll begin to affect the local economy. We don't have the manpower to spare, and there haven't been many heroes in this area recently. Seems like the perfect opportunity to build trust between our communities."

"That's actually a really good idea."

"You're more than welcome to participate yourself. Here." The quest displays in the corner of my vision.

Quest Alert. *You have been offered the quest "Save the Farms." Monsters have been destroying crops and killing livestock around Lynchton. Find and kill the monsters before the economy begins to suffer. Bring the head of the slain monster to the town mayor to claim reward.*

Reward: 1 silver per monster.

"If you don't mind me asking, what is the currency here? We haven't had much need for money in the forest."

The mayor laughs at my comment. "Ah, to be a troll. You'll find that out here, money rules everything. Bronze is the most common, with one hundred bronze coins for every silver, ten silver for every gold, and 10 gold for every platinum. Platinum is the currency of royalty, so I wouldn't set your eyes on acquiring that any time soon. There is a branch of the Royal Bank in every town, where you and other trolls can safely store coins if you desire. It is all regulated and insured by the master banker in Vanaria."

One silver for slaying a monster sounds like a pretty fair price for the dangers involved. If he only knew how many gold coins Limery and I had between us.

"If I had to guess, I think your monster problem will be handled in short order. Limery, what do you say we go track down some of these troublemakers?"

"Oh, yes! Limmy wants more monies." He drains the rest of his beverage in one chug.

I accept the quest and several markers appear on my map, displaying areas where the monsters have attacked.

Before we leave, I want to take some time to check out some of the shops. I have all of this gold; it'd be a shame not to use it.

"Want to do a little shopping before we hit the road?"

Limery's eyes light up with excitement. I'm sure he's aching to spend his stolen coins.

Staying true to his nature, the first thing he spends his money on are various smoked meats. We have to exchange some of our gold coins for smaller denominations at the bank in order to pay for it.

After sampling some of the meats, I'll give it to the humans, they know their way around a spice rack. They really play off the different flavors in ways that roasting meat over a fire simply doesn't.

We're in and out of the tailor in a flash. Aside from a pretty cool cloak, there's not much that tempts me away from the freedom of my loincloth. The blacksmith offers some sturdy weapons, but nothing that outclasses my Petrified Staff or Forlorn Scepter. Limery picks up a small silver dagger for a couple of silver, but with his fire magic, I'm sure it's more for show.

If we want the good stuff, I think we'll need to go to a larger city or hit up some dungeons.

We pass a small jewelry shop next to the Dancing Donkey, and Limery refuses to let me pass by without entering. Inside, it's full of rings, necklaces, and bracelets. Some with quality enchantments, but most of them not. I wonder if NPCs can analyze the items like I do.

Limery presses his fingers against the glass display case, eyeing a pendant in the shape of a blue flame. The owner's face contorts at the smudged surface, when the door behind us opens and a shimmering knight clanks through.

Pressley Allen
Level 23
Knight
Human

With each step, the knight's armor clanks and jingles. Each piece of silver plate mail is pristinely polished and in far better shape than any of the guards' in Lynchton. Beneath it, vibrant chainmail protects any weak spots. My reflection stares back at me from his helmet as he passes, unconcerned with my presence.

He lifts his hand and a purple amulet falls out, dangling from a golden chain. "How much?" he asks the shopkeeper, cutting right to the chase.

The shopkeeper inspects the amulet, pulling out some sort of magnifying glass with a green lens. She mumbles to herself as she turns it over, examining every inch of the jewelry. "Two gold."

"Done." The knight doesn't even try to haggle for a better price.

"Wait," I interrupt. "What is it?"

The knight takes the amulet back and shows it to me. "An amulet of protection. I looted it from a dungeon two days ago."

Tiny yellow bolts run through the amulet's center, like a tropical thunderstorm. I focus on the item and its stats appear.

Item. Amulet of Grounding. *Protects wearer from the elemental effects of lightning-based abilities. Does not block damage, but does negate stuns, chains, and explosions associated with electric attacks.*

The memory of the wisps from the faerie dungeon comes to mind. The cluster of shocking puffs of energy would have killed me if not for Limery. This amulet would have allowed me to walk straight through the first level unimpeded.

"You don't want it?" I ask. It seems like a pretty valuable item to me.

"It's not a matter of wanting it. I want gold. Lots of gold. I'm not going to stop to rest until I have enough." He lifts the visor of his helm and brown eyes flecked with gold look at me with authority. His dark complexion is pronounced against the silver of his armor. "I don't care about the trolls. I don't care about the squabbles of the other heroes. I care about gold. So, unless you want to pay me more than two gold for this amulet, I don't care about you either."

"I think I'll pass." Three gold is a lot to spend on something I don't really need. "What are you saving up for anyways?"

He stares at me before answering. "This is a do-over. Most of these clowns don't see that. They want to kill and backstab and plot. Prison didn't teach them a damn thing. Me? I want an empire and ain't nobody on this island gonna stop me from getting mine." He hands the amulet to the shopkeeper, and she gives him two gold coins. "You understand, though." He looks me up and down, as if surveying me. "Yeah, you know what's up."

I stand in stunned silence. An empire, huh? I just want to have a little fun.

"That's enough chit-chat for today." He shuts his visor with a clank. "I've got to restock and get back on my grind. I'll see you around, troll."

As quick as he entered, the knight is gone. Off to whatever adventure awaits him next. I'm glad to know that there are other players in here for things besides vengeance. Players who actually want to play the game. Maybe some of them actually want to be rehabilitated. I wonder what Pressley is in prison for anyways. He's not short on ambition, and he's got the levels and mindset to make the most of this world.

"He come in here a lot?" I ask the shopkeeper.

"Oh, yes. Sir Allen is one of my greatest suppliers. Quite the adventurer, that one."

Limery points to a small silver ring with a red stone. "That one."

"Five silver."

He hands the shopkeeper a gold coin, and she gives him the ring and his change.

"What'd you get?"

He slips the ring on his finger and it magically adjusts to his size. "Something to makes Limmy stronger." He snaps his finger and flame erupts in his palm. It seems denser and more vibrant than before.

"Get out!" the shopkeeper yells. "Get out before you burn the whole place to the ground!"

Outside the shop, I pull up my map, searching for the nearest location of the mayor's quest.

CHAPTER 14
COMMUNITY SERVICE

THE LOCATIONS of the quests are marked on my map with red exclamation marks. There are over a dozen areas that have been ravaged by monsters. The closest farms are only a few miles away.

Far off in the distance, something gleams on the horizon, reflecting the bright sunny day. I wonder if it might be Pressley the knight heading off to his next adventure.

At level twenty-three, he's the strongest player I've met so far. He must have really been grinding to get that high. If he really does want an empire, then he's going to be grinding for a while. With each new level, it becomes increasingly more difficult to get to the next.

I can't even imagine how much gold it will take to start a town, much less advance it to a kingdom. It sounds like a lifetime of work.

Ping!

My message icon flashes, and I pull up my new message.

Incoming Message (Taryn): *Yo Chode! Just kidding, bro. I'm getting close to the forest. Where should we meet?*

Message (Chod): *Call me that again and I'll spawn-camp your little noob self all the way back to level one. We're at a group of farms outside of Lynchton. I think we're going to complete a few quests for the mayor. If you make it here in time, you can help out. That is, if you're strong enough.*

Taryn doesn't respond, so I assume he is on his way. There's no point in just standing around and waiting for him to show, especially when there is a silver to be earned for every monster we kill. We should head to one of the farms and find out what's causing all the damage.

The first farm we come upon is a small hut with a thatched roof, surrounded by acres of crops. A wooden fence to the rear separates horses and a few goats. A trail of upturned soil snakes through several rows of cabbage. Nearby, some sort of coop or building lies in shambles, with pieces of wood scattered everywhere.

The farmer trudges behind a plow being pulled by a donkey as it re-plows his mangled garden.

"Excuse me!" I shout, giving him plenty of time to prepare before we are face to face. "The Mayor of Lynchton sent us. He said you were having problems with monsters destroying your crops."

The farmer lifts his straw hat and raises an eyebrow. "The mayor sent you? Now ain't that something. Us countryfolk are usually left to fend for ourselves." He wipes sweat off his brow with a dirty sleeve. "We can't pay heroes, and the townsfolk never seem to have enough men to part with. If you're looking for money, we don't have any to spare, not with the attacks."

"No need to worry about payment. The mayor thinks it is in the best interest for all parties if we eliminate this threat as quick as possible. We're at your service. And before long, there should be several other trolls to help put this problem to rest. I'm Chod. This is my companion, Limery."

"I've never been one to turn down good help. Especially if it's free. You can call me Dewitt." He takes off his hat and places it over his chest.

"So, Dewitt. What is it we're dealing with here?" It looks to have been a pretty big creature, judging by the tracks left behind.

"Moulhaugs. I've never seen them down this far in the grasslands before. Normally, they call the foot of the mountains home, but recently, more and more have been showing up." He leads us over to the upturned earth and points at giant hoofprints sunk into the ground. "You see, they love eggs. Normally, they ram their giant horns against trees to knock them from the nests of large birds. Out here, they can seem to smell our chickens from a mile away. I rebuilt the damn coop twice, and twice, it got destroyed. I'm not even bothering with it again. If I don't have chickens, then the moulhaugs won't be destroying my crops."

If he doesn't have chickens, then the townspeople don't have eggs. "Leave it to us and the moulhaugs won't be troubling you again. Now, how do we go about finding them?"

The farmer laughs at my question. "I don't think that'll be a problem. Follow the trail of destruction and you'll come on them eventually. Just be careful when they're sleeping. Their mossy backside looks like a giant boulder when they're not moving. Their horns are powerful, even for someone as big as you."

"Good to know. Thanks." Sounds an awful lot like my Camouflage ability.

"I wish I could help you more, but I have seeds that need sowing. Or else the townsfolk might start eating one another." He chuckles before returning to his crops, leaving Limery and I standing over the giant hoofprints.

"Pretty big, huh?" The hoofprint engulfs my own as I step inside it.

"Very bigs. Very, very bigs." Limery hovers from one footprint to the next.

"It's not like we haven't faced bigger. We did kill a giant wyrm." Plus, they can't be that high of level if they are around here.

We follow the trail of the moulhaug from one farm to the next. Each farmer has the same story, with a promise to forego eggs as long as it saves their livelihoods. I don't blame them.

At the fourth farm, we come to another destroyed chicken coop. This one sits right next to a massive boulder covered in green moss. A soft snoring noise comes from the giant rock.

Moulhaug. *Level 18. A hulking, moss-covered quadruped with a single horn in the center of its snout. Generally peaceful creatures, moulhaugs scavenge for eggs from high in the treetops by swinging their massive horns like a battering ram. When provoked, they will lock onto a target until it is no longer visible or dies.*

"How in the hell is this thing level eighteen and hanging out around Lynchton?" No wonder the townspeople can't do anything to help. They'd be massacred.

"Theys comes from the mountains." Limery points to the range in the distance, its snowcapped peaks rising high. "Monsters is toughs up there."

Remembering the wyrm, I'd have to agree. Everything is coming together. If the moulhaugs are typically found near the mountain, then of course they are a higher level. They aren't in their natural habitat. Which means that whatever caused them to leave is even stronger than they are.

We'll deal with that later. For now, we have a beastie to kill.

"I'm going to summon a bunch of horrors while he's sleeping," I tell Limery, and three horrors appear in a puff of smoke. "Go and scout the surrounding areas for more moulhaugs while I prepare." We don't want to accidentally attract more of them while fighting. One, we can take. More and it starts to get tricky.

"Limmy's on it!" The imp disappears as I continue to summon new horrors as soon as the cooldown allows.

With a one-minute cooldown on each horror and a ten percent life decay every minute they are out of combat, I'll be able to summon thirty horrors just as the first set begin to die. Once the battle starts, there's no limit to how many I can have active at once.

At level eighteen, I'm sure the moulhaug has a substantial amount of health. Could exploding all thirty horrors be enough to kill it? It'll cost me three thousand mana just to summon all of them. If there is more than one moulhaug nearby, more than half my mana will be gone along with my horrors. My mana regen is pretty fast, but it's still a risk.

Once the horrors are all summoned, I equip my Petrified Staff for the added attack range on my physical attacks and wait for Limery to return. As each of the old horrors fades away, I summon a new one in its place. They grumble and snarl, my own personal army. Some of the Horrors of Vitality ram their horns against one another in boredom, and the Horrors of Finesse ride the Horrors of Power like a mount.

Limery zooms around the farmhouse like a bat out of hell. "Two monsties in the next field. Both is sleeping."

That's good. They're far enough away that our fight likely

won't disturb them. That makes this the perfect opportunity for a test run.

"Ready?" I ask.

Limery nods, and two fireballs erupt in his palms.

"Alright, light 'em up!"

I use Petrified Staff's ranged attack at the same time as Limery tosses his fireballs. They connect with the mammoth bulldozer of a creature and it stumbles to its feet, eyes red with rage. The damage is barely noticeable against the moulhaug's thick hide. It lets out a vicious snarl, displaying teeth that, while not sharp, could probably crush whatever it bites like a trash compactor.

This is going to take the big guns. "Limery, start working on a mega fireball. When I give the word, I want you to throw it with all you've got."

The moulhaug paws at the earth, leaving craters where its hooves smash.

Limery hovers next to me, his hands overhead as a vortex of fire swirls into a sphere.

The rhino-like creature charges, each step a miniature earth-quake. It swings its head side to side as it tramples across the field, destroying what's left of the crops. I run out of the way as it comes pummeling through and order my horrors to do the same, but several of the furry Horrors of Vitality are not quick enough in the thick soil of the garden and explode as the moulhaug's horn snuffs them out of existence.

I quickly summon more as the moulhaug turns for another charge. I forego my ranged attacks, since they seem to have little effect against the tough monster.

The beast charges again, and I lose several more horrors that are not quick enough to escape. Right now, I'm wishing I had an actual weapon that could stab and slice as it goes by instead of a glorified walking stick. That's what I need to spend my gold on.

"Ready!" Limmy shouts, and I send my horrors toward the moulhaug just as it turns again.

The few Horrors of Vitality left manage to slow the creature somewhat as they wrap their furry little arms around its tree-trunk legs.

"Now!" I order, and Limery lets the fireball fly. It soars across the field, torching the plantlife beneath its path and distorting the surrounding air.

When the fireball is several feet away, I cast Kamikaze, exploding all but my Horrors of Power. Half of the beast's HP vanishes in an instant, and the fireball collides in an explosion of heat and fire. The backdraft of the explosion singes the hair on my arms and causes my eyes to water.

Smoke clears and the moulhaug still stands with a quarter HP remaining. One tough motherfucker. Its mossy backside is burnt away, revealing tough, gray, rock-like skin.

My Horrors of Power attack, goring their tusks into the creature's legs while it thrashes its horn about like a giant wrecking ball.

Limery erects two flame walls along both sides of the monster and its HP drops slowly. He sets my horrors ablaze in the process, but they continue their savage attack until their life disappears.

Favoring one leg, the moulhaug crashes to the ground. With a great amount of effort, it rises again, its skin blistered and legs in tatters. Ropes of flesh hang from where the horrors gored it. It lets out a cry. A bellow of pain that reverberates out across the plains.

A moment later, a resounding call answers.

Shit.

CHAPTER 15

GET RICH OR DIE TRYING

LIMERY BLASTS the moulhaug with fireballs, slowly whittling away at its health, but not nearly fast enough to kill the creature before its friends show up to ruin our party. I summon horrors as quickly as I can, all the while slinging ranged attacks from my Petrified Staff, but it just doesn't seem to be enough.

If I don't do something more than what we've been doing, we'll lose the kill and we might not get another chance with a moulhaug alone. I feel bad for the townspeople if that's the case.

Screw it. There's no way I'm letting this kill escape. If I'm going to be the baddest player on the island, then I need the XP. I need to find ways to defeat enemies when the going gets tough.

I sprint toward the moulhaug, switching to Forlorn Scepter as I do so. The obsidian shaft is cool to the touch. Its added range for summoning allows me to drop the horrors right on top of the beast as I run. One by one, I summon and explode them, taking out small chunks of health. Just not nearly enough.

The creature is slow with its injured legs, no longer capable of charging, but its horn still has the power to kill. One wrong move and I'll be respawning in the forest.

Using the built-up rage from all my previous attacks, I activate Bite and Claw and leap for the moulhaug.

Its powerful horn slams into my side like a battering ram, cracking several of my ribs and knocking the breath completely out of me. Limery flies down to me, concern radiating from his face.

"Chods, is you okay?" His bulbous eyes are full of worry.

"I'm fine," I get out between painful breaths. "Just...keep attacking."

Pain shoots through my ribs as I stand. Is this what being hit by a truck feels like?

The other moulhaugs will be showing up any minute now, and this one still has five percent health.

Five percent. That's all that stands between us and victory.

Time to go all in.

I activate Berserker Rage and my vision goes red. Increased Strength bulges my muscles and raw power flows through my veins. The pain in my side vanishes as my health rapidly recovers from the attack and my bones begin to mend themselves. I ready Bite and Claw, this time approaching the beast from the rear.

With a running start, I leap onto its back and bury my claws into its side. They rake along the moulhaug's burnt skin, tearing flesh and spilling blood. The beast thrashes about, trying with everything it has to throw me off. Its horn swings with enough ferocity to bludgeon me to death if I'm unlucky enough to land in its path. I dig my claws in deeper until they scrape against bone. Hot blood coats my hands and runs down the moulhaug's side.

I sink my tusks into its back and the silky, hot taste of iron fills my mouth. Fireballs connect all around me, damaging both of us.

The Phoenix Feather I wear in my braid and increased healing from Berserker Rage mitigates most of the damage.

The moulhaug sways, blood loss causing the creature to move slower. Its thrashing grows less erratic as its HP trickles down. A trumpeting cry sounds nearby at the same moment as the moulhaug collapses to the ground.

"Run!" I tell Limery. "We can come back for the body later, but right now, we need to get the hell out of here."

The mourning cries of the other two moulhaugs can be heard over a mile from where we left the body. Their long resounding wails sprout goosebumps down my spine.

Once I feel we are far enough away, I stop to catch my breath. Even though forest trolls have more speed than other troll races, we weren't built for sprinting long distances. We're predators, built for the attack. My heartbeat pounds in my ears with each breath. Limery lands on a fence post and doesn't even seem winded.

How fast is he truly capable of going? Or any imp for that matter. They're like gazelles of the air, never running out of energy. It makes sense that they would be great messengers.

"Good job, Chods. We beats the monsty." He curls his tiny hand into a fist.

"Yeah, now we just need to find a way to take its head off without the others finding us." I don't relish the idea of carrying that giant horn all the way back to Lynchton, but silver is silver.

"Theys will go to sleeps soon. Theys mostly come out at night."

"Alright, we'll give them some time and then head back over."

I focus on my messaging tool and compose a quick message for Taryn. Maybe we can finally meet up in the downtime.

Message (Chod): *Dude, you are slower than my grandmother. Where the hell are you?*

A minute later, I receive a reply.

Incoming Message (Taryn): *And you're about as impatient as mine. Heaven forbid a new player actually try to explore the game instead of rushing to meet you. Suck on a butterscotch, and I'll see you when I get there.*

Sarcastic asshole. I love it. He's only ever that outspoken and crude with me. For a big guy, he's awfully quiet and reserved. It takes time for Taryn to open up to new people. Put him in a room with strangers, and it's like he lost his voice. Even when we would play together, he'd talk so much shit, but as soon as the stream went live, he'd go silent.

Incoming Message (Taryn): *I just passed the first farm. Where are you?*

    Message (Chod): *Stay away from the farms! We had a bit of a SNAFU. It is not safe right now, especially for you. Meet me here.*

I send him my location on the map and hope the other moulhaugs don't accuse him of killing their brother.

Several minutes pass by with no response, so I take a moment to clear my mind and reorient myself. After a fight, I'm always on edge until I have a chance to calm down and breathe a little. Even when I just played online, a good fight would send my pulse racing.

I sit down and lean back against a post, letting the gentle breeze wash over me. The air smells so clean, not like New York where it was all smog, car exhaust, and street vendors. Not to mention the occasional homeless person that took a shit on the sidewalk.

Today is beautiful and sunny. Fluffy, white clouds float by overhead and I lose myself in their shapes. My muscles relax and the tension I've been holding begins to disappear.

I'm admiring a cloud in the shape of an axe when a small red bird flies down and perches on a post near Limery. Little does it know the danger it has just placed itself in.

The bird watches me intently, cocking its head and fixing one yellow eye on me. Limery licks his lips when he notices the bird. He has such an affinity for birds that I wonder if he has ever eaten fried chicken. If not, I bet it would blow his little imp mind. My mouth waters at the memory of that deep-fried goodness.

The air around his hands shimmers and a flame bursts to life in his palm. A quick flick of his wrist sends the fireball hurtling at the poor bird.

The fireball hits the bird, and there's an explosion of feathers as the bird transforms into a short, stout man. He falls off the fence with a thud.

"Ouch! Ouch!" he screams, patting his smoking body. "What the hell did you do that for?"

Limery already has two fireballs ready for the follow-up when the man puts his hands up in surrender.

"Chod! Call him off! Call him off!" he squeals.

"Taryn? What the hell? Is that you?" He scoots away from Limery's wrath. This makes absolutely zero sense. How was he a bird? "Limery, it's okay. This is my friend I was telling you about."

I take a moment to analyze him, just to make sure.

Taryn Jones
Level 9
Druid
Ebony Dwarf

A dwarf and a druid? Quite the change from his normal support or tank role. Looking at the pint-sized dwarf before me, aside from the color of his skin, he's about as different from the real Taryn as possible. His normally giant afro has been replaced with thick dreadlocks. Outside the game, Taryn is built like a linebacker, tall with broad shoulders. The dwarf lying before me can't be over four feet tall. He has the typical bushy dwarven beard, and it's segmented with golden clasps that are engraved with runes. He lays on a dark green cloak and next to him lies a gnarled staff tipped with a boar's tusk.

Limery's eyes dart between Taryn and me. "Yous sure? This is yous friend?" I can't blame him for being untrusting of a bird that just transformed into a dwarf.

"I'm sure. Limery, meet Taryn. Taryn, this is my partner, Limery."

The imp extinguishes his flames and offers Taryn a demonic smile. I'm not sure if it's welcoming or terrifying.

Taryn slowly stands. "Thanks for the warm welcome." He brushes dirt off his arms and shoulders.

"How were we supposed to know you were a bird? You didn't tell me anything about you, so I think you had it coming." I wrap him in a massive bear hug. "Congrats on being the first dwarven hero."

He smiles at that, revealing a set of pearly whites that contrast with his dark complexion. "Oh man, they love me up there. Honest to goodness, they treated me like royalty. Though they were a little disappointed I wasn't a battle mage or a cleric. Still, I got some nice items to start out with for free."

"Why druid, anyway? It's never really been your style. And why were you a bird?"

He laughs. "If you're impressed by that, you've got another thing coming. That's a level-one druid ability. I can transform into animals. Mostly basic stuff, but I can upgrade it later on." He bends down to pick up his staff. "Why did I choose druid? I don't know. I guess because I've spent my entire life living in a city." He kicks the bottom of his staff and it swings forward like a pendulum. "You know, I've never even been to upstate New York. The only experience I have with nature is Central Park, and you're just as likely to see a man's dong as an animal. This seemed like a good time to see what it's all about. Nature, not the dongs."

I burst out laughing at his explanation. "You're always so chill about everything. I think you'll be a great druid. What other abilities are you packing?"

"Let's see. Right now, I have six abilities. I have another point to spend, but I'm saving it for a special ability that unlocks at level ten." His eyes have a far-off look to them, like he's looking at something we can't see. I wonder if I look like that when I check my stats. "I started out with Transform, Lightning Bolt, and Strong Wind. Transform lets me transform into any creature my level or under that I've seen in the past twenty-four hours. I get one animal that I can always turn into. For me, it's a red bird. I don't get any special abilities they may have, but I look and sound just like them. It's really good for traveling without being noticed. Lightning Bolt is just what it sounds like. I call a nasty bolt of electricity from the sky. Strong Wind increases my movement speed and that of anyone around me."

Taryn pauses to adjust his cloak and satchel. Limery eyes him cautiously, as if debating whether or not to trust the dwarf.

"I've since unlocked Restoration, which heals me while I am communing with nature, Nature's Aegis, which makes me immune to elemental effects like stuns and slows; and then Nature's Bulwark, which means animals will only attack me if I provoke them. What about you?"

I take a few moments to describe my abilities to him, how I am a double-class barbarian and summoner and my chosen summoner class plays well off my race.

"That's pretty cool. I'm guessing that dead monster back there is your handiwork?"

"Yeah, we're working on a quest for the Mayor of Lynchton. Each one of those moulhaugs is worth a silver."

"Only a silver?" He arches an eyebrow. "Those things are a much higher level than anything else in this area. You're being robbed."

I scoff at him. "This isn't the dwarven capital where people wipe their butts with golden coins. Money is hard to come by around here. Plus, we think they wandered down from a higher-level zone. Once we get you leveled up, I'd like to go and see what could have driven them off. But first, we need to get that thing's head and take it back. Maybe let the mayor know that people should be doing this quest in groups."

"I hope you don't expect me to help you lug that thing

around." In a flash, he transforms in a small red bird again and lands on my shoulder.

Incoming Message (Taryn): Carry me on, noble steed!

CHAPTER 16
EBONY AND IVORY

THE MOULHAUG HEAD is cumbersome as I drag it by the horn down the dirt road. It leaves a trail of dark red ichor in our wake. If I would have known how big they were, I might have purchased a wagon before leaving Lynchton. I feel like ten gold would definitely be enough for a wagon and some horses.

I offered the rest of the moulhaug body to the farmer who lived there. He said the meat could be used for jerky, but otherwise wasn't really palatable to humans. He seemed grateful that we eliminated one of the threats to his crops and wished us a speedy return. I only wish we could have taken care of the other two, but it won't be long before more trolls show up. If they manage to clear the area and win the farmers' favor, that will do a lot of good for our reputation.

As I carry the giant head, Limery perches on one shoulder while Taryn sits on the other, still in bird form. We've been communicating through the messaging system about Mythos Games and the outside world. Things that Limery doesn't need to know about.

Message (Chod): So how long are they letting you in for?

Incoming Message (Taryn): A month to start with. My parents will get an automatic deposit each week, so I don't have to worry about that, though I can request to be pulled at any time if I want. I still think it's strange how the system malfunctioned when you were pulled out. I mean, that's weird, right? I wonder if it's had the same effect when others have been pulled?

Message (Chod): I don't know about the others, but it's definitely weird. It makes you wonder if our minds are anything more than just points of data if the system can just lock onto them like that. The whole concept makes my head hurt just thinking about it. Like how we are even here at all, feeling, tasting, and smelling while our bodies are being fed and cleaned by tiny robots.

Incoming Message (Taryn): No kidding. It's easier not to think about it.

Incoming Message (Taryn): Can I ask you a question?

Message (Chod): Yeah, what's up?

Incoming Message (Taryn): With as real as this game seems, do you feel pressure to stay and play? I mean, I know it's awesome. Everything about it feels more real than outside. I'm a tiny dwarf, but I actually feel like a dwarf, you know? Every person I met at Seascape, they felt as real as you and me. Each one had their own quirks. I did a quest for an old lady who couldn't find her cat. And I haven't been here as long as you. You and Limery, I can tell you have a connection. And not a 'pet in a video game' connection. It's real. Don't you worry about what would happen to him if you let the system fail?

Message (Chod): Yeah, that's easier not to think about, too.

Taryn transforms back into his dwarven form and slides off my shoulder. "I could get used to that. I see why you keep him around, Limery."

"Limmy likes Chods. Chods is Limmy's best friend." He pats me on the shoulder.

"We've got that in common then. Do a lot of imps go adventuring?" Taryn asks.

"No. Mommy says we used to be great messengers. We's used to travels all over, but not Limmy. Limmy wasn't a baby yet."

"But here you are now, leveled up and kicking ass." Taryn winks at Limery, and I have a feeling these two are going to get along just fine.

A few hours later, we arrive at Lynchton.

Shocked faces stare at us as I drag the moulhaug head through the gate and drop it in the town center. Twilight is nearing and the market has shut down for the day, but there are still people about the town. Several men sit on the porch of The Dancing Donkey drinking ale and having a laugh.

Luka, the stable worker, comes over and greets me. He holds a brush in one hand and a small pick in the other. "Now that is a mighty beast. You kill that thing all by yourself?"

"I had a lot of help from Limery here."

"You're doing the gods' work, I tell you. It will not be a pleasant day in my house if we don't have eggs. It's not my fault, but the wife'll take it out on me all the same." He shuffles his feet. "Well, these horses ain't gonna groom themselves. Take care."

No sooner has Luka left than I see a red-faced mayor marching in our direction. "Get. That. Out of here!" I'm afraid for a minute his head is going to explode as he spits out the words.

"What? How else am I supposed to prove that I killed the beast?" I grab the moulhaug head by the horn and show it to him. "I thought you'd be grateful."

"I— I am," he stutters. "You didn't have to bring it inside. It's going to rot and stink up the whole town. Here, take your silver and get that blasted thing out of here!"

I do as I'm told and deposit the head outside of the gate, not that I think it will do much for the stench when it begins to decompose. The mayor really should have thought of a better way to confirm completion of the quest. It would save a lot of time and traveling for those who are completing it if they don't have to bring the head all the way back to town after every kill.

Jameson, the guard, stands slack-jawed as I leave the head and return to the town. "What am I supposed to do with that?" he asks.

"Take it up with the mayor." I turn to Taryn. "What do you say we get a room at The Dancing Donkey tonight and head out in the morning?"

"Works for me. I have some gold I need to deposit anyway."

We catch several glares as we enter the inn, but everyone moves out of our way and lets us pass. Someone in the group of drinkers makes a comment about a troll, a dwarf, and an imp walking into the bar, but we don't stay to hear the punchline. We pay for our rooms for the night, which also includes dinner, and take a seat at one of the tables on the bottom floor.

A serving maid makes her rounds, and a bartender pours drinks at the bar.

We're able to see the entire room from our table in the corner. Its dark wood is stained from years of use and tiny gashes are permanent reminders of the many men who have stabbed their blades in drunken revelry. The smells of roasted meat and smoking tobacco intertwine to form a savory and spicy aroma. In one corner, a man sits smoking a pipe, the fog around him so dense his face is barely visible. At another table, a group of travelers watch us out of the corners of their eyes and steal brief glances when they think we aren't looking.

"First round's on me," offers Taryn. He sets his staff down and returns a moment later with three mugs full of amber liquid.

Limery's is a quarter of the size of the other two, but he holds it with pride.

"Cheers." We all tap our mugs together.

"I haven't seen many dwarves south of the mountains." I take a sip of my drink and it bubbles down my throat, malty and delicious. "Only one, actually, and that was at Vanaria. He was working as part of some trade agreement with the dwarven kingdom."

"Makes sense. They—I mean we—have a beautiful kingdom. The ivory dwarves are masterful stoneworkers. Plus, I kind of get the feeling that they like to keep to themselves." The golden clasps in his beard catch the light of the sconces on the nearby wall.

"Ivory? What's that all about? I noticed that you are an ebony dwarf." The first dwarf I've ever seen rocking dreadlocks.

Limery lets out a loud belch, causing the other guests to turn and look. He looks shocked that the noise escaped him. "Excuse Limmy."

"Nice one." Taryn fist-bumps the imp. "They're different sub-races. Like the forest and mountain trolls. The ivory dwarves are what most people think of when they imagine dwarves. White skin, thick beards, work in the mountains. Really good craftsmen that make weapons and build things. The ebony dwarves are the lowland dwarves. We originated in the desert between the mountains and Seascape. We're more the hunter-gatherer type, but amazing craftsmen as well. We make some of the finest jewelry on the island. Our towns are so well hidden that you might pass them by if you didn't know where to look. And then there are the blood dwarves. Known for their dark red skin, they used to mine obsidian in the heart of the volcano when it was still active. They say the fire and lava permanently turned their skin red and that lava runs through their veins. They are the rarest of the bunch."

"Wait, there's another volcano on the island?" I remember Kassidy saying that the stone for the walls and towers in Vanaria were raised from a dormant volcano. This is the first I've heard about one in Seascape.

"It's dormant. The entire city of Seascape is built on its remains." He takes another long draw of his ale, draining half the mug. "It's kind of crazy how there are so many ecosystems on one island."

"Ecosystems," I laugh. "When did you become such a nerd?"

"Since I knew the only way I was making it out of the block was with an education. Well, until I had this opportunity." His face goes serious for a moment. "Do you think I did the right thing? Skipping out in the middle of the semester to come play this—" He lowers his voice to a whisper. "—game?"

"You can always go back." I pat him on the shoulder. "The money you'll make while you're here, that'll really help your family. Stay here long enough and you might not even have to work at the burger joint when you go back."

His smile returns. "Yeah, you're right. I didn't even think of it like that. Want another round?"

Limery sways back and forth, his bulbous eyes glazed over.

"Sure, why not? I think Limery can sit this one out. He's tanked."

Not long into our second drink, Limery passes out at the table. He curls into a ball and a tiny balloon of snot bubbles from his nose with each snore.

"Lightweight," jokes Taryn.

"Maybe so, but he could kick your ass." I give him a playful shove and accidentally push a little too hard, nearly knocking him off the bench. "He's been with me in almost every fight and is only a couple of levels below me now."

Taryn returns with another round, noticeably more intoxicated.

"I never knew you liked to drink," I say, taking the mug.

He flashes me a goofy smile. "I didn't. I tried one of Pop's beers once. Tasted like piss. I don't know if it's because I'm a dwarf or what, but it goes down so easy now. Not to mention the feeling. It's like my whole head is vibrating, like a gentle buzz." His eyes light up like he just had a realization. "Wait! No way! Is that why they called it being buzzed?"

My deep laugh startles the nearby table, causing one man to knock over his drink. "I guess so. You know, I can't eat fruit since becoming a troll. My palate has completely changed. I can eat raw meat, but I can't eat fruit."

"That's wild, bro."

Several hours pass as we drink and chat. It feels so good to have Taryn here, to let my guard down and just chill out like before. Eventually, we both stumble to our rooms.

When I close the door, I'm greeted with a notification

Welcome to The Dancing Donkey! *You may set your respawn point in your room for as long as you are staying here. Once your stay is over, your respawn point will be reset to its previous location. Would you like to bind here?*

I decide not to, since we are only staying for the night. It's a useful feature if you are paying for an extended stay.

Limery grumbles as I carefully place him down on the bed, but he doesn't wake. The little guy is out cold.

Feeling completely content, I drift off to sleep.

CHAPTER 17
THE BEAR NECESSITIES

SUN SPILLS through the window of my second-story room at The Dancing Donkey. The daylight assaults my sensitive eyes, so I bury my head beneath the blanket. My head pounds, like a tiny gnome has crept into my brain with a sledgehammer. Not to mention my parched mouth. I stumble from the bed in search of the pitcher of water and accidentally knock Limery to the floor. He falls on his head with a thunk, letting out a confused groan. When he stands up, he looks every bit as hungover as I feel. His bulbous eyes are bloodshot and squint at the burning light as he sways back and forth searching for his balance.

"Some night, huh?" I ask.

He responds with incoherent babbling.

We gather our belongings and I head to Taryn's room to check the damage he inflicted on himself. He opens the door with a smile.

"You look like hell." He laughs. "Both of you." He's already packed and stands there, staff in hand, with his satchel tossed over his shoulder.

"Why aren't you hungover?" I ask.

He shrugs. "Dwarven immunity?"

Limery clings tight to my shoulder. "Chods, more quiet, please," he whispers.

"You two need some breakfast," suggests Taryn, grinning. "It'll fix you right up."

True to his word, breakfast does wonders for our hangovers. After devouring loads of eggs and sausages, we leave The Dancing Donkey.

We slept through most of the morning and the sun sits high overhead. When we step out into the market, Taryn grabs me by the arms and points to the square.

"Aren't those your people?" he asks.

There are several groups of trolls spread around the market in pairs.

"Yeah, but they shouldn't be here yet. Not without Lillith and the imps."

Malak and Jojin stand in front of a table laden with knives. So many types of knives that I don't even know the uses for them all. Some are short, others long. Most are plain, but a few are embellished with jewels or engraved with runes. I don't remember seeing this table here when I left yesterday. It must be new.

The two guardian trolls carry some of the looted armor from the village. They must be here to trade. Malak sets the weapons down on the table and picks up a knife, examining it with great interest. With such sharp claws, trolls don't really need knives, but trading the weapons away will bring the two sides together.

I want to say hi, but something tells me to stand back and watch the interaction. There are no imps here yet, so they can't communicate other than by pointing at the items they wish to trade. Why would Chief Rizza send out the trolls without translators? It doesn't make any sense.

The man behind the table eyes them suspiciously. He wears a royal blue tunic, much finer than most others in the market. My guess is that he travels from village to village selling his items. His acquaintance seems to be his muscle, clad in all black with broad shoulders and a sword by his side. His bald head is scarred in several places.

We step up behind the two trolls, quiet so that they don't notice. The man selling knives must not recognize who I am because he talks freely to his companion. "They kill these people's men, then they bring their weapons back to trade. Isn't that messed up?"

The other man nods. "That's why you don't negotiate with savages. They can't be trusted."

Taryn makes to say something, but I put out my arm to stop him. I send him a message, telling him to let this play out.

Malak holds the knife in front of him in one hand and the weapons in the other, offering the exchange.

"No," says the man. "For you, coin." He reaches into his pocket and pulls out a silver coin. "Coin," he says again.

"Coin," Malak repeats.

The man in black questions the other. "You really think they have coin?"

"Does a troll shit in the woods?" He snickers. "You think all those poor souls who died in the forest never had coin on them? You think that hero that kept dying kept all his money in the bank? No, they have gold. I'm sure."

Jojin reaches into his pocket and pulls out a gold coin. "Coin," he says to the man.

The man's eyes light up. "Stupid trolls," he tells his partner. "That knife can't be worth more than five copper." He reaches for the gold coin.

"Enough!" I shout, pushing Malak aside. "How dare you take

advantage of them because they can't speak your language. Malak, Jojin, leave us be. I will explain in a moment."

The two trolls move out of the way, and I'm leaning across their table before I know what I'm doing. The man in black draws his sword and points it at my throat.

His partner gives me a sniveling smirk and raises his eyebrows. "This is why we don't trade with savages. They only know violence."

"You were about to rip them off simply because they don't know any better," I roar. I'm the only reason he didn't.

"It's a free market. And they are free not to purchase. They can learn their lessons just like the rest of us."

Taryn pulls on my arm. "Hey, Chod. I think we should leave them be. We're drawing a crowd."

Fire courses through my veins. I turn around to see the entire market has gone silent.

Screw them. I'll tell them where they can all go. "All of you ca—"

Incoming Message (Taryn): *Bro, take a deep breath. You can't let one bad seed ruin it all.*

He's right. I don't need to be causing problems before I leave

I heed Taryn's advice and take a breath, trying to rein in my temper that has so often gotten me in trouble. If anything, I should be educating the trolls so that they don't become victims.

"What's going on here?" The mayor steps out of Ms. Mcgee's spice shop.

"Nothing," I say. "Just a misunderstanding. Trolls, would you come with me outside the gate? We need to talk."

I want to thank Taryn for keeping me in check, but when I look for him, he's disappeared. I glare at the shady knife salesman as we leave. He's smirking at me when something splats on his shoulder. He lets out a yell of surprise. "Are you kidding me? I've been shit on by a bird."

Up above him on the palisade, a red bird sits on the fence. It winks at me as we leave.

Outside the gate, all of the trolls look confused.

"Chod, what is the meaning of this?" asks Malak.

"That man was going to take advantage of you. That coin you were going to give him, you could have bought half that table."

"So? The trolls have no need of gold. What does it matter as long as it gets me what I want?"

I bury my head in my hand. "It's the principle of the matter. If you let him take advantage of you, then pretty soon they all will. And then the trolls will have nothing left to trade. Why are you here anyway? I thought you were waiting on the imps?"

Malak hangs his head. "I did not want to wait. I am ready to see the world."

I grab him by the shoulder. "The world will still be waiting when the imps return, I promise you. It can't be much longer."

"Fine," he grumbles. "Let's return to the forest."

Is this what it is like to have children? Constantly needing to watch out for them so that they don't hurt themselves or get taken advantage of. Or if you're my parents, hiring a nanny.

"You did good back there." Taryn pops up behind us. His brilliant smile pokes through his beard. "I'm glad you didn't murder that guy."

"Me too. It just made me so angry to see them taken advantage of like that." I clench my fist at the memory. His bodyguard has no idea how lucky he is.

"Some things they'll have to learn for themselves. You can fight their battles, but you can't run their lives."

"Yeah, you're right. It's hard not to feel responsible for them, though. Thanks for taking care of that prick for me."

"Anything for you." He laughs. "Now, what do you say we get me leveled up?"

Several miles from Lynchton, I'm only half paying attention when Taryn casts Lightning Bolt and a giant flash of raw energy cracks into an unsuspecting deer, giving him the XP he needs to hit level ten. Daydreams of cleaving the knife merchant in two keep popping into my mind. The way he looked at us, so smug, so superior. I should have rearranged his face.

"Chod, are you listening?" Taryn glares at me. "I said I can finally unlock Tame."

"Tame, what's that?" I hope he hasn't already told me, or he's going to be pissed. If I could only get out of my own head.

"It allows me to tame any beast that's less than five levels above me. All I have to do is get it down to five percent health." His eyes glaze over as he unlocks the ability.

"That's pretty cool. Is there a limit to what you can tame?"

"Yeah, I can't wait to try it out. It only works on beasts, though —nothing capable of talking. No unique monsters, and for every new pet I tame, I lose five percent influence over all pets I have. So if I have ten pets, they may not listen to me half the time. And I can only tame something new every six hours."

"That's probably for the best. I can imagine some people getting into bad situations with an ability that lets them tame their peers." Glenn comes to mind. "Is there a limit to how many creatures you can have tamed at once?"

"I don't think so, but the more I have, the less they will listen to me. They'll just be pets, so I don't have to monitor them, not like your horrors that you are capable of controlling. I can give them orders, but I can't actually enforce them."

"Well, let's go test it out." I try to push the thoughts that are bothering me to the back of my mind. I'm here with my best friend, playing the most awesome game on the planet. *Enjoy it*, I tell myself.

I cast a few horrors, and we move further north. The mayor's quest can wait for the other trolls. "What type of pet do you want first? There's a pretty good variety around here."

"I don't know." He shrugs, then runs his fingers through his beard. "I always thought it would be cool to have a pet bear."

I laugh. "At your size, you could probably ride it."

Taryn's eyes light up at the thought, and I think I just gave him an idea.

For the next few hours, we see dozens of animals, but not a single bear. Deer, warthogs, coyotes, even a few kobolds and gnolls. But of course, the moment we're looking for a bear, it's like they went extinct.

"Come on, T. Can't you just settle for a warthog or something? If you grind a little, we can probably even get you a moulhaug."

"Dude, a little patience." He cuts his eyes at me. "What are you in such a hurry for? I'm going to take to the skies. Maybe I can spot one from higher up. Limery, want to join me and leave this crybaby alone?"

Limery sticks his tongue out at me and takes to the air. A moment later, Taryn transforms into a bird and flutters away. I take the time to rest against a tree while they scour the area.

It doesn't take long before I receive a message from Taryn telling me he's spotted a mother and her cubs. He shares his location with me, and I set off to join him.

I find Taryn and Limery hiding behind a tree, watching the mother bear and her cubs as they play around an old tree stump. The three young cubs fight for supremacy, knocking each other to the ground. The mother bear is level eight, but the cubs are level one.

"What's the plan?" I ask. I don't think he wants a bear cub, but it also seems downright cruel to take the mother from her spawn.

"We wait for them to leave and follow them. Hopefully, they'll lead us to their den," he says without looking away.

I roll my eyes at him. "Great, more waiting."

Taryn whacks me on the side of the head with his staff, and Limery bursts out laughing, startling the bears and sending them running. I guess that's one way to get them moving.

We have to run to keep up with the surprisingly agile creatures. Even the cubs are faster than I would have expected. They lead us across a field and up a hill into a thick copse of trees.

We're following them into the trees when a massive brown bear appears out of nowhere. It rises up on its hind legs, easily taller than Taryn.

Umber Bear. *Level 12.*

The reddish-brown bear roars at us, arms outstretched, warning us to stay away from its family. Its dark muzzle reveals powerful teeth capable of snapping bones in half. There's a beauty in its power and brutality.

Without warning, Taryn casts Lightning Bolt, hammering the unsuspecting bear with a stream of raw energy. The bear charges him, and Taryn casts Strong Wind, giving himself added speed as he runs away.

"You gonna help me or not?" he yells.

I forgot he only has the one offensive ability, and he's unlikely to smack the bear to death with his staff. How did he manage to get to level nine only using Lightning Bolt?

"Limery, let's help him out. No matter what, do not kill the bear." I cast a Horror of Vitality, slowing the bear's charge, and then follow up with Horror of Power and Finesse.

The three horrors attack the bear, drawing its attention and filling my rage meter. I activate Claw, and along with the attack bonus from Horror of Power, my next attack drops its health by forty percent.

A couple of fireballs from Limery drop it further. The bear sinks its teeth into the Horror of Finesse, crushing the poor thing with its powerful bite. Horror of Power gores the bear with its tusks just before a mighty strike sends it to a sliver of HP.

Another bolt of lighting zaps the bear, dropping its HP into the required area for Tame to work.

The bear stands there, stunned, as Taryn moves into position. A green aura surrounds him, and his hands glow a vibrant yellow. The bear looks almost hypnotized as Taryn steps into its attack radius. It places all four feet on the ground and huddles into itself, allowing Taryn to place his hands on the bear.

When he touches the creature, the yellow glow from his hands transfers to the animal. The bleeding wounds stop flowing and begin to mend themselves. Slowly, the bear's health recovers until it's like the fight never happened.

The bear uncurls and looks around, the menace gone from its eyes.

CHAPTER 18
MARSHLANDS

LEAVING the rest of the bears in peace, Taryn, Limery, and I set off in search of our next battle. We need to level up Taryn so that he can actually be useful in a tough fight. It won't take long if we can find the right monsters.

"Tell me, how is it you managed to get to level nine with one offensive spell?" After witnessing Taryn's battle with the umber bear, it's clear he'd have a tough go at fighting creatures without my help. The cooldown on Lightning Bolt isn't quick enough for him to spam it, and the staff he carries isn't made for bludgeoning. His abilities are nice, but he's better off as part of a team early on. Once he's tamed enough beasts, they can do his dirty work for him. Just like my horrors.

"Very carefully," he says. He rides on the back of the umber bear as it traipses across the meadow. We're heading back east, away from the moulhaugs and the mountains for now, to an area that should be more suitable for leveling. After using Tame on the creature, it seems to obey Taryn's commands, all of the fire gone from its eyes. "I'm sure it's easy for you, using brute strength to plow through monster after monster. For those of us who didn't go melee, and aren't the equivalent of a walking fridge, it's an actual grind to level up. You can kill a bear by yourself. For me, I have to slay a hundred bunnies. I got lucky and completed several quests in the capital, but most of it has been a real grind. But now that I have Berry, here, we'll be a formidable force in battle."

"Berry? Seriously?" I shake my head. "You cannot name your pet bear, Berry."

Taryn turns to me, his face scrunched. "And why not? You don't think he looks like a Berry?"

"Unless they're a fat old man with an alcohol problem, nobody looks like a Berry. You're riding him into battle, the least you could do is give him a proper name. He's a beast, not a fruit."

Taryn shrugs me off, petting the bear behind the ear. "Don't listen to him, Berry."

Limery snickers on my shoulder.

"You think this is funny?" I scowl at him.

He flashes me his sharp teeth. "Oh, yes. Limmy likes Berry."

Taryn slows the bear's pace, mirroring my own. "Now that I've got a pet, why don't we try to find some tougher competition. The sooner I level up, the sooner we can find out what it is that's driving the moulhaugs south."

"What'd you have in mind?"

"I was thinking maybe we could try to find a dungeon. I heard there might be one in this area. Normally, we'd need to hire a guide or buy a map, but if I take to the air, maybe I can spot the entrance."

"There's an easier way." My map practically shows me where every dungeon is just based on the location of the ley lines.

"What do you mean?" Berry comes to a halt and Taryn stares me down, his dreadlocks dancing in the breeze beneath his antler helmet.

"When I agreed to complete the first quest for Chief Rizza, she gave me access to a map that only the trolls have. It shows the ley lines that run across the entire island. If I look at the concentrated areas of magical energy, that usually means there is a dungeon nearby."

"You've got to be kidding me." He turns his head up to the heavens. "Could you be any luckier?"

"Hey, it was a hard road getting to where I am right now. I didn't have a tutorial. I got dropped in the forest and had to find my way. Yeah, maybe I got a little lucky here and there, but everyone who wasn't a troll would have killed me on sight a month ago. Everything I have now, I worked for." If he thinks this has been easy for me, he's clearly misinformed. Fighting the mana-infused wyrm wasn't easy. Nor was the faerie dungeon. Hell, I plotted the entire battle that defeated Glenn and his army.

"Yeah, yeah, yeah. Poor baby. Poor six-hundred pound, seven-foot-tall, double-class, hero of your people, and friend to King Favian, baby. Cry me a river. But first, how about you point me in the direction of the closest dungeon?"

I should make him beg me for my information, but it's more important to level him up than stoke my pride, so I pull up the map and locate the nearest ley line. Several miles from our location, there's a small cluster of magical veins. Nothing big, but hopefully something that'll give Taryn a level or two.

I share the location with Taryn. "Lead the way, your bearness."

He just strokes his beard and carries on. A half-hour later, the meadow grows soggy, transforming into a marsh.

My feet sink into the muddy earth. The water line is just barely below the surface. Reeds and other tall grasses blow in the wind. Occasionally, we startle a flock of birds, and they take to the air, but not before Limery torches a few for himself.

There are no trees or large bushes, just miles and miles of wetlands. Frogs croak and splash into the surrounding pools as we navigate toward the cluster of magical veins. Brightly-colored fish dart between the reeds, stirring up mud and silt.

"Is this it?" asks Taryn. His bear struggles to move through the muddy earth the same as I do. Each step is twice as hard as normal with the mud suctioning to our feet.

"Almost. Looks like it's about a half a mile that way." I point in the direction of the ley line.

Sick of sinking into the mud, I equip my Aquatic Boots. My prize from completing the faerie dungeon, they allow me to walk on water. Their magical properties prevent me from sinking into the mud.

"Hey, no fair," quips Taryn as his bear struggles with the new terrain. Beasts like that were not made for these environments.

"It's going to be tough to fight here. Maybe we should find another area that's more forgiving."

"We're already here. Let's just see what it has to offer. I'm going to scout ahead. This should help you and Berry keep up." The boar tusk on the tip of his staff glows blue and a strong gust seems to push me from behind.

You have been targeted with Strong Wind. Your movement speed has been increased.

Suddenly, Berry's feet move a little quicker through the mud. It's still tough for him, but it doesn't slow us as much.

Taryn transforms into a red bird and disappears into the sky.

I wonder where this dungeon will be. There are no trees or rock formations for as far as I can see, and it's unlikely to be underground with all the surrounding water. As if to answer my question, I receive a message from Taryn.

Incoming Message (Taryn): *Dude, this is wild. There's some kind of design formed by the water that runs through the marsh. It looks like a giant symbol.*

Message (Chod): *Any idea what it means?*

Incoming Message (Taryn): *Not sure, but I'm guessing it has something to do with the dungeon. On my way back.*

Up ahead, Taryn waits for us, perched on a swaying reed. When we're close enough, he returns to his dwarf form and his feet sink into the marshy earth.

"This is the edge of the symbol." He points to the water just before where we are standing. "It runs in a circle several hundred yards that way."

I pull up the map again. We're definitely in the right place. "Ready to see what it's all about?"

He nods, and we step forward. As soon as my feet touch the water, I'm greeted with a notification.

Marshlands. *Would you like to enter?*

I confirm and take another step forward. Taryn follows my lead, legs wrapped around Berry as he floats alongside me. A second later, there is a flash of light that runs through the water, not just in front of me but throughout the entire circle Taryn pointed out. A translucent barrier appears around the circle's edge, keeping others out but also keeping us in.

"Looks like we found our dungeon," I say.

Limery flies from my shoulder and touches a finger to the barrier. It clinks when his nail taps against it. I follow him and do the same. The barrier feels like glass, but it's made entirely of magical energy. He throws a fireball at the barrier, but it does nothing to the forcefield.

I've never seen a dungeon like this. No rooms, no levels, just wide-open space.

"What now?" asks Taryn.

"Now, we explore." I walk atop the water like some biblical prophet. It's strange, expecting to sink but walking on firm ground.

With Taryn riding him, Berry's nose is only a few inches above the water. Limery flutters in the air not far behind us.

The water gently splashes as we follow nature's path through the marsh. Berry disturbs the waterbed, making it impossible to see anything below the surface. The sun has only just begun to descend, so we still have a few hours before darkness. Not that it matters much to me or Limery with our night vision.

"Do dwarves have night vision?" I ask. With all the mining they do, it is certainly possible.

"Not quite." The water deepens and Berry's front legs wade through. "We have dark vision. It allows us to see better in dimly-lit areas, but not in complete darkness."

"Better than nothing."

All around us, insects rattle, birds chirp, and frogs croak. Where are the monsters?

Taryn stops moving and points a short dark finger to the marsh ahead. I don't immediately notice what he's showing me, but then I spot two orange eyes just above the water's surface and about a foot away, two nostrils.

I try to focus on it to reveal its stats, but there's not enough of the creature visible. Taryn lifts his staff and motions towards the monster.

I nod. A second later, there's a thunderous crack overhead and a bolt of lightning rips into the creature. It roars in pain before emerging from the muddy depths.

Mutated Crocodile. *Level 14. Mutated by the ancient rune magic* *of the Marshlands, this reptile walks on powerful hind legs capable of jumping long distances. They are fierce brawlers with unnatural strength.*

The crocodile that emerges looks more like a dinosaur than anything I've ever seen on the Discovery Channel. Burnt orange scales tipped with black match its fiery eyes. When it stands, the beast is easily seven feet tall. I hope Taryn is ready to party.

He dismounts and sends his bear on the attack, but in the water, it doesn't have the same attack speed it does on land. Even when he rises on his hind legs, the bear is still waist deep in muddy water. The crocodile lunges at Berry, sinking its teeth into the Berry's front leg. With a powerful strike, the bear smashes the crocodile in the side of the head, releasing its hold.

We need to get in there and help. "Limery, hit it with fireballs."

I summon my horrors while Limery pelts the reptile with fire. The flames sizzle against its orange scales but do little damage. My horrors float through the water like children at a pool party, unable to gather enough speed for an attack.

"Dammit, we need to get out of the water and onto the bank. It's muddy, but it's better than this." The water is the crocodile's element.

As soon as the cooldown allows, Taryn casts another Lightning Bolt. It stuns the creature in place, allowing Berry to land a few blows before retreating to the high ground. I gather my floating horrors and toss them onto land. Taryn casts Strong Wind, helping him and Berry make land.

"Got any bright ideas?" I ask.

Taryn's eyes are focused on the croc. "If you tank the damage, Limery and I can take him down with ranged attacks."

I summon a Horror of Vitality on the monster, slowing the crocodile's movement as it crawls out of the water. A wall of fire blocks its path, forcing it to go around just in time for Taryn to hit it with another bolt, dropping its health to sixty percent.

With a powerful leap, the bipedal crocodile covers the distance between it and me in a single jump. It crashes into me, and I fall onto my back in the sandy mud. The Aquatic Boots only keep my feet from sinking, not my whole body. We scrape, claw, and bite at one another as we roll through the muddy marsh. The crocodile grips me with his arms and kicks out with its legs, shredding my own legs with its talons. Berry tackles the creature, pulling it off me. I activate Claw, and jump back into the fight, piercing its scales and drawing blood. My own legs are streaked with blue. I manage to stand, and a powerful kick sends me stumbling away.

My legs sting like I just walked through a thorn bush naked, so I take a moment before rushing in. Summoning more horrors does no good. Each new one is so slow in the muddy terrain that the crocodile punts them away like soccer balls, so I resort to exploding them as soon as they summon, taking out chunks of health in droves.

When a bolt of lightning finally stuns the monster again. I sink my tusks into its neck and score a critical hit.

"Finish him off!" I tell Taryn so that he will get the kill bonus.

"Lightning Bolt is on cooldown." He lifts his arms as if not knowing what else to do.

"Use your brain."

A moment later, he transforms into an exact copy of Berry and the two maul the crocodile for its last bit of health.

"Woohoo!" yells Taryn after transforming back. "Now, that's how you get experience. A couple more of those and I'll be level eleven." He comes over to where I'm sitting and treating my wounds. "Ooh, that's nasty." He grimaces.

I down one of the health potions I crafted, and my wounds

slowly begin to heal. "Here, give this to Berry." I hand him one of the potions.

"Thanks, but we don't need it." He tosses me the potion. "Check this out." He calls Berry over and has the bear sit beside him. His fur is matted with blood, and gashes from the crocodile cover his body. Taryn closes his eyes and begins chanting, both hands on Berry. As he does, a green aura surrounds their bodies. The gashes that run along the bear's sides quit bleeding and soon close. A moment later, he's completely healed.

"What was that?" I toss my empty clay vial back into my satchel, feeling better already.

"Didn't you listen when I was explaining my abilities? It's called Restoration. I can recover HP for me and my pets while communing with nature. The only downside is that I'm immobile while I do it, so I need someone to watch my back to make sure I'm not attacked." He climbs on the back of the freshly-healed bear. "Now, how about we see what else this dungeon has to offer?"

CHAPTER 19
PEST CONTROL

THE MARSHLANDS. Or as I like to call it, The Suckity Swamp, also known as a great way to use all your health potions while helping your scrub friend level up in the worst terrain possible.

For the next few hours, we slay mutated crocodiles the size of a small truck, go half-deaf fighting bats that do sonic damage, and fend off a nasty school of barracuda. Taryn uses his level eleven stat point to learn Imbue, an ability that increases the size of a summoned monster or pet. I stay back as much as possible, so I'm still a ways off from hitting level twenty.

Imbue is actually a pretty cool ability. He can even cast it on my horrors, effectively doubling their size. The long cooldown means Taryn can usually only imbue one pet at a time unless it's a super long fight. Berry is the chosen target more often than not, and when imbued, he even towers above me. He tanks the monsters and when the fight is over, Taryn heals him back to full health. The crocodiles fall a lot easier when he's tanking the brunt of the damage. Once we put a little armor on him, he'll be a force of nature.

There's not a lot of good loot from the monsters we've killed, so I'm holding out hope that whatever boss we stumble upon has all the spoils.

"That's my last potion." After another battle with a crocodile, I toss the vial into my satchel. "I'll need to search for ingredients to craft more once we're done with this place."

"You think we'll finish by dark?" Taryn gazes towards the horizon. We can't have more than an hour of daylight left.

"Doubtful. And I don't think that barrier is going down until we beat the boss." In the twilight, the barrier is even more pronounced. It seems to have its own ethereal glow.

As the day comes to a close, the rattle of insects grows louder. Limery and I will be fine to fight at night, but Taryn doesn't have our night vision. And this is definitely not a suitable place to camp, when creatures are lurking just below the surface.

Berry comes to a stop, pawing at something buried in the mud.

"What's this?" Taryn dismounts to get a better look.

Berry continues digging around the object. It's some sort of shell, dark brown and about the size of a trashcan. It looks almost like a cocoon with its layered ridges.

"I don't know, but I'd rather not find out. Go ahead and smash it. Maybe you'll get some free XP."

Taryn takes the end of his staff and jabs it against the shell. The shell doesn't break, but a small crack forms. Then, the shell shakes, something moving inside.

"Limery, burn it before it hatches," I order.

He tosses a fireball, but it doesn't explode the shell. Instead, the shell absorbs the heat, turning a vibrant red. A claw breaks through the crack where Taryn stabbed it, and the shell begins to crumble from the inside.

Without warning, the shell explodes, raining bits of debris all over us as a giant winged creature emerges. It flaps its wings, taking flight, and a deep rattle resonates from its chest.

Glouwseeker. *Level 15. While fragile and harmless in their larva state, once evolved, these winged insects are deadly warriors. Their stingers are coated with a paralyzing venom, capable of immobilizing even the liveliest of enemies. Like most insectoids, they have a fascination with lights.*

Great. Giant bugs.

Fully unraveled, the bug is monstrous. A good five feet with double the wingspan. A dangerous proboscis, capable of stabbing or drawing blood, protrudes between giant, bubble eyes. Six long, spike-covered legs attach to its thorax, and a nasty-looking stinger extends from the bottom of its abdomen, coated in a slimy substance. Two translucent wings flap rapidly, keeping it afloat.

This bug was made for battle.

Taryn draws first blood, hitting the giant bug with a lightning bolt. The energy runs through its exoskeleton, briefly revealing its hollow insides.

The bug dives for Taryn, ripping the dwarf from his mount with its serrated legs and flying off. I quickly cast a Horror of Vitality and sling it by its horn at the glouwseeker, exploding it at the same time as Limery's fireballs burn through one of its wings.

Our attacks cause the insect to drop Taryn, and he lands in the mud with a splat.

With only one wing, the bug falls to the ground on top of him. Once he's downed, it's pretty easy to finish him off.

"That wasn't so ba—"

Something wet plops against my back. A second later, my back burns like hell and I turn to see three more of the bugs hovering in the air. One of them spits a green ooze from its proboscis that goes sailing by my head.

"Watch out for the ooze! It burns like hell." The stinging pain doesn't fade as I get into position. "Limery, take out their wings."

A lightning bolt crashes into one of the insects, while another dives for Taryn. They must really have a thing for dwarves.

Limery zooms through the air, slinging fireballs and lighting up the sky with his personal brand of fireworks. He takes out the wings of one of the bugs, and I turn my attention to the other two. The wingless one can wait.

Berry stands at his full height, protecting Taryn as one of the bugs harasses them. It changes course at the last second, extending its stinger and injecting the bear right in the chest before zipping away.

Paralyzed, Berry falls to the ground. Taryn rushes to aid his downed mount.

"Leave him," I order. "You can heal him after the battle. Right now, I need your help."

In response, he calls another bolt of lightning. This time, it lets off a chain reaction, jumping from one bug to the other. Their exoskeletons glow as electricity courses through them. I try to swat at them with my staff, but they flutter just out of reach. Limery zooms through the air, but the bugs seem determined to avoid his fireballs.

The one downed bug crawls across the marsh toward Berry, its long legs refusing to sink in the mud.

I take off toward the insect and tackle it into the water. Its chitinous shell cuts against my body like barbed wire. Even with my thick skin, it stings pretty bad. I wrap my hands around one of its barbed legs, using my strength to crack it in two. A dark yellow substance drains out like rotten crab legs. Activating Claw, I rip a hole in its abdomen, spilling its innards. It sinks to the bottom of the marsh.

One down, two to go.

Back on land, Limery has downed another bug. Without wings, it moves in a grotesque manner, bending several sets of knees like something out of a horror movie.

Taryn calls forth another lightning bolt, and this time, it's lucky enough to stun. He then transforms into a replica of Berry and rips two of the bug's legs off one side before the stun wears off. Imbalanced, the bug stumbles in the mud and Taryn moves in for the finishing blow, ripping its head off and spilling yellow ichor into the marsh.

Limery and the final glouwseeker play a game of dodgeball in the air. Limery tosses his fireballs and the creature shoots its acidic projectiles, each one missing by only inches.

I summon two horrors and toss them at the insect, exploding them just before impact. The bug turns towards the distraction, which is all Limery needs to damage one of its wings.

"Thanks, Chods!" he shouts.

By the time we kill it, Taryn is already healing Berry.

"Good job, guys. That was some quick adaptation."

Taryn is oblivious to my comments as he communes with nature to heal himself and his bear. Limery flies over to the decapitated glouwseeker and dips his finger in the yellow goo that spills out of its neck. He licks it and then spits it out.

"Yuck, Limmy no like." He scrunches his nose and continues spitting like a cat that just licked a lemon.

I use my empty vials to milk some of the venom from the glouwseekers's stingers.

Item. Glouwseeker Venom. *When injected into the bloodstream, glouwseeker venom immobilizes target. Length of stun dependent on size of target, resistances, and amount injected.*

"Pretty neat," I say as I describe the effects to Taryn.

"Berry caught the full stinger to the chest, no wonder he froze. Almost to level twelve, though," says Taryn. He pats Berry on the head and the bear grunts softly, no traces of its previous wounds. "It's getting dark. What should we do now?"

"I've got an idea that might bring a few more glouwseekers to us now that it's dark." And hopefully some easy XP.

With the remaining daylight, we gather reeds, dead bushes, anything that seems the least bit flammable, and the bodies of the fallen glouwseekers. We pile them together on the densest plot of mud we can find, until we have a pyre that is five feet tall.

"You think this is going to work?" Taryn looks skeptically at the pile of debris and body parts.

I shrug. "If not, I think we are mightily fucked." Truthfully, I've got a very good feeling about this.

"That's reassuring." He turns to Berry. "If we die, it was nice knowing you." Berry gives him a sad groan.

"Alright, I'm going to step away now. All of this experience is for you and Limery. Don't screw this up and maybe we can get the hell out of here." I give them a wide berth and wait for Camouflage to take effect, saying a silent prayer that just because we're in a fantasy game, some things never change.

When I'm far enough away, lightning shoots from the sky, hitting the pyre and starting a small fire. Two orange balls of flame erupt in Limery's palms. He tosses them into the pyre and it rages even higher, sending flames shooting into the night sky.

The call of insects roars across the open expanse as the fire crackles.

Dark shapes begin moving across my night vision. Suddenly, a giant fireball explodes as one of the glouwseekers barrels into the flames. A bolt of lightning zaps the pyre, sending a thousand tiny embers drifting through the air.

The air around me fills with buzzing as dozens of glouwseekers and other insects are enraptured by the giant beacon. One by one, they burst into flames, drawn to death's beautiful and fiery embrace.

For half an hour, I sit back and watch as they add their bodies to the pyre, growing it higher and higher. Eventually, the winged meteors become less and less frequent as the population dies off, until finally minutes pass between deaths.

"You genius!" Taryn pushes me when I return. "That was bloody brilliant! I got three levels off of that. Three levels!" He grins from ear to ear. "I went ahead and upgraded Lightning Bolt to level two so that it deals more damage and cuts down on the cooldown."

"'Bloody brilliant?' You want some tea and crumpets with that?" I roll my eyes. "What about you, Limery?"

Limery gives me a devilish grin and then explodes into flames. Not just his hands, but his entire body. Even from several feet away, I can feel the heat radiating from him. I have to put my hand up to shield my eyes.

"Limmy doesn't just makes fire. Limmy is fire," he laughs at his own joke.

With the experience from all those kills, Taryn is now level fourteen. Limery is not far behind me at level seventeen. All in all, our squad is pretty strong. I wonder if anyone else thought to power-level this way. I don't imagine too many people choosing to tackle this dungeon at night.

The marsh is eerily quiet with the glouwseekers gone. There's the occasional splash and slither in the depths, but the slosh of Berry's footsteps is the loudest thing around.

"Could you be any louder?" I ask Taryn.

The torch he carries made from a glouwseeker leg leaves nothing to the imagination when he flashes me a rude gesture.

"Oh, I'm sorry that I don't have a pair of magical boots for me and my bear."

"Three levels and he thinks he's the king of the world. I'm just trying to help you out. Making that much noise, you'll be the first target if—"

A shrill hiss cuts me off.

CHAPTER 20

DRAGOMANDER

WATER SPRAYS US AS A LARGE, dragon-like creature emerges from the marshy waters. It's at least ten feet long from nose to tail, shaped like a salamander, and perfectly fitted to conceal its massive body beneath the shallow depths of the marsh. From an orange and black speckled head, two large, glossy black eyes stare at us, reflecting the flame from Taryn's torch. Its slick, scale-less skin shimmers against the dancing light.

We're going to need more than a single torch for Taryn to see well enough to fight.

The creature's mouth is wide and curved, unlike the pointed snout of most dragons. It hisses menacingly before a forked tongue extends and tastes the air. Two small wings that look more for show than flying adorn the shoulders of the long, winding creature.

Dragomander. *Level 17. This amphibious, fire-breathing dragon is equally dangerous whether on land or water.*

With each predatory step, webbed feet keep it from sinking as they splat against the mud. It takes a few more steps before hissing again, making a show of dominance.

"You think this is the boss?" asks Taryn. He plants the torch in the mud and grips the fur of Berry's neck with one hand while holding his staff in the other, ready for a fight.

"I don't know. Usually, bosses are a little more unique." It looks tough, but one single monster for all of this seems a little too easy.

"It's a dragon-salamander. How does it get more unique than that?" He gives me a bug-eyed look and shrugs.

"I guess we'll—"

Another splash cuts me off as a second dragomander appears from the water. This one is twice as large, with two heads.

Twin-headed Dragomander. *Unique Monster. Level 20. Mutated by the ancient rune magic of the marshlands, both heads are capable of emitting elemental magic.*

Awesome. If fire-breathing wasn't enough, this one gets elemental magic, too. The twin-headed dragomander steps beside the lesser beast. As it stands there, the coloring of its skin changes from orange to yellow to blue, like a rotating advertisement in Times Square. It doesn't just reflect the firelight, the coloring of its skin seems to come from within, much like my own mana-infused skin.

Both heads let out a hiss, and the other dragomander joins in. A moment later, a third dragomander, this one level seventeen, crawls from the water.

"I don't know how many more there are, but I suggest we get to fighting before they call in any more friends." I grip Forlorn Scepter tight, readying my mana for a brawl. This is going to be a tough fight, seeing as how they already out-level us and I don't have any horrors at the ready.

Poor foresight on my part.

A lightning bolt smashes into the boss monster, starting the battle. The flash of lightning ignites the sky for a moment, and the twin-headed dragomander launches at Taryn with ridiculous speed, knocking Berry aside with its massive body and sending Taryn flying through the air. It lunges at his floundering body as Taryn is tossed skyward. At the last moment, Taryn transforms into a red bird and zips out of the way, leaving the monster snapping at air.

I don't waste any time watching the battle unfold before jumping into the action and summoning three quick horrors. Limery pummels the dragomander closest to him with fireballs, drawing its attention and leaving the final monster to me. A jet of flame pours from its mouth, setting the three horrors ablaze. I quickly use Kamikaze to explode them, taking out a chunk of health and dealing as much damage as I can before my horrors perish.

Fire. "Why is it always fire?"

"Limmy likes fire!" the imp shouts from over my shoulder.

I turn to see him, body aflame, riding the other dragomander like a cowboy as it tries to buck him off. His tiny hands hold onto the dragomander's small wings while the rest of him bounces with each thrashing movement. The beast's health slowly fades from Limery's radiating heat.

Pain flares through one entire side of my body as fire engulfs me. Flames sear my flesh, and the heat distorts my vision. My health drops by ten percent from a single attack, and the lingering burn damage takes slivers of HP each second. Half my body burns, but I try to fight through the pain as I attempt to locate the monster, but before I can, another wall of flame scorches my backside. A quarter of my health is gone in an instant.

Abandoning all thoughts of fighting, I run toward the water. Toward safety. When I jump, my Aquatic Boots keep me from its cool embrace. Without thinking, I take off the boots and toss them aside, sinking into the muddy water. The burning slowly fades, and I suddenly realize what a big mistake I've made just as something slimy and cold coils around my midsection, pinning my arms to my sides.

I'm only a few feet below the surface, but the clenching tightness around my body weighs me down as the dragomander attempts to crush my ribs and drown me. I fight the coiling dragon, but this is what it was made for. I'm in its element now. Its grip is ironclad against my body. The more I struggle, the tighter it becomes. As my lungs beg for air, stars dance at my vision in the blurry water.

I hope Taryn and Limery are having better luck than I am, because I'm about to be dead.

Not knowing what else to do, I activate Berserker Rage. The ability that has saved my life more times than I can count. My body grows stronger from the increased stats, putting even more stress on my bones as they fight against the mounting pressure. My health regenerates rapidly, healing my burned body and mending my tired muscles, but it does nothing for the fact that I am a sinking weight in the muddy marsh water. I try to walk, to grip anything, but the silty bottom only sucks me deeper.

I feel a rush of water around me, and claws dig into my shoulders. My body slowly moves toward the bank.

The claws shred my skin, but I'm grateful for the pain when my head breaks through the surface and air rushes into my lungs. Not enough air to fill my lungs, but enough to put the stars in my vision at bay.

Berry unleashes a monstrous roar as he tries to peel the dragomander from around me. His teeth sink into the dragon's neck, but the creature only grips tighter. It would rather die than release me.

Thank God for that bear. If I make it out of this, I'll never make fun of his stupid name again.

Limery zips through the edge of my vision, and I turn just in time to see a bolt of lightning shooting into the air, missing him by inches.

Why in the hell is Taryn shooting lightning at Limery?

Berserker Rage ends and my muscles reduce to their normal size. The momentary slack in the dragon's coil gives me enough leeway to squeeze my arms free. With a full rage bar, I activate Claw and rip through the dragomander's flesh. It lets out a shrill hiss and squeezes tighter around my midsection. It hurts like hell, but at least now I can fight back.

The dragomander's body goes hot as it erupts a stream of flame, but the fire shoots into the sky, burning no one. Berry still has his teeth sunk like a vice into the monster's neck, able to aim the blast like a firehose. My body jerks with each massive heave as Berry pulls at the dragomander's neck like a dog playing tug-of-war.

I quickly burn through all my rage, clawing the dragomander until its ribs are exposed and my sharp claws can puncture its insides.

I bury my hand inside its body, my sharp nails ripping through organs until finally, the tension releases and I can take my first full breath since the fight began. I barely enjoy my first unencumbered breath before a cannonball of ice knocks me on my ass.

"Chods!" Limery's voice rings out from somewhere nearby as I suck at air. "Chods, is yous okay?" That should be his catchphrase at this point. His warm hands grip my shoulder as I stumble to my feet. He grabs me by the tusk and forces my head towards him, his giant yellow eyes examining me.

"I'm fine. What the hell just happened?" The huge ball of ice that nearly killed me sits in the mud, slowly melting.

With my dragomander dead, Berry has already joined another fight. He charges the two-headed beast, his muscles rippling beneath thick fur with each step.

I look around, but Taryn is nowhere to be seen, though I do spot the corpse of the other one-headed dragomander.

There's no time to search out Taryn. Berry and Limery's safety depend on me finding a way to defeat this monster. If Taryn is dead, he will respawn. They won't be so lucky.

Berry is a few steps from the twin-headed dragomander when its skin changes from light blue to yellow. It rears back one of its heads and a stream of lightning explodes from its mouth, setting Berry's hair on end and stunning him in place. The second head changes color, turning back to light blue and unleashing a stream of ice that freezes Berry for even longer. The bear's fur is covered in a thick layer of ice as he stands there, unable to move. The two attacks drop his health by half.

Now, I understand. Each color that the dragomander changes to affects the elemental attacks it uses.

Rather than let the bear die while I stand by watching like a jackass, I jump into action, summoning three horrors and tossing them at the dragomander. I explode them when they are in range. Without my Aquatic Boots, I sink into the mud with each step, making it hard to gather any speed for a physical assault.

Whatever Taryn and Limery did to fight the beast worked, because its HP is over halfway gone. It's not very tanky; the damage it deals is our main source of concern. Getting close enough to deal damage to it is the problem.

There's a rustle in the nearby bushes and Taryn appears from a thicket with nearly three-quarters health.

"Thanks for holding it off while I healed, Limmy." He lifts his staff and a bolt of lightning strikes the monster. "Chod, glad you could finally join us."

The dragomander shoots flame in his direction, but he swiftly transforms into a bird and dodges the attack. A moment later, he returns to his dwarven form, unleashing another bolt of lightning. He's mastered the ability to use Transform as a defensive maneuver.

He casts Imbue on Berry, and the bear nearly doubles in size. The spell also grants him a small boost of health.

Limery summons a flame wall between the dragomander and Berry, protecting the bear from being trampled while he's stunned. The imp follows up with a barrage of fireballs.

Both dragomander heads turn dark blue and spit out a blast of water, turning Limery's fireballs into puffs of steam.

I continue throwing horror bombs as quickly as they become available. Each explosion takes out a fraction of the monster's health.

Fire, ice, water, and electricity cycle through the dragomander's attacks. We dodge what we can, but the twin heads act of their own accord, seemingly attacking at random. The lightning attacks are the worst, as there is no rhyme or reason to their path of madness. They explode out of the dragomander's mouth, zigzagging until finding a target.

Poor Berry takes a massive beating. He and I are the only ones willing to get within the monster's range and he lacks my mobility, even with Taryn's Strong Wind buff increasing our movement speed.

He and I spread out, taking opposite sides and keeping the dragomander from focusing on either one of us for too long. When the monster charges, Taryn and Limery attack it from the rear, drawing its attention to the other side. When it charges again, they repeat the process.

Limery, Taryn, and I slice down the monster's health from afar with fire, lightning, and exploding horrors until it eventually collapses.

When the dragomander falls, the barrier around the Marshlands vanishes. Several notifications clutter my vision, but I focus them away for now. My muscles bulge slightly, letting me know without checking that I just hit level twenty.

A glowing stone falls from the dragomander just as tiny bubbles form in the marsh's waters. They grow bigger, until they are the size of my head. For a moment, I'm afraid the battle isn't over. Then I notice several chests have floated to the surface. Each one has a faint aura around it. Runes run along their weathered lids.

"Sweet! We've got loot." I slosh through the marsh and gather two of the wooden chests, piling them on land. Each one is waterlogged and slimy. Who knows how long they have sat at the bottom of this marsh. The metal clasps are rusted, and the wooden corners have been weathered to a smooth surface.

Limery sways through the air, his eyes full of greed as he carries a chest nearly as large as he is. Nearby, Taryn focuses on healing Berry. The fiery surroundings offer him enough light to see by.

By the time Taryn finishes communing with nature, Limery has already cracked the ancient lock. He flips the lid and buries his head inside.

His lips pout when he lifts a water-filled jar from the chest. Flashes of white clink against the jar, barely visible in the muddy water. He opens the lid and pours out its contents, letting them fall through his fingers.

Item. Jar of Teeth. *Nothing special, just a jar of teeth.*

"Limmy no likes." His frown grows larger.

The teeth fall to the ground and disappear into the mud.

"Maybe if you weren't so greedy," I offer, but Limery has already buried his head back in the chest, riffling through its contents.

Taryn takes a chest for himself and sets it down beside me. "Let's hope I fare a little better." He strikes the lock with his staff and it comes undone.

"Wait." I stop him. "First, I want to know how both of you killed the first dragomander." I'm a higher level and almost died to one. They killed the first and put a dent in the boss monster, too. It doesn't make any sense.

Taryn waits to open the chest. "You can thank Limery for that. He basically boiled the dragomander alive. I guess they mimic their temperature to their surroundings like most reptiles and amphibians, because he did his little flame thing and pretty soon, its chest exploded. We were able to tag-team the big one, until I noticed you were getting your ass kicked and sent Berry to help you."

"And a good thing, too." I pat him on the shoulder. "I owe you one for that."

"How about we loot this treasure and call it even?" He flashes me a toothy grin.

"Deal."

Taryn lifts the lid and reaches in. After a few seconds, he pulls out a gnarled and waterlogged staff. It looks like trash, much like the chest, with a cloudy stone set in the tip. I focus on the staff and analyze its stats.

Item. Staff of the Marshes. *+1 Intelligence. An enchanted staff, capable of muddying any water source.*

"Dude, this is so lame. When would anyone ever have a need for this?" Taryn jabs the end of the staff into the mud and searches for more items. "What a crappy dungeon."

Limery continues to take items out of his own chest. So far, he has a soggy boot, a couple of empty jars, and a sack of bronze coins. Hardly a treasure.

After pulling out the other matching soggy boot, he kicks the chest away and crosses his arms. "Hmmph." He pouts.

Berry sits on his butt watching the show unfold. The next item Taryn pulls out is a bow. The string is made of some kind of marsh weed, and the wood looks like it might snap with the least bit of pressure.

"Oh, wow..." Taryn's sudden change of tone has me interested.

Item. Bog Bow. *Capable of firing arrows underwater as if on land. Arrows will fly as true as the archer's aim.*

Wow, indeed. "That's actually a damn good weapon."

"Yeah," echoes Taryn. "But realistically, when would we ever use it? Neither one of us can breathe underwater. How often are we going to be battling sea creatures?" He lays the bow aside.

The seaside trolls would have a use for it. "I bet it'll fetch a high price at an auction."

Next, he pulls out a brown orb. It looks like a coconut, but with a green weed dangling out of it.

Item. Bog Bomb. *An explosive with a waterproof fuse.*

"Pretty cool. There's two of them." Taryn's smiles as he looks them over. "Okay, these we can definitely use. There's one more chest. Do you want to do the honors?"

I twist the lock and the wood creaks as the latch gives way. I lift the lid in anticipation of the crappy loot that awaits.

The first item is a vial of dark purple liquid.

Item. Infernal Darkness Potion. *Covers opponent in a veil of darkness, making them unable to see or smell their surroundings for one minute.*

Not bad. I pull out another vial. This one is a deep pink color with a layer of black silt on the bottom.

Legendary Item. Angel of Death Brandy. *When drinker falls* *below 1HP, a metaphysical event will occur, rewinding time for the user to two seconds prior to death.*

Taryn and I both just stare at each other. Essentially, we just found an extra life. One with no penalties, no levels lost, and no respawns.

"Holy shit, this is huge." I carefully place the vial aside.

"No shit. Is there anything else?"

I rake my fingers against the bottom of the chest and touch something metal. It's heavy as I lift it, one end weighing far more than the other.

The chest must be enchanted, because what I pull out couldn't possibly fit inside.

When I take the item out, the trident shimmers with the reflection of the surrounding flames. Runes run all along its golden shaft, and there is an indentation beneath the barbed spears for attaching an enchanted stone.

Item. Sea Scorpion. *An enchanted trident capable of taking on the property of 1 enchanted stone. Bonus: deals splash damage. +3 Strength.*

The only other weapon I've seen capable of taking on enchanted stones was Peacemaker. They must be pretty rare.

I equip the trident and feel its weight in my hand. The six-foot-long spear gives me plenty of reach. I know I have my staffs, but this just feels so much more natural. I'm not meant to stand back and cast spells. I'm meant to be in the action, fighting side by side with my horrors as we overwhelm opponents with brute force and violence. With Taryn leveling up, I can get back to my more natural role.

What's the point of having this strong body if I'm just going to play it safe? I practice a few thrusts. I could skewer several enemies at once on its pointed tips.

"What makes you think you get the trident?" asks Taryn. He stands beside me, arms crossed in expectation.

"Because I can actually lift it without falling over."

He stares at me for a moment before bursting into laughter. "You got me there." The metal clasps in his beard jingle against one another as his chest rumbles. "What do you say we get the hell out of this shithole and make camp?"

After retrieving my Aquatic Boots, we divide the rest of our loot, setting aside what we will keep and what we will trade. In the end, Taryn takes the Bog Bombs and the Infernal Darkness Potion. We elect to auction or sell the Bog Bow and the Staff of the Marshes. Not sure of how to handle the Angel of Death Brandy, I hold on to it for now. I'm sure it could fetch a small fortune. It's probably something even kings would fight over. For now, we'll keep it hidden. Limery's items are all returned safely to the chest he pulled them out of, minus the teeth that have by now settled into the mud.

"Wait a sec!" I suddenly remember the stone that fell from the dragomander and rush to the monster's corpse. The glowing stone has submerged into the mud, but it still casts a faint glow from beneath.

I dig my hand in and pull out the stone. It cycles through the same colors as the host it came from.

Item. Elemental Stone. *10% bonus to elemental attacks.*

The stone would be great for Limery or Taryn, seeing as how they both use elemental damage, but I have the feeling that Taryn could use the boost more than the imp right now.

I hand him the stone and he uses it to replace the boar tusk that was attached to his staff. I didn't realize his staff was capable of taking enchanted stones.

"We'll get you something next time, buddy." I try to comfort

Limery, but his inner greedy pig refuses to be placated for the moment.

He sits on my shoulder, stewing as we make our way back to solid ground.

Now that we are in the boring part, I pull up the notifications I discarded earlier.

You have defeated a unique monster: Twin-headed Dragomander.

Item. Elemental Stone. *10% bonus to elemental attacks.*

Congratulations! You have reached level 20. +1 stat point to distribute. +1 Strength and Constitution racial bonus.

New ability unlocked.

Sweet, it's been a while since I've gotten a new ability. Too bad I don't get another ability point until level twenty-one. I pull up my abilities, focusing on the ones that haven't been unlocked. They are separated by the class or trait that unlocked them.

Barbarian:

Iron Will. *Immune to slows and stuns for 30 seconds. Cost: 50 rage. 180 second cooldown.*

I'm Always Angry (Passive). *Once rage meter is at 50%, it will not deteriorate below 50% when out of combat.*

Both of these seem like a waste of an ability point now that I have better abilities.

Melee:

Cleave. *Your next attack causes bleed damage, dealing 1% of opponent's health per second for 5 seconds. Cost: 10 rage.*

__Battle Cry.__ You let out a ferocious roar, increasing rage by 20. No Cost. 60 second cooldown.

Cleave could be useful. I wonder if it stacks with Claw or Bite?

__Wisdom:__

__Perception.__ For 10 minutes, gain increased awareness of your surroundings. Spot hidden objects, as well as unusual sounds, odors, and tastes. Cooldown: 6 hours.

This is nice, but not much better than what I can already craft with a perception potion.

*__*New* Summoner:__*

*__*New* Champion.__ Summon a copy of the most recent enemy you have defeated. Decays 10% every minute out of combat. Cost: 50% of mana pool. Cooldown: 6 hours.*

Holy smokes! The ability to summon whatever I have killed recently. Imagine summoning a dragomander or a mana-infused wyrm. They could turn a fight instantly. The mana cost is pretty high, as well as the cooldown, but that ability will be a game-changer once I unlock it.

I briefly glance over the rest of my unlocked abilities. None of them are a priority and half of them are easily covered by abilities I already have. Aside from Perception, I doubt I will be using a hard-earned ability point on any of them.

When I analyze Taryn, it looks like he has gained another level, too.

All in all, not a bad day.

CHAPTER 21

SMALLTOWN

As soon as we are out of the Marshlands, we make camp for the night underneath a towering oak. Its leaves rustle together in a gentle lullaby. After so much fighting, Taryn and I are both pretty wiped out.

The ebony dwarf uses his cloak as a blanket as he lays against the soft fur of his bear. Limery takes his normal sleeping position in my arms.

The last of my horrors pops out of existence nearby. They are steadfast guardians until their health fades to nothing. Since finding myself unprepared in the marsh, I try to keep a constant supply at the ready when we are traveling. Unless I know for a fact we are safe, it pays to be prepared.

"I know that we got some pretty good items." Taryn pulls his cloak up like a blanket, obscuring everything but his bearded head. "But that place really was a shithole. I'll be happy if we never go back. I say we stick to solid ground from now on."

"I respect that. Perhaps tomorrow we can go see what scared

away the moulhaugs. Now that you've leveled up a little, I don't feel so worried about you dying at the drop of a hat."

Taryn mumbles something about saving my ass before drifting off to sleep. Limery snores softly, blowing warm breath against my bicep.

His bulbous eyes shift underneath his closed lids. I wonder what he is dreaming about. Killing birds or stealing coins, probably. He doesn't look it, but Limery has grown into a powerful imp. The day I met him might be one of the luckiest moments I've had in my life. At level eighteen, he could rival almost any of the other heroes in a duel. And his power, it's raw, elemental magic, never seeming to fade. That, combined with his blinding speed and small target zone, makes him a force to be reckoned with. Not to mention his never-ending desire to make sure I don't die.

Better than all of that, he's a great friend. Sure, he's wild at times, but he's still young. In time, I have no doubt that he will outgrow his less endearing qualities.

Closing my eyes, I let the sounds of the night lull me to sleep.

The next thing I know, the smell of roasting meat wakes me. I open my eyes to find Limery turning a spit loaded with four birds over an open flame.

"You're up early." I wipe the sleep from my eyes.

Berry sits next to Limery, drooling in anticipation of a delicious treat. After yesterday, I'd say he's earned it.

"Limmy was hungry. Didn't wants to wake Chods." He takes one of the birds off the spit, grabbing it with his open palm, and hands it to Berry without so much as a wince.

I guess all the fire he handles makes him pretty much immune to burns. Berry devours the bird in only a few bites and hungrily waits for more.

"Where is Taryn?" I ask. He's nowhere to be found, but his

bags are still next to the tree. It seems like I was the last one to wake.

"He goes flying. Saids he wants to look ahead." Limery pulls off another bird and tosses it to me, then takes one for himself. His razor-sharp teeth rip the meat apart.

Truth be told, transforming into a small bird might not be the smartest option for Taryn.

I take my time with breakfast, electing to actually savor what I eat. As I'm gathering our belongings, Taryn appears on a branch above my head, his short stubby legs dangling just above my eyesight.

"Morning," he says with a smile.

"What has you so chipper?" I toss my satchel over my shoulder and grab Sea Scorpion. The trident feels more natural almost every time I hold it.

"Have you ever watched the sun rise from a thousand feet in the air? Without a building in sight to block the view?" His smile grows a little wider, reaching all the way to his dark brown eyes. "I'll never get used to it. Birds might not be the toughest of creatures, but damn, do they get a view."

I've never watched the sun rise from a thousand feet, but I get what he means. The little things about this game are what make it so unique. What will make it a hit if it ever goes mainstream. It's not always about fighting and weapons, but those small experiences that actually make you feel like you are here, that you are a part of something bigger. Here, the fantasy is real.

"See anything good while you were up there?" I gaze out to the mountains looming in the distance.

"More moulhaugs moving south. Whatever is happening at the base of the mountain, they want no part in it." He slides from the branch and lands with a soft thud.

"Let's check it out then."

The journey to the mountain is boring and uneventful. We make our way back to the Mythroad and pass a few travelers as we head north. Most of them are clad in dull rags. I'm sure the sight of a troll, an imp, a dwarf, and a bear is quite alarming, because many of the other travelers clear the road altogether, stepping aside or hiding behind trees or bushes.

This is all still new to them and will be for some time, so I try not to take offense. We're so far away from Vanaria and its protections that I'm sure these people are used to fending for themselves.

"If you weren't so ugly, they probably wouldn't be so scared," Taryn teases. "The rest of us are pretty lovable." He winks.

Limery snorts on my shoulder and I conveniently stretch, raising my arms overhead and knocking him to the ground. He frowns at me and crosses his arms, before sticking out his tongue and flying ahead.

There are not many houses or farms this far from Lynchton. According to my map, the closest settlement is a small trading post at the base of the mountain.

With the Greystone Mountains looming ever larger, they appear almost insurmountable. Their snow-covered peaks reach above the clouds in places and stretch from one side of the isle to the other. The only way to travel from the southern half of the island to the north is by climbing over. No wonder the two kingdoms don't trade more.

Fast-travel could change all that. The ability to get from Vanaria to Seascape in a matter of minutes instead of weeks. Too bad the portals are closed. Perhaps forever. Hiding whatever dark secrets loom on the other side.

No, they wouldn't be there if they were going to remain closed forever. There are other continents out there. Other races. More quests and objectives. If the portals are still there, then there has to be a quest to unlock them. The next time we are in a capital city, I need to spend some time investigating.

When I first logged into *Isle of Mythos*, I saw the world. It was large and sprawling. This small island is but a blip on the map. There's—

"Snap out of it." Taryn whacks me on the shoulder with his staff. "You see that?" He points to a giant boulder in the distance.

It sits off to the side of the road next to a lone oak. Now that I think about it, I haven't seen any boulders for miles. Kind of a random place for a rock so large.

The wind changes direction and I'm hit with a whiff of rotting flesh. Then I realize that it's no boulder. "Moulhaug?"

Taryn nods, covering his nose with his cloak.

When we arrive, the moulhaug is rotten to the core. Exposed ribs frame a rancid cavity filled with squirming maggots. My stomach turns at the sight, and Limery casts a fireball, holding it close to his nose. Even Berry lets out a dissatisfied groan.

"Something big had to have caused this. Something, really, really big. You see that?" He points to the moulhaug's face. Several gashes run along the side of its head. Big, seeping gashes. "Those are claw marks."

Remembering our own encounter with a moulhaug, it was like fighting a bulldozer. It would take something truly powerful to inflict that kind of damage. "Limery, can you burn the body? Let's try to do everyone within a mile radius a favor and end this smell?"

Limery plugs his nose and erects two fire walls on both sides of the carcass. He then hits it with several fireballs until it begins to cook. Cooked meat, even if it's rotten, will smell a hundred times better than the current situation.

Over the next few hours, we burn two more moulhaugs before arriving at the small settlement at the base of the mountain.

The settlement is just that, not nearly big enough to be called a town or a village. It has a small inn, a shop, and a stable. There are no houses or huts, so I can only imagine that the workers all live at the inn.

A small sign in front of the inn reads, "Welcome to Smalltown."

How original.

First, we step into the shop. Berry waits outside with my horrors. I'm sure a troll, a bear, and several dozen demonic looking creatures would be a little much for whoever waits inside.

The inside of the shop is filled with basic necessities for traversing a mountain. Spikes, pickaxes, ropes, satchels, and blankets adorn one wall. Another has potions and pots filled with herbs and powders. A bin in the center has an array of basic weapons. A rack of dull black tunics and cloaks sits beside it.

"All of this is way overpriced." Taryn holds one of the potions in his hand. "Kind of like running out of gas in the desert."

I don't have much experience with potion prices, but I'll take his word for it.

An old, balding man with a fluffy gray beard sits behind the counter with his eyes closed. I tap a bell sitting in front of him and it rings, startling him awake.

"Uhnn." He looks lost for a moment. "Uh, sorry. How can I help you?" He sits forward and adjusts his tunic. The ends of the fabric are tattered, and several holes adorn one shoulder.

"We're just passing through. We saw the moulhaug carcasses on the way in. I was wondering if you had any information on what was killing them?"

"Not in the slightest." He shrugs. "Not many people come through these parts nowadays. Most of our staff have left to safer areas. Those of us that remain, we don't get out much. Too many dangers to risk one's life."

"What do you mean, 'too many dangers'?" I ask.

He sighs, and then scratches his beard, making it look even fluffier. "Monsters killing moulhaugs. Bandits robbing and killing travelers. No offense to you, I'm aware of the king's peace with the forest trolls, but the mountain trolls and goblins are always a problem to anyone passing through the mountain. They say that the heroes are supposed to set the world right, but it seems they bring more problems with them."

"Have bandits always been a problem?"

"Never before. But with half a dozen attacks this week, people are afraid to venture north. The western passages may be safer. I've sent a raven to the king, but this far north, I doubt we'll receive help."

Taryn and I make eye contact. "This has the smell of Glenn and Jude all over it. They know they can't set foot in a shop, so they are killing people and taking their belongings."

Taryn steps forward. "If we find these bandits, we'll make sure they pay for all the trouble they've caused."

"Heh." He looks Taryn square in the eye. "What's a life worth to someone who never dies?" An awkward silence hangs in the air. "If there's nothing I can help you with, there's plenty of room in the inn."

Outside of the shop, Taryn finally speaks. "Damn, he really has something against heroes. And you're a troll hero. That makes you a double whammy."

"Don't worry, Chods. Limmy likes yous." He puts his hand on my neck.

"Thanks, buddy."

We have no intention of staying the night in the inn, so we set out along the base of the mountain. Since we are low on potions, I use the time to level up my herbalism skill and make more health potions. I still have a fair amount of bloodfennel, but I need more horned thimbleberry and powdered crow's feet to complete the potion.

"Limery, do you think you can track me down some crows' feet?"

He gives me a wicked grin and then disappears into the trees.

I activate my herbalism skill, and the outlines of all the plants I have identified glow in the distance. It makes it easy to locate exactly what I'm looking for, since I can filter out specific plants to locate. I wish I had spent more time with Yashi to learn more. Perhaps, when we return. Actually...

"You're a druid, right?" I ask Taryn.

He cocks an eyebrow. "What gave it away?"

"I mean, that means you have a strong knowledge of plants and wildlife, right?"

"Yeah, so?"

"Then you can help me increase my herbalism skill by showing me new plants. Right now, I'm looking for horned thimbleberry. But once I have enough, I'd love to learn some more. What level is your skill anyway?"

His eyes glaze over for a moment. "Right now, I'm a journeyman. You?"

"Still a novice, so I'm sure there is a lot to learn."

I find some horned thimbleberry in a thicket of bushes. The thick, brambled stems run through the bushes, making the fuzzy leaves and large pink berries difficult to reach for predators.

I take the stem and berries and mash them together in my mortar with the bloodfennel and a drop of my own blood. While I wait for Limery to return with the final ingredient, Taryn introduces me to a few new varieties of plant.

"These are called golden buttons." He points to a tiny plant that grows at the base of the tree. A patch of small green leaves hugs the bark. "The flowers come out at night. They are poisonous to humans, but other races seem just fine around them. It's said that long ago, the dwarven king Voluck Lighthorn served ale brewed with golden buttons at a feast and all of the humans died. That was the beginning of what was later known as the Button War."

"How do you know all this?" That's an awful lot of detail for one plant. It's almost like he's reading from a book.

"Comes with the territory." He gives me a devious grin. "Seriously, though, my passive ability for being a druid allows me to identify certain plants and animals. My knowledge base increases as I level up." He pats me on the lower back. "Brains over brawn, my friend."

"You know you're not a dwarf in real life, right?"

"True. I've got the best of both worlds."

I roll my eyes at his stupidity. "Just show me some more plants."

Next, he shows me echo hedge, a plant that absorbs sound; spiky poppy, a beautiful yet dangerous flower; jester broadleaf, used to make laughing potions; and oboil, whose secretion causes anyone unlucky enough to brush against it to erupt into violent boils.

All the new knowledge increases my herbalism skill another level.

Congratulations! You have leveled up the skill 'Herbalism.' You are now a level 6 Herbalist (Apprentice). Increase your skill and learn advanced techniques for herbalism by finding an advanced herbalist (journeyman or above). Ranks: Novice, Apprentice, Journeyman, Expert, Artisan, Master, Grandmaster.

"Sweet! I'm an apprentice now." That makes herbalism my

highest ranked skill. Close behind is my apothecary skill, used for potion-making.

Limery returns carrying a handful of crows' feet. Their bodies are nowhere to be found, but his stomach does seem to be protruding a little more than usual.

I take the feet and grind them to a paste in the mortar, then I add in the rest of the ingredients. They mix together, forming a deep red liquid that I pour into several vials. With all of this, I'm able to make a half-dozen health potions.

I offer several to Taryn, but he scrunches his nose. "Not sure I want to drink anything that has your blood in it. I think I'll stick to my natural remedies."

"You are turning into a hippy." I laugh. "Want me to gather you some flowers so you can put them in your hair and beard?"

"Save some for yourself and maybe people won't be so scared of you." He crosses his arms, waiting for my comeback.

"Whatever. At least I can reach the top shelf." That shuts him up for a minute.

We search our surroundings for clues on the giant beast, but there's no evidence of the creature that has been killing the moulhaugs. No giant footprints. Nothing. Whatever it is, it seems to be pretty selective of moulhaugs, because the trees are still full of birds. Deer and other animals roam the forest. Even wolves skulk in the shadows.

What could be singling out the moulhaugs? And why?

Hours pass as we continue our search. I'm afraid that night may come, and we'll be forced to wait until tomorrow to continue. Limery and I could search in the dark, but giving Taryn a torch to see by would draw all kinds of predators to our direction.

Taryn comes to a halt, extending his staff to block my path. "Do you hear that?"

"What?" I try to use my advanced hearing to sense anything out of the ordinary.

There are animals scurrying along the forest, insects rattling, newborn birds loudly squawking somewhere nearby on the ground. I listen for the thunderous footsteps of an apex predator, but there's nothing out of the ordinary.

"What am I listening for?" I ask again.

"Babies." His face is stone cold as his eyes scan our surroundings.

"The mighty Taryn, afraid of a few baby birds?"

"Those aren't birds," he whispers. "We need to leave and come back with a plan. Before the mother retur—"

A shrill caw flares through my eardrums, and echoes across the forest. I call my horrors to my side, and we slowly back away. What is it that has Taryn so spooked? I have a full army of horrors. I'm sure we can take whatever it is.

Something silver and gray moves between the trees. It paws at the earth as it approaches, releasing threatening high-pitched screeches with each step. All other signs of wildlife have fled the scene.

A golden beak huffs in agitation as the half-eagle/half-lion walks towards us. I've seen this monster before. In Vanaria.

Griffin. *Unique monster. Level: 30. Known as the 'King of Beasts,' the griffin is one of the oldest and wisest monsters. Both proud and intelligent, they will only fight with their masters, not for them.*

Something about this one is different than the one the king rode. Something is out of place. One of its wings hangs lopsided, almost like it's broken.

"We need to go," says Taryn. Urgency coats his voice.

"It's injured." I'm sure we can take it if it can't even fly.

"How do you know?"

"I've seen one before. This one's wing is broken. Look how it hangs to the side."

"You've seen a griffin? How? Nope, not the time." He shakes his head. "We still need to go. Griffins are smart. I don't care if it is injured. You've seen what it did to those moulhaugs."

The griffin marches towards us, head held high. Even injured, it stands its ground with pride.

"We need to help it." This isn't just an animal. This is an intelligent creature, as smart as any one of us. We can't just leave it like this.

"We most certainly do not. You and I might come back if it kills us, but I don't want to risk Limery or Berry's lives on something this stupid. There's a reason they call griffins the king of beasts. Their claws are sharper than most metals. They're fast. And they attack with foresight."

We continue to backpedal as we talk, trying not to make any sudden movements. I still don't get what Taryn is so afraid of.

"We have to. It's killing the moulhaugs because they eat eggs. The moulhaugs would have killed its babies. It did the only thing it knew would drive them away. If you heal it, it will go back to the mountains."

He doesn't say anything for a moment, then lets out a resounding sigh. "Dammit. How in the hell do you propose we subdue this thing long enough for me to heal it?"

That is a very good question.

CHAPTER 22
A MURDER MOST FOWL

Even in its injured state, the griffin is a beauty to behold. It carries itself with pride. A creature with the head, wings, and front-quarters of an eagle, the hindquarters of a lion, and the regality of both. King of land and air all rolled into one. Its left wing flutters in agitation, but the right wing just hangs limp.

It screeches again, and I can't help but wince at the cutting sound. Limery cups his hands over his massive ears. He must be in awe of the creature, because he hasn't said a word since we spotted it.

It's safe to say this is one bird he won't be eating.

"You're gonna have to subdue it." Taryn's golden clasps jingle as we continue our backpedal.

The griffin hasn't charged us yet, but it keeps our pace, making it undeniably evident that we are not welcome here.

"Why me? Can't you lull it to sleep with some of your druid magic?"

"First, this is your stupid idea. And second, I'm not sending Berry within a hundred feet of that griffin. It's twice his level and will rip him to shreds." He pats Berry on the head. "Dwarves have a healthy respect for griffins. Working high in the mountains, we've seen what they are capable of. There are ancient stories of dwarves being carried off by griffins, never to be heard from again."

I wonder if that is why King Favian has taken the griffin as his sigil?

Berry makes a sad groan, letting us know that he has no desire to die today.

My horrors grumble as I force them to retreat. Several puff out of existence and I summon three more to replace them. With sixty active, I have an additional 2,736 health, bringing my total to over seven thousand as long as they stay alive. My attacks hit for an additional sixty percent as well. Both will rise and fall like the tide once a battle starts. If only there was a way to keep them out of harm's way during a fight so I could have a permanent health boost.

The griffin paws at the ground again, its sharp talons ripping through the earth. What the hell are we supposed to do? Attacking it will only make it angry. Plus, we're trying to help the creature, not hurt it. Neither Taryn nor Limery have any crowd-control abilities. All I have are my Horrors of Vitality with their slows.

So here I am, a level twenty troll forced to subdue one of the island's most dangerous creatures, and it's ten levels ahead of me.

Fuck.

It's not like I haven't been in this position before, though. The mana-infused wyrm that blocked the ley lines was out of my level. But that was different—I had to kill it, not restrain it. A massive amount of critical hits saved my ass that day. That won't work here.

"Alright. Stand back. I'm going to try and subdue it. Don't move in until I give the okay."

Taryn says something to Limery, and the imp and bear move back even further. Taryn has his staff at the ready. He just shakes his head.

This really is a stupid idea.

I urge my horrors to move forward. "Come on, man. We've got this. We're heroes. Let's do something stupid and heroic." The griffin bows its head and unleashes another warning caw.

"It's your funeral," says Taryn.

"Yours too, if I fail."

Taryn buffs us with Strong Wind, but we move forward slowly. Cautiously. I need to play this smart. The griffin shuffles its wing in agitation once more. It must sense that something has changed. I summon another round of horrors to the rear of the line. The weakest ones are stationed at the front. They'll be the first to die.

I hold Sea Scorpion tight. I don't want to injure the beast, but it might help me keep it at bay. Maybe I could use the prongs to pin one of its legs to the ground.

Hoping for the element of surprise, I lift one of my Horrors of Vitality and sling it by the horn at the griffin. I'm hoping its passive slow will give me a slight advantage.

As the orange and blue fluffball flies through the air, the rest of my demonic army charges.

The griffin plucks the horror out of the air like a trained seal eating fish. With blazing speed, it pounces forward, the powerful feline hind legs closing the distance between us in a single leap.

Before I even have my trident raised, the griffin decapitates half a dozen horrors, snapping its beak in a blur. I summon three more horrors, but the griffin rips through my line quicker than I can replace them.

I dive for its neck, hoping I can tackle it to the ground, but a sharp talon wraps around my arm and slings me to the side. The wound hurts like hell, blue blood spilling down my arm.

Up close, the griffin is even larger than I imagined, standing several feet taller than me. It pecks at my horrors like a chicken eating bugs. The force of its snap severs them in half. They don't even have time to pile on the creature before it ends their short lives.

I attempt to subdue it from behind. Maybe if I can wrangle it from the rear, then I can pull it to the ground and pin it. With a running jump, I soar toward its backside.

I land on its back and wrap my trident around its throat, pulling with everything I have in an attempt to make the catbird pass out. It cocks its head back, smashing the back of its skull into my face. My nose crunches at the impact and blood pours from it like a fountain, but I don't let go.

With a massive leap, the griffin carries me through the air. It lowers its head when we land, tossing me from its back.

I duck and roll, avoiding damage, but my satchel catches on a bush and snaps, spilling its contents across the forest floor. Jira warned me I needed to work on my leatherworking, but I didn't listen. I dive for a health potion, chugging it quickly as I cast a few more horrors. At this point, they are nothing more than a distraction. The slow of Horror of Vitality seems to have little effect. Either it's not working, or the griffin is even faster than I thought.

If only there was a way to stun the creature. Taryn's Lightning Bolt has a random chance of a stun, but if the griffin turns on him, he's toast.

Then it hits me. A vial of bright yellow liquid litters the ground with the other contents of my satchel. Glouwseeker venom.

Item. Glouwseeker Venom. *When injected into the bloodstream,* *glouwseeker venom immobilizes target. Length of stun dependent on size of target, resistances, and amount injected.*

The glouwseeker sting froze Berry completely, even when he was imbued. If I can somehow inject the griffin with the venom, it might paralyze the creature long enough for Taryn to heal it.

The griffin pounces for me, and I barely dodge the attack. The talons smash into the earth, destroying several health potions.

"Taryn! A distraction please," I beg for anything to give me a second to breathe and form a plan.

A moment later, an arc of lightning rips through the canopy, setting limbs ablaze as it crashes into the griffin. The creature turns towards the source of the attack, but Taryn has already transformed into a red bird and zips through the trees. It pounces after Taryn as he swerves amongst limbs.

I use the time to open a vial of glouwseeker venom and pour it on the barbs of my trident. I use two whole vials for good measure, and by the time I'm done, the prongs glisten with a vibrant yellow sheen.

Casting another horror, I toss it at the griffin, regaining its attention. I send Taryn a quick message.

Message (Chod): *As soon as it comes for me, hit it again. I need the element of surprise.*

The griffin lunges through the air toward me, clearing twenty yards in a single bound. Mid-stride, a bolt of lightning strikes the majestic creature, setting its hair on end. The blow barely does any damage as it crashes to the ground in front of me.

I dive behind a tree just in time for it to turn again, searching for the dwarf. I use the opportunity to plant my trident in its rear haunch. I bury it as deep as I can. The griffin lets out a cry of pain. It turns, talon raised to swipe at me, when suddenly it freezes in place.

"Get over here quick! I don't know how much time we have."

There's no witty banter as Taryn takes his position. He falls to his knees and begins casting Restoration, a faint green glow enveloping him and the griffin.

Sooner than I would like, the griffin begins shuffling its paws. Taryn isn't even close to healing the wing yet, so I uncork another vial of venom and make a cut along the griffin's back with my own claw. I pour the entire vial into the open wound, and the griffin grows statuesque once again.

I watch as the wounds heal, and the broken wing retakes its normal shape. Once it is mended, I pull the trident from its hindquarters. The final piece of the puzzle is the glouwseeker venom being expelled and the punctures closing.

The griffin rises to its feet like a newborn horse, knocking Taryn aside in the process. I step in front of him, trident extended. A handful of horrors remain at my side.

We are locked in a stare-down, neither of us blinking.

A powerful screech sets my hair on end. The griffin shuffles its wings. When it realizes they are no longer broken, it extends them fully. The wingspan is angelic, nearly twenty yards when fully unfurled.

No wonder King Favian likes to ride above the clouds. He could fly forever on wings that broad.

The griffin retracts its wings, then steps forward. It clicks its beak together several times before bowing its head. Taryn and I return the gesture. A sound resembling a purr comes from its throat, and then it turns and saunters away.

Taryn collapses to the ground next to me. "Bro, I almost shit my pants."

"I'm thankful for both of us that you didn't." I extend my hand and help him to his feet. "Good work. We helped a lot of people today."

"Yeah, I guess we did the right thing after all." He bends down and picks up the last vial of glouwseeker venom. "What do you say we get a room at the inn tonight and you can work on your leatherworking skills?"

Gathering my belongings and stuffing them in a makeshift pouch made out of the scraps of leather, I'm surprised it lasted as long as it did.

CHAPTER 23
THE MOUNTAINS ARE CALLING

Congratulations! You have leveled up the skill 'Leatherworking.' You are now a level 3 Leatherworker (Novice). Increase your skill and learn advanced techniques for working leather by finding an advanced leatherworker (Apprentice or above). Crafting Ranks: Novice, Apprentice, Journeyman, Expert, Artisan, Master, Grandmaster.

I set my satchel down on the table at the Smalltown inn and admire my handiwork. The stitches are a little more uniform, the thread a decent quality.

The materials cost me a pretty penny, due to the exorbitant prices this far out, but my leather satchel is patched and repaired. It's amazing what a difference a needle and quality thread can make in holding the seams together.

Miss Velma, one of the owners of the inn at Smalltown, is a pretty talented seamstress. She seemed happy to teach me a few new techniques once she heard we had removed the threat to the moulhaugs.

"Much better." I fit the last of my belongings back into the satchel. Once again, I find myself out of health potions due to the griffin smashing them all.

"Congrats, you've advanced from kindergarten to first grade." Taryn laughs from the table beside mine where he enjoys a frothy ale. "Honestly, I'm surprised your giant fingers could hold a needle." He smirks. "You could just buy a quality satchel. For a few gold, you can even buy one with an expandable inside."

"What? Do you mean like a Bag of Holding?" I examine my bag again. It might not look the best, but it gets the job done.

"Pretty much. How do you think I managed to fit the Bog Bow, Staff of the Marshes, and everything else we've looted in a bag the length of my arm?"

I hadn't really thought about it, but now it makes perfect sense. Undoubtedly, his magic bag is another benefit of starting out in an actual city. It's not like I really need one, though. I'm a big troll. I can carry a lot.

"Here's your dinner." Miss Velma sets down a piping hot bowl of chowder in front of all of us. She has a warm, motherly demeanor about her, but living this far out, I'm sure she's tougher than she looks. "I'll be feeding the scraps to that bear of yours. I'm sorry he has to stay in the stables, but rules are rules."

"We understand." I take the bowl from her. "If you make an exception for us, then you have to make one for everyone."

She gives me a warm smile. I wouldn't have expected such a motherly woman to be this far out near the mountains. Maybe her gentle exterior is just a front.

"Yum!" Limery pours the steaming chowder into his mouth without waiting for it to cool.

I rip off a chunk of bread and dip it in my bowl. The chowder is savory and delicious, with chunks of meat and hearty vegetables. I wash it down with a dark brown ale.

My vision goes hazy around the edges by the time I'm finished. Alcohol really does take the edge off.

When the sun sets, the door to the inn opens and the bearded man running the shop steps through. His heavy boots clank against the floor as he approaches us.

"Velma told me what you did." He places his hand on the back of a chair at my table. "We're grateful. It's not often outsiders come through these parts willing to help. Most are just looking to pass through. Mind if I sit?"

"Be my guest." I motion to the chair in front of me. I'm probably better company than Taryn, at least until he gets a few more beers in him and comes out of his shell.

Velma brings over another bowl of chowder and a mug of ale for the man. She kisses him on the forehead before going back to her work.

"Name's Keaton. Me and Velma have been running Smalltown for many years now. Our children help out when they can, but our boys are usually in the mountains. They guide those unfamiliar with the area from one side to the other." He blows on his chowder before taking a bite.

"Is it a difficult journey?" I ask.

Limery laps at the last drops of his chowder, already finished.

"There's a lot of dangers in the mountains. Dangers most lowlanders have no knowledge of. Usually, my boys aren't gone more than a week." He sets the spoon down before continuing. "My boys are tough. They're warriors. Had more than their fair share of run-ins with goblins, beasts, and even a few mountain trolls. But it's been ten days and I haven't heard nothing." He takes a swig of ale. "Maybe it's nothing, but maybe it's not. An old man like me isn't fit for hiking the mountains. If you'd be willing to check in on them, I'll outfit you with whatever supplies you need for the journey."

I turn to Taryn. He sets down his mug, froth coating his burly mustache. "We'll be happy to help, but if the mountains are as treacherous as you say, I'm taking another pet."

Quest Alert. *You have been offered the quest 'Find my sons.' Ten days have passed since Keaton and Velma last heard from their sons. They expect trouble. Travel into the mountains and search for signs of the men.*

Reward: None.

Bonus: By accepting this quest, you will be given items for your journey.

We walk through the forest at the base of the mountain. The area where the griffin had nested is now empty. Cracked eggs and white feathers that drift aimlessly are the only memory of the powerful creature and its young. I suspect they are now tucked away somewhere high in the mountains.

"You want a moulhaug?" I ask Taryn again. That's a mighty big creature to tame.

"Why not?" Taryn gazes out into the forest depths atop Berry, searching for a sign of the large beast. "They're big, they're strong, and they can tank for us. What's not to like?"

He has a point. They are powerful beasts. And one more layer of protection for whatever comes next. "You're right. And if this whole adventuring thing doesn't work out, you can always join the circus."

"Haha, make fun of the little guy." He rolls his eyes. "You should really get some new jokes. I'm going to take to the air and see if I can spot any. With the griffin gone, they should be coming back soon."

In a flash, Taryn transforms into a red bird and disappears

into the trees. Out of all the creatures he could transform into, I still don't get why he chooses a small red bird.

"You don't want to join him?" I ask Limery.

The imp quits flapping his wings and lands on my shoulder. "Limmy wants to stay with Chods." He puts a small hand on the back of my neck.

"Everything okay?"

"Limmy like Chods, but sometimes he misses Mommy and Leo. And Daddy, too." He sighs.

He's homesick. "I'm sure they miss you too. You can always go back home if you need to. I would understand." I never once thought that he might miss his family. Just because I'm better off without mine doesn't mean that everyone thinks that way. Some people have families that love them. That show them love.

The closest thing I have to a brother is Taryn, and he's here with me. I'm sure Limery misses his own brother, even if Leo does pick on him. And his dad, Limery hasn't seen him since he sold himself into slavery in an attempt to save Leo's life.

"Limmy will stay with Chods. Chods needs his help." He gives me a half-smile. A smile that would scare anyone who didn't know him. "Mommy says it's okay to be sad. She says it's okay to miss Daddy. It means we loves him."

I don't know why, but I feel a hollowness in my chest. It feels both empty and full at the same time, like a giant ball of nothingness is threatening to explode from within. Or swallow me whole. I can't imagine ever having a talk that real with my mother.

She was the queen of hiding her emotions. She and father both.

"Your mother is a smart woman." I try to smile but it's only skin deep.

Luckily, a message from Taryn pulls me from my sobering thoughts.

Incoming Message (Taryn): *I've got one. Level eighteen. The quicker you get over here, the quicker we can get back to the mountain.*

He sends me his location. It's about a mile away.

When we arrive, I find Taryn, still in bird-form, sitting on the horn of the moulhaug as it basks in the sun.

Message (Chod): *What are you doing?*
    Incoming Message (Taryn): *Chilling.*
    Message (Chod): *I can see that. Do you want to die before we get to you?*
    Incoming Message (Taryn): *Did you forget about my passive? Nature's Bulwark. Animals will only attack me if they are provoked.*
    Message (Chod): *Well, if you sat on my nose, I'd definitely say it was provocation.*

With a flap of his wings, he takes to the air, flying towards Limery and I.

Message (Chod): *Don't even think about it.*

With an explosion of feathers, he returns to his dwarven form.

"You're no fun." He looks at me and his face softens, the mischief vanishing from his eyes. "Everything okay?"

"Just having an off day." I don't really know how to put it better than that.

He nods. It's not the first time Taryn has seen me affected by my relationship with my parents. More often than not, I can hide it, but sometimes, I just wish I had what others do.

"Come on." He pats me on the lower back. "It's nothing fighting a giant monster won't cure."

He raises his staff, calling a bolt of lightning into the slumbering creature. The moulhaug jerks to life, a scorch mark smoking from its backside.

With four of us, we are able to bring the moulhaug down to five percent without taking any damage. Berry and I hold the creature down while Taryn uses Tame to bond with his new pet.

True to his word, by the time the battle is over, Limery and I both have smiles on our faces. Berry, on the other hand, seems a little jealous as he walks beside the moulhaug. Every time the moulhaug's head swings Berry's way, the bear's lip curls up in a snarl.

The moulhaug even seems rather content, considering we just beat the snot out of it. I wonder if Tame makes them forget about the battle that just took place, or if they just don't care anymore?

Atop the moulhaug's back, Taryn towers above us all. "Now this is what I'm talking about." The only thing he is missing is a howdah, the resplendent Asian carriages that used to sit atop elephants and carry the wealthy over long distances.

He looks natural on his new mount. The level eighteen creature is the size of a large van. It sways its head from side to side as it walks. I still remember the force of the moulhaug horn that smashed me near Lynchton. The creature's mossy gray skin blends nicely with Taryn's dull green cloak. Traveling through the mountains, they might not even be noticed at a distance.

With the newest member of our party, we make one last stop in Smalltown to gather supplies before we leave. Keaton offered anything we needed for the journey at no cost. Aside from a few potions, I think we have everything we need to make do. However, Taryn really wants to load up on free supplies.

I guess it has something to do with his life back home. He's never really had excess. Free goods don't have the same luster to me.

In the shop, Taryn carries a wicker basket, filling it to the brim with potions and other supplies. "I've never been on a shopping spree before." His eyes light up as he tosses in several strips of jerky.

I leave him to his shopping and find Keaton in the backroom, bringing out more stock to replace what he is giving away. "Thanks again for the supplies."

He sets the wooden crate down on the floor. "No, thank you. I just pray it isn't too late."

"From what you've told us, your sons are tough. Whatever they've gotten themselves into, they will be fine. Here, let me help you with this." I pick up the crate and set it out in the main shop. "While I've got you here, I was wondering if you could send a raven to Lynchton. I want to let them know that the moulhaugs will be returning north and that there is no reason for them to be killed any longer."

"I can take care of that for you." He scribbles the message on a piece of parchment and ties it with a string.

Taryn pushes a large satchel into my hands. "I know you worked really hard on the other one, but this will really serve you a lot better on the road. I mean, look at that stitching. Miss Velma has a gift."

I can't argue that the bag doesn't look a million times better than the one I made, but I made mine. It's something I can be proud of. "I think we've taken enough of their supplies. I'll make do with what I have." I give a final nod to Keaton. "Time to hit the road."

CHAPTER 24
SHOOT THE BIRD

THE MOULHAUG TRUDGES up the mountain. For all its power, it is as slow as molasses. Taryn has loaded it up with a satchel on each side. They are cinched around its massive frame with rope from the shop in Smalltown. Limery clings to the moulhaug's horn, enjoying the rhythmic bobbing as it marches along. He reminds me of a pirate searching for landfall from the crow's nest. Berry pulls up the rear, a kid's teddy bear compared to the moulhaug.

I know from experience that moulhaugs can charge with surprising speed, so I have no idea why it walks like an elderly snail when out of combat.

"Can't you speed this thing up?" I ask Taryn.

He looks down from the moulhaug's back, finally taller than me. "And what? Cause a rockslide?" He pats the moulhaug's spine. "I'd rather not kill us all because you can't slow down and enjoy the moment."

"You think Keaton's sons are enjoying the moment?" I counter. "We have no idea what has happened to them."

"You can go ahead if you want, but there is nothing I can do about Stompy here." His mustache curls up at the edges when he reveals his new pet's name.

"Stompy? Really?" I guess I should consider myself lucky he didn't name it Horny.

The pass that goes through the mountains is a bit daunting. It clings along the edge of the mountain, curving and winding. At times, it's steep, then levels out for miles. We go up and down, traversing from one mountain to the other.

The thing about climbing mountains is that we can't just go straight up and over. It's too steep, so instead, we journey for hours and hours in a roundabout way.

"We'll need to camp soon," says Taryn. The sun has already dipped below the mountains, engulfing the entire side in shadow. "The path is too dangerous for us to travel at night."

For now, our mornings will be bright and our evenings dull, until we cross the other side and it will reverse.

We find a shallow cave to settle in for the night. Limery kills a mountain goat for dinner, and we roast it over a small fire near the back of the cave. Smoke gathers overhead, choking us in the enclosed space, until Taryn has the genius idea to cast Strong Wind. Even though we aren't moving, the breeze that accompanies the spell clears the smoke.

Stompy lies at the front of the cave, concealing most of the entrance. His hide is a similar color to the surrounding stone, so nothing passing by will have any idea we are inside.

"What do you think happened to them?" Taryn asks me as he cuts off a piece of goat meat with one of the knives he took from the shop.

"Could be anything. Goblins, monsters...trolls. They could have gotten lost or had an injury." I take a piece of goat for myself, slicing it off with my sharp claw. "Sounds like a dangerous place by the way Keaton told it."

"Hopefully, we find them soon and then get on the way north. I really think you'll like the dwarven kingdom." He finishes eating and snuggles up next to Berry in the warmth of the fire.

I curl up against the cool cave wall with Limery tucked between my arms.

Day two in the mountains is much the same as day one. A lot of slow walking, narrow passes, and echoes. A single rock bouncing down the canyon walls seems to carry for miles. Unlike in New York City, where the city seems to swallow every noise and spit it back all at once.

A strong gust of wind shakes the trees, so even this desolate location feels alive with trouble. Even though we seem so isolated and alone, I can't help but feel like there are threats lurking around every bend or inside every cave we pass.

Not knowing what to expect has me constantly alert, so I keep my horrors at the ready. They grumble and bump against one another in the narrower passes, and several times, I lose a horror to the depths below.

As the day drives on, we avoid fighting monsters when we can to prevent drawing attention to ourselves. The few times we are forced to fight, we destroy our opponents with no restraint in an explosion of horrors, lightning, and fire.

When a small host of spear-carrying lizard men ambush us from a cave, I block their retreat by throwing my horrors against the mountain and exploding them to create a rockslide. Then Stompy takes the lead along the narrow pass and shovels them aside like a plow on a snowy day.

The mountainsides are filled with so many caves that the threat of danger waits around every corner, but so far, we have been lucky. We make camp for the night and as the temperatures drop, we huddle a little closer to the fire.

On day three, Taryn decides to take to the skies.

"The mountain range is too wide for us to find anything following a single path. We don't even know if this is the trail they followed." He stares up at the mountain peak, where a hawk circles high overhead. "From up high, I'll be able to get a better view."

"Alright, just be careful."

He pats Stompy on the head before transforming into a red bird and disappearing into the sky. The rest of us carry on with our march, climbing ever higher like some twisted version of *The Fellowship of the Ring*. Judging by the map, we are about halfway through the mountain pass.

Taryn is right. This is like finding a needle in a haystack. There's no way to know which path Keaton's sons took. Neither one of us are rangers or have very good tracking skills. Hopefully, Taryn can find a sign of their whereabouts from up above.

After a few hours, I check in with him.

Message (Chod): *Any luck?*

Incoming Message (Taryn): *Not yet. There are lots of paths up this high. The tree-cover makes it hard to see much of anything happening on the ground. I did see a few goblins, though. They disappeared into a cave carrying pickaxes. Mining, I suppose.*

Taryn returns and we stop for lunch. As he transforms from bird to dwarf, I'm hit with a fascinating question.

"Do you ever eat worms when you're in bird form?"

He just cocks an eyebrow and stares at me.

"I mean, I just wonder if they taste different when you're a bird? I ate a raw rabbit when I first got here."

He rips off a piece of jerky and stuffs it in his mouth. "No, I haven't eaten worms," he says in a deadpan tone.

"What about bugs?" I fight the grin that hides at the edge of my mouth. I toss the bone from a deer leg I'm eating to one of my Horrors of Power as a distraction, and it crushes it in its strong jaws.

"Limmy eats worms sometimes." He flashes a toothy grin. "Limmy likes birds and worms."

"I think Limmy just likes to eat," I tease, poking him in the belly.

He erupts into laughter. "Stop, Chods."

"If we don't find his sons, what then?" Taryn is stoic. Maybe that's why he didn't laugh at my jokes. "Do we just abandon the quest? It seems wrong, don't you think?"

He's starting to feel the same way I do about this game. There are no random NPCs here. Abandoning a quest means they face the consequences. "I don't know. We'll make that decision when the time comes. For now, we keep our eyes peeled."

He returns to the sky, and another hour passes before I hear from Taryn again.

Incoming Message (Taryn): I think I found something. There's smoke coming from a cluster of trees. I'm sending you the location.

It pops up on my map. The location is only a mile or two from where we are. I'm checking our route when I receive a second message.

Incoming Message (Taryn): *Chod, get here quick! I've been shot. I don't think I can make it back.*

"Shit!" I say aloud. How the hell did he get shot as a small bird? I send Taryn a quick message telling him I'm on the way, but there's no reply.

Limery turns to me, his bulbous eyes full of alarm.

"We need to get moving. Taryn is hurt." I don't know how serious the injury is, or if he's still stuck in bird form. All I know is we need to get there ASAP.

"Limmy will fly ahead. Makes sure Taryns is okay."

Before I can stop him, the imp has left. I pray he doesn't get shot, too. Is this what happened to Keaton's boys?

"Dammit! Why does everything have to always fall to shit?" I yell. Berry lets out a huff of agitation.

I jump on the back of the moulhaug and use the rope that keeps the satchels in check for balance. "I know Taryn told you to go slow, but we need to get moving. Berry, lead the way."

The bear trots ahead of us, and the moulhaug starts moving. Trudging at first, it seems like it's going to keep its slow pace, but then its movement increases. Rocks fall from the mountainside with each thunderous step, and pretty soon we're moving like an avalanche, leaving a dust cloud in our wake. My horrors rush to keep up as we barrel down the mountainside in search of my friend.

Taryn's location grows steadily closer until we turn a bend and I see smoke wafting up from a recess in the mountain. The crevice goes back pretty far, like someone hit the mountain with a giant axe, leaving an enormous gash in its rocky exterior. A small forest has grown in the crevice, concealing what lies within its depths.

Limery stands guard over a green lump of clothing on the ground, squaring off with a handful of goblins. He holds two fireballs, and even though he's half their size, the goblins look hesitant to attack. Some hold spears, others pickaxes or small bronze swords.

The goblins stand there, weapons pointed at Limery. They exchange glances, none of them wanting to attack first. Limery has an almost feral rage in his eyes as he stands his ground. The goblins have dull green skin, lanky arms, and pointed ears. Their eyes are a dark shade of orange, and tiny noses hook over a wide mouth full of sharp, triangular teeth. They are all dressed in rags or scraps of leather, and each one has a thick metal collar around their neck.

They jump with surprise at the sight of a charging moulhaug with a troll on its back, before screaming and retreating deeper into the recess.

Taryn stirs beneath his cloak, and I'm thankful that he is still alive. I jump from the moulhaug and rush to his aid.

"Ungh." He grimaces. When he emerges beneath the cloak, an arrow protrudes all the way through his bicep. "The little bastards shot me right through the wing." He touches the arrow and flinches in pain. "If you can get it out, I'll be able to heal myself."

The arrow is tipped with a stone arrowhead on one end and feather fletchings on the other.

"I'm going to have to break it in half. It might hurt a little."

He nods and closes his eyes, extending his arm to me. As quick as I can, I snap off the end of the arrow and pull it through his arm. It slides out with ease, leaving a hole that trickles blood down Taryn's bicep and drips to the dusty ground.

He runs to a nearby tree and takes a knee, letting the green aura of Restoration envelope him.

When he returns, he looks much healthier. The color has

returned to his face. He looks past me, eyes wide, toward the area where the goblins were and points.

When I turn, my stomach drops. Several muscle-bound mountain trolls emerge from the trees carrying stone clubs. The small goblins snicker at their feet.

CHAPTER 25
KRONAN THE BARBARIAN

The center troll smacks his club ominously against his palm like some sort of street thug in an eighties movie. His muscles flex with each motion. Two other trolls flank his side, and the goblins we scared off flit between their legs. Each one of these trolls is built like a bodybuilder, and they range from level fifteen to twenty-two.

I remember the character creation screen saying that the mountain trolls were the strongest of all trolls. Looking at these three, I believe it. I'm no chump, but these dudes are ripped. Thick, corded muscle covers every inch of their bodies. Their arms are like braided steel, veins pulsing with every movement.

The center troll is the biggest of the three. His plum-colored skin is scarred in many places, with a pronounced lilac scar running diagonally down his chest. His shoulders and arms are dotted with speckles of gray, allowing him to blend in with the surrounding mountains. A long hawk nose nearly touches his lips, and two short, girthy tusks jut upwards from the corners of his mouth. His hair is braided into a long mohawk that runs down his back.

The trolls beside him look in a similar fashion, but with shorter mohawks. They all stare at us, furious, their muscles twitching.

"I hope you have a good reason for setting foot on mountain troll lands?" the deep voice of the center troll rumbles. "Outsiders stick to the gaps or they pay the price."

"We're looking for two travelers. Two humans." I stand my ground. "Have you seen them?"

The center troll looks to his comrades and they all burst into laughter, even the goblins laugh in a shrill, high-pitched tone.

What's so funny? Considering I'm not cracking jokes right now, their laughter sets me on edge.

Taryn steps up beside me. "I have a bad feeling about this," he whispers.

So do I.

A few of my horrors pop out of existence, but I wait to cast more. It feels like we're in a volatile situation and I'd hate to accidentally set it off.

"You travel with a dwarf and search for two humans. Who are you?" He lets his club fall by his side.

"I am Chod, hero of the forest trolls." I say it with all the authority I can muster. These guys look tough, and we don't know how many of them there are beyond those trees. Perhaps my confidence will make me seem higher than the level twenty that I am. At least I have Conceal to hide my true level.

"A hero, you say? You don't look like any forest troll I have ever seen." One of the goblins bumps against his leg, and he swats it on the head. The goblin falls to the ground and then scurries to safety, cowering behind a different troll. I wonder what type of relationship the two races have, because they definitely seem to be on the same side.

"I would like to speak with your leader. If she will see me, then I can explain everything."

"She?" The three trolls roar with laughter. "Okay, you truly are a forest troll." A laughing goblin steps too close, and he smacks it away. "Follow us, and I will take you to the chief. You may keep your weapons, but know if you raise them against us, we will have your heads, Chod, hero of the forest trolls."

So this isn't the same female-led society as the forest and seaside trolls. What else do they do differently?

He turns and kicks another goblin, sending it sprawling to the ground. The goblin squeals before running ahead and vanishing into the trees.

The sun dips below the mountain, leaving the sky bright but casting the mountains in shadow. We walk among the pines, passing dozens of goblins that sit around small fires. Some roast birds, others squirrels or some mystery meat. They all look up warily at the passing trolls.

Eventually, we exit the trees and enter a clearing that extends into the mountain. A half-dozen caves line the sides. A massive fire rages in the center of the clearing, and next to it, in a wooden cage, a group of men press their faces against the bars.

Behind the fire, a plum-colored troll, much larger than the other three, sits on a stone throne. A fur shawl covers his broad shoulders. One of his tusks is cracked at the tip. He wears his hair in a braided mohawk with the braid hanging over his shoulder. When I analyze him, I see he is level twenty-five. On a smaller throne to his left sits a female, and several other females sit on the ground next to her. She holds a small troll in her lap, feeding him strips of meat from a stone platter held by a goblin. The females are built more like the female forest trolls, slender but still muscular. They have the same white or gray hair as the males, but their mohawks are much wider.

Goblins run about, some carrying flanks of roasted meat to the trolls, others bowls of water. One stands on a platform behind the chief, waving a fan made of a strip of leather tied between two branches.

Each goblin wears the same metal collar around its neck. Are they slaves?

The troll on the larger throne looks in our direction as we approach, then leans towards the troll to his left and whispers something in her ear.

"Chief Kronan," the most muscled of the three trolls addresses the chief. "It seems a forest troll and his companions have wandered onto our lands."

"He doesn't look like any forest troll I've ever seen." The chief stares me down.

"He claims to be a hero." The muscle-bound troll laughs.

It's a condescending, mocking, assholish laugh that makes me want to smack the sneering grin off his face.

The king smirks. "I suppose we can test that easily enough."

The last of my horrors vanish. Even though I am surrounded by potential enemies, their health continues to decay unless I am actually engaged in battle. I pull my mana to my fingertips so that it is ready to cast at a moments notice. My anger simmers beneath the surface as these goons mock me. If I didn't think that summoning a horror would set them off, I would have summoned more already.

Looking at the mountain trolls, there is no doubt they are strong, but we have magic. The great equalizer.

Limery grows warm against my shoulder, and I know he must be thinking the same thing.

If things go to shit, Taryn and I don't risk a lot by dying other than losing our items and a level, but Limery and the others are not so lucky. I don't even trust that Limery could fly out of here unharmed after what happened to Taryn.

"Speak, troll," the chief bellows. "What business does a forest troll and his companions have with the mountain trolls? Speak wisely, hero, or we may just put that claim to the test."

This is so not the welcome I received with the forest or seaside trolls. This guy puts Gord to shame on the dick-o-meter. I clench my fist, fighting back my rising anger. That innate desire to pop off. I need to choose my words carefully. Our lives depend on it.

I take a deep breath and try to remain calm. "I am on a quest to find two men that have gone missing on their journey. I also have an offer of peace from King Favian of Vanaria. He wishes to make peace with all of the troll races, to build a better future together."

A goblin approaches the chief to fill his cup, but the chief smacks him away, spilling the liquid and knocking the goblin to the ground. The female trolls murmur behind him.

"Silence!" he roars, and the crag goes quiet. Clearly, I said the wrong thing. "The forest trolls were once a mighty race. They took what was theirs and they ruled our people with pride. Even the mountain trolls followed their lead. And now, here they are, ruled by their females, doing the bidding of humans, and taking offers of peace. How the mighty have fallen." He spits at the ground. "In the mountains, we take what is ours." He points to the men in the cages. "These men wandered onto our lands and they will pay the price. We will dine on their bones tonight." He looks down into the fire before making eye contact with me. "You will not come onto my lands and disrespect me with demands and offers of peace. The only peace we will have is the peace we take by force." The three trolls behind me beat their chest at his words. "Brutus, kill the troll, and throw the others in the cages. Dwarf sounds especially delicious tonight. Forest troll, if you are a hero, then tell your king what I think of his peace."

Before Brutus can lift his club, I have my trident pointed at his throat. "Attempt to harm me or my companions and I will kill you before you lift a finger."

His eyes radiate hatred, but he doesn't move.

Limery's fireballs crackle next to my ear, and behind me, the moulhaug snorts in agitation.

The three trolls stare at me, none of them willing to make the first move.

I call to the men in the cages. "Are you Keaton's boys?"

"We are. What is going on? Can you get us out of here?" one of them shouts back.

I ignore his questions. Right now, I need to figure out how to get us out of here without dying. I don't want to let Keaton's sons die, but if it is them or Limery, I will save my friend.

"You will die for this." Brutus leans his neck against my trident as he says it, letting the blade prick his skin as he snarls. "And I will pick my teeth with the bones of your friends."

Incoming Message (Taryn): *What's the plan here?*
Message (Chod): *Follow my lead, and try not to die.*

We are fucked. So, so fucked. I do the only thing that I think might give us a chance at getting out of here alive.

"Chief Kronan, I challenge you to a duel."

The clearing goes quiet. The only sounds are the crackling of the fire and the breathing of the animals.

"A duel?" There's amusement in his eyes. "Is that how you

southerners do things? What do I have to gain from dueling you that I wouldn't take already by letting my trolls kill you?"

"For one, I don't kill Brutus right here and now." I press my trident a little harder into Brutus's throat until a trickle of blood runs down his chest.

Brutus doesn't flinch. He's the type of warrior that would run to death and call it glory. I'm sure Kronan is the same way. People don't get that kind of bravado by running from fights. I'm just hoping that as leader of the mountain trolls, maybe Kronan has at least a little brains.

"Go on." He runs a clawed finger down his jawline. The amusement is gone, replaced by something else. Curiosity.

The time has come to see if I can bluff my way out of this. "You may talk big, but I know the truth. Alone up here in the mountains, your people are slowly dying. Losing more trolls will cripple you further. You may pretend that the goblins serve you because of your power, but the truth is that you don't have the power to take care of everything without them. You are slaves to them just as much as they are slaves to you. You hide away in your mountain caves, capturing those who walk through your lands, and call it power. But tell me, what is the real reason you don't set foot off of these mountains?"

The chief's lip curls up, and he stares daggers at me. He says something to one of the goblins, and it runs toward a giant gong near the fire, smashing it twice with a large bone. The gong reverberates throughout the crag, echoing over itself several times.

A moment later, goblins descend from the mountainsides, and a patter of footsteps comes from the caves that line the mountains. Torches glow from within their depths, and soon, dancing shadows begin to appear. Goblins and trolls emerge from the caves and gather around the chief. A trail of goblins from one cave all carry pickaxes. Some of the ones that descend the mountain carry spears or bows. They all chatter amongst themselves, no doubt wondering what has happened to leave Brutus with a trident pointed at his throat.

By the time the caves empty, there are over one hundred goblins and maybe thirty trolls. Only a handful of troll children are among them. Unless there are other tribes, there are even fewer mountain trolls than I thought. Perhaps I hit way too close to home with what I said.

"Everyone, gather around." The chief stands from his throne. At full height, he is even taller than I thought. "Tonight, I show this forest troll how we do things in the mountains." He removes his shawl and tosses it to the female troll sitting next to him.

When he steps forward, two giant scars that cross his chest in an X shimmer in the firelight. Several more scars cover his arms and shoulders. It's evident that he has fought many battles. He's stronger than me and has at least a foot height advantage.

The chief orders his people to form a circle in the back of the crevice near the caves, and they pack in tightly. The goblins we passed on the way here have joined the spectacle as well.

"Release Brutus and choose your weapon."

My heart pounds in my chest. What have I gotten myself into? I have no reason to trust that they won't attack us once I remove my trident from Brutus's throat other than the fact that I believe the chief values his strength above all else. A gamble that I'm betting all our lives on.

I pull back Sea Scorpion, and Brutus grunts at me.

His lips curl up in a devilish smile. "Let's see what you're made of, hero."

Taryn rushes to my side. "Chod, are you sure about this?"

"This is our only way out. You heard what they said they were going to do to you. At least this way, we have a shot at survival. If it looks like I am going to die, use the distraction to take Limery and flee."

He gives me a grave nod, before patting me on the backside. "Good luck, friend."

"Chods will win. Limmy knows it." Limery jumps from my shoulder and hovers beside Taryn.

"Lock the others away," orders Kronan.

Brutus and another troll take Taryn by the shoulders and lead him and Limery to a cage next to the men.

As I approach the ring of trolls and goblins, one of the men in the cages shouts at me, "What's going on?"

I ignore him. Right now, I have bigger problems than calming this fool who managed to get himself caught.

Kronan cracks his knuckles and paces as he waits for me. "Choose your weapon, hero." The way he says 'hero' is like it's the most disgusting word he's ever heard.

"I'll use my trident." I display the golden weapon for him to see.

He smirks. "We are a long way from the sea. Rholi, bring me Crusher."

One of the other trolls who brought us here disappears into a cave. A minute later, he returns carrying a giant silver warhammer that glitters in the dull light. It reflects the flames onto the ground like a speckling of fireflies.

Kronan turns to his own people. "For anyone who attempts to interfere, I will kill you myself." He faces me. "Brutus, if his companions attempt to escape or interfere, kill them. And when I slay this so-called hero, we'll prove once and for all that the mountain trolls have no equals."

The other trolls beat their chests, and the goblins squeal with delight.

Kronan twists the warhammer in his hands, feeling its

weight. The massive weapon looks like it was meant to hammer trees into the ground. It must weigh at least a hundred pounds. He gives it a few practice swings, and the metal sings as it swipes through the air. A few hits from that, and I'll be respawning far, far away.

That just means I better not get hit. Forest trolls are known for their agility, after all. At least compared to the other troll races.

I summon a round of horrors and they pop to life on the battlefield. Gasps hiss all around me. Clearly, they didn't believe that the group of horrors that came in with us were my summons. That must mean they don't have any magic users in the mountains. The horrors follow me around as Kronan and I circle one another.

To the outsider, which one of us looks like the predator?

Kronan makes the first move, swinging his warhammer at me, and I dive to the side. It crashes into the ground, sending a spray of rock and debris into the air, literally ripping the ground open.

I quickly summon three more horrors and send them to the ring's edge. I back away from Kronan as he readies his hammer for another attack. Until I get an idea of how he fights, I need my horrors to stay out of the way, and most importantly, stay alive.

We circle each other, and every time the cooldowns are up, I summon more horrors. When Kronan charges me, I keep as much distance between us as possible. He swings with a mighty force, but once he has selected his target, there is no adjusting the blow. The warhammer carries him like an anchor to his chosen target. His weapon crashes into the stone, leaving gashes that will remain long after our battle is over, tattooing our fight on the mountain he calls home.

"Are you so afraid to meet your doom?" He lifts his hammer from the newly-formed crater and holds it over his chiseled shoulder.

For all the force he puts into his swings, he doesn't seem to be tiring. Not yet, at least.

Without warning, he leaps through the air, the warhammer raised above his head. I dive between his legs and roll out of the way as his hammer connects to stone with an ear-aching crash.

I could attack him as he lifts his weapon, but I'm playing the long game. There's no room for error. Before I attack, I need to make sure I can win.

He grunts as he lifts Crusher. "No wonder the forest trolls are ruled by females. Even their heroes are cowards."

The crowd laughs at his comment.

For any other forest troll, that comment might have baited them into attacking. For Gord, I know it would have. Not so long ago, it might have baited me.

I smile at him. It was a good effort, I'll give him that, but this isn't my first rodeo. I've been baiting innocent players into attacking me for years. One of my greatest strengths as a streamer was taunting other players into attacking before they were ready.

I focus on my breathing, making sure to keep enough distance between us. I grip my trident tight. Sea Scorpion is light to my adrenaline-fueled muscles.

I cast three more horrors in rapid succession, bringing my total to twenty-one. As I circle around our makeshift arena, it's beginning to look more like a warzone than a clearing. Chunks of rock litter the area next to hammer-sized holes.

Kronan lunges for me again, and this time, I barely dodge the attack when my foot slips on the rubble.

He laughs at my near fall. "Time is running out, hero." He lifts the warhammer again, readying his swing.

"You're right." I summon three more horrors and instantly use Sacrifice on all twenty-four of them. Their bodies vanish in a puff of smoke, and the crowd erupts into a dull roar of murmurs. My Strength, Constitution, and Dexterity increase by eight points each. My muscles bulge with the influx of stats, and in only a matter of seconds, my size rivals Kronan's.

I flex my newly-invigorated muscles, feeling their promise of power. Hell yes!

His eyes go wide for a moment, before returning to their angry slits.

He swings his warhammer at me, and I parry it with my trident. They clink against one another, and the hammer explodes the earth. I kick Kronan in the side, and he tumbles to the ground, taking his warhammer with him.

I leap towards his downed body, trident pointed at his neck, but he lifts his warhammer, pressing its shaft between the spears of my weapon. With a swing of his hips, he kicks my legs out from underneath me, sending me sprawling to my back.

Heat emanates from Kronan's body as he crawls to his feet, his rage building.

He brings the warhammer across his body in a sweeping strike, and I jump in the air. The weapon hums as it passes underneath me.

Mid-air, I jab Sea Scorpion into his shoulder, drawing first blood. Kronan grimaces at the wound, and in the same motion of his first swing, brings his warhammer overhead and smashes it into the ground beside me. The force of the blast sends rubble spraying into me like a shotgun blast.

He lifts the hammer, and takes a step back. His chest heaves with each breath, and sweat steams off his skin.

I use the moment to summon three more horrors, sacrificing them and increasing my stats again.

I take the offensive and lunge at Kronan several times with my trident. He parries each of my jabs, using the massive head of his warhammer as a shield. Sparks fly, and the ding of metal on metal echoes against the walls of the crag.

He grunts with each swing of the warhammer as he presses again. His attacks still move with amazing speed, but I watch my footing, dodging each blow as he pounds the mountain to gravel beneath us.

"Fight me!" he shouts after I dodge another attack. "Fight me, you coward." He beats his free hand against his chest, and the trolls in the crowd do the same.

It sounds like a stampede as they beat their chests like drums of war. The goblins join in with shrill yodels that cut through the bass.

A wicked grin crosses Kronan's face, and my vision goes fuzzy.

Warning! You have been targeted with Goblin Battle Cry. Effects: Confusion.

What the hell? That's cheating. I try to say the words, but they get stuck in my throat. All I see are fuzzy silhouettes all around me. I can't pinpoint Kronan to save my life.

Something collides with my side, cracking several ribs and knocking me off my feet. The impact sends my trident flying through the air, and it drops my health by ten percent.

I try to scurry away from the looming silhouette that follows me around, but it's like there is a water tank on my head, sloshing with each step I take. If this confusion doesn't wear off soon, I'm done for.

Another sharp pain flares through my other side as I try to stand, knocking me on my back. Everything around me sounds like muffled buzzing. The beating chests, squealing goblins, and Kronan's taunts all muffle together.

Every breath I take sends pain down my sides. There's no telling how many broken ribs I have.

Taryn sends me a message, but the words come through as squiggles. This confusion, it effects everything but the thoughts in my own head.

Another hit drops me down to fifty-percent health. I must be bleeding internally, because my health continues to drop as I writhe on the ground.

Kronan is toying with me, otherwise he would have caved my head in with the warhammer. This is bad. I can't even focus on my Tiger's Eye Pendant long enough to activate its ability. There's only one way that is going to get rid of this confusion.

I activate Berserker Rage, and the world comes spinning back together, like I just traveled through a wormhole.

Kronan stands over my body, arms outstretched, basking in the glory of his people.

My blood pumps as Berserker Rage takes effect, allowing me to see everything clearly and rapidly replenishing my health. Kronan still hasn't noticed I'm no longer confused, so I lie on the ground, waiting for my moment.

Kronan lifts his warhammer over his head. "This is what happens to anyone who would challenge the mighty Kronan."

He swings for my head, and I kick out, sweeping Kronan off his feet. He falls with a thud, but I'm already halfway across the ring searching for my trident. I find it sticking out from the rubble just as Kronan stands, and I pick it up.

"Still has a bit of fight left in him." Steam continues to rise off his muscled body. "Not for long." He tilts his head back and lets out a monstrous roar, silencing the crowd. In that moment, the air around his body distorts as he goes into a rage.

We charge at one another. My vision is red, and all I see is Kronan. I level my trident at his throat, ready to end this here and now.

He rears back his warhammer. When he swings, our two weapons collide with a crash of metal on metal that sets my ears ringing. Both weapons fly from our hands, disappearing high into the sky.

Kronan lunges for me, and we lock our hands together in a show of strength. We push one another with all of our rage-fueled might, but neither of us budge.

With a full rage-meter, I activate Bite. I extend my arms, pressing them out wide, and sink my tusks into Kronan's shoulder. He brings his knee up to my stomach, the impact forcing me to release my grip.

"Fine." He smiles. "We will finish this like our ancestors." He swipes at me, and the tips of his claws rake across my chest.

I jump toward him, tackling the mountain troll to the ground. We claw, bite, and kick one another in a primal brawl.

My Berserker Rage is the first to end. I kick Kronan away and retreat to temporary safety. He chases after me, and I cast a Horror of Vitality in an attempt to slow him down, but due to his Berserker Rage, it has no effect. He does stop for a moment to attack the furry horror, killing it in one strike and granting me a brief reprieve.

Picking up a giant rock, I hurl it at Kronan like a major league pitcher. The rock goes wide to the right and crumples in the face of an unlucky goblin.

I search for my trident, but it's nowhere to be found. However, I do catch the gleaming face of Kronan's warhammer.

His rage wears off, and he spots the warhammer at the same time I do.

We both take off toward the weapon, hand-checking one another the entire way. Our claws shred each other's skin as we race across the battlefield, covering us both in a thick layer of blood. I'm thankful for the Dexterity bonus from my horrors. It grants me just enough to keep up with a troll five levels higher than me. I summon another Horror of Finesse and use Sacrifice. The additional bonus point in Dexterity allows me to pull ahead by a few inches. I dive for the warhammer and feel the cold metal against my palms.

With the warhammer in my hand, I roll over, keeping it out of reach of Kronan. He grasps for it in a panic, but I manage to kick free. Rising to my feet, I swing the hammer as he tries to grab it, connecting with his ribs.

He picks up a boulder and tosses it at me, but the warhammer easily smashes through it. He slowly backs away from me, knowing I have the upper hand. Without a weapon, he's finished.

I cast Horror of Vitality, and the furry ram-demon charges ahead of me. Kronan stomps the horror into the ground, but not before its crowd-control slow takes effect.

The warhammer connects with Kronan's knees, shattering his left kneecap and knocking him off his feet. He grimaces at me as I stand above him.

"Go ahead. Finish me." His eyes are full of hatred. Self-hatred.

I unleash a guttural roar as I raise the warhammer in the air. It looms above him. Heavy. One motion and it would all be over. I hold the fate of his people in my hands.

I could kill him. Kill him, gain a load of experience, and probably take his ancient warhammer as my prize. But then where would the mountain trolls be? They need leadership to avoid extinction. Perhaps Brutus would take over. But he has already proven to be much the same as Kronan.

I drop the warhammer beside his head. "Save your people, before there are none left to save."

The crowd stands in shocked silence. They part before me

without a word as I leave Kronan lying on the ground. On my way to the cages, I spot Sea Scorpion's gleaming shaft among the rubble and retrieve it. Brutus looks on in disbelief as I release the prisoners from their cages.

"Don't talk. Just go," I tell them.

CHAPTER 26

GREAT, MORE WALKING

My horrors hiss and grumble as we travel down the mountain with great speed in an attempt to put as much distance between us and the mountain trolls as possible. Occasionally, a Horror of Vitality will lose its footing and be trampled underneath Stompy's massive hooves.

The mountain trolls were so shocked by the turn of events that they let us leave without a problem, but that doesn't mean they won't change their mind once they take stock of the situation.

I may have defeated the chief, but if a hundred goblins come chasing after us, we're gonna have a serious problem.

"Thank you so much," one of Keaton's sons says for the tenth time. His curly brown hair hangs against his broad shoulders. His forearms are brawny from years of wielding a sword. He wears tattered clothing, and his face is covered in dirt and soot, remnants of his time in captivity. His only possession is a stick for walking. All their belongings must have been stored in one of the caves, because there was nothing near the cages. "They were going to eat us. They were actually going to eat us." He shakes his head at the thought. His face is pasty white beneath the layers of dirt.

"What were you doing on their lands to begin with?" I cast three more horrors to pull up the rear. "Your father said you were warriors."

When I analyze them, I see that they are indeed warriors—level five, in fact. Which makes it all the more stupid that they would be on troll lands.

"It wasn't us," his brother answers for him. He looks much the same as the other one, aside from having short black hair. He also seems more composed and less shell-shocked. "We've been through these mountains a thousand times. We know better than to stray too high." He cuts his eyes at the other two men we rescued. The ones who have yet to say a word. "These two had the bright idea that there would be hidden treasures in the high caves. Said that we wouldn't be paid unless we took them to investigate. We'd have been within our right to let them die."

"What did you think you would find in the caves?" I ask the two men.

They just stare at me with wide eyes. Their clothes are of a finer quality than Keaton's sons. Even in their ripped and tattered state, the stitch quality is noticeable. The tan lines on their fingers tell the story even further. The trolls probably brought in quite the spoils from these two, not counting whatever goods they were traveling with.

"Good luck getting them to talk," the black-haired son says. "Neither one of them has said a word in three days. It's like talking to a wall. They were traders of some sort, that's all I know. They brought treasures from the south to trade with the dwarves.

This was their first time using the pass at Smalltown. I expect it will be their last."

Up ahead, Taryn leads the way on Stompy, while Limery rides beside him on Berry. I'm glad I'm not the imp's personal mount for a change.

We reach far enough down the mountain that the trail forks in two directions. One leads back towards Smalltown. Keaton's sons and the merchants will be on their own from here. There are still several mountains to traverse, but each step will take them farther away from the trolls and goblins.

The other trail leads to the north, but at a much lower elevation.

I empty my pack and give the humans enough of our supplies to get them home. Taryn reluctantly parts with a dagger he took from Keaton's shop. The black-haired son gives us directions for the quickest and safest route through the mountains.

"Be safe out there." I watch them as they go, the two traders following Keaton's sons like dogs on a string.

"You think they'll make it back in one piece?" Taryn watches them leave.

Stompy snorts and paws his feet, ready to be on the way again.

"The two sons seem like they know what they're doing. The other two might need some serious counseling when they return." I slap Stompy on the backside and he starts moving. This time, we take the lower route.

"We haven't had a chance to talk about it yet, but damn, where did you learn to fight like that?" Taryn cast Strong Wind on us, increasing our speed. Since we aren't on such an incline, we can quicken our pace without worry. "Back there, that was on another level than what I've seen you do. It was brutal. And I know your scrawny ass can't fight like that in real life, so what gives?"

"I don't know, man. When my rage takes over, it's like I'm running on autopilot." I kick a rock and it goes tumbling off the trail. "My body sets out to destroy anything that's in my way. It's like when you learn a new ability and you just instantly know how to use it." I try to find the words to accurately explain what it feels like, but I can't. "It's hard to explain. Like with herbalism, once you learn a new plant, you can see its outline without even having to search for it. Fighting is just like that; my body just knows what to do. I think my mind and years of gaming are what give me an edge."

Taryn runs his fingers through his beard, thinking. "Hmmm. I guess it's the same with me. I don't know how to actually pull lightning from the sky, I just do it." His eyes light up when he has a thought. "Wait, do you think you'll know how to fight when you log—when you go back?" He turns to Limery, to see if the imp caught his slip-up, but the imp is fixated on my horrors that pop in and out of existence.

I laugh at the absurdity of his question. "Do you think you'll be able to call lightning from the sky?"

"If so, they'll be calling me Black Lightning." He grins. "And you can be my sidekick, White Thunder." He leans back and cackles, nearly falling from the moulhaug.

Following the directions from Keaton's son, we make it through the mountains in two days with no problems. At one point, we pass an area that has a pretty sizable number of ley lines, perhaps some hidden mountain dungeon, but Taryn is so excited to show me the dwarven side of the island that we don't stop to investigate.

When the mountains finally end, and we find ourselves in the valley beneath them, a beautiful meadow stretches for miles.

Flowers are in full bloom, and the wind sweeps across it in waves, like a turbulent rainbow sea.

Stompy goes to the side of the trail and gathers a mouthful of flowers. Taryn tries to lead him back to the trail, but the moulhaug will have none of it.

"All of that power and he eats flowers and eggs." Taryn shakes his head as Stompy rips another massive bouquet and chews it up.

"You survived on soda and fast food, so you aren't that different." Those were good times. I can remember so many nights when that was all we ate. Soda, chips, Chinese delivery or pizza.

"What's fast foods?" asks Limery. "Limmy is fast. He can catch all the foods."

"I'm sure you can," says Taryn, grinning. "Fast food is when I take a piece of meat and throw it at you really fast. You have to catch it out of the air."

"Ooh!" Limery claps his hand together. "Can we plays fast foods?"

"Yeah, we need some food first." Taryn laughs. "You want to catch us something?"

"Limmy's on it!" He zooms away among the flowers.

"You know he is going to want to play fast foods about twenty times a day now, right?" I watch Limery as he zips above the flowers, hurling fireballs at birds and other creatures hiding in the underbrush. Limery's fascination with food knows no bounds.

He returns with several dead birds and a nest full of turquoise eggs. Standing proudly, he presents his spoils to Taryn. We stop for lunch, and they roast the food over an open fire.

I lean against the moulhaug's side, eating a bird wing and watching Taryn throw pieces of meat at Limery, who flies to catch them. No matter how fast or how far Taryn tosses it, Limery zooms through the air, never missing a piece.

I can't help but smile at their antics. At home, on the rare occasion we had dinner as a family, we ate our meals in silence. The sounds of slurping water and mastication were enough to drive anyone mad. Mom and Dad would talk business; I would sit quietly.

This wouldn't fly there.

The few times I had dinner with Taryn and his family, it was the complete opposite of my home life. His family laughed and joked. They talked about their day. They even asked me questions. It felt so different, so welcoming.

Taryn might not have grown up with money, but he had something far more valuable. Family.

"Go long." I load an egg in my palm and point far into the meadow.

Limery takes off, and I launch the egg. It soars through the air, so high that I can't even see it against the blue sky. Farther than any baseball player could possibly throw a ball.

The imp soars into the sky and a moment later, I hear his cheer as he catches the egg.

Once we cycle through the remainder of the eggs, we're back on the road.

As we journey away from the mountain, the flowery meadow begins to thin out. We walk beside a stream as the terrain transforms into grassland, and then gradually, the grass grows sparse and becomes nothing but sand. When the stream of water disappears underground, we come to a stop.

Ahead, there is nothing but desert for as far as I can see. When I pull up my map, I see it stretches even farther.

"We should stock up on water now." Taryn dips his leather canteen in the stream. "We'll need to reconnect with the Mythroad, and we might not find another water source along the way." He puts the cork in his canteen. "Once we reconnect with the Mythroad, that'll lead us straight into Sandholde."

"Sandholde?" I've never heard of it, but to be fair, the only dwarven city I know is Seascape, and that's because it's the capital.

"Yes, it's the second largest dwarven city on *Isle of Mythos*. It also happens to be the home of the largest ebony dwarf population on the island, located in the center of the desert."

Judging by my map, we are at least a day's journey from the Mythroad, the massive road that runs from Vanaria to Seascape, connecting the two kingdoms. We never reconnected with it after the Marshlands, instead following smaller roads that led us to Smalltown. I wonder if the Mythroad passage through the mountains is a safer journey.

Looking closer at the map, the Mythroad is the only major road that goes through the desert. There's only one city in all of the sand-colored landscape, so I assume that is Sandholde. The Mythroad is the shortest and most direct route to Seascape, and it passes straight through Sandholde.

Roads and towns surround the desert on both sides, but the desert is short and wide, shaped like a saucer, so it appears that it would double our travel time to bypass it. Plus, I wouldn't get to see the native home of Taryn's people.

As we travel, Taryn tells me all he knows about Sandholde. "It's an oasis among the desert. Truly remarkable. If I hadn't been on my way to meet you, I could have spent days there." His eyes light up with excitement as he talks about the architecture and fashion. "It's said that in ancient times, Sandholde refused passage to outsiders for various reasons. Without enough water to make it back to safety, many men were laid to waste outside their gates begging for entrance."

"That's harsh." I wipe sweat from my brow. The desert sun is already beating down upon us. "What would cause them to close their gates?"

Taryn shrugs, his dreadlocks swaying back and forth. "Who knows? War or politics would be my guess."

He pulls his cloak over his head. Since entering the desert, he has exposed very little of his body to the sun, keeping his cloak around him like a tent. To me, it seems like that would cook him like an oven, but he doesn't complain.

Limery, whose body is a natural furnace, doesn't seem affected at all. He zooms ahead at times, occasionally returning with some slithering creature he's managed to catch.

Berry moves sluggishly behind us. The fur-covered bear wasn't meant for these conditions.

Taryn orders the moulhaug to stop. Climbing down from Stompy, Taryn gives the bear some water from his leather flask and pats him on the head. "You can do it, buddy. I promise it'll be worth it."

The bear weakly grunts. His beautiful umber coat has grown a lighter color from all the sand.

The day drags on, and the blistering heat of the desert sun beats down from overhead. There's nothing but sand for as far as I can see. Why would anyone want to live in such a desolate and angry place? The plants are covered in spikes or needles, and the monsters are all venomous. The entire area is hellbent on killing one another.

We come across a dune and something shifts beneath. Sand ripples like crystallized water as the monster beneath rises up. Grains of sand fall off its body, concealing its true form beneath the facade of a sandy ghost. It thrashes forward, revealing a worm-like monster with dozens of sharp teeth that spiral down into its throat. It has a hardened exterior with rows of spiked barbs that run down its body.

I would expect nothing less from such hellacious terrain.

Sandworm. *Level 18. These eyeless predators attack from below ground. Without eyes, they track their prey by feeling movement in the sand. The sandworm's circular mouth is capable of ingesting enemies whole.*

The sandworm rockets from the sand, mouth open, and dives for my horrors. It devours several of them in one bite before disappearing beneath the sand.

I wipe the sweat from my brow and get into position. It's too damned hot for this.

Following the ripples in the sand as the sandworm moves below, I ready Sea Scorpion for attack when the sandworm breaks the surface.

My weapon clinks against its hardened exterior, doing no damage as it passes by, and the worm ingests several more of my horrors.

"Its shell is too hard to damage with melee weapons," I tell the others.

Taryn cast Lightning Bolt from Stompy's back, but the electricity only runs along the sandworm's exterior, doing very little damage.

Stompy unleashes a powerful war cry and paws at the sand.

When the creature rises again, displaying its open mouth, it reminds me of our battle with the mana-infused wyrm. I see an opening. "Limery, dive down its throat!"

Without a moment's hesitation, the imp burst into flame and darts at the sandworm's open mouth. Its teeth chomp down as Limery enters, but it's too late. He's is already barreling down its throat.

Heat radiates from the sandworm's body as Limery crawls along its insides. It rears up, unleashing a demonic cry before collapsing to the ground.

A moment later, Limery burns a hole through the creature's side and emerges, covered in mucus. He shakes off his arms and the slimy substance splats in the sand.

"That's one way to do it." Taryn walks over to examine the body for loot. "Nothing worth taking. It's mostly shell."

Not long after, we come across another dune and a sandworm rises to attack. We're all grouchy from the heat, so before it can even attack, Limery turns into a scorching ball of flame and flies straight into the creature's throat, cooking it from the inside. Taryn and I stand back, watching the imp roast it alive. His molten temperature burns through the creature's stomach as it curls up in agony. We leave it to bake in the sun.

***

Night comes, and we finally connect with the Mythroad. Sand covers the road, but its even elevation and worn path leaves no doubt that it's what we are looking for. Looking around, there's not a soul in sight in either direction. I don't know why I thought there would be. The two kingdoms don't really trade. They send ambassadors and workers to go to the other kingdom and show them their ways.

We're only a few hours from Sandholde, so we decide to push through instead of camping in the desert, where predators are more likely to attack at night. Once we're there, we can find a nice inn and wash some of this sand away. It's in my toes, in my braid, and I'm pretty sure I could build a sandcastle with what has found its way into my ass-crack. For the first time since coming here, a hot shower sounds amazing.

Limery perches on my shoulder, and soon soft snores ring in my ear.

We make better time now that we are on a main road. The buff from Strong Wind has us all moving at a fast pace.

The desert is a strange place. Eerily quiet most of the time. Occasionally, a creature howls or something slithers in the sand, but for the most part, the only sounds we hear are our muffled steps on the sand-covered Mythroad, and the grumbling of my horrors.

I tilt my head back and look to the stars. Millions of them twinkle overhead, and they are like nothing I have ever seen. Millions of stars, but not a single recognizable constellation. It makes me appreciate the detail that went into this game even more. It's not a copy of Earth. It's something brand new. A world with its own history, its own future. The choices that I and these other heroes make will decide that future.

That's pretty wild.

To my left, Taryn hunches atop Stompy. In the darkness, with his cloak covering his features, he looks like some shadowy villain.

Up ahead, something twinkles in the distance, catching my eye. The longer I look at it, the more I see until it's an entire line of twinkles.

I'm pondering what type of monster we're about to fight when I notice the outline running beneath the twinkling. It's a wall. And those twinkles are fires.

We've made it to Sandholde. The outline becomes clearer the closer we get, until I can see the entirety of the wall as it towers above the sand. It's massive, stretching for many hundreds of yards. A citadel in a wasteland of nothingness. A faint glow escapes from inside, projecting on the humongous palm trees that tower above the walls. With so many, it looks like a tropical paradise is waiting on the other side.

A large crowd surrounds the gate, waiting for entrance. I hear laughter before I ever see their faces. There are several wagons covered in canvas. A few of the people are extremely tall and lanky, and I wonder if they are some race I haven't heard of.

Then one of them rears its head back and blows out a stream of fire, igniting the emblem on the side of one of the wagons.

A red lion. The same red lion I saw before on the door of the Underground Circus.

CHAPTER 27
WHERE'S WALDUR?

A MAN with a painted face approaches us from the circus crowded at the gate. He wears a multi-colored striped tunic, billowing pants, and fanciful shoes that curl up at the end.

"Hawkin?" I recognize the bard from the Underground Circus as he gets closer. His face is painted white, with a green clover painted over one eye and a black diamond over the other. The colors match the rest of his outfit. "What are you doing up all the way up here?"

"I should be asking you the same thing." He flashes me a smile. "I took your advice. We've brought the Underground Circus on the road." He walks closer to Taryn, examining the moulhaug. His eyes follow it from its horn all the way down its massive body. "Now, this is a fascinating creature. You don't happen to be in need of employment, do you, Mr. Dwarf?"

"I'm afraid not. We're just passing through." Taryn removes his hood, and his dreadlocks fall beside his face.

I take a moment to introduce the two. "And you haven't

formally met Limery." I point to the imp, still asleep on my shoulder.

"You travel in rare company, Mr. Troll." He flips a golden coin with his thumb. It's similar to the one he gave me the first day we met.

"How has it been on the road?"

"Life outside the capital has been absolutely marvelous. Most of the townsfolk have never seen our brand of entertainment. And the dwarves, they love us. They view us as performers, not just freaks." He beams. "If things hold up, we may never return to Vanaria again."

"Wow, that good?" I look over at the wagons. They are loaded to the brim with crates and bags. How is it possible that they left after me but still managed to make it to Sandholde ahead of us? "How did you manage to get your caravan through the mountain in one piece?" Most of the wagons look like they could topple over at any moment.

He looks at me with confusion. "What do you mean?"

"It took us five days to cross the mountains. I can't imagine navigating some of those passes with all that cargo."

"You didn't take the Mythroad through the mountain?" He cocks his head in bewilderment.

"No, why?" No one gave us a road-map with directions.

"It's the safest route. There's a tunnel that goes straight through the mountain, carved by magic long ago. You have to pass through dwarven customs. They are very particular about what they let into their country, but the time it saves makes up for the hassle. The only ones who travel through the mountains are adventurers, criminals, or those with something to hide."

No wonder Smalltown is so small. Keaton and his sons are smuggling items from one kingdom to the other.

And what about Glenn and Jude? Does that mean they had to cross through the mountains to avoid being detected?

"Hawkin, we're through!" someone yells from the front of the caravan, and they begin filtering in through the gate.

"I must take my leave now, but we will be having a show tomorrow. I hope to see you there." He leaves to rejoin his people.

When Hawkin is out of earshot, I turn to Taryn. "Why didn't you tell me the Mythroad went straight through the mountain?" It would have been some nice information to have. That way, we would have at least had the option.

"I didn't know. I flew through the mountains to save time." He shrugs nonchalantly. "Who would have thought that sweet, old couple from Smalltown were part of a smuggling ring?"

"Tell me about it. They seemed so nice."

Limery stirs on my shoulder as we approach the gate, grunting and looking around in confusion.

Several dwarven guards block our entry as soon as the circus passes through. They range from level fifteen to twenty, and stand side by side, holding obsidian spears tipped with gold. They each wear silk loincloths and sandals, with a golden sash wrapped around their waists. The white fabric stands out prominently against their dark skin. Golden necklaces shimmer as they hang across their bare chests. Each dwarf has a thick, black beard similar to Taryns, but they all wear their hair fairly short.

Taking them all in, they look more for show than actual battle. With no armor, all their weak points are exposed. Kind of like me, I guess. Maybe I shouldn't be so quick to rush to judgment.

"What is your business in Sandholde?" one of them asks in a deep baritone voice. He wears his hair in a mohawk and has a brilliant sapphire ring on one hand.

"We're just passing through." Taryn steps forward. "I wanted to show Chod here one of the greatest cities in the world on our way to the capital."

The dwarves stand a little taller at the compliment, puffing out their chests.

"Keep a wary eye," says the dwarf to his right. "Several dwarves have been reported missing. If it keeps up, I expect our gates will be closed to outsiders soon."

Taryn and I exchange glances. Missing people? This has Glenn and Jude written all over it. If he's started gathering another army...

The guards step aside, allowing us entry into the city.

A sprawling road leads down the center of the city for several hundred yards to a giant pyramid that rises high into the sky. The center road is pristine with thousands of neatly-laid bricks. The mortar between each brick is visible, without a grain of sand caught between. Numerous fountains gurgle along the side of the road, with lush gardens surrounding them. Brightly-colored tropical flowers blossom in the moonlight.

Taryn was right, this place is an oasis. You'd never know it from the outside, but I haven't seen this much life since the meadow at the base of the mountains. This feels like paradise.

Farther out from the road, there are lines of beautiful buildings made from sandstone. Eclectic patterns are carved into them, almost like Egyptian hieroglyphics, except the images are all dwarves and monsters.

"You might want to lift your jaw up off the ground or you're going to trip over it." Taryn gives me a smug grin.

"This place is beautiful." It's almost too much to take in. I can't imagine what it will look like in the daylight. "I don't know what I was expecting, but it wasn't this."

"We can explore tomorrow. I think we're all pretty beat. Let's find us an inn." He hops down from Stompy and leads us down a side street.

Taryn scratches Berry behind the ears and the bear nuzzles against his arm, glad to finally have some attention.

The manicured streets are eerily quiet at this hour. That's until we turn a corner and hear drunken revelry on the steps in front of a sandstone building.

White columns surround a porch filled with dwarves. Above the entrance, there's an engraving of several enormous mugs of ale.

As we approach, the raucous noise becomes more distinguishable. Many of the dwarves are singing a song about a maiden in the mountains. They clink their tankards together, and their drinks splosh on the ground.

Candlelight flickers from inside the open door.

Taryn instructs Berry and Stompy to wait outside while we make arrangements for the night. Many of the dwarves shout "Welcome, brother!" to Taryn as we pass. They're all clad in similar forms of canvas robes or silken loincloths. Many of them wear gaudy rings, gold bracelets, or necklaces. I notice that a few of the dwarves don't have beards, and I can't help but wonder if they are the females. If that's the case, there is very little to distinguish them. They stumble along merrily. Some eye me cautiously as we pass, but I don't hear any of the rude comments I heard in the southern towns.

A beardless dwarf stands behind a marble counter as we enter. The dwarf wears a long silken robe, with a gold sash tied around the waist. "Welcome to The Sand Dune Inn." The voice has a softer tone than Taryn's or the other male dwarves I've met, so I assume my hypothesis is correct. Still, I don't trust it enough to test it and allow Taryn to do the talking.

"I'd like two rooms for me and my friends. And a place for my pets in the oasis." He slides a gold coin across the counter.

The hostess rings a bell, and a dwarf appears from a back room. She whispers something in his ear, and he hurries past us.

"Right this way, please." She motions towards an immaculate staircase. It's engraved and set with jewels along the balusters. A hammer is carved into the knob at the end of the handrail.

Limery's eyes linger on the jewels as we pass.

"Don't even think about it," I warn, and he blows out of his nostrils.

Taryn falls in step beside me. "So, what do you think? Pretty nice, huh?"

"This place is amazing. You didn't have to spring for something so fancy." Honestly, we're just sleeping here. All we need is a bath and some food.

"I didn't. This is actually on the cheaper side." He laughs. "Believe it or not, there's not a lot to do in the desert, and dwarves are master craftsmen. Mix boredom and sandstone and you get inns that look like royalty stays here."

The hostess shows us to our rooms. "Food is available downstairs, and the hot spring is located in the rear." She smiles, revealing a set of pearly white teeth. "Enjoy your stay."

"Did she say hot spring?" I toss my bags on the bed and race downstairs.

In the courtyard outdoors, a stone-walled tub steams in the moonlight. There are several torches burning nearby, and a shirtless dwarf sits in the pool, drinking a frothy liquid and relaxing.

"Hop on in," says Taryn. "I'll grab us some drinks."

We should be resting, but how can I pass this up? It may be hot, but clean skin is worth the price.

I stand on the ledge, wondering if I should leave my loincloth on or let my trollberries swim in all their glory when the dwarf looks up at me.

"I promise not to bite if you don't." He chuckles and takes another swig of his beverage.

I climb down into the hot spring. It's definitely dwarf-sized, because when I sit my butt flat against the bottom, the water barely comes past my stomach. Still, it feels amazing and I'm beyond grateful for a chance to wash away the dirt and sand.

"You're a big lad." The dwarf looks on with amusement.

"That's what they keep telling me." Dirt cakes off my skin as I rub at my forearms.

Limery dips his toes in the water, then scrunches his face. "Limmy goes to bed. Goodnights, Chods."

"Good night, buddy. I'll see you in a few." I splash water against my face and taste the saltiness as it washes away days worth of sweat.

Taryn returns with two mugs, passing Limery as he leaves. "Who knew you were actually blue under all that dust?" He laughs as he hands me my mug. The liquid inside is creamy and white.

"What is this?" I take a sip and it's a mixture of sweet and bitter.

"Fermented goat milk. It's an ebony dwarf specialty." He sets his mug on the edge and climbs in.

"Cheers to that!" says the other dwarf. "Name's Krenshaw Glassbreaker. What brings a troll to the finest city in all of the dwarven kingdom?"

"We're visiting the capital," answers Taryn. For being such a quiet and shy person around new people, he seems awfully chatty with the dwarves. "But I didn't think a visit to the north would be complete without a stop at Sandholde."

"Aye, I'm actually on the way to the capital myself." He drains the rest of his mug. "They say the king is planning a great announcement in the coming days. I'm hoping for a tournament myself. It's been a good while since we've had a dwarven tournament. There's word that a hero has finally been blessed to the dwarves. It'd be a sight to behold if he showed up."

Taryn and I exchange glances.

"We may just have to check it out." The edge of Taryn's mustache twitches. I guess the dwarves really do love their heroes.

I wake up the next morning ready to explore the city. My first dwarven city! If it's anything like what I saw on the way to the inn, I'm in for a real treat. After relaxing in the hot spring last night with Taryn and Krenshaw, I feel as rejuvenated as ever. Maybe it was something in the fermented goat's milk.

Limery sits on the end of the bed, watching me. I don't know how long he's been up, but he looks like he's been expecting me. His bulbous yellow eyes stare intently. He grins, showcasing his both frightening and endearing smile. "Good mornings!"

When I open the door to the hallway, a dwarven guard waits outside. "You have been summoned by Lady Brollen to the great pyramid." He is dressed in the same garb as the dwarves from the entrance, but instead of a spear, he carries a shortsword that hangs by his side.

"Is Taryn awake yet?" I ask. We're not under arrest, so I can only assume that this is a cordial visit. She must have somehow found out that two heroes were in her city.

To answer my question, the door across the hall opens, and Taryn looks out in surprise.

"We've been summoned," I say.

He raises his eyebrows. "Do we at least get breakfast first?"

"Food will be provided," says the dwarf. His fingers rap against the hilt of his sword. "If you'll follow me." He takes off down the stairs.

We hurry to follow him, leaving our belongings in the room for later. He's surprisingly swift for such a stocky fellow. Taryn's stubby legs practically run to keep up.

Downstairs, the inn is crowded with dwarves, and the smell of roasting coffee wafts across the room. I try to take a gander at some of the platters, but the dwarven soldier is out of the door in a flash, forcing us to catch up.

Bright light blinds me for a moment as we step into the street. In a matter of seconds, I'm already sweating. Forest trolls were not made for this type of environment.

In the daylight, the city is even more resplendent than I imagined. To our left, a pyramid towers over the rest of the city. I don't know how I didn't notice it last night. We pass fountains of dwarves that spout water out of hammers, axes, horns, and shields. The beautiful engravings almost pop off the buildings. Tropical birds flutter through the city streets, flying from one fruit tree to another.

One fountain is drained, and a group of dwarves unload a cube of marble from a wagon. Another dwarf looks on, holding a hammer and chisel.

Several dwarves sweep the city streets. That explains why everything looks so clean.

"Why do you think they want to see us?" I ask Taryn. "Did they ask to see you last time you were here?"

Taryn runs beside me. Without his mount, he forced to keep up on his own. He shakes his head. "I have no idea. I didn't tell anyone we were heroes, so I don't know what they could possibly want."

Two guards wait outside the entrance to the pyramid, guarding a gleaming golden door that depicts a fight between a dwarf and a sandworm. Our guide says something to them, and they move aside.

Inside, we're hit with a rush of cool air. The cold air jolts my sweat-covered body, sending chills down my spine. Limery shivers on my shoulder for a moment before his feet grow warm.

There's a low ceiling and a path that meanders between several pools of water covered with flowering lily pads. Brightly colored fish swim just beneath the surface. The pools themselves are cubical, and the entire room looks like a giant game of Minesweeper with the way the path leads through the pools.

A dozen different doors surround the perimeter of the room. They must lead into the rest of the pyramid. At the far end of the room, a dark-skinned, beardless dwarf with long, curly, black hair, and wearing a silken white robe, sits on a throne of glass. The throne has glass spikes that stick up from the back of it, and they shimmer with the light of the surrounding torches. Several guards stand off to each side.

I focus on the dwarf on the throne and her stats appear.

Lady Brollen. *Level: ???*

Of course, she has her stats concealed. I wonder how powerful she truly is.

"It's not every day that we have the great honor of housing two heroes in our fine city." When she smiles, her face lights up. I'll never get over how beautiful ebony dwarf teeth look against their dark complexion.

"How do you know we are heroes?" asks Taryn.

"No one can hide their identity from city officials." She looks at me and winks. "But you have no need to worry. It is a great honor to host you. Please, come and join me for breakfast." She rises from the throne. "We shall dine in my chambers."

Limery licks his lips at the prospect of food, and I have the strong urge to toss him in the fish pond.

When Lady Brollen stands, her robe clings to her body. She's built very differently from the female dwarves I saw at the inn. Less stocky, more curvy. There is no confusion that she is a female.

Taryn stares on in wonder.

She leads us through a door at the rear of the room and up several flights of stairs. Inside of her room, the slanted walls are lined with floor-to-ceiling windows. They must be painted or enchanted on the outside, because I don't recall being able to see into the pyramid from the street.

We must be near the top of the pyramid, because the windows offer a complete three-hundred-and sixty-degree view of the city. The center street is visible, along with the homes and inns in one corner of the city. In another, I spot a lake as blue as sapphire surrounded by trees and vegetation. There are fields full of crops and from this high up, dwarves move among them like tiny ants.

Two dwarven soldiers take their post by the entrance.

"Please, have a seat." She gestures to two sofas surrounding a golden table loaded with grapes, figs, bread, roasted fowl, and fish.

Limery reaches for a piece of fish before we even sit down.

"Thank you." I take a seat, admiring the rest of the room. Marble floors with a swirled pattern of tan and aqua blue feel cool against my feet. Several miniature sculptures adorn a desk littered with papers, scrolls, and heavy tomes.

"What do you think of our fair city, Chod?" Lady Brollen asks.

"It's lovely. How do you manage to keep it so lush in the middle of the desert? And how is the pyramid so cool?" Air conditioning is a luxury of my past, yet, here we are.

She picks up a grape, grasping it between her fingers. Tiny veins of ice spread out from where she touches it, covering the grape until it has a layer of frost surrounding it. She places the grape on the table and it clinks against the gold.

An ice mage!

"One thing my people are known for is making sure that those with power find themselves in the right places." One side of her mouth curls up in a mischievous grin.

"You're an ice mage?" asks Taryn, his mouth wide open. "That's awesome."

"Indeed, I am. Controlling the temperature of the air around me is one of my specialties." She picks up another grape and seductively bites on it while staring at Taryn.

Even his dark skin can't hide the blushing as blood rushes to his cheeks.

She eats the other half of the grape and returns her gaze to me. "The water gardens, the lake, the forest, and the plants, all that is the work of our druids and water mages. They are the reason Sandholde is the most beautiful city on the island."

I can't argue with her about that. I have yet to see a single part of the city that couldn't appear on the cover of a travel magazine in the real world.

Limery picks up an entire fowl and sinks his teeth into it. Lady Brollen watches him with fascination. We really do need to work on his manners.

"I hear you are on your way to Seascape." She leans back against the sofa, waiting for our response.

I wonder how many spies she has placed throughout the city. Maybe even the dwarf in the hot spring is in her employ.

"That's right," Taryn says between bites. He gives her a goofy grin, and I'm not sure if he's playing it cool or trying to be sexy.

I settle back and enjoy some of the food while Taryn does whatever it is that Taryn does. The roasted fowl and fish are delicious. They have a certain spicy flavor to them that I haven't tasted before. Probably some ethnic herbs and spices.

Lady Brollen watches us for a moment before speaking. "I can't wait to see what crazy idea the king has this time. If he knows you'll be in attendance, I'm sure it'll be extra special." She sighs. "But truth be told, I've called you here for more than simple chat. Over the past week, several of our people have gone missing. There have been no signs of foul play. No blood or anything that would suggest a struggle. Not so much as a note explaining why they left. But the sheer number of vanishings point to something more at play. Even my own brother, Waldur, has disappeared without a trace." She leans forward, her icy blue eyes piercing my own. "You may be headed north, but I don't believe it is blind chance that brought you upon our fair city. Keep your eyes open, and if you notice anything suspicious, here or on your travels, I implore you to investigate. Find out what has happened to our people, and you will be greatly rewarded."

Quest Alert. *You have been offered the quest "Where's Waldur?" Discover where the missing dwarves have gone and to what end. Return to Lady Brollen with information to claim your reward.*

Reward: Unknown.

Bonus: Return with Waldur.

Not the greatest quest, but if these missing people have anything to do with Jude and Glenn, then we're already on the trail.

"We will do our best." Taryn nods.

"I cannot ask for more than that." Her gaze lingers on Taryn. "Now if you will excuse me, I have important matters to attend."

When she doesn't move, it becomes clear that we are the ones expected to leave. Apparently, I am the only one who notices, because I have to jab Taryn in the side before he takes his eyes off Lady Brollen.

He scowls at me before rising. "Ugh, thank you, my lady." He bows, the clasps in his beard clinking.

When we are outside of the pyramid, I burst out laughing. "Somebody has a crush."

Limery echoes my enthusiasm, pointing a skinny red finger at Taryn. "Somebodys has a crush," he chants.

"Oh, knock it off. I was just being polite." He tries to play it off, but his red cheeks give it away. Even though he was the tall, dark, and handsome type in real life, his shyness kept him from being a hit with the girls at school.

"Don't you mean 'knock it off, my lady'?" I let out a deep and boisterous laugh. "Tell me, do you even know what color her eyes were?"

"Dude, shut up. She was pretty." He shoves me in the side. "What do you want to do now?"

"The circus performance isn't until this evening. We can explore the city until then and head out tomorrow?" I suggest. A bead of sweat runs down my brow. "I'd love to check out that lake."

"Sounds good. I think it might be time for me to upgrade my outfit too." He looks over the tunic and cloak he's wearing. "I picked these up in Seascape. It'd be nice to get something more climate appropriate."

Our first stop is a tailor for Taryn to buy some new clothes. He ends up purchasing a tan cloak, light brown pants, and a white cotton shirt that laces up the front.

I settle for a patterned white and green shawl that wraps around my head and shoulders. The tailor said it will help to cool me off in the heat. I've grown accustomed to wearing nothing but a loincloth, and I don't plan to stop now that I have money.

After trying it on, I ask Limery if he would like one.

"Limmy doesn't need it. The hots is fine."

Imps. They don't get tired. They don't get hot. The little guy doesn't know how good he's got it.

With our new clothing, the heat does seem a bit more bearable. I guess the lightweight fabric has a way of reflecting the heat back or something.

We follow a narrow stone path through dense vegetation that leads us to the lake. Several dwarf children splash about in the water, and on the far side, I spot Berry and Stompy relaxing beneath the shade of a palm tree. When Berry sees us, he takes off running toward Taryn.

"What are they doing out here?" I ask. I figured they would be in the stables.

"Perks of the inn. They take great care of pets and mounts here. They can pretty much roam free in the park as long as they behave."

Berry leaps on Taryn, tackling the dwarf into the sand. Meanwhile, Stompy sits basking in the shade, barely acknowledging us.

A strange-looking camel catches the corner of my eye. When I focus on it, I notice it has a large silver protuberance sticking out of its head.

Unicamel. *Level 5.*

That's just too weird. A camel-unicorn hybrid. I point it out to Taryn and his face lights up for a moment. It's quickly replaced by a frown.

"I wish I could have one. Stompy would take offense if I got another horned creature." He gazes at the unicamel longingly.

"Sounds like Stompy is running your life now." I watch the camel as it leans down to take a drink from the lake. With its long, skinny legs, it wouldn't be much use in a battle, not unless that horn has some special powers, but I'm sure it's an excellent mount, especially in this climate. It probably couldn't carry me, though.

"Admiring The Gore Queen, are you?" a husky voice calls from behind us. When I look at him with confusion, he elaborates. "That's what I call me mount. She's a right beaut."

I stare at him for a moment. Not because of anything he's said, but because I'm shocked to see an ivory dwarf in Sandholde. He wears a light blue tunic with a white undershirt, keeping most of his skin from exposure to the sun. Thick leather boots cover his feet, a battle helm protects his head, and a vibrant red beard hangs across his chest. It matches the color of his sunburned nose. His tunic has a patch of a golden hammer sewn on one sleeve. In one hand, he holds an iron scepter that trickles water out of the end. In the other, a flask.

He looks more out of place than I do.

"She is quite gorgeous," says Taryn. "I didn't think the mountainfolk visited Sandholde often?"

"Eh, we don't. Wee bit of bad luck on my end." He pokes the end of his staff into the ground and takes a swig of his mystery beverage. When he unstops it, a faint whiff of alcohol hits me. "It's been quite a time since a water mage has been born in Sandholde. Until they can supply their own, water mages from the capital are sent on rotation to keep the city alive. It's a beautiful city, but damn if she isn't a pain in me arse."

"Wait, do you mean that Sandholde isn't actually an oasis? All of this is dwarven-made?" Taryn's mouth hangs open in shock.

I smack him on the back of the head. "Lady Brollen told us this not even an hour ago, but I guess you were focused on other things."

The water mage bypasses my snide remark. "That be the truth of it. In the next life, if I ever find the dwarf who thought this would be a good idea, I'll kick him in the balls meself." He lifts his helm and wipes at his perspiring forehead. Bright red hair is matted with sweat. "That's enough chatting for me. I need to top off the lake, and then water the crops." He gives us a two-finger salute and takes off toward the lake.

I imagine it's quite the change from living in the cool mountains to spending his entire day in the desert sun.

"Do you mind if we tag along?" asks Taryn. "I'd like to see how it's done."

"Be me guest."

A flock of brightly-colored birds lands in a palm tree overhead. Limery hops from my shoulder and takes off after them.

"Limery!" I shout after him. "We are guests. Do not go killing any of their wildlife."

He gives me such a pitiful frown that I think he might cry. I just shake my head at him. It's not going to kill him to learn a little restraint.

Berry galumphs along behind Taryn as we head down to the bank of the lake. Several of the children have gathered around the water mage. They must know what is about to happen.

On the far side of the lake, dwarves are fishing. A few canoes paddle in the open water.

The water mage lifts his scepter into the air and a stream of water shoots out of it into the lake. At first, it trickles like a faucet, and I can't help but wonder how he will ever fill the lake with that weak of a stream. Then, the water flow sputters, like it's backed up. The water shoots outs in jolts, a little at a time, then suddenly a geyser erupts from the end of the scepter, like someone popped the lid off a fire hydrant. The water shoots out for twenty or thirty yards, creating a rainbow as the sun is refracted through the mist.

Children rush into the lake, standing under the torrent of water, laughing and playing. Their parents watch from the bank, soaking in the sun.

For the next thirty minutes, water continues to pour from his scepter. Taryn stands beside the mage, watching with amazement.

I try to focus on the mage, but his stats are unreadable. For him to have that much continuous power, he must be pretty strong.

The water flow stops to wails of disappointment from the children.

"I come here every day, and every day, they cry when I leave. It's off to the crops for me."

"Take care." Taryn waves at the mage before turning back to me. "Can you imagine? Having the responsibility of keeping an entire city with water. I know he hates it down here. I mean, he must be roasting alive."

"Yeah, but the good thing is that the king is keeping the city alive. The unhappiness of one to save thousands. Not to mention the Mythroad would be useless without Sandholde."

We take a seat in the sand next to Stompy. The moulhaug raises his head for a moment before plopping it back in the sand. Of course, Taryn had to make a pet out of one of the laziest and most stubborn creatures in this game.

"We haven't talked about this new quest yet." He pulls out his flask, takes a drink of water, and passes it to me. "What do you make of it?"

"It sounds like the work of Glenn. Probably Jude too, if they are working together." I hope we can find the missing dwarves before they suffer the same fate as those in the forest. So many villagers lost their lives attacking the trolls because he convinced them to fight for him.

"How does he do it?" Taryn stares off in the distance, watching the dwarf families as they play in the lake. "How does he just convince them to follow him, no questions asked?"

I can tell by the way he is watching them that he no longer

views them as NPCs. How could he? Spending five minutes alone with any of them and it's impossible to believe they are just numbers in a system.

"I don't know. Valery said he was a psychopath. Maybe that has something to do with it. Maybe he has some special abilities because of it." If so, that seems like a seriously fucked up thing to do. Or could it be like what happened with me? Is it possible that the game adjusted to him based off the way his brain works?

"If what you say is true, then we're better off finding them before they find us."

CHAPTER 28

THE GREATEST SHOW ON MYTHOS

THE STRIPED TENT of the Underground Circus stands tall in the center of the main thoroughfare. Against the backdrop of the city, it looks out of place, like something from another era altogether. Bright colors against a sandy landscape.

A large man with a black beard stands by the entrance. He wears a black tunic emblazoned with a red lion's head. I recall him as the man who took my coin when I first visited the Underground Circus all the way back in Vanaria. His mismatched eyes are hard to forget. One brown, the other a brilliant sky blue.

He takes coins from each dwarf as they enter.

"Welcome back." He winks, refusing our coin and ushering us through.

Limery sits on my shoulder, and Taryn walks beside me.

"I went to a circus once," he says. "Mom took me and my sister when we were younger. At the time, I thought it was pretty awesome."

"I'm sure this will be on a whole other level." If my underground encounter was any indication, they have quite a few tricks up their sleeves.

We walk down a tented corridor into a giant auditorium. Hundreds of seats fill one side, with a stage at the bottom. There's no way that all of this should fit inside the tent we saw outside.

"It has to be enchanted, right?" I ask.

Taryn nods. "I don't see any other way." He looks around, taking it all in. "I've heard of enchanted bags, but not an enchanted tent. The cost to make something so large, how could they afford it?"

"Maybe they didn't have to buy it." Considering Hawkin is a bard, it's very possible that they have an enchanter in their midst. Probably others who are magically inclined as well.

"Mr. Troll!" a childish voice calls out to me and I look over to see Brock, the young black-haired boy who snuck into my chamber at the castle. He carries a platform around his neck filled with popcorn. No longer dressed in tattered clothing, he wears a well-made red tunic similar to the man at the entrance. "Hawkin told us you might be coming. It's a surprise to see you all the way up here."

"I'm sure it is. Are we in for a good show tonight?" I honestly don't know what to expect. When I went to the Underground Circus, it was more of a party than a performance.

"It's gonna be great, I tell ya." He smiles. "Enjoy the show."

I attempt to buy a bag of popcorn from him, but he refuses my money. "I insist. Keep it for yourself." I press the gold coin into his palm, and he smiles.

Many of the seats are already filled, so we take a spot near the top. Being that I'm about twice the size of everyone else here, I don't want to be the dickhead that blocks their view from the show.

After we take our seats, I spot a man wearing a cat mask

walking through the crowd. He wears the emblem of the circus and carries brightly-colored drinks that fizzle and smoke. The dwarves are going crazy over them, and he sells out in a matter of seconds. The circus doesn't disappoint, however, and as soon as he is gone, another man steps up with a new batch.

If these are anything like the drinks I had, then the dwarves are going to be ecstatic.

Taryn waves the man down and tries to buy a round for the three of us.

The man pushes away his coin. "On the house."

I take the cup of fizzing blue liquid. Tiny bubbles jump out at me, tickling my chin as they pop. I sip at the drink and it fizzes all the way down my throat.

Limery chugs his beverage, downing nearly half of it in one gulp. He hands me the cup, and his face contorts. He places his small hand over his stomach. "Limmy don't feels so good."

I laugh at him as dozens of bubbles fly out of my mouth. They billow in the sky.

Forgetting his pain, Limery reaches out and pops one with his finger. He laughs and bubbles spout from his mouth. Every time we laugh, more bubbles fill the air.

Below us, many of the dwarves' drinks have the same effect. Some blow steam out of their ears, others smoke from their nostrils. The show hasn't even started yet and the circus has already won them over.

As we wait for the crowd to filter in, the stands are alive with a maelstrom of bubbles, smoke, and steam.

Taryn points down to the front row. "Look, it's Lady Brollen." Bubbles float from his mouth with each word.

"Yeah, are you wanting to go sit in her lap?" I joke, but Taryn just rolls his eyes.

Eventually, every seat is filled and the candlelight dims to almost complete darkness.

A single spotlight falls upon the center of the stage. It doesn't flicker like candlelight, but burns steadily.

A woman steps before the light, her golden hair shimmering. I recognize her face and her lion-like hair that falls down her shoulders. Leona.

She opens her mouth and a mighty roar carries across the tent. The roar of a powerful beast. She bows, then disappears into the darkness. A moment later, Hawkin steps into the light.

He wears his juggler's attire, but this time, the pattern is all black and red, matching the circus.

"Welcome to the Underground Circus." He holds his hands together like he is praying as he talks. "Tonight, you will enter a land of whimsy, where anything is possible if you only believe. Tonight, you will see things that shouldn't be possible, things that are not possible, but for tonight, they will be."

He claps his hands together and an explosion of smoke obscures the spotlight. The light goes out, and for a moment, we are enraptured in total darkness. Then, the candles reignite, and light slowly returns as their flames grow. The stage is now filled with many silhouettes. They become more visible with each passing second.

Music surrounds us. The slow strum of a violin, then horned instruments, and drums. Only it appears to be coming from around us, from overhead, from behind.

Braziers erupt on the stage, igniting the performers in light. A dark-skinned man with fiery red dreadlocks dances across the stage, flipping and spinning. He somersaults through the air and his dreadlocks burst into flame.

Above him, a man and woman with splotched skin swing on a trapeze. The woman lets go of the trapeze, and for a moment, she flies through the air unencumbered before grasping hands with the man. He rockets her through the air, and she catches the next trapeze with the back of her knees.

The crowd erupts into applause.

Giant men on stilts step on the stage, juggling as they walk amid the flying acrobats. More dancers join them, and it descends into organized chaos. Every person has a place, a job, and they intertwine perfectly.

The music slows and the dancers file away into the darkness. There's a whistle, and a red lion with a black mane steps out into the spotlight. It roars as it paces. Several men appear, holding burning hoops. The lion roars and then jumps through. As it passes through the hoop, its mane erupts into flame. The lion stalks to and fro, huffing when it comes too close to the crowd, before running and jumping through another flaming hoop.

Next, flame-spitters and sword-swallowers take the stage. The crowd oohs and ahhs at their performances. The flame-spitters spit out cones of flame that turn into birds and dragons and fly around the tent. When one flies up to where we are sitting, the heat emanating from it is reminiscent of Limery's fiery form.

With so many fire elements, I can't help but wonder if there is a fire mage in their midst.

Hours pass as show after show mesmerizes the crowd. One oddity after another does a performance, each receiving grand applause. Drinks flow freely and one thing is certain: dwarves appreciate quality entertainment.

Limery sits enraptured on the edge of his seat, clapping and laughing with delight. I'm sure he's never seen anything so grand.

After a performance where a woman balances two swords tip to tip on her forehead while riding a unicycle, the tent goes dark and the spotlight reappears. Hawkin steps forward holding his fiddle.

He pulls the bow and visible neon soundwaves shoot out across the room. The soundwaves seep into the bodies of the crowd, turning their clothes the color of the soundwave that hit them. As his rhythm speeds up, the waves grow short, and when he slows down, they grow thick and seem to waft through the air.

I receive a notification, but I push it away for now, not ready to break my immersion.

The light of the candles changes to pastel before sending up plumes of glowing smoke that billow above our heads. The clouds absorb the soundwaves, pulling them in as tiny sparks of lightning form inside.

Thunder rolls across the tent. Then, with a final pull of his bow, the candles extinguish, and rain falls on our heads. It patters against everyone, and I imagine Limery and I alone are the only ones who can see in the darkness. There's a final crash of thunder, the rain stops, and the candles reignite. On the stage, there is no trace of the performers. The entire audience is covered in splotches of pastel, like a watercolor painting vomited all over us.

One by one, the performers retake the stage. When they are all there, they bow, and the crowd goes wild. Dwarves clap and yell and beg for more.

"Dude, that was awesome!" says Taryn. His beard looks like cotton candy from all the pastel raindrops.

Limery looks like he was dumped in a bucket of chalk.

While the crowd filters out, I check my notifications. There's actually two of them.

You have been targeted with Aura of Vigor. +1 Constitution for 2 hours. All debuffs have been cleared.

You have been targeted with Rains of Contentment. You will feel an overwhelming joy for the next hour.

A show and a buff. Not a bad way to spend an evening.

CHAPTER 29
DESERT STROLLS

WE RISE EARLY the next morning and stock up on provisions before leaving. With a satchel full of food and water, we won't have to stop to hunt. The quicker we are out of the desert, the better.

Our stay in Sandholde was brief, but it has been memorable. We have a new quest, and I have an overwhelming curiosity for what the king may be announcing. Maybe it's another regional event. And Taryn, well, he has hearts for eyes right now.

He looks around as we exit the city gates. I guess he was expecting Lady Brollen to see him off.

"You'll see her again. Especially if we find her brother." I try to console him, but he seems lost in his own head. If I didn't know any better, I'd say he was under some kind of charm.

With my shawl covering my head and shoulders, we set out into the miles and miles of desert before us. Strong Wind increases our pace, but we still have several days before we reach Seascape.

After spending two nights resting in an oasis, Stompy is in a bit of a mood, huffing and puffing as we travel. He and Taryn are perfect companions for one another right now.

I keep to myself as we walk. The monotonous sandy tones are all I see. It reminds me of the lab at Mythos Games, all white and pristine. Boring. I think about sending Valery a message, but I don't really have anything to say. I'm not ready to log out, and if she had news from my parents then I'm sure she would have reached out to me. Over a month and a half that I have been in this game, and I've heard nothing from them.

I notice I'm clenching my fist and try to push the thoughts away. Nothing good will come of thinking about them. I've made my own family in this world. Honestly, if Taryn wants to stay, I may never go back.

"—Chod?" Taryn calls my name, and I realize I've been on autopilot, putting one foot in front of the other like a mindless drone. "I said I'm going to fly overhead and get a view of our surroundings."

I give him a thumbs-up, and he transforms into a red bird. With a quick flap of his wings, he's off.

Watching him flutter through the air, it makes me wonder why he didn't pick something more capable of traversing long distances, like a hawk or a falcon. No one has ever been scared of a red bird.

I focus on the road ahead. It's nothing but sand for as far as the eye can see. Hills and mounds of sand. My new shawl makes it more bearable, but my ass cheeks still drip sweat like a snow cone in July.

Eventually, Taryn returns.

"See anything good?"

"Not really." He scratches Stompy behind the ears. "Some interesting-looking rock formations to the east, but nothing we'd want to waste our time with. Full steam ahead to Seascape."

"Can I ask you something?"

"Yeah, what's up?"

"Why a red bird? You can change into pretty much any creature you see. Why pick something so small?"

He smiles before answering. "It's my mom's favorite animal. It's my little way of keeping her with me."

"Do you miss them?" It's a stupid question, but I ask it anyway. Why wouldn't he miss them? He has an amazing family.

His smile fades, and he stares off into the distance. "Yeah. This is great and all, and I'd be lying if I said there weren't times when I was so caught up in it all that I didn't think about them, but they're my family. Even with school and work, there were always a few minutes each day where we just sat down and talked. I think I miss that most."

I don't respond. How can I? I have no idea what that is like. One thing is clear, and that's that no matter how much Taryn loves this game, he'd never come here for good. How could I blame him for that?

He's here now, though, and that's all that matters. It's not like I'm stuck here permanently. Any time I want to leave, I can. I just have to accept the fact that if I do choose to stay, he won't be here with me.

That's enough being emo for one day. I can deal with all of that when the time comes. For now, we need to get to Seascape, find out what the king has planned, and shut down Jude and Glenn before something bad happens.

As we travel, we eat jerky and bread. Without a need to cook anything, we can eat without needing to stop. Limery sits on Berry's back, and my horrors pop in and out of existence.

The new ability that I haven't had a chance to unlock crosses my mind.

Champion. *Summon a copy of the most recent enemy you have* *defeated. Decays 10% every minute out of combat. Cost: 50% of mana pool. Cooldown: 6 hours.*

I can't wait to try it out, but I still need to hit level twenty-one for a new ability point. The spell itself seems highly volatile. The fact that I could only summon the most recent being I've defeated means I would have to be super selective about what I kill. Summoning a twin-headed dragomander would be awesome. Summoning a rabbit would not.

Using the ability in a dungeon would mean I'd have almost no control over what the creature would be. Unless I find myself in the perfect situation, my horrors will always be my bread and butter.

Something moves across the road up ahead. At first, I think my eyes are playing tricks on me, but the closer we get, the bigger it becomes. It crosses the road and trudges slowly through the sand, carrying something behind it.

It can't be.

Desert Troll. *Level 15.*

The desert troll is a dull tan with dark patches of toffee-colored skin on his shoulders and neck, allowing him to blend in with the sandy terrain almost seamlessly. His hair is a vivid orange, pulled into a ponytail, and his tusks are short and thick surrounding his stumpy, bulbous nose. His body looks far less muscular than the forest or mountain trolls. A thick layer of fat covers whatever strength he may be hiding underneath, but even from far away, I can tell he is several feet taller than me and much wider.

He carries a massive bone club in one hand, and wears bone armor lashed with strips of leather around his forearms. A tattered loincloth drapes over his upper legs. Long arms hang down to his knees as he lumbers through the sand. In his other hand, he drags a dead scorpion twice his size by the tail.

"Hey!" I cup my hands around my mouth like a megaphone.

The troll looks over his shoulder, but then carries on with his slow pace.

"Wait up! I just want to talk." I increase my speed and the others fall in behind me.

"Chod, are you sure you want to do this?" Taryn urges Stompy to keep up with me as I jog toward the troll. "Don't you remember our encounter with the mountain trolls?"

"It's the first desert troll I've seen. I can't just not say something." I might not have another opportunity.

"Alright, but if this blows up in our faces, it's on you."

When I'm about fifty yards away from him, the troll stops moving, freezing in place.

"Hey, I'm Chod, the, uh, hero of the forest trolls. I just wanted to say...Hi. I've never met a desert troll before." I step forward, making sure to keep my horrors far behind me. For a lone troll in the desert, I'm sure we can be quite intimidating.

"Leave me be." His voice is a deep baritone. The words come out slow, dripping from his mouth like molasses.

"We mean you no harm."

"Leave me be," he says again. His head turns slightly, and his orange eyes lock with mine.

"I'm sorry. We just wa—"

He turns and unleashes a mighty roar. Tilting his head forward in an act of dominance, spittle flies out from his mouth and his cheeks flap like sails in the wind. The roar carries on for seconds and when it's finished, the desert troll's chest heaves. He clenches giant fists that look like sledgehammers.

"I think we should give him his space." Taryn has his staff lifted, ready to attack the moment he feels threatened. "Not everyone wants to be your friend."

"Alright." I put my hands up and slowly back away. "We'll leave you be."

The troll doesn't move a muscle as we leave. Even after we have rejoined the Mythroad and are half a mile away, when I look back, he's still frozen.

"What the hell was that?" I cast a few more horrors, replenishing the ones I lost while trying to be nice.

"He's was not a nice trolls." Limery floats over and lands on my shoulder. "It's okays, Chods."

"A troll who didn't want you in his business." Taryn takes a final look over his shoulder. "If I had to guess, that scorpion was food for his tribe. He probably thought you were out to steal it."

"Well, that's ridiculous." I pull up my map and sure enough, there is a cluster of magical veins a few miles from where we spotted the troll. That could be where they live.

"Is it?" He casts Strong Wind, and my legs move faster. "Put yourself in his position. You live in a harsh climate where finding food is already a struggle. You have people depending on you, and then one day, a group consisting of an ugly-ass forest troll, an imp, a devilishly handsome dwarf, and an army of tiny little monsters approaches you, wanting to talk, while you're alone on a sand dune. What do you do?" He doesn't wait for me to answer before continuing. "You run, and you lose your dinner. You fight, and you might die. Your best bet is to try and intimidate them into leaving you alone. I say good for him. Not everyone has to like you, you know?"

"What's that supposed to mean?" I stop in my tracks. That's the most ridiculous thing I've ever heard. "I don't need everyone to like me."

Taryn cocks an eyebrow at me. "Really? Come on, man. If you want to be real, let's be real. You used to stream because you wanted followers. You were shy in real life, just like me, but online attention, you thrived off that. When you first started, people liked you for you. Because you were genuine. When you screwed up, you laughed about it. You did crazy things that others wouldn't try, and most of the time you failed but occasionally, you'd win and it'd all be worth it. You got addicted to the comments and the views, and you wanted more. So you tried to be funny. The worse things got at home, the meaner your jokes became. When we played together, things were fine, but when you played alone... Man, you could be a savage. Over a game. Over nothing. I think it has a lot to do with how your family treated you, and that's on them, but it doesn't change the fact that you have always been searching for something you never felt at home. Appreciation."

We stand in silence for a moment. The tension is like an invisible wall. Limery has no idea what just happened, but the way his eyes dart between both of us, he knows something is up.

"You're a dick." I say it, and I mean it. My face grows hot, and I know that if I don't leave, I'm going to snap. What does Taryn know about my home life? About not being loved. His family had everything. How in the hell could he possibly know what I feel?

"Bro, come on."

"Nah, you're a dick. Leave me alone."

He cuts his eyes at me, and I know I've hurt his feelings, but I don't really care. He pats Stompy on the side of the head and they take off down the road.

"Chods—" Limery starts, but I cut him off.

"Go with Taryn. I need to be alone."

His bulbous eyes well up with tears, but he doesn't argue. He doesn't understand what's going on, but I don't have the time or energy to comfort him right now. He flies away and lands on Berry's back. I hear sniffles before I turn away.

I sit down in the sand. Not thinking, just fuming. If there was anything around me besides miles of fucking sand, I'd break it. My horrors slowly pop out of existence, and I don't care enough to replace them. One by one they vanish until I am completely alone.

I let out a deep breath, trying to let go of some of my anger with it. The sun's warm rays blaze against my back. I don't need people to like me. Taryn is full of shit. I want people to like me, but I don't need it.

Do I?

My heartrate slows and the anger that threatened to boil over has almost receded entirely. Our argument replays in my mind. There's probably some truth to what he said. Why else would I have freaked out on Taryn like that? He's my best friend, and he's never said a bad thing about me. I just didn't want to hear it.

God, I'm an asshole.

I turn around to find them, to apologize, but they're gone. I wonder how long I have been sitting there stewing, because I can't see them at all. Long enough for my horrors to die and then some. Jumping to my feet, I scan the area. There's no trace of Berry or Stompy's giant moulhaug butt on the horizon. Did I piss off Taryn enough that he used Strong Wind and left me behind?

Limery would never let that happen. I just need to catch up to them, to make things right.

I could send Taryn a message, but it needs to be in person.

I take off at a near sprint to find my friends. Sweat pours down my back as I push my body to its limits in the raging heat. I continuously summon horrors, and they struggle to keep up.

After twenty minutes of running, I feel like I am going to die. My head pounds, my heart races, and cramps run through both legs and my side. Forest trolls were most definitely not meant for desert sprinting.

I bend over, hands placed on my knees, when I hear a crack of thunder in the distance. I look up to see a multitude of dark blotches on a distant dune.

Fuck. They're in trouble.

With my stamina depleted, there's no way I'm going to make it there in time to help, so I do the only thing I know how. I activate Berserker Rage, replenishing my stamina, and take off toward the battle.

While Berserker Rage is active, I feel like I could run a marathon in the desert, but it ends far too quickly, and my stamina begins to deplete once again.

The battle grows clearer with each step, and eventually, I can make out what is happening. Taryn and Limery are squared off against a group of giant scorpions. They look identical to the one the desert troll was pulling—golden, with a black stripe running down their backs. There's at least five of them, and each one is the size of a small car. They scurry around, clicking their pincers and striking with their stingers.

Limery tosses fireballs and occasionally, a lightning strike rips into one of the creatures, scorching its shell.

"I'm coming!" I yell, but they can't hear me above all the chaos.

A stinger stabs into Stompy's rear leg, and he bellows in pain. Berry launches himself at one of the scorpions and rips off one of its legs with his teeth. It walks lopsided in the sand, but it manages to grab him with one of its giant pincers.

Berry roars as the pincer rips through his fur. He tries to push it away, but the creature's grip is strong. While he is subdued, the scorpion stings him in the neck and the bear goes limp. Venom drips from the tip of the stinger.

He's going to die if I don't get there in time.

I sacrifice all the Horrors of Finesse I have summoned, taking their speed boost and sprinting with everything I have. I arrive just in time to tackle the scorpion's tail as it prepares to sting Berry again.

For being so large, the scorpion is surprisingly lightweight. It tumbles with me and we go rolling down the dune. I wrap my legs around its tail and pull with all my might. Something cracks, and the tail breaks free, spraying me in a squirt of bodily fluids. The tailless scorpion turns on me, but I take my trident and stab it through the center of its body until its legs curl up in death.

Berry whimpers as he crawls through the sand, leaving a trail of blood behind him. He's on his last bit of health.

"Taryn, save Berry! I'll hold the others off."

He leaps from Stompy, transforming into a red bird and fluttering over to Berry.

"Taryn, I'm—"

"Not now," he says as he returns to dwarven form. He leans over Berry, casting them both in a green glow.

My horrors battle against the other four scorpions. Several of them are chopped in half by pincers, and more fall to strikes from stingers. A few Horrors of Vitality are able to slow one scorpion enough for Limery to erupt a fire wall underneath it, cooking the monster alive.

That leaves three level sixteen scorpions against me, Limery, a limping Stompy, and about a dozen remaining horrors.

Piece of cake.

One scorpion sees Taryn hunched over Berry and makes an attempt at an easy kill.

"Limery, wall!" I order.

A flaming wall ignites beside Taryn, stopping the scorpion's advance. I grab the creature by the tail, and with one good spin, I toss it as far away as I can like a hammer thrower at the Olympics. Limery pelts it with fireballs as it soars through the air.

The two other scorpions surround Stompy. He thrashes his

head from side to side, warning them to back off. One of the scorpions strikes, but Stompy parries the blow with his horn. The action leaves his other side exposed and the second scorpion jabs its stinger in his side. A string of yellow slime stretches from the wound to the stinger. Stompy bellows in pain and swings his horn to the other side, but the scorpion has already retreated out of range. His health trickles down as the venom takes effect.

Over my shoulder, Limery bursts into flame and darts for the lone scorpion, leaving me and Stompy with the other two. Taryn is taking longer than usual to heal Berry, and I don't know if it is the lack of plant life in the desert or something else entirely.

Whatever the reason, it means I'm essentially on my own to finish these two off. I use Intimidation, unleashing a roar that momentarily confuses the two scorpions. Their eyes glaze over, and I realize each one has several sets. Two up top and another pair on each side of its mouth.

As they sway back and forth, I quickly use my trident to stab out all three sets of eyes on the scorpion nearest me, completely blinding it. When Intimidation wears off, the blinded scorpion lashes out at no one, striking with its tail and lunging with its pincers. It'd be comical if my friends weren't dying all around me. I leave him for later and focus on the other.

I try to stab out its eyes, but it blocks the blow with one of its pincers. Stompy lets out an angry bellow beside me, but his wounded leg makes it impossible for him to charge.

These scorpions are dangerous, but at the end of the day, they're just giant bugs. Bugs with hard shells and very little muscle.

I stand in front of the scorpion and wait for it to strike. When it does, the strike is too quick for me to stop, so I take a stinger straight to the chest. Before it can retract the stinger, I wrap my hands around it and pull with all my might. The scorpion tries to pull it back, but I refuse to let go. The venom burns like hell as it creeps through my veins.

The scorpion's pincers reach for me, but I jump over them. I twist the stinger until it snaps off and then slam the pointed barb down hard through the creature's head. Venom to the brain is super effective! My health continues to tick down and my racing heartbeat thumps in my eardrums.

I use my Tiger's Eye Pendant to cleanse the venom from my body and bask in the sweet relief.

It doesn't last long, though. A sharp pain plunges into my backside, and a fresh influx of venom enters my veins. My luck must be pretty fucking shitty today for me to be the victim of a blind scorpion.

There's a flash of lightning, and suddenly, I can't move. When the stun wears off, the blind scorpion retracts its stinger. The creature's body smokes from the lightning attack. I just happened to be unlucky enough to be attached to the end of it.

The scorpion lunges at nothing in particular. Then, a fully healed Berry sinks his teeth into the creature's pincer arm and bites it clean off. The scorpion strikes at Berry, but without sight, the stinger hits nothing. When Berry rips off the second pincer, the weight of the scorpion's tail topples the body over, revealing its soft underbelly, which the bear has no trouble tearing open.

With the threats gone, I collapse to the ground, exhausted.

"Here, take this." Taryn's face gives very little away, but his voice is soft. He hands me a health potion he purchased in Sandholde.

"Hey, man. I'm sorry—"

"I know." He smiles and the corners of his mustache twitch up. It's not a smile born of laughter, but of love.

"No, I need you to hear this." I hold the health potion in my hand, not ready to take it until I've made peace. My back burns and the venom creeps through my shoulders and arms, but I need to say this. "You were right. About all of it. I was a dick a lot of times just to be a dick. I hated my home life, and it gave me a sense of power to tear others down, a sense of control. But mostly, I did it for the attention. My parents wouldn't notice me, so it felt good when others did. They noticed me, but they didn't like me. How could they like someone like that?" I wince as a fresh bolt of pain goes through my shoulder. "This has been a chance at a do-over. The friends I've made here, it's been because of who I am, and because of the choices I have made. I'm sorry I took what you said so personally." He's one of the few people who have always been there for me. I hope my apology is enough.

"Hey, I know you're a good guy. That's why we're friends. I just want you to know that you don't need the entire world to like you in order to be important. You're important to us." Taryn wraps his arm around me. "Now, will you take the damn potion?"

I uncork it and pour the red liquid into my mouth. Immediately, the potion soothes my aching veins and my health slowly restores.

"And Limery..." I turn to find the imp standing sheepishly behind me. "I'm sorry I yelled at you. You've been my best friend since coming here. You've looked after me, had my back time and time again. You deserve better than to be dismissed."

He flies over to me and wraps his tiny arms around my neck. "Oh, Chods. Limmy is yous best friend."

I hug him back, thankful for his wonderful, crazy self.

We gather up the stingers and pincers and stuff them in my bag. The venom will probably sell well in Seascape, and the pincers could make for decent weapons.

As I put them away, I notice I have a new notification. I must have missed it due to half my body being ablaze with venom.

Congratulations! You have reached level 21. +1 stat point to distribute. +1 Strength and Constitution racial bonus. +1 ability point to distribute.

I use my new ability point to unlock Champion. It's kind of cool knowing that I can summon a giant scorpion any time I need one. I have two skill points, but I'm not sure where to allocate them at the moment. Dexterity or Intelligence seem like safe bets, since Strength and Constitution are through the roof due to my racial bonus. However, with Champion depleting my mana pool by half, it might be smarter to invest in mana regeneration, so maybe Wisdom.

I leave it be for now. If nothing else, I can debate the pros and cons on the fifty miles of desert we still have left.

With our emotional meltdowns behind us, we set off for Seascape.

CHAPTER 30
SEASCAPE

MY HEART JUMPS when I see the first signs of plant life returning. Beautiful green plant life. It doesn't happen all at once, but slowly, the desert fades and we walk next to green grass and towering oaks.

No longer surrounded by sand and dust, I remove my shawl and stuff it in my pack. Limery zooms through the trees, chasing the birds he has missed for many days. There's a certain weight that's lifted just by the change in environment, which is fine for me. I'm happy to put what happened in the desert behind us.

As the day goes on, we eventually come to a crossing where the roads that bypassed the desert on both sides reconnect with the Mythroad. According to my map, we will arrive at Seascape within a day.

Lots of dwarves are on the road, coming and going from both sides. Most take the road north to Seascape, some go east or west, but no one seems interested in taking the Mythroad to Sandholde.

There's a mixture of ebony and ivory dwarves in the crowd.

The ebony dwarves that live outside the desert dress more like the ivory dwarves, wearing tunics and pants. Some even wear armor.

Taryn makes chit-chat with other dwarves as we walk, and they speculate on what the king could be announcing. Apparently, he sent out a regional alert before we crossed the mountains, because almost everyone in the kingdom knows about it.

"Haven't seen this many dwarves on the road since the king's seventy-fifth birthday feast," says an ivory dwarf pulling a cart loaded with burlap sacks.

"He's that old?" Taryn asks.

The dwarf burst out laughing. "Old? I expect he's still got a few hundred years in him."

Taryn's eyes go wide. "Do dwarves really live that long?"

"Blood dwarves do."

Taryn turns to me. "I had no idea that the king was a blood dwarf. I mean, I knew they were rare, but why did no one tell me our king was one? It's kind of a big fact to leave out." Whenever it comes to dwarven knowledge, he just can't get enough.

"Maybe they thought everyone knew," I offer.

"Yeah, maybe." He turns back to the other dwarf. "What else do you know about blood dwarves?"

I listen in on their conversation as we walk. I don't really care that much about blood dwarves, but it beats staring at the trees. Limery sits on Stompy's horn, bobbing along as the moulhaug and the bear take up the majority of the road, blocking anyone from passing us. Strong Wind moves us along, even as we make our way uphill.

"Blood dwarves are very rare," the dwarf continues. "And they are dying out. It's said that whenever they have children with one of the other dwarf races, their red skin doesn't come through. So most blood dwarves only marry other blood dwarf families. They can recognize one another by their skin color, but if you take away that, they're no different than you or me. You only really see them in the capital these days. The families have grown smaller over time. They say that magic is strongest in the veins of blood dwarves, and that they have produced more paladins, clerics, and mages than the other races combined."

Taryn hangs on every word, absorbing the knowledge of his people.

By the time Seascape comes into view, I know more about dwarven culture than I ever cared to.

For being a city by the sea, Seascape appears more like a mountain that rises from the ocean. We cross a bridge that goes over a ravine, separating Seascape from the mainland. The smell of saltwater comes up in gusts from the violent tides below. Seascape itself juts high into the sky, steep cliffs on all sides protecting it from interlopers. The only way on or off Seascape is the bridge we are crossing.

At the end of the bridge, there's a drawbridge guarded by a dozen well-armed sentries. They all wear resplendent plate mail, engraved with images of warhammers and axes. I find it strange that the dwarves are so defined by the things they make and the tools they use. The sentries' beards are braided, and beautiful red cloaks embroidered with golden thread adorn their shoulders. The bridge remains down, and they stand aside as the crowd filters through. With the king's announcement, I'm sure that the influx of dwarves has been nonstop.

Since they aren't checking those entering, Glenn and Jude might have made their way inside the city. If they were on dwarven soil when the king's announcement went out, then they are aware that something big is happening. I doubt they would miss it. And since King Favian's laws have no merit here, Jude and Glenn are free to travel without worry.

I suddenly feel uneasy, like I could be attacked at any moment. My towering blue body is hardly inconspicuous among all these dwarves.

Once we pass the bridge and return to solid ground, the road zigs and zags, ascending toward a masterpiece of dwarven architecture.

The castle reminds me of something out of history books. Dozens of towers, spires, and flying buttresses reach for the heavens. It dominates everything in sight. Sculptures of dwarves adorn each of the hundreds of stained-glass windows that depict imagery from their long history. There are gargoyles and intricate carvings along almost every inch of the castle.

It's a beauty to behold, simultaneously fragile and imposing. A mixture of fine lines and details on a behemoth of a structure.

When my eyes are finally able to look away, I take in the rest of the city. It's just as magnificent as the castle. Every building is made from brick or stone. Even the outermost shops and homes, where the poor would normally live, are far beyond anything I saw in Vanaria, save the castle. We pass jewelers, armorers, more blacksmiths than I can count, pubs, and dozens of inns. Everything is so tightly packed together that they had no choice but to build vertically.

As much as I try to look away, my eyes are drawn to the city's beauty. One detail leads into the next, drawing me into a maze of architecture. "I thought Sandholde was beautiful, but this is something else. It's like a gothic New York."

"I know. It's crazy that something like this could be made without machines." He looks on with lust at the surrounding structures.

We pass a rowdy tavern named The Slobbering Ogre, where dwarves sing loudly inside; and an inn called The Merry Kobold, where several dwarves who traveled with us stop to leash their ponies. As we journey deeper into the city, it seems like there is a tavern on every corner.

"Want to stop for a drink?" Taryn stares up at a sign with a dog standing on two legs. The Dancing Hound.

"Maybe we should find an inn first. With so many people coming into town, I'd like to make sure we have rooms for tonight, and somewhere for Berry and Stompy to stay."

Dwarves filter around the beasts' massive bodies while we are stopped in the street. Limery is focused on an imp gargoyle on the side of a nearby building.

"Yeah, that's a good idea." Taryn licks his lips one last time before turning away from the tavern. "I know of a nice inn near the castle. I stayed there when I first came here."

As the sun sets, the windows of the castle come to life, the stained-glass glowing from the light of hundreds of torches. Even though it is made of stone, the castle feels alive. No matter where we go in the city, its towers are always visible. Always watching.

The streets become less crowded the closer we come to the castle. At the top of the hill, we enter an open courtyard in front of the castle gates. It is beautifully designed, arranged so that the different colored bricks depict images of warhammers and axes. In the center of the courtyard, there's a tall and elegant archway, almost identical to the one in Vanaria. Dozens of plainly-clad dwarves surround it, looking on with awe. Runes and symbols run along the sides of the arch. It's slightly elevated from the surrounding area, with a mosaic of stones circling outward from its base. The entrance to the arch is sealed with stone, but a dark purple energy radiates from between the stones

"That's different." The portal in Vanaria didn't have any sort of energy around it.

Taryn turns from the rows of buildings. "Yeah." He scrunches his brows at the arch. "That's...odd."

"What's odd?"

"That energy. It wasn't doing that last time. It was sealed, but you could walk right up and touch it."

"You think this has something to do with the king's announcement?"

"I wouldn't doubt it." He stares intently at the portal.

Limery jumps from Stompy's horn and flutters to my shoulder. "Limmy doesn't like. There's is evils coming from thats." He points a long skinny finger at the arch.

I feel it too. There's something off about the portal. Something unsettling.

On the other side of the courtyard, near the castle gates, dozens of guards stand at attention, covered in heavy battle armor. Their helmets sit low upon their brows and the nose guards conceal all but their eyes and beard from view.

"That's a lot of guards." I analyze them. Each one is a member of the kingsguard, all level twenty-five.

"They take protecting the king very seriously," says Taryn.

One of the dwarves near the portal reaches out to touch it. When he does so, the dark energy strikes out like lightning. There's a loud scream, and the dwarf falls to the ground. He doesn't move.

A female dwarf rushes to his side, screaming. "Help! Someone help! Someone help my husband!"

The guards don't move. No one comes to the man's aid, so I sprint over, parting the crowd.

One look at the body, and I know he's dead. His eyes are open, yet unseeing. Why does no one else seem to care?

"Why would he do that?" I ask the woman, but she just weeps loudly over her fallen husband. I put my hand on her shoulder, but it does nothing to ease her pain. The rest of the crowd doesn't even seem to notice the dead dwarf in front of them. They all just stare at the portal with longing.

Another dwarf reaches out, and I pull him away. It takes a moment before his eyes register what's happening. He shakes his head, as if coming out of some fog.

"Uhn, what happened." He looks down and sees the dead dwarf. "Oh, no. Did I—"

"You almost touched the portal. Whatever that energy is, it's deadly. I suggest you go home." I step in front of the portal, blocking his view.

"Th-thank you, sir. I don't know what happened. I remember looking at it. It was so beautiful, and then...and then, you pulled me away." The dwarf blinks rapidly. "I must be going."

When I turn around, Taryn and Limery are ushering the other dwarves away. They all have the same realization as the dwarf I stopped. It's like they were transfixed by the energy. No longer enraptured in the portal's spell, some of the dwarves help to carry the dead husband away. To where, I have no idea.

After the crowd leaves, the energy that radiates through the portal dims. Is it possible that the power grew as more dwarves looked on it?

"That was weird." Taryn strokes his beard as he looks at the portal. His eyes droop a little and his words begin to slur. "Why did no one else help them?"

I grab him by the shoulder and make him face me. Whatever affected those dwarves, it seems to be having a similar effect on him.

The guards stand as still as ever. Berry and Stompy remain where we started, almost as if they are wary to come any closer to the portal.

"Let's get the hell out of here." I shake his shoulder. "Where's that inn you were talking about?"

"It's right around the corner." He rubs his head like he's fighting a headache. "Closest inn to the castle. It'll cost a gold a night, but we'll be right in the action."

I take one last glance at the arch. "Honestly, I'd prefer to stay a little away from the action."

We enter the front door of The Golden Hammer, and the place goes quiet.

The tavern has thick stone walls. Black banners with a golden hammer sigil hang from the ceiling. Mounted heads of various beasts adorn the walls with torches blazing in between. A mighty fire roars in the fireplace against the far wall. There's a bar on one side and plenty of tables on the other. A handful of dwarves are scattered around the room. The barkeep leans forward, whispering to a lone patron at the bar.

"You've got some balls on you," says a dwarf at the closest table. An ivory dwarf with a jet-black beard. He wears golden chainmail under red leather armor. "I saw what you did. I've seen many a dwarf lured to their death in front of that portal. There's no helping them once they've fixed themselves on it. The priests and paladins are the only ones who can go near it without feeling its pull. You're lucky to be alive."

Then why the hell was no one blocking it off?

"How many people have died to the portal? And why wasn't anyone there to warn us?" Taryn scowls at the dwarf.

"More than I can count. Most of us natives know to stay away. Only the outsiders venture through the castle square these days." He takes a swig of his drink. "Shoulda been someone telling you to turn away, but my guess is they either felt the pull and left, or they were one of the ones that got caught in its snare."

"The pull?" I ask. I didn't feel a pull, but it certainly looked like Taryn did.

"Whatever ancient power has awakened in that portal, it calls to the dwarves like a siren song." He shakes his head. "The only ones who don't seem to be affected are the blood dwarves and those with holy magic. Still, not a dwarf that has touched the energy has lived to tell the tale." He lifts his mug. "Have a seat, grab a drink, celebrate the fact that you didn't die."

I don't think either one of us feel like celebrating right now after watching an innocent dwarf die. And his poor wife... I just want to lie down.

Taryn walks over to the barkeep and orders us two rooms.

"Our large beast stables are farther down the street. Does that work for you?" the barkeep asks.

"As long as they are safe, that'll be fine."

The barkeep snaps his fingers, and a dwarf who was sitting in the back of the tavern rushes out the door.

Taryn leans against the bar. "After all that, I think I need a drink." He looks over to me. "You in?"

We take a seat at the table, and the barkeep brings over two of the biggest mugs I have ever laid eyes on. Big enough that they actually fit my troll hands.

"And one for the little one." He places a smaller mug in front of Limery.

Taryn lifts his glass. "To the king."

"To the king." We clink our glasses.

The dwarven ale is delicious. A deep dark brown, it's nutty and smooth and goes down like water.

True to his nature, after a few sips, Limery's head begins to bobble back and forth.

More dwarves filter in as the night goes on, and after a few more mugs, we forget all about the troubles with the portal.

"I love you, bro." Taryn places his hand on my arm. "I'm sorry I hurt your feelings."

"Don't worry about it. I needed a wakeup call. You're a good friend." I slap him on the back, making his dreadlocks dance and causing him to spill a little ale as he tries to take a drink.

A red-haired dwarf with a matching beard takes a seat on the bench beside Taryn. He gazes at me with a drunken stare. "You're a big fella. I bet you're strong. What do you say we put it to the test?"

I laugh at him and scoot back a little from the table. I guess you haven't really lived until you've been in a dwarven bar fight.

He slams his elbow down on the table. He flexes his hand a few times before extending it to me. "Loser buys the winner a beer?"

Arm wrestling. He wants to arm wrestle me. A drunken smile crosses my face, and I put my own elbow on the table. "You're on."

The other dwarves take note of our challenge and gather around the table. Taryn takes bets on who they think will win.

When we grip each other's hands, the red-haired dwarf speaks. "You're about to find out why they call me Uluf Steelgrip."

Another dwarf pipes in over my shoulder. "We call you Uluf Steelgrip because that's what yer mother named ye."

The entire bar erupts into raucous laughter. They countdown from three, and then we square off.

The dwarf is pretty strong for his size. His forearms are built like a baseball player, all thick, corded muscle and bulging veins. His face goes red as he flexes, pushing against my arm with all he has. At level sixteen, he's a strong dwarf. He could probably beat Taryn. Unfortunately for him, he just happens to be going against a level twenty-one forest troll.

I slam his wrist against the table. "I'll be taking that beer now."

He scowls at me before heading to the bar.

One by one, the other dwarves line up, each of them eager for the opportunity to test their strength against a troll. Pretty soon, our table is filled with empty mugs, and the world dances in and out of focus. Taryn and Limery cheer me on.

The rest of the night passes in a blur, but I have visions of daggers stabbed into tables, dice games, and an endless flow of beer.

And most of all, laughter.

CHAPTER 31

BATTLE ROYALE

REGIONAL ALERT! King Orso Brightgaze will be making an announcement at noon in the castle square.

My head throbs, which has become a common occurrence on the days following an evening of drinking with Taryn. I focus the notification away and pull the feather-stuffed pillow over my face.

"Uhn," I moan. I'm a giant blue monster, why is it that Taryn can drink me under the table?

"Uhn," Limery echoes my sentiments from the floor.

I have no idea why or how he happened to end up on the floor. Blurry visions of daggers, drinking, and arm-wrestling flutter through my mind.

There's a knock on the door and by the time I sit up, Taryn enters. He has returned to the clothing he wore the first time I saw him in-game. A dark green cloak and a tan tunic. He hits me in the foot with his staff.

"Get up, you bums. We want to get a good spot for the announcement. It's not every day you get to see a king in person."

299

He pulls the covers off the bed. "Up! I've already ordered breakfast for you lightweights."

I crawl out of bed and my head threatens to roll off my shoulders. Limery stands up and runs straight into the bedpost. I've never second-guessed letting the imp drink. Honestly, I don't know how old he is. Young for an imp, but he could be older than me for all I know. Besides, what's the drinking age on the island? No one has ever refused him service.

Taryn leads us downstairs to the tavern. Raucous applause greets us, resounding in my head like thunder.

"There's our champion!" Uluf Steelgrip slaps me on the back. "Strongest troll I ever did see."

I nod, not quite ready to engage in conversation.

Uluf is bright-eyed and full of cheer. The room is nearly packed with dwarves, and not one of them is nursing a hangover.

"Eat up." He laughs. "It'll take the edge off."

A platter of sausages, eggs, ribs, and potatoes waits for us. Next to it, a mug of frothy ale.

My stomach lurches at the thought of more ale.

Taryn notices my hesitance. "Hair of the dog." He motions for us to sit. "It'll set you right."

By the end of the meal, I'm feeling better and can finally focus enough to listen in on other conversations.

"Could be he wants someone to encase the portal in stone," says one dwarf.

"Maybe he knows what's causing it," says another.

"Could be a blood dwarf cursed it. How else do you explain that it doesn't affect them?"

"Maybe the volcano is alive again. You know that the castle is built on its ruins."

They shout out speculations, one after the other. Some plausible, some downright ludicrous.

"You ready?" Taryn asks the moment I take my last bite. He stands from the table.

I'm not going to be the one to kill his enthusiasm. "Let's go."

When we step out the door, the streets are packed. The sun shines high overhead. It must be almost time.

Limery sits on my shoulder, and I bulldoze my way through the crowd. There are a few angry faces, but once they look at me, they part with ease. Taryn follows closely in my wake.

There are only a few yards between the door of The Golden Hammer and the castle square. Most of the square is empty. Nearly a hundred armed guards keep the crowd pressed back, creating a barrier between us and the portal. Where were these guards yesterday?

A dozen or so red-skinned dwarves stand back against the stairs that lead up to the castle entrance. Blood dwarves. Some wear robes, others wear armor. There are a few females in the mix. Holy energy surrounds them as they stand at attention, but their black eyes give them a sinister look.

Once we make our way close enough to the front of the crowd, I lift Taryn into the windowsill of one of the shops. The ledge is deep enough for him to stand on without falling.

"What's going on?" I ask.

"No idea." He scans the square and then looks out behind us into the crowd. "This is all kinds of weird."

I'm watching the blood dwarves, when a bright glare catches my eye. Across the courtyard, standing in one of the streets that empties into the square, a large knight towers above the surrounding dwarves. Pristinely polished plate armor gleams in the sun.

Pressley Allen

Level 24
Knight
Human

The last time we saw him was in Lynchton, when he sold that amulet to the shopkeeper. What the hell is he doing here? He's gained a level since we last saw him, and at his level, that takes some work.

I wonder how he found out about the king's announcement. Maybe he thinks there will be gold. If there is gold to be had, then he is the one hero I would expect to be here. I still remember his words, "I only care about gold."

Pressley leans over, whispering something to a smaller man in a red cloak. It takes me a moment, but I realize I've seen him before as well. A thick, black chain hangs from his neck.

Richard Hummel
    Level 18
    Cleric
    Human

The cleric who serves the God of Chaos. He wears the same red robes and black chain as when I met him in Vanaria. He's a long way from The Green Giant Inn. What is he doing here, and why is he with Pressley?

I've got a very strange feeling about this. If those two are here, I'm sure Jude and Glenn are here somewhere, too. And who knows who else.

I should have an army of horrors on hand, but with so many

people here, there's no way to summon them without causing a scene. As if I don't have enough eyes on me just for being a giant blue troll.

"There are other heroes here," I whisper to Taryn.

"Where?" He scans the crowd.

"Across the courtyard. Giant knight and cleric with the red hood."

"They could just be curious." He stares in their direction.

"For them, maybe, but it means Jude and Glenn might be here, too. Keep an eye out for any more humans. If they tried to attack the king, it could start a war."

"I'll see what I can do." He transforms into a bird and flies over to the roof of a nearby building. He hops along the edge of the roof, surveying the crowd beneath.

Bells ring from inside the castle. Several of them. They echo through the streets, and everyone falls silent.

The large metal doors of the castle open, and a small crowd of dwarves step through. A half-dozen kingsguards in their silver armor and red capes. A priest stands to one side, clad in a white robe that only draws more attention to his red skin. In the center stands the king.

He is at least a foot taller than the other dwarves. His skin is the dull red of cooling magma. He has bushy black hair that falls to his shoulders, and a black beard intricately braided and adorned with silver clasps. He wears a black tunic and black cloak, each embroidered with silver thread. A red breastplate engraved with a silver warhammer protects his chest, and a glowing red crown sits atop his head. The tines of the crown have alternating battleaxes and warhammers.

When I focus on him, his level is unreadable.

King Orso Brightgaze. Level: ???

At the edge of the stairs, the kingsguards move aside and the king steps forward. I can only imagine what it must look like for him up there. Standing on that precipice and seeing his kingdom before him. Lands that stretch for miles. Thousands of dwarves packed in the streets of his city, all watching him.

He holds his hand in the air and there is absolute silence. When he speaks, his voice carries over the crowd like a loud-speaker, as if magically amplified.

"Thank you all for joining me here today. For many years now, the Kingdom of Seascape has lived in peace. It has been many ages since we were last at war. Longer still since our people battled the dark one before he retreated, sealing all the portals with him. With the closing of the portals, we lost contact with the other continents. As great monsters patrolled the seas, sea travel vanished.

"In the time that has passed since the day the portals closed, most of the island has forgotten the atrocities we witnessed, that our forebears faced." He pauses, looking across the crowd. "Some of us are not so lucky. Ever since I was a young dwarf, I have been reminded of the last great war. Of what it may mean if the dark wizard should turn his gaze upon us once again. For years, I have been reminded, but for years, we have lived in peace. That peace may be coming to an end."

The crowd stirs. Whispers begin snaking in waves, causing the guards to adjust their stances.

The king lifts his hand, bringing quiet with it. "I do not say that to frighten you. I tell you so that you may prepare. The Seascape portal has been reactivated. The enchantments put on it by the dark wizard still hold, but dark energy swirls within it. The energy calls to most, luring them to their doom, but it does not seem to affect the dark races. Blood dwarves, imps..." His gaze finds me and lingers. "Perhaps others. You may be asking yourself, 'What does this have to do with me?' A valid question.

Most of you are aware of the curse of the blood dwarves. That whenever we mate with those outside our race, our most defining feature is lost. Many of you may have the blood of my ancestors running through your veins, and you don't even know it.

"We did not build our empire by sitting idly by while kingdoms rose and fell all around us. Nor do I want to sit idle while our enemies gather on the other side of our portal. I want to break through the enchantment and discover what is lurking on the other side before they are ready for us. Our clerics and paladins of the castle have tried to break the enchantment to no avail. Maybe one of you have the ancient power within you. Maybe one of the so-called heroes from the south have that power. All I know is that the portal must be opened. Therefore, I am offering a keep, and all of its attended lands, to anyone who can break through the wall that blocks our portal. Who will answer the call of your king?

"You're more than welcome to participate yourself. Here." The quest displays in the corner of my vision.

Quest Alert. *You have been offered the quest "Open the Portal." Dark magic has arisen in the Seascape portal and the king wants to take action. Find a way to open the portal so that he may discover what is on the other side.*

Reward: Dwarven keep and all attended lands.

The crowd murmurs like a pot about to boil. Several dwarves around me speak in hushed voices, wondering if it is possible that they are descended from blood dwarves.

Message (Chod): *See anything?*

Incoming Message (Taryn): *I've spotted a few humans in the crowd, but none of them are heroes. There's so many people. It's impossible to see everyone.*

"I will answer the call!" a deep voice booms from the street behind me.

The crowd parts, and a stocky ivory dwarf with a scraggly brown beard steps forward. His tunic is tattered in places, and his pants are ripped at the knees. The warhammer he carries shimmers, but the leather bindings along its shaft are old and flaky in spots.

The guards allow him to pass. He approaches the portal, and the eyes of the clerics and paladins follow his every movement.

"Who are you?" asks the king.

"I be Tramond Volcanobreaker, Yer Highness." He bends down to one knee. "I am but a farmer from the small village of Oakside. My great-great-grandfather was a blood dwarf. This warhammer belonged to him and has been passed down through me family fer generations."

The king nods at the dwarf.

He approaches the portal cautiously, as if worried the energy will lash out at him. No doubt the stories of the portal's power have circulated throughout the city.

He lifts the warhammer over his shoulder. With a heave, he swings it against the enchanted stones that block the entrance.

The warhammer connects with the stone, and an explosion of energy catapults the dwarf and his warhammer into the crowd.

Shit! The portal blasted him like a cannon.

"Next," says the king.

"I will try!" someone yells from several streets over.

He makes his way to the guards, armored from head to toe in brilliant plate mail. A flowing yellow cloak trails behind him. When he steps past the guards, someone tries to pull him back, grabbing his cloak.

"You know yer not a damned blood dwarf!"

"Quiet, you!" the ivory dwarf curses at the dwarf who tried to stop him. "I am Brimgurd Proudsword, Your Highness."

The king nods and the dwarf approaches the arch, head held high. He carries a double-headed battleaxe. As he walks closer, his gait changes. His head begins to droop and the swagger he carried himself with before all but vanishes. The axe falls from his hand, clinking against the stone. He reaches toward the portal and a bolt of dark energy strikes his hand. The dwarf falls to the ground, his platemail clanks against the square and the gasp of the crowd sounds like all the air has been sucked from the world.

Limery's claws dig into my shoulder.

I can't help but wonder if this is all for nothing. Those with blood dwarf ancestry might be lucky enough to fight another day. But for the rest, is a keep worth risking their lives? Not to mention what might be on the other side of the portal.

Several clerics rush to the body and carry it away.

I guess he wasn't a blood dwarf after all. What a prideful idiot.

"I will open your portal!" a crisp, clear voice that couldn't possibly belong to a dwarf shouts.

"Step forward and reveal yourself," says the king.

A moment later, a tall, blond man wearing massive blue and silver armor steps forward. A billowing blue cape trails behind him. I'd recognize that heavenly glow anywhere. He was Jude's partner back in Vanaria. Have the two teamed up again or is he here of his own accord?

Michael Didato
 Level 19
 Paladin
 Human

The armor swallows him whole and might actually fit me if I were to put it on. He's replaced his warhammer with a new broadsword at least four feet long. His enormous shield is emblazoned with a white raven on a blue background. Either he finally found the one we took from him outside the dungeon or got it replaced. Everywhere he steps, golden light shines down upon him.

He bypasses the guards and stands before the king.

"I am Michael, paladin and hero to the people of Vanaria, but I have come to answer your call."

"What makes you think you can unlock this portal?"

"Only light can repel darkness. Your blood dwarf paladins and clerics may not be affected by the pull of dark energy, but neither can they combat it. I will open your portal, and then I will take a keep by the sea."

"Very well."

Michael the Paladin steps toward the portal. For a moment, his stoic pose falters, but then he lifts his sword and a ray of light showers him. His entire body takes on an ethereal glow. He swings his sword, gathering momentum, and brings it down upon the enchanted stone.

Black lightning explodes from the portal, instantly defusing the paladin's holy glow. He screams in agony before collapsing to the ground. His body shakes violently, rattling his armor. Then, in a flash, his body vanishes, leaving only his armor behind.

A dwarven paladin moves forward to pick up Michael's armor and weapons when someone yells at him to stop.

"Wait!" Pressley the Knight moves through the crowd. "Wait!" Richard the Cleric skulks close behind.

"Yes?" asks the king.

"I will open the portal, but when I succeed, I will take the paladin's armor as well." He brushes through the guards and their armors scrape against one another.

The king laughs. "So be it."

Pressley unsheathes his sword and gives it a few practice swings. The cleric tries to move past the guards, but they block his passage, apparently under orders to only let one person in at a time.

"He's with me," says the knight.

They allow the cleric to pass, and he brushes off his robes once he is through, as if rubbing against the guards made him dirty. He takes position behind Pressley and begins chanting. I can't quite make out the words, but as he does so, a purple aura envelopes the knight. It seeps into him, turning his armor from silver to a dark plum.

Sparks of lightning run along Pressley's sword as he stalks toward the portal. He raises his weapon and brings it down with a slash across the enchanted stones. Black energy jumps out from the portal and runs along the knight's blade. It sticks to the blade like goo, slowly trudging toward his body. He attempts to relinquish his weapon, but the dark substance crawls through his gauntlets and into his suit of armor.

He screams, his wails of pain setting my hair on end, as he crumples to his knees. His head falls forward, his helm resting against his breastplate.

We all stare on, waiting for his body to vanish and his armor to crash to the ground.

It never happens.

Instead, his head rises.

"Oh, noes." Limery grips me tight on the shoulder.

I don't know what's going on, but if Limery is worried, I think I should be too.

The knight stands. The purple aura that surrounded him is now black. Something buzzes from inside his armor. Pressley lifts his visor and all I can see is blackness.

The guards all turn from their positions, swords and spears pointed at Pressley.

"What the hell is going on?" I ask no one in particular.

"Fall back," a guard orders. "Protect the king."

Something about Pressley has changed, but nothing that would warrant that kind of reaction. Then I analyze him and see why they are so afraid.

Pressley Allen
    Level 24
    Death Knight
    Human

A death knight. The townspeople try to run away in the crowded streets, but those far away have no idea what is happening. Pandemonium takes over as hundreds of dwarves push against one another.

Suddenly, the pieces all fit together. The tower in Vanaria blessed by a cleric. The tapestry of men fighting skeletons. The dark wizard. The dark energy that transformed Pressley into a death knight.

The dark wizard was a necromancer. One who brought death on *Isle of Mythos* before. A fear that both humans and dwarves share.

Pressley raises his sword and points it at Richard. "You said this would work! You said it would allow me to open the portal."

The cleric laughs. "What can I say? God works in mysterious ways."

Pressley stabs the cleric through the chest. There's half a scream before empty robes fall to the ground. The crowd fights to escape him. He hasn't done anything, and yet his very presence is enough to cause a panic. The death knight picks up the fallen paladin's armor and disappears into the escaping crowd.

As most of the dwarves shove to get past me and down the hill, a rather large group marches toward the portal from the other side. Among them, two humans are giving orders.

A force of at least thirty or forty dwarves moves across the square. To one side, stands Jude. His beard is shaggier than ever. He walks shoulders first, hunching like a predator. He carries two shortswords, and several daggers hang from his belt.

Glenn marches on the other side. He walks with a deadly swagger. The only armor he wears is a bit of chainmail beneath his tunic.

"Taryn!" I call out. Shit is about to get real ugly.

"I see." He appears in his dwarven form right beside me. "What's the plan?"

"I don't know, but if they want to get near that portal, then I'm pretty sure we don't want to let that happen."

We move past the escaping dwarves and into the castle square. The king's guards line the stairs, but they hold their position for now. They must be letting this play out.

Why? I don't have a fucking clue.

I pull up Glenn's stats to try and gain an idea of what we are dealing with.

Glenn Orickson

 Level 12

 Warrior

 Human

Only level twelve. He must not have been power-leveling like Taryn has. I guess he had more important things on his mind. He'll be easy enough to handle.

As he marches forward, I can't help but think that I've never seen a plainer looking man in my life. He has such a forgettable face, like someone you could pass on the street and forget about as soon as they are out of vision. And yet, he commands followers so easy.

Is it his Charisma? When I increased mine, it was like a drug. I felt I could do anything, convince anyone of anything. Could his psychotic tendencies be the reason he has such an effect on others?

Fire crackles as Limery prepares for battle on my shoulder. I summon a quick array of horrors and wait.

Glenn, Jude, and their followers march with purpose.

"What are you doing?" I ask Jude. Of the two, he's the only one I have a chance of reasoning with. "Why would you follow a man like Glenn? He's nothing but trouble."

Jude laughs. It's a cruel laugh, absent of joy. "He's the only one who sees you for what you are. Trouble. You kill other heroes for no reason. You make threats and demands to the king. And then...and then, you are rewarded for it." He spits at the ground. "What kind of justice is that? King Favian is not around to protect you now."

I had a reason for every one I killed. My people were dying. The humans treated us like dirt, and I had to send a message that it wasn't okay. Remembering the way he talked about the trolls, like we were nothing, it has my blood boiling.

I analyze his stats as we square off. Despite losing a level at King Favian's feast, Jude has managed to level up to nineteen. Most of the other dwarves range from level five to ten. Whatever happens, Jude is the top priority.

"So what, you're going to kill me?" I shrug. "I'll just come back and find you. You already saw what I did to Glenn. We can put this behind us right now, and no one else has to die."

"Once we open the portal, we'll be under the king's protection. If you attack us, we'll wipe the forest trolls off the map." He snarls. "Hell, we might do it just for fun."

I have to hold back the anger that wells up in me. No one threatens my people. "And how do you expect to do that? You saw the others fail."

He flashes a devious grin. "There's strength in numbers. Attack!"

Their march turns into an all-out sprint as the dwarves raise their weapons in attack.

I don't want to hurt these dwarves, but I can't let Jude and Glenn accomplish whatever sick and twisted goal it is they have in mind.

"Limery, fire wall!"

He flies into the air and erupts a wall of flame in front of the charging dwarves. The dwarves don't stop. They run straight through the flames, their clothes and hair catching fire.

The guards on the step look to the king for orders, but he stays silent.

With fifteen horrors summoned, I send them out with instructions to wound but not kill. I don't want the blood of innocent dwarves on my hands if I can help it. If we can kill Glenn, then whatever influence he has over them will end. It happened in the forest the first time I ever saw him.

My horrors collide with the flaming dwarves, momentarily slowing them. The Horrors of Power sink their tusks into the legs of the dwarves, knocking a few to the ground. The overwhelming number of armed dwarves quickly ends them.

"We need to kill Glenn," I tell Taryn and Limery. "Kill him, and they'll stop."

Glenn is at the back of the fracas, avoiding combat. He wears a demented grin, watching the chaos unfold. This isn't like the forest, when he was on the front lines, enjoying the pain and suffering he brought on the trolls. He has something planned.

We all three take off towards him, when a glowing dagger from Jude stabs me in the ribs. "I don't think so. You're mine." He readies another dagger.

"You two deal with Glenn. I've got this asshole." At level twelve, Glenn should be easy work for the two of them.

Poison from Jude's dagger enters my veins, burning me from the inside. I elect to save my Tiger's Eye Pendant for now, in case I'm attacked again. I have more than enough health to handle a few minutes of poison.

I cast more horrors and send them at the dwarves. Jude marches toward me, spinning a glowing dagger around his finger. The dwarves have stopped their march and now surround Glenn, ready to defend him as he squares off with Taryn and Limery.

Several dwarves lie in the square with either broken or bleeding legs.

Jude throws another dagger at me, but this time, I swipe Sea Scorpion and send the blade ricocheting down the street.

Dammit! I'm torn between fighting Jude and helping my friends. I was hoping to save Champion, but unless I use it now, I'll lose the ability to summon a giant scorpion and be stuck with a level five dwarf instead.

Casting Champion, half of my mana drops in an instant and the giant demon of an insect appears in a cloud of smoke. It's the same as the scorpion I killed, only its color has changed. It's now gray, with a black streak running down its back. It clicks its pincers, and the stinger on its tail pulses a violent red.

I send it to help Taryn and Limery, and it scurries away, armed with three horrors on its back.

Jude unsheathes his swords and charges at me. His outline blurs with each step.

When he's several feet away, I stab my trident at him, but he dodges to the left, leaving a distorted blur in his wake. Before I retract my weapon, he stabs me in the side.

He's gotten faster since the last time we fought.

I swing my trident in an arc, but he jumps back, leaving a shadowy version of himself in his place. The shadow disperses into smoke as my trident cuts through it.

"You might be big and strong, but good luck catching me." He crosses his swords in an X and then his body splits in two. Two mirrored versions of himself laugh at me.

He's like a ninja with a doppelganger, and I can't tell which one is real.

Thunder cracks and lightning flashes nearby, but I don't have time to take in the action. Jude might be two levels under me, but I've proven before that levels aren't everything. He wants to see me hurt, and he has the speed to do it.

The two Judes spread out, splitting to both sides of me. With his speed, if I sit still, he is going to pick me apart. But if I go on the offensive, he might do the same. My only hope is that he makes a mistake. One mistake is all I need to crush his shaggy little head.

I jab my trident at the Jude to my right. He dodges the blow, leaving a blur behind, and before I've even fully extended my arm, another sharp pain flares in my side.

My health continues to trickle down from the poison. I lash out at the other Jude, and am rewarded with a sword to my blind side.

We continue our game of cat and mouse until I'm down to fifty percent health.

I'm fast for my size, but I'm not that fast. I summon a Horror of Vitality near the Jude on my left. Its passive effect slows him, and I stab with all my might. If the blow lands, it will pierce him completely.

Sea Scorpion stabs through Jude's heart and he explodes into gray smoke just as another attack cuts against my ribs.

Taryn's cry of pain causes me to lose all focus, and I turn to see my friend lying on the ground. My blood runs cold. For a moment, I forget that we are in a game, because to me, this isn't a game anymore. I let out a breath of relief. I have no idea what happened, but Limery stands over his body, flaming walls erupted on three sides of them. He pummels fireballs at the dwarves that try to push through, and a mound of bodies pile up at the edge of his fire walls. My scorpion is nowhere to be found.

A sharp pain in my shoulder is the price I pay for my lack of awareness.

Forget Jude, I need to help Taryn. I need to help my friend.

Abandoning all thoughts of Jude, I take off for Taryn, but something stabs through my calf, causing me to fall to the ground. My trident bounces off the stonework just out of my reach.

I'm crawling toward the fight when a trumpet blares from down the street. It carries on for a moment, like a declaration of war. Then, there's a loud crash and the sound of wood splintering, followed by thundering footsteps.

The blade in my calf twists, just as Stompy barrels around the corner, eyes red with rage as he plows through the escaping crowd. Berry follows close behind, both pets drawn to the battle by their psychic bond with their master.

The moulhaug smashes into the group of dwarves, head

swinging like a wrecking ball and tossing their bodies like bowling pins.

I let out a sigh of relief. Taryn is going to be okay.

"Where do you think you're going?" Jude asks. He grabs me by the foot and pulls me. The stone floor grates against my open wounds.

That's when I realize that during our game of cat and mouse, he has lured me right beside the portal. Its dark energy moves in waves around the arch.

Jude pulls a vial of yellow liquid from a pouch on his belt and splashes it on my body. The liquid stings against my open wounds, and suddenly, I can't move. I can't reach my Tiger's Eye Pendant to activate its debuff. I'm helpless.

My only choice left is Berserker Rage.

I activate the ability just as Jude rolls me against the portal.

CHAPTER 32

BLESSINGS

I ROLL against the enchanted stone and tendrils of dark energy surround me. Everything goes black.

I'm no longer stunned, but I also can't move. There's nothing but darkness. I try to remember where I last set my spawn point, but I can't. I could end up in the forest for all I know.

Words appear in my vision. Blurry at first, but slowly, they come into focus.

Blessing of the Forest Trolls Activated.

A massive force explodes against my back, and the blackness peels away from my eyes as I'm launched into the castle courtyard. My senses overload as I land back in a world of color and smell. Everything smells of sulfur. Stone and rubble fall all around me. Berserker Rage continues to cleanse my body of poison and stitch my cuts back together.

A notification pops up, but I push it away. I try to gain my bearings.

To my left, dozens of dead or injured dwarves litter the courtyard. Stompy and Berry sit beside Taryn's slumping body. He's not dead, or his body wouldn't be there.

What the hell just happened?

Limery's ferocious scream catches my attention and I look over by the portal to see him with his tiny hands wrapped around Jude's throat. Limery's body burns a vibrant red, flames licking at the air all around him. Jude's skin melts from his neck and face before he suddenly vanishes.

Behind Limery, the stone wall that blocked the inside of the arch is gone. The black energy has vanished as well, replaced by a peaceful white swirl. Several of the runes around the arch's edge glow a dull red. Others don't glow at all. They're just empty carvings now.

There's movement on the stairs as the king makes his way down.

"Limery," I try to get the imp's attention.

He turns to me, his eyes bloodshot and filled with tears. "Chods?" In a flash, he's by my side. "Limmy thoughts yous was dead."

"I'm okay, buddy. What happened?"

He wipes his eyes. "The bad mans, he throws you in the portals."

I remember Jude pouring something on me. Something that paralyzed me. Was it glouwseeker venom?

Out of the corner of my eye, I see two bodies enter the court-yard at a full sprint from one of the side streets.

"Get them!" the king shouts, and his guards race from the stairs.

Glenn and Jude run across the courtyard toward the portal. They must have set their respawn points nearby. The two men have a head start, and before the guards are even halfway there, both men leap through the swirling arch. As they disappear, the runes flare for a second and then return to a dull glow.

"Dammit!" the king shouts. "Form a perimeter! I want this portal secured at all times. Detain anyone or anything that comes through." He turns to one of his kingsguard. "Yorn, gather enough men for an envoy. I want to know what is on the other side of these portals by nightfall."

Escorted by several clerics and paladins, the king approaches me. At full height, he's barely taller than I am sitting. "How did you destroy the dark energy?" His tone is urgent as his black eyes bore into me.

"I—I honestly don't know. I think it was the troll blessing."

"Troll blessing?" He looks to one of the clerics. "What do you know of this?"

The cleric strokes his beard for a moment. "If I recall, the trolls were one of the few races unaffected by the dark wizard's temptations. Perhaps it is a form of protection."

The king kneels next to me. "This blessing, can it be replicated?"

Thinking back on the dance and the chants that the forest trolls did before I left, I would imagine it could be. "I think so."

"Good. Kurzol, I want a raven sent to King Favian and one to the forest trolls. Let them know what has happened. Let them know how to unlock the portal." He looks back at the arch. "Tell King Favian that once the portal in Vanaria is open, I request an audience with him."

I struggle to my feet, only half-healed by Berserker Rage. "Do you know where they went?" Wherever it is, it's far away from here. Whoever is on the other side has no idea how dangerous those two can be.

"It's impossible to tell. Each of the red runes are portals that are open on other continents. The empty runes are portals that remain closed. This one..." He points to an empty rune in the shape of an R. "That is the lair of the dark wizard. Our portal hasn't been opened in my lifetime, but I have prepared for this all the same. I did not see which rune activated when they stepped through. They could be on any one of them." He pauses, looking at the devastation all around him. "My council advised me not to interfere in the battles of heroes. They warned me that you all had your part to play. I should have known that there are bad seeds in every bunch. My inaction has caused much needless death here today. Gather your companions and wait for me in the castle. There is more to discuss, but first, I must address my people."

A cleric leans over Taryn's body, healing him with holy light. When the light fades, Taryn stands up groggily. "What the hell happened?"

"Jude and Glenn escaped through the portal."

His eyes go wide when he sees the swirling white vortex. "How did they manage to open it?"

"They didn't. It was me. On accident."

He scrunches his face.

"I'll tell you all about it inside."

We're led into an intricately decorated throne room. Columns carved with Celtic-looking knots ascend into a vaulted ceiling. The walls are engraved with mighty battle scenes. Even the ceiling is painted with brightly colored images of days past. Statues of great dwarven kings stand on pedestals against the walls. But for all of the decoration in the throne room, the throne itself is simple. One large chunk of obsidian carved with clean edges. No ornamentation.

As the king addresses his people outside, his voice carries

through the castle. He speaks of the opening of the portal, the threat of days to come, but also of the hope that we may unite with the other continents to put a stop to the darkness once and for all.

I tell Taryn everything that happened to me, explaining the blessing and the explosion. "It protected me from the dark energy somehow. It's like I overloaded whatever spell was holding it in place."

Limery holds tight against my shoulder as I recount the events. Ever since I came back from the portal, he hasn't let go. That's twice now that I've scared him into thinking I was dead.

Taryn shakes his head. "What happens now?"

The door to the throne room opens and King Orso enters, escorted by his kingsguards. Taryn drops to one knee as the king passes and takes the throne.

"These two men that entered the portal. They are enemies of Vanaria, yes?" The king's red skin is prominent against the black throne.

"How do you know that?" I thought their wanted marks would vanish once they entered the north.

"Others may not see, but a king sees all. Especially on my lands." He leans forward. "If they are enemies of Vanaria, then henceforth, they are enemies of Seascape as well. The world as we know it is on the verge of change. Once the portal to Vanaria is open, I intend to make plans for what comes next. Make no mistake, a war is coming. The dark energy that has sealed these portals is old, and it is strong. A day will come when the dark wizard opens his own portal once more, and on that day, we will need the heroes of this world on our side. You must use this time wisely. Strengthen your bodies, your minds, your very bonds with one another. For when that dreaded day comes, we will need all the help we can get."

A long silence passes as we take in the king's words. Several dwarves have gathered around the throne, waiting for their orders.

The king is right. For the people of *Isle of Mythos,* their world is about to change. I trust that King Orso and King Favian will prepare their people for what comes. No one knows what waits on the other side of that portal, but if war is coming, I need to make sure I am strong enough to answer the call. And with a little luck, maybe I can rally more heroes to our cause.

ACKNOWLEDGMENTS

Congratulations! *You have finished* Sentenced to Troll 2.
  2 of 6 completed.
  +1 stat point to distribute.
  +1 Review to leave.

Thanks for reading! I hope you had as much fun reading about Chod and his adventures as I did writing them. This adventure is just getting started. If you enjoyed the book, please consider leaving a review. Reviews and word-of-mouth are the lifeblood of indie authors. The more positive reviews I have, the more likely it is that others will take a chance on this series.

As always, there are so many people that helped make this book possible. Cindy, you helped me to add emotion and depth to every single page with your comments and feedback.

My patrons: Peezy, Tim Krason, Sean Amy, Richard Hummel, Patrick Short, and Michael Didato. You may recognize some of them as prisoners stuck in the game alongside Chod. If you'd like to be one of the unnamed prisoners yet to be unveiled, stop by my Patreon.

My beta readers: Brian Walker, Bryan O'Bannon, Ian Mitchel, and Rickie Brookes.

Eric Martin, the fantastic narrator of Sentenced to Troll. He is a wonderful talent and brought my characters to life better than I could have imagined.

Finally, I'd like to thank everyone who read Sentenced to Troll, the reviews and feedback have been nothing short of amazing and I can't wait for you to see where this series goes.

If you're looking for more books similar to my own, check out LitRPG Books.

About the Author

S.L. Rowland is a cozy fantasy and LitRPG author known for crafting immersive worlds filled with adventure, heart, and a touch of humor. A lifelong gamer and fantasy enthusiast, he draws inspiration from tabletop RPGs, video games, and the fantastical. When he's not writing, he enjoys weightlifting, hiking with his Shiba Inu, and enduring the heartbreak of being an Atlanta sports fan.

SLRowland.com

Patreon-For signed paperbacks, advanced chapters, exclusive short stories, art, merch, and more.

Newsletter: For updates on new releases, sales, and behind the scenes content!

Email: slrowlandauthor@gmail.com

Find out more at https://linktr.ee/SLRowland

ALSO BY S.L. ROWLAND

Tales of Aedrea

Cursed Cocktails

Sword & Thistle

The Halfling's Harvest

There Be Dragons Here

Pangea Online

Pangea Online: Death and Axes

Pangea Online 2: Magic and Mayhem

Pangea Online 3: Vials and Tribulations

Sentenced to Troll 1-6

Path to Villainy: An NPC Kobold's Tale

Collected Editions

Pangea Online: The Complete Trilogy

Sentenced to Troll Compendium: Books 1-3

Sentenced to Troll Compendium 2: Books 4-6

9 781964 567044